The Best
AMERICAN SHORT STORIES 2016

The *Best* AMERICAN SHORT STORIES® 2016

Selected from
U.S. and Canadian Magazines
by JUNOT DÍAZ
with HEIDI PITLOR

With an Introduction by Junot Díaz

MARINER BOOKS
HOUGHTON MIFFLIN HARCOURT
BOSTON • NEW YORK 2016

www.hmhco.com

ISSN 0067-6233
ISBN 978-0-544-58275-0
ISBN 978-0-544-58289-7 (pbk.)

Printed in the United States of America
DOC 10 9 8 7 6 5 4 3 2 1

Contents

Foreword

THIS WAS MY tenth year as the series editor of *The Best American Short Stories.* A decade! How quickly we grow older. I had my children—twins—near the end of my first year reading for this series, and now the twins are in third grade, physical reminders of my tenure at this job. I used to try to read them stories when they were strapped in their bouncy seats. It never went well. One would cry, the other would scream. A bottle would spill on *The New Yorker.* Someone would gum the latest *Southwest Review.* Now they navigate technology better than I can. My son collects Pokémon cards and is enamored of Minecraft and pizza. My daughter listens to Taylor Swift and Rachel Platten and loves animals.

Over the past ten years, the world has grown noisier. Within seconds, my kids can find the answer to whatever question they can conjure. I don't have to tell anyone that we now have more information at our fingertips than at any time in history. The first year that I read for this series, the iPhone had not been introduced to the public. Nor had Instagram, Pinterest, or Tumblr. Nor had Amazon's Kindle, Google Chrome, or Netflix streaming.

Right now, as I write this foreword, Donald J. Trump is running for president of the United States. NASA just announced that for three consecutive months, the earth has broken high-temperature records. Americans passionately, dangerously disagree over everything from Syrian refugees to gun control to when and how a new Supreme Court justice should be nominated. There is no shortage of subjects with the power to hijack our attention.

Here are some other things that held my attention this year: Ta-

Nehisi Coates's *Between the World and Me;* Maggie Nelson's *The Argonauts;* Lily King's *Euphoria;* Emily St. John Mandel's *Station Eleven;* the *Harry Potter* books, which I am reading to my kids; the movies *Brooklyn* and *Spotlight;* the TV shows *Transparent, House of Cards,* and *American Crime Story: The People v. O. J. Simpson.* My children, my family, our bank account, my elderly father, my new dog, my friends, my email inbox, my Facebook account, my Twitter feed. Over the past year, I published and toured for my second novel and edited *The Best American Short Stories 2015* and *100 Years of the Best American Short Stories.* I worked to develop a new short story app. I wrote book reviews, consulted, and began writing my third novel.

Still, I don't suspect that my life was much busier than anyone else's—anyone else who reads fiction.

Right now, writers of short fiction face more competition for readers' attention than ever before. We, as writers and editors, need for our work to remain relevant and engaging and compelling and new and honest. More than anything, honest. Thankfully, none of these things are impossible.

Each year, I read more than three thousand short stories. The best ones not only hold their own when faced with the noise of the world, they silence it. They command our attention with eloquence and honesty and guts. In this age of information overload, these three characteristics are rare yet necessary. A good short story can ground the reader. It can give hope, solace, comfort—things that are more crucial than ever.

Over the past ten years, while reading for this series, I've had the joy of encountering for the first time writers such as Lauren Groff, Mia Alvar, Adam Johnson, Maggie Shipstead, Megan Mayhew Bergman, Roxane Gay, Taiye Selasi, Daniyal Mueenuddin. A great pleasure of my job is the rush that comes with discovery. Sometimes, reading so many pages of so many stories has a lulling effect. I feel my mind slow, my focus wander. I must work to pay attention to the words before me. And then, when I least expect it (for great writing can appear in any magazine at any time), I'm reading a new story and not checking how long it is or what time I have to pick up the kids. I'm reading and feeling and thinking and, if I'm lucky, laughing too. I'm not working at all. A great story has that power: it removes you from your life. It lifts you away for a while.

Junot Díaz and I found much to discover this year: Caille Millner, Yuko Sakata, Meron Hadero, and Lisa Ko, for starters. This year, the best stories presented themselves clearly. Some years there is much back-and-forthing between me and my guest editor, but Mr. Díaz presented me with his list and I saw that it nearly matched my own. We talked through a couple of stories. He introduced me to a few that I hadn't found myself, and that was that. I am grateful to Mr. Díaz for his commitment to these stories and to the form, and for his generosity and openness.

A quick plea: I am able to read only the stories that are submitted to me. I receive relatively few stories from online magazines. To all editors of online magazines that publish short fiction: please send hard copies of your stories to me at the address below.

The stories chosen for this anthology were originally published between January 2015 and January 2016. The qualifications for selection are (1) original publication in nationally distributed American or Canadian periodicals; (2) publication in English by writers who have made the United States their home; (3) original publication as short stories (excerpts of novels are not considered). A list of magazines consulted for this volume appears at the back of the book. Editors who wish their short fiction to be considered for next year's edition should send their publications or hard copies of online publications to Heidi Pitlor, c/o The Best American Short Stories, 125 High St., Boston, MA 02110.

HEIDI PITLOR

Introduction

I'VE SPENT THE past twenty years reading and writing short stories—which, given some careers, ain't all that much, but it is more than half my adult life. I guess you could say I'm one of those true believers. I teach the form every year without fail, and when I'm asked to give a lecture on a literary form (a rarity), the short story is inevitably my craft subject du jour. Even now that my writing is focused entirely on novels, short fiction is still the genre I feel most protective of. The end-of-the-novel bullshit that erupts with measles-like regularity among a certain strain of literary folks doesn't exercise me as much as when people tell me they never read short stories. At these moments I find myself proselytizing like a madman and I will go as far as to mail favorite collections to the person in question. (For real, I do this.) I hate the endless shade thrown at the short story—whether from publishers or editors or writers who talk the form down, who don't think it's practical or sufficiently remunerative—and I always cheer when a story collection takes a prize or becomes a surprise bestseller (rare and getting rarer). I always have at least one story collection on my desk or near my bed for reading—and there's never a week when I don't have a story I just read kicking around inside my head.

I am as much in awe of the form's surpassing beauty as I am bowled over by its extraordinary mutability and generativity. I love the form's spooky effects, how in contradistinction to the novel, which gains its majesty from its expansiveness, from its size, the short story's colossal power extends from its brevity and restraint.

Or, as Dagoberto Gilb has said, in the story "the small is large, strength is economy, simplicity, not verbosity." If the novel is our culture's favored literary form, upon which we heap all our desiccated literary laurels, if the novel is, say, our Jaime Lannister, then the short story is our very own Tyrion: the disdained little brother, the perennial underdog. But what an underdog. Give a short story a dozen pages and it can break hearts bones vanities and cages. And in the right hands there's more oomph in a gram of short story than in almost any literary form. It's precisely this exhilarating atomic compound of economy + power that has entranced readers and practitioners alike for generations, and also explains why the story continues to attract our finest writers.

But such power does not come without a price. This is a form that is unforgiving as fuck, and demands from its acolytes unnerving levels of exactitude. A novel, after all, can absorb a whole lot of slackness and slapdash and still kick massive ass, but a short story can unravel over a pair of injudicious sentences. And while novels can dawdle for chapters before sparking into brilliance, the short story needs to be about its business from its opening line. Short stories are acts of bravura, and for a form junkie like me, to read a good one has all the thrill of watching a high-wire act. When the writer pulls it off sentence by sentence scene by scene page after page from first touch to last, you almost forget to breathe.

Novels might be able to summon entire worlds, but few literary forms can match the story at putting a reader in touch with life's fleeting, inexorable rhythm. It's the one great benefit of the form's defining limitation.

Stories, after all, are short, just like our human moments. (We're all Tyrion, narratively speaking.) Compared to the novel, stories strike like life and end with its merciless abruptness as well. Just as you're settling into the world of a story, that's usually when the narrative closes, ejecting you from its embrace, typically forever. With a novel there's a more generous contact. When you read a novel you know implicitly that it ain't going to end for a good long while. Characters might die, families might leave their home nations, generations might rise and fall, but the world of the novel, which is its heart, endures . . . as long as there are pages. A novel's bulk is a respite from life's implacable uncertainty. You and I can end in a heartbeat, without warning, but no novel ends until that last page is turned. There's something deeply consoling about that contract the novel makes with its reader.

No such consolation when you read stories. That's the thing —just as they're beginning they're ending. As with stories, so with us. To me this form captures better than any other what it is to be human—the brevity of our moments, the cruel irrevocability when those times places and people we hold the most dear slip through our fingers.

Some friends have told me that their lives resemble novels. That's super-cool. Mine, alas, never has. Maybe it's my Caribbean immigrant multiplicity, the incommensurate distances between the worlds I inhabit, but my life has always worked better when understood as a collection of short stories than anything else. Thing is, I'm all these strange pieces that don't assemble into anything remotely coherent. Hard for me to square that kid in Santo Domingo climbing avocado trees with the teen in Central NJ bringing a gun to school with the man who now writes these words on the campus of MIT. Forget the same narrator—these moments don't feel like they're in the same book or even the same genre. Those years when I was running around in the South Bronx, helping my boys drag their congas to their shows—that time feels like it happened to someone else. (*That world! These days it's all been erased and they've rolled it up like a scroll and put it away somewhere. Yes, I can touch it with my fingers. But where is it?*) I guess some of us have crossed too many worlds and lived too many lives for unity.

Here's the funny part, though. For all that rah-rah on how super-duper-amazing stories are, I didn't actually start out wanting to write them. Surprise surprise: I started out like a practical fiction person—wanting to write novels.

Was there some moment when I chose the novel over the short story? Dark Side or Light? Nope. I'm not sure I even thought about it. I chose to be a novelist . . . because that's just what a normal person did. Didn't matter that three of my biggest literary heroes at the time—Los Brothers Hernández and Sandra Cisneros—were short story writers. Didn't matter that in those days Carver was ascendant, that *Where I'm Calling From* was prominently displayed in every bookstore and on every fiction writer's shelf. Didn't even matter that my undergraduate writing professor was a storywriter by trade and a damn good one. I'd heard the rap about how the story wasn't going to get you shit and swallowed it whole hog. (Didn't help that when my mentor went up for tenure on the strength of his stories he got denied—no pass go.) The simple fact was that stories were treated then as they are treated now—like daughters are treated in third-world patriarchies—and when you're a kid who grew up trapped on the margins, the last place you want to be is on the margins. As unthinking as an insect turning toward a flame, I went straight for literature's big fat brass ring: the novel.

Only problem was I reached my MFA with my Great Dominican Novel still in its "development stage" (a condition from which it never recovered). Since I was obligated to hand in writing for my workshop at a regular clip, my plan was to draft a couple of short stories to cover my ass while I got my novel game up to speed. Bang a few of these bad boys out and by the end of the semester my novel would be up and running and I'd never look back.

Yeah, that was the plan. But you know what they say about plans. Those first September weeks in Ithaca, when a balm seemed to hover over the place and the students still splashed in the gorges, I churned out my first story and handed it in to my workshop. I didn't expect a lot of problems. To be honest, I was so confident that the story was good that I didn't give it much thought at all; was more caught up reading about Trujillo and the U.S. invasion of 1965—you know, doing my real work, my novel work. Workshop rolls around and I still remember the feeling on my face as I watched my story get *gutted*. I'd caught beatdowns before, but this one was a graduate workshop beatdown and I felt those lumps for days. Sure, there was some mild praise about the setting and a few of my lines got checkmarks next to them, but the overwhelming reaction was negative. Even the students of color I felt affinity for were underwhelmed; one of them wrote extensive notes about everything that was wrong with my story. Like, three pages, if I remember. In little type.

All right, a bad first story—that can happen to anyone. It wasn't like I had plans to be a storywriter anyway, so it would have been easy to switch to the novel and fuck short stories forever. But try as I might I couldn't quite get over my embarrassment at that first attempt. My own prejudice turning on me. *I thought you said stories are bullshit—so why can't you write one?* Pure dumbness—writing good stories don't make anyone a great novelist and vice versa, but that's where I was at. (The fact that my peers were turning in excellent short work only added to my burn.)

So after a lot of deliberation, I decided to write another story —mostly to clear the bad taste out of my mouth. (Translation: pride.) But this time I went, as the kids like to say, *in*. I attacked the form with a fury—like my life depended on it. Started eating breathing shitting short stories. I've always had this immigrant's ability to turn it on in times of trouble, but that first semester at Cornell I didn't just hit beast mode; I went Super Saiyajin. Not only did I read my peers' work with a Talmudic intensity, writing up long-ass reports on what they did right, but I began locking myself up at the Olin Library every single morning after my run, with the mandate to read at least a hundred pages of short fiction minimum. I got recommendations from my peers, from my professors, picked up names from the discussions in workshop and from prowling around the stacks and the new arrivals shelf. If there was a short story collection, I pulled it and read it. Didn't matter who wrote it or if it was any good. I devoured *everything*.

What happened during that intense blaze of reading was that a new aesthetic standard began to establish itself in me. I went from a grudging tolerance of the short story to a surprised admiration. It dawned on me finally that this was no intermediate form, a step en route to the novel, but an extraordinary tradition in its own right, not easily mastered but rich in rewards. I started yammering on to my friends about the form's surprising complexity, its power, its mutability—how structurally instructive it was.

And when I wrote my second story and it didn't go over so well in workshop, instead of giving up I ended up doubling down. By then it was already too late. I was too hooked to quit. My enthusiasm had kindled into a purer form of devotion.

Call it love.

It's the classic love story turn. We start assured of what we want and don't want, only to have life turn our desiderata upside down and inside out.

On my way to the novel I fell in love with the short story. That's the absolute shortest version. Naturally I didn't forget my dream of a Great Dominican Novel—some shit is too deeply entrenched to be cured of easily—but I didn't feel the passion for it anymore (not yet). For my next three years I wrote strictly stories, nothing else. It took a while for me to improve. When my first book, *Drown,* came together and got picked up and was about to be published, my editor suggested very diplomatically that we might consider calling the book a novel. It wouldn't have been a big stretch. I'd seen plenty of less coherent works earn that appellation. And it sure would help the sales of the book, I was told. After all, not a lot of people read story collections.

I refused, of course . . . for a number of reasons. But one of biggest was simply that I was proud of the form and didn't want to see it shortchanged like that.

Changes.

A lot of what I've just written was on my mind as I read the 120-odd finalists for this year's *Best American.* It had been a long time since I'd read that much short fiction in one jolt and in a way it was something of a homecoming. Brought back the old days (has it been twenty years already?), when I hadn't yet published a word, when I was still figuring it all out, the marathon reading sessions in that corner of Olin Library, the faith I had that reading could save me from my troubles. Brought back the thrill of encountering a story that had something to teach me, that I knew was about to take up residence in my head and my heart awhile. And it brought back above all else the many reasons I fell so hard for the form in the first place.

It's always better to let the stories speak for themselves, for the introducer to get out of the way, but I'd be remiss if I didn't offer a few remarks. There is, after all, much to marvel at here. Take Louise Erdrich's masterful "The Flower," which packs a novel's worth of incident and character into a taut tale of colonial love and colonial murder on the Ojibwe frontier. Also the spectral head of a poisoned trader makes an appearance. "Sometimes it propelled itself along with its tongue, its slight stump of a neck, or its comically paddling ears. Sometimes it whizzed along for a few feet, then quit, sobbing in frustration at its awkward, interminable progress."

The dead return (isn't that their way?) in Karen Russell's "The Prospectors." They also dance, kiss, pose for photographs, and burn the knowledge of their own deaths "like whale fat." "Perhaps the knowledge of one's death, ceaselessly swallowed," Russell's grifter narrator muses, "is the very food you need to become a ghost." Russell's story, like Erdrich's, begins in the precise empirical language of realism, and how both writers pivot into the fantastic is an act of literary legerdemain worth reflecting on.

The uncanny also underpins Ben Marcus's "Cold Little Bird." A child suddenly turns into a suburban Midwich Cuckoo, cold, intelligent, and hostile to his parents' affections. As chilling an allegory of "family bonds" as I've ever read.

Love and its discontents are an evergreen in short fiction; you'll certainly find them here, but the stories that are the biggest heartbreakers describe intimacies at their phantom stages—love, in other words, at the lowest frequencies. Andrea Barrett's "Wonders of the Shore"—another master class in compression—tracks the unconventional friendship of Daphne and Henrietta, two unmarried "naturalists" at the turn of the century. "Firmly rooted" Henrietta walks away from a suitor who turns out to be her last chance at a family, "so that for barely more than a week, she could feel" a painter's "hair against her lips."

Héctor Tobar's quietly affecting "Secret Stream" touches upon a similar decision. Here is Nathan and his tentative attempt to connect with Sofia, a self-proclaimed "river geek" who is mapping the surviving traces of LA's waterways. Both a love letter to LA and a tough look at how we are often our own worst enemies: "The hour of their meeting came and went and Nathan didn't leave home. It was the way he'd handled relationships with women since his wife left him; he preempted disappointment."

In Chimamanda Ngozi Adichie's powerful "Apollo," our middle-class Nigerian narrator recounts with a devastating clarity his adolescent infatuation for his family's former houseboy, Raphael. Despite the vast distance in circumstance, the boys bond over a shared love of Bruce Lee and martial arts until a bout of pinkeye—the story's Apollo—exposes the yawning gulf that determines the lives (and the deaths) of Nigeria's haves and have-nots.

Set in the darker pits of neoliberalism's economic abyss, Tahmima Anam's "Garments" follows Jesmin, an impoverished sweatshop girl on the verge of being evicted. Desperate to secure a room from a landlord who prefers married tenants, Jesmin agrees to become the third wife of a coworker's boyfriend. That this scheme qualifies as "not bad" speaks volumes about these women's straits.

"Jesmin decides it won't be so bad to share a husband. She doesn't have dreams of a love marriage, and if they have to divide the sex that's fine with her, and if he wants something, like he wants rice the way his mother makes it, maybe one of them will know how to do it."

There is so much to recommend. Meron Hadero's "The Suitcase," which dramatizes perfectly the politics of immigrant luggage and how the smallest of gifts crammed inside a suitcase helps hold diasporas together. Caille Millner's depiction of an academic meltdown in "The Politics of the Quotidian" absolutely sizzles; this is a writer I cannot wait to read more of. Sarah Shun-lien Bynum's canny tale of a William James scholar, recovering from a miscarriage, is as eerie as it is fine. Smith Henderson's bruising portrait of brotherly rage in "Treasure State" and Mohammed Naseehu Ali's depiction of a coup in "Ravalushan" play for keeps, as does Lauren Groff's unsparing "For the God of Love, for the Love of God." Then there are the newer writers—Lisa Ko, Yalitza Ferreras, Daniel J. O'Malley, Yuko Sakata, and Sharon Solwitz—whom I expect we'll be seeing much more from.

Clearly it's time for me to go, but since this is an anthology about "the best," let me finish with two stories that were arguably "my best": John Edgar Wideman's "Williamsburg Bridge" and Ted Chiang's "The Great Silence." Wideman is one of the nation's literary treasures, and his contribution is a dazzling, delirious achievement: as his narrator, perched on edge of the Williamsburg Bridge, prepares for suicide, he delivers a cri de coeur that ranges from Sonny Rollins to the Yalu River and becomes nothing less than a meditation on the extraordinary resilience of ordinary black lives in the American Century.

Chiang's profoundly moving story is another farewell letter, but this one from a most unlikely source: Puerto Rican parrots driven to the point of extinction by human activity. (The first story I ever tried to write was about a parrot, so there's something fitting about this being the last story I read.) As they contemplate the Great Silence that will soon extinguish their voices forever, Chiang's parrots reflect on the irony of the nearby Arecibo telescope. "The humans use Arecibo to look for extraterrestrial intelligence. Their desire to make a connection is so strong that they've created an ear capable of hearing across the universe.

"But I and my fellow parrots are right here. Why aren't they interested in listening to our voices?"

Querida reader, ultimately I hope these stories do for you what they've done for me—at the very least I pray they offer you an opportunity for communion. A chance to listen, if not to the parrots of our world, then to some other lone voice struggling to be heard against the great silence.

JUNOT DÍAZ

The Best
AMERICAN
SHORT
STORIES
2016

Apollo

FROM *The New Yorker*

TWICE A MONTH, like a dutiful son, I visited my parents in Enugu, in their small overfurnished flat that grew dark in the afternoon. Retirement had changed them, shrunk them. They were in their late eighties, both small and mahogany-skinned, with a tendency to stoop. They seemed to look more and more alike, as though all the years together had made their features blend and bleed into one another. They even smelled alike—a menthol scent, from the green vial of Vicks VapoRub they passed to each other, carefully rubbing a little in their nostrils and on aching joints. When I arrived, I would find them either sitting out on the veranda overlooking the road or sunk into the living-room sofa, watching *Animal Planet*. They had a new, simple sense of wonder. They marveled at the wiliness of wolves, laughed at the cleverness of apes, and asked each other, "Ifukwa? Did you see that?"

They had too a new, baffling patience for incredible stories. Once my mother told me that a sick neighbor in Abba, our ancestral hometown, had vomited a grasshopper—a living, writhing insect, which, she said, was proof that wicked relatives had poisoned him. "Somebody texted us a picture of the grasshopper," my father said. They always supported each other's stories. When my father told me that Chief Okeke's young house help had mysteriously died, and the story around town was that the chief had killed the teenager and used her liver for moneymaking rituals, my mother added, "They say he used the heart too."

Fifteen years earlier, my parents would have scoffed at these stories. My mother, a professor of political science, would have said

"Nonsense" in her crisp manner, and my father, a professor of education, would merely have snorted, the stories not worth the effort of speech. It puzzled me that they had shed those old selves and become the kind of Nigerians who told anecdotes about diabetes cured by drinking holy water.

Still, I humored them and half listened to their stories. It was a kind of innocence, this new childhood of old age. They had grown slower with the passing years, and their faces lit up at the sight of me, and even their prying questions—"When will you give us a grandchild? When will you bring a girl to introduce to us?"—no longer made me as tense as before. Each time I drove away, on Sunday afternoons after a big lunch of rice and stew, I wondered if it would be the last time I would see them both alive, if before my next visit I would receive a phone call from one of them telling me to come right away. The thought filled me with a nostalgic sadness that stayed with me until I got back to Port Harcourt. And yet I knew that if I had a family, if I could complain about rising school fees as the children of their friends did, then I would not visit them so regularly. I would have nothing for which to make amends.

During a visit in November, my parents talked about the increase in armed robberies all over the east. Thieves too had to prepare for Christmas. My mother told me how a vigilante mob in Onitsha had caught some thieves, beaten them, and torn off their clothes—how old tires had been thrown over their heads like necklaces, amid shouts for petrol and matches, before the police arrived, fired shots in the air to disperse the crowd, and took the robbers away. My mother paused, and I waited for a supernatural detail that would embellish the story. Perhaps, just as they arrived at the police station, the thieves had turned into vultures and flown away.

"Do you know," she continued, "one of the armed robbers, in fact the ringleader, was Raphael? He was our houseboy years ago. I don't think you'll remember him."

I stared at my mother. "Raphael?"

"It's not surprising he ended like this," my father said. "He didn't start well."

My mind had been submerged in the foggy lull of my parents' storytelling, and I struggled now with the sharp awakening of memory.

My mother said again, "You probably won't remember him. There were so many of those houseboys. You were young."

But I remembered. Of course I remembered Raphael.

Nothing changed when Raphael came to live with us, not at first. He seemed like all the others, an ordinary-looking teen from a nearby village. The houseboy before him, Hyginus, had been sent home for insulting my mother. Before Hyginus was John, whom I remembered because he had not been sent away; he had broken a plate while washing it and, fearing my mother's anger, had packed his things and fled before she came home from work. All the houseboys treated me with the contemptuous care of people who disliked my mother. Please come and eat your food, they would say —I don't want trouble from Madam. My mother regularly shouted at them, for being slow, stupid, hard of hearing; even her bell-ringing, her thumb resting on the red knob, the shrillness searing through the house, sounded like shouting. How difficult could it be to remember to fry the eggs differently, my father's plain and hers with onions, or to put the Russian dolls back on the same shelf after dusting, or to iron my school uniform properly?

I was my parents' only child, born late in their lives. "When I got pregnant, I thought it was menopause," my mother told me once. I must have been around eight years old, and did not know what "menopause" meant. She had a brusque manner, as did my father; they had about them the air of people who were quick to dismiss others. They had met at the University of Ibadan, married against their families' wishes—his thought her too educated, while hers preferred a wealthier suitor—and spent their lives in an intense and intimate competition over who published more, who won at badminton, who had the last word in an argument. They often read aloud to each other in the evening, from journals or newspapers, standing rather than sitting in the parlor, sometimes pacing, as though about to spring at a new idea. They drank Mateus rosé—that dark, shapely bottle always seemed to be resting on a table near them—and left behind glasses faint with reddish dregs. Throughout my childhood, I worried about not being quick enough to respond when they spoke to me.

I worried too that I did not care for books. Reading did not do to me what it did to my parents, agitating them or turning them into vague beings lost to time, who did not quite notice when I came and went. I read books only enough to satisfy them and to answer the kinds of unexpected questions that might come in the middle of a meal—What did I think of Pip? Had Ezeulu done the right thing? I sometimes felt like an interloper in our house. My bedroom had bookshelves, stacked with the overflow books that did not fit in the study and the corridor, and they made my stay feel transient, as though I were not quite where I was supposed to be. I sensed my parents' disappointment in the way they glanced at each other when I spoke about a book, and I knew that what I had said was not incorrect but merely ordinary, uncharged with their brand of originality. Going to the staff club with them was an ordeal: I found badminton boring; the shuttlecock seemed to me an unfinished thing, as though whoever had invented the game had stopped halfway.

What I loved was kung fu. I watched *Enter the Dragon* so often that I knew all the lines, and I longed to wake up and be Bruce Lee. I would kick and strike at the air, at imaginary enemies who had killed my imaginary family. I would pull my mattress onto the floor, stand on two thick books—usually hardcover copies of *Black Beauty* and *The Water-Babies*—and leap onto the mattress, screaming "Haaa!" like Bruce Lee. One day, in the middle of my practice, I looked up to see Raphael standing in the doorway, watching me. I expected a mild reprimand. He had made my bed that morning, and now the room was in disarray. Instead, he smiled, touched his chest, and brought his finger to his tongue, as though tasting his own blood. My favorite scene. I stared at Raphael with the pure thrill of unexpected pleasure. "I watched the film in the other house where I worked," he said. "Look at this."

He pivoted slightly, leaped up, and kicked, his leg straight and high, his body all taut grace. I was twelve years old and had, until then, never felt that I recognized myself in another person.

Raphael and I practiced in the backyard, leaping from the raised concrete soakaway and landing on the grass. Raphael told me to suck in my belly, to keep my legs straight and my fingers precise. He taught me to breathe. My previous attempts, in the enclosure of my room, had felt stillborn. Now, outside with Raphael, slicing the air with my arms, I could feel my practice become real, with soft grass below and high sky above, and the endless space mine to conquer. This was truly happening. I could become a black belt one day. Outside the kitchen door was a high open veranda, and I wanted to jump off its flight of six steps and try a flying kick. "No," Raphael said. "That veranda is too high."

On weekends, if my parents went to the staff club without me, Raphael and I watched Bruce Lee videotapes, Raphael saying, "Watch it! Watch it!" Through his eyes, I saw the films anew; some moves that I had thought merely competent became luminous when he said, "Watch it!" Raphael knew what really mattered; his wisdom lay easy on his skin. He rewound the sections in which Bruce Lee used a nunchaku, and watched unblinking, gasping at the clean aggression of the metal-and-wood weapon.

"I wish I had a nunchaku," I said.

"It is very difficult to use," Raphael said firmly, and I felt almost sorry to have wanted one.

Not long afterward, I came back from school one day and Raphael said, "See." From the cupboard he took out a nunchaku—two pieces of wood, cut from an old cleaning mop and sanded down, held together by a spiral of metal springs. He must have been making it for at least a week, in his free time after his housework. He showed me how to use it. His moves seemed clumsy, nothing like Bruce Lee's. I took the nunchaku and tried to swing it, but only ended up with a thump on my chest. Raphael laughed. "You think you can just start like that?" he said. "You have to practice for a long time."

At school, I sat through classes thinking of the wood's smoothness in the palm of my hand. It was after school, with Raphael, that my real life began. My parents did not notice how close Raphael and I had become. All they saw was that I now happened to play outside, and Raphael was, of course, part of the landscape of outside: weeding the garden, washing pots at the water tank. One afternoon, Raphael finished plucking a chicken and interrupted my solo practice on the lawn. "Fight!" he said. A duel began, his hands bare, mine swinging my new weapon. He pushed me hard. One end hit him on the arm, and he looked surprised and then impressed, as if he had not thought me capable. I swung again and again. He feinted and dodged and kicked. Time collapsed. In the end, we were both panting and laughing. I remember, even now, very clearly, the smallness of his shorts that afternoon, and how the muscles ran wiry like ropes down his legs.

On weekends, I ate lunch with my parents. I always ate quickly, dreaming of escape and hoping that they would not turn to me with one of their test questions. At one lunch, Raphael served white disks of boiled yam on a bed of greens, and then cubed pawpaw and pineapple.

"The vegetable was too tough," my mother said. "Are we grass-eating goats?" She glanced at him. "What is wrong with your eyes?"

It took me a moment to realize that this was not her usual figurative lambasting—"What is that big object blocking your nose?" she would ask, if she noticed a smell in the kitchen that he had not. The whites of Raphael's eyes were red. A painful, unnatural red. He mumbled that an insect had flown into them.

"It looks like Apollo," my father said.

My mother pushed back her chair and examined Raphael's face. "Ah-ah! Yes, it is. Go to your room and stay there."

Raphael hesitated, as though wanting to finish clearing the plates.

"Go!" my father said. "Before you infect us all with this thing."

Raphael, looking confused, edged away from the table. My mother called him back. "Have you had this before?"

"No, Madam."

"It's an infection of your conjunctiva, the thing that covers your eyes," she said. In the midst of her Igbo words, "conjunctiva" sounded sharp and dangerous. "We're going to buy medicine for you. Use it three times a day and stay in your room. Don't cook until it clears." Turning to me, she said, "Okenwa, make sure you don't go near him. Apollo is very infectious." From her perfunctory tone, it was clear that she did not imagine I would have any reason to go near Raphael.

Later, my parents drove to the pharmacy in town and came back with a bottle of eye drops, which my father took to Raphael's room in the boys' quarters, at the back of the house, with the air of someone going reluctantly into battle. That evening, I went with my parents to Obollo Road to buy akara for dinner; when we returned, it felt strange not to have Raphael open the front door, not to find him closing the living-room curtains and turning on the lights. In the quiet kitchen, our house seemed emptied of life.

As soon as my parents were immersed in themselves, I went out to the boys' quarters and knocked on Raphael's door. It was ajar. He was lying on his back, his narrow bed pushed against the wall, and he turned when I came in, surprised, making as if to get up. I had never been in his room before. The exposed light bulb dangling from the ceiling cast somber shadows.

"What is it?" he asked.

"Nothing. I came to see how you are."

He shrugged and settled back down on the bed. "I don't know how I got this. Don't come close."

But I went close.

"I had Apollo in Primary 3," I said. "It will go quickly, don't worry. Have you used the eye drops this evening?"

He shrugged and said nothing. The bottle of eye drops sat unopened on the table.

"You haven't used them at all?" I asked.

"No."

"Why?"

He avoided looking at me. "I cannot do it."

Raphael, who could disembowel a turkey and lift a full bag of rice, could not drip liquid medicine into his eyes. At first, I was astonished, then amused, and then moved. I looked around his room and was struck by how bare it was—the bed pushed against the wall, a spindly table, a gray metal box in the corner, which I assumed contained all that he owned.

"I will put the drops in for you," I said. I took the bottle and twisted off the cap.

"Don't come close," he said again.

I was already close. I bent over him. He began a frantic blinking.

"Breathe like in kung fu," I said.

I touched his face, gently pulled down his lower left eyelid, and dropped the liquid into his eye. The other lid I pulled more firmly, because he had shut his eyes tight.

"Ndo," I said. "Sorry."

He opened his eyes and looked at me, and on his face shone something wondrous. I had never felt myself the subject of admiration. It made me think of science class, of a new maize shoot growing greenly toward light. He touched my arm. I turned to go.

"I'll come before I go to school," I said.

In the morning, I slipped into his room, put in his eye drops, and slipped out and into my father's car, to be dropped off at school.

By the third day, Raphael's room felt familiar to me, welcoming, uncluttered by objects. As I put in the drops, I discovered things about him that I guarded closely: the early darkening of hair above his upper lip, the ringworm patch in the hollow between his jaw and his neck. I sat on the edge of his bed and we talked about *Snake in the Monkey's Shadow*. We had discussed the film many times, and we said things that we had said before, but in the quiet of his room they felt like secrets. Our voices were low, almost hushed. His body's warmth cast warmth over me.

He got up to demonstrate the snake style, and afterward, both of us laughing, he grasped my hand in his. Then he let go and moved slightly away from me.

"This Apollo has gone," he said.

His eyes were clear. I wished he had not healed so quickly.

I dreamed of being with Raphael and Bruce Lee in an open field, practicing for a fight. When I woke up, my eyes refused to open. I pried my lids apart. My eyes burned and itched. Each time I blinked, they seemed to produce more pale ugly fluid that coated my lashes. It felt as if heated grains of sand were under my eyelids. I feared that something inside me was thawing that was not supposed to thaw.

My mother shouted at Raphael, "Why did you bring this thing to my house? Why?" It was as though by catching Apollo he had conspired to infect her son. Raphael did not respond. He never did when she shouted at him. She was standing at the top of the stairs, and Raphael was below her.

"How did he manage to give you Apollo from his room?" my father asked me.

"It wasn't Raphael. I think I got it from somebody in my class," I told my parents.

"Who?" I should have known my mother would ask. At that moment, my mind erased all my classmates' names.

"Who?" she asked again.

"Chidi Obi," I said finally, the first name that came to me. He sat in front of me and smelled like old clothes.

"Do you have a headache?" my mother asked.

"Yes."

My father brought me Panadol. My mother telephoned Dr. Igbokwe. My parents were brisk. They stood by my door, watching me drink a cup of Milo that my father had made. I drank quickly. I hoped that they would not drag an armchair into my room, as they did every time I was sick with malaria, when I would wake up with a bitter tongue to find one parent inches from me, silently reading a book, and I would will myself to get well quickly, to free them.

Dr. Igbokwe arrived and shined a torch in my eyes. His cologne was strong; I could smell it long after he'd gone, a heady scent close to alcohol that I imagined would worsen nausea. After he left, my parents created a patient's altar by my bed—on a table covered with cloth, they put a bottle of orange Lucozade, a blue tin of glucose, and freshly peeled oranges on a plastic tray. They did not bring the armchair, but one of them was home throughout the week that I had Apollo. They took turns putting in my eye drops, my father more clumsily than my mother, leaving sticky liquid running down my face. They did not know how well I could put in the drops myself. Each time they raised the bottle above my face, I remembered the look in Raphael's eyes that first evening in his room, and I felt haunted by happiness.

My parents closed the curtains and kept my room dark. I was sick of lying down. I wanted to see Raphael, but my mother had banned him from my room, as though he could somehow make my condition worse. I wished that he would come and see me. Surely he could pretend to be putting away a bed sheet or bringing a bucket to the bathroom. Why didn't he come? He had not even said sorry to me. I strained to hear his voice, but the kitchen was too far away and his voice, when he spoke to my mother, was too low.

Once, after going to the toilet, I tried to sneak downstairs to the kitchen, but my father loomed at the bottom of the stairs.

"Kedu?" he asked. "Are you all right?"

"I want water," I said.

"I'll bring it. Go and lie down."

Finally, my parents went out together. I had been sleeping, and woke up to sense the emptiness of the house. I hurried downstairs and to the kitchen. It too was empty. I wondered if Raphael was in the boys' quarters; he was not supposed to go to his room during the day, but maybe he had, now that my parents were away. I went out to the open veranda. I heard Raphael's voice before I saw him, standing near the tank, digging his foot into the sand, talking to Josephine, Professor Nwosu's house help. Professor Nwosu sometimes sent eggs from his poultry and never let my parents pay for them. Had Josephine brought eggs? She was tall and plump; now she had the air of someone who had already said goodbye but was lingering. With her, Raphael was different—the slouch in his back, the agitated foot. He was shy. She was talking to him with a kind of playful power, as though she could see through him to things that amused her. My reason blurred.

"Raphael!" I called out.

He turned. "Oh. Okenwa. Are you allowed to come downstairs?"

He spoke as though I were a child, as though we had not sat together in his dim room.

"I'm hungry! Where is my food?" It was the first thing that came to me, but in trying to be imperious I sounded shrill.

Josephine's face puckered, as though she were about to break into slow, long laughter. Raphael said something that I could not hear, but it had the sound of betrayal. My parents drove up just then, and suddenly Josephine and Raphael were roused. Josephine hurried out of the compound, and Raphael came toward me. His shirt was stained in the front, orangish, like palm oil from soup. Had my parents not come back, he would have stayed there mumbling by the tank; my presence had changed nothing.

"What do you want to eat?" he asked.

"You didn't come to see me."

"You know Madam said I should not go near you."

Why was he making it all so common and ordinary? I too had been asked not to go to his room, and yet I had gone, I had put in his eye drops every day.

"After all, you gave me the Apollo," I said.

"Sorry." He said it dully, his mind elsewhere.

I could hear my mother's voice. I was angry that they were back. My time with Raphael was shortened, and I felt the sensation of a widening crack.

"Do you want plantain or yam?" Raphael asked, not to placate me but as if nothing serious had happened. My eyes were burning again. He came up the steps. I moved away from him, too quickly, to the edge of the veranda, and my rubber slippers shifted under me. Unbalanced, I fell. I landed on my hands and knees, startled by the force of my own weight, and I felt the tears coming before I could stop them. Stiff with humiliation, I did not move.

My parents appeared.

"Okenwa!" my father shouted.

I stayed on the ground, a stone sunk in my knee. "Raphael pushed me."

"What?" My parents said it at the same time, in English. "What?"

There was time. Before my father turned to Raphael, and before my mother lunged at him as if to slap him, and before she told him to go pack his things and leave immediately, there was time. I could have spoken. I could have cut into that silence. I could have said that it was an accident. I could have taken back my lie and left my parents merely to wonder.

Ravalushan

FROM *Bomb*

I

THE MUSIC WE heard on our radios that morning was nothing new to our ears; it was what the soldiers played whenever they make a coup. The brassy, instrumental military music had been playing since dawn, and every now and then a deep male voice interrupted with the same announcement: "Fellow countrymen and women. The New Ghana Proletariat Revolutionary Council, N.G.P.R.C., is now in full control of the Castle and the radio stations in all nine regional capitals. We advise everybody to remain calm and to stay tuned for a speech. By the Leader of the Revolution. At ten o'clock."

Revolution?

It was the first time we had heard the word, and it sounded more serious than coup d'état, which we were used to. At five to ten, the music stopped abruptly. It was followed by what sounded like an argument or scuffle in the background. Everything and everybody —even the lizards that roamed the street's crevices bobbing their heads wantonly—froze. "Good morning, comrades, countrymen and women." The new leader's voice, loud and hoarse, shook the tiny speakers of our transistor radios. "My name is Sergeant Francis Wilberforce. I am speaking on behalf of the New Ghana Proletariat Revolutionary Council." We immediately noticed how different his tongue was from ours. He sounded like someone who had lived overseas for a long, long time. His *blɛ*, some even swore, was a true Englishman's English.

"We seized power in order to give it back to you, the people," the new leader continued, his voice awe-inspiring and uplifting. "We seized power in order to correct the injustices that have taken place in this country since independence. Education is not meant for only one tribe, affluence is not created for only one section of the population. The wealth of the nation must be shared and distributed equally among all our citizens. We will apply every military might at our disposal to stamp out the kalabule that has infested the moral fiber of this country, to usher in a new era of probity and accountability!"

Listening to his angry speech, one could have sworn by the Quran that Sergeant Leader, the name we instantly gave the new head of state, was sent by Allah himself to rescue us. To lift up Zongo Street from its poverty, to give us the opportunities other tribes enjoyed, to buy some respect for us and all the common folks in this land. The speech lasted not more than six minutes and, before concluding, the Sergeant Leader explained that some anti-revolution soldiers were trying to stage a coup to counter his "uprising," and that in order to stabilize the situation, a six-to-six curfew had to be imposed nationwide, "until further notice."

Wallahi, this man is a man of action, we cried. A man of the people!

"The Soviet people themselves orchestrated this revolution, and they handpicked this new leader," commented Mr. Rafik at Gado's barbershop, where a small crowd had gathered to listen to the speech. The barbershop was the hangout for book-long types like Mr. Rafik and Dr. Azeez. They spent half the day reading the newspapers and listening to GBC, BBC, and Voice of America, and then wasted the other half challenging each other's views and punditing to whoever cared to listen. And in true fashion Dr. Azeez didn't even allow the air to blow over Mr. Rafiq's statement before he countered, "You got it all wrong, Mr. Man. The white people of England, and not the Russians, are the ones in charge of this mutiny. The British people are coming back to colonize us all over again, and I here"—the doctor placed an open palm on his chest—"fully support the move."

Himself, Gado Barber didn't grant any opinion. He was a serious man, and quite notorious for his mood swings. As the shop's crowd grew, Gado—tall, lanky, with a slight back hump that was a result of how he bent his extraordinary long upper body—rose

from the lone barber's chair and announced a haircut morato-
rium. "Not until we know the state of affairs in this land," he declared. "These are grim times." He returned to his chair, tilted
his head toward the shop's rain-damaged plywood ceiling, and in
solemn silence twisted his thick mustache.

Right then, an out-of-towner squeezed himself into the shop's
center and proceeded to ask for a trim. "Are you so stupid you
don't realize the gravity of this day?" yelled Gado. He chased out
the baffled customer, waving a pair of scissors in the air. "Idiot, I'll
cut off your ear, not your hair!" he screamed amid a cacophony
of laughter. He would have done it too: Gado had been known to
give a bloody ear to kids who wouldn't sit still during a haircut.

Across the street at Mallam Sile's teashop, the mood was lighter.
The children, enjoying an automatic holiday from the Catholic
school and the madrasa, milled about the shop's entrance. They
were excited, in the way small pikins are when things, good or bad,
happen to people. Sile's adult patrons, however, had worried looks
on their faces as they sipped their hot beverages. The dwarfish
tea-seller, known to readily engage in idle chatter, was noticeably
silent, his mind obviously on the morning's upheaval.

In the mosque's yard, meanwhile, Mallam Imran, the self-ap-
pointed spiritualist, addressed a small gathering of his talibai and
the mendicants that patrolled the compound. "This so-called ravalushan was revealed to me in the wahai I received last night, but
I predict it will not last," swore the boka in his usual soft-spoken
manner. "By Allah's grace I give it maximum"—he paused, fixed
his eyes on the cloudy skies, then added, "four weeks, Insha Allah!"
His listeners quietly shook their heads up and down in the devo-
tional manner of religious supplicants.

The main road was suddenly filled with people, who after listening to the speech in their houses came outside to see what a
revolution looked like. Our two resident lunatics, Ee Hey and Mr.
Brenya, were there too, at their regular spots by the palace assembly shed, carrying on with their antics. Ee Hey, the giant thong-
wearing lunatic was deeply engaged in his favorite pastime: he
laughed deliriously at the sounds from the stereo speakers of a
nearby pirate music store. The other madman, Mr. Brenya—who
for twenty-seven years had neatly kept and read the same newspaper articles—stood at akimbo position, murmuring vocabulary
words to himself. Typically Mr. Brenya hardly said a word to any-

body, except when he challenged passersby to a word-definition contest, the passion that consumed his life. "I know English pass the Englishman himself," he often boasted. Ee Hey and Mr. Brenya didn't only entertain us; they protected the street at night from vandals and petty thieves, who walked on at the sight of these men. But that February morning was not a day for humor. By the harshness of the morning's rising heat and the discordant sound of the white man's music, we felt that the tranquil, naive state of our lives was about to be altered in a way and manner we couldn't have ever imagined.

As we mulled over Sergeant Leader's speech, wondering what it all meant for our poor lot, a loud roar erupted from the five corners of the city. Soon a massive, jubilant crowd that numbered into the thousands came marching toward our street. Taxi and trotro drivers bleated their horns. Women took off their veils and waved them in the air. "Power to the people!" they chanted, and stamped and kicked their feet in the air, creating a cloud of dust. "Yay, a luta! Yay, a luta continua!" the marchers wailed. Half-naked children galloped behind the throng. We joined the demo people and sang their songs of protest though the real meaning of the words and lyrics weren't clear to a great number of us. We railed and wailed. Against Disenfranchisement. Against Kleptocracy. Against Tribalism. Against Capitalism. Against Nepotism. Hastily assembled, crooked placards screamed: DOWN WITH CORRUPTION. REVOLT OF THE MASSES! WE NO GO SIT DOWN MAKE DEM CHEAT US EVERYDAY!

We loitered for hours at Justice Park, where the march ended. And with all the singing and dancing that went on, it seemed to everybody that a rally was about to begin. We would discover later on that the demo was not organized by any person or group in particular; it sprung from the spontaneous giddiness that had followed Sergeant Leader's speech.

By late afternoon the city's food hawkers and drink vendors—always on the lookout for large gatherings—had planted their carts and trays all around the park's perimeter. Tricksters, magicians, aphrodisiac peddlers, quack gonorrhea doctors, and box-cinema operators had all got wind of the "rally," and they too had set up shop with their rickety umbrellas. The dust from all these activities, coupled with the harmattan smog, created a dense, bleary atmosphere. And amid the heightened state of celebration, we lost track of the rhythm of our inner clocks. The intoxicating beat and comforting words of the songs of struggle drowned out the cautious drumbeat of old that had for generations guided our actions. We only came to our senses when somebody from our street shouted in Hausa, "Curfir yakai!" One look at the Prempeh Assembly Hall clock—it was ten to—and we borrowed the gazelle's legs, disappearing in no time. Others in the crowd immediately understood their folly too and joined us in flight. A great stampede ensued. Luckily for us, Zongo Street was only five hundred meters from the park, and we made it into the safety of our compounds before the siren. But the story was not the same for the marchers from Ash Town, A.E.B., Asafo, and Bantama.

At the strike of six, hundreds of gun-carrying soldiers—it appeared that they had all the while lain in wait in nearby alleys —descended on the marchers. People ran helter-skelter into compounds in which they knew nobody. We sheltered those that managed to escape and gave them mats to sleep on in our courtyards. The unfortunate ones who couldn't escape would for the rest of their lives rue that day. Through the cracks in our windows, we saw them being beaten to the ground, mercilessly, as if they were prey. With crude batons. With gun barrels. With metal-toed boots. Some were even shot dead. The dusk air was filled with the wailings of trapped victims, the screams of soldiers, the cracking sound of bullets, the thud of objects to body and body to ground.

Deep into the night gunshots and mortar shells rang and boomed from distances across the city. By daylight, more than fifty people were dead, at least that was the figure told us by Mansa BBC, the eminent rumormonger of Zongo Street. Sources from other neighborhoods pegged the total dead at thirty. But since none of the newspapers made mention of the march or the attack, we had no way of knowing the actual number of people killed on the first night of the revolution.

We quickly became accustomed to the new way of life under the curfew. We and our sheep, goats, chickens, and ducks locked ourselves in our compounds well before the dreaded siren. Young children cornered their grandparents to spin one Gizo tale after another until sleep-time. Meanwhile Sergeant Leader and his people created new laws every day. We gathered around our radios every morning, to listen to new rules, which always ended with the warning that "All citizens must comply with the new directives. Or face the consequences."

Then came the introduction of the People's Vigilance Committees. The PVCs, we were told, were created to facilitate a neighborhood-by-neighborhood discussion about a new thing they called "Grassroots Democracy," a term not even Mr. Rafik and Dr. Azeez could explain properly. Mr. Rafik posited that the "Grassroots" had something to do with Sergeant Leader's effort to make Ghana produce its own food and stop importing from overseas. Dr. Azeez's explanation for the term was much fuzzier, but we were confident that his was closer to the truth. "It means every man is going to be a farmer, and is allowed only one hoe and only one wife and only one vote," he chimed. When asked to define the new phenomenon, English maverick Mr. Brenya simply said, "Dem all crazy," finally betraying the authoritative command he was known for on matters of the Queen's language. But no sooner had the PVCs been formed than it became clear that the main mission of its members was to spy on and root out the Against People, the Enemies of the Revolution.

"Snakes in the grass, that's what they are, those PBC ravalushan boys," said Mansa BBC.

The inauguration of the Zongo Street PVC ushered in an era of social upheaval in our small community. Respect for the elders, a sacred practice in our Hausa Islamic culture, quickly disappeared among some youth, who felt it was time the old folks realize the changing zaman. If the song changes, the dance too must change, they asserted.

Soldiers in armored vehicles, carrying heavy firearms, went from house to house in the city proper, and from store to store at Central Market, searching for kalabule goods and the people who hoarded them. Operation Clean House, it was called. Shop owners locked their doors. Trading came to a halt across the city, causing a scarcity of provisions and foodstuffs we had never seen before. A spell of hunger and suffering threatened to erode what little dignity we had left. And so consumed were we with our struggles that the disappearance of Ee Hey and Mr. Brenya didn't come to our notice until a week after it had happened. It never occurred to us that mad folks too were bound by the laws of the revolution. We never saw Ee Hey again. Mr. Brenya eventually returned to us, but

never was he the affable wordsmith we had known. His face bore a
sad expression, unsmiling, foreboding.

On the day we discovered that our beloved lunatics had been
abducted, the remaining bit of jollity in our lives evaporated into
the dense fog of the revolution. Even Hamda One, the latrine man
and the so-called Laughing Hyena of Zongo Street—who, despite
his horrendous vocation and low social class, was the most cheerful person in the neighborhood—lost his sense of humor. He
avoided eye contact with people and sped on, the latrine bucket
precariously balanced on his head. For weeks, not a single laugh
was heard on Zongo Street, not even from the children, who are
usually immune to such absurd realities.

2

For a stretch of time Zongo Street was spared the carnage of the
revolution. Not a single house was bombed—instant justice was
meted out to the landlords in whose houses kalabule goods were
found. And nobody, other than the two madmen, had been abducted by soldiers from Gondar Barracks. Baba Ila—the only truly
rich person on Zongo Street—was a God-fearing merchant who
imported stockfish and other dried goods from Nigeria and the
Ivory Coast. Assured in our minds that he was not in harm's way,
we discreetly supported the assault on the city's wealthy folk, on
whose head Sergeant Leader placed the blame for the poverty of
folks like us and for all of the country's economic and social problems. We watched in tacit silence as soldiers lined up businessmen,
market women, and ordinary citizens, stripped them naked, and
flogged their backs and buttocks in the market square.

Then at exactly six-thirty a.m. on the fourth of May, five lorries
packed with abongo men descended upon our street like seasonal
locusts. There must have been a hundred of them, armed heavily
with machine guns, rifles, and grenades that hung loosely from
their waistbands. A number of the soldiers stood at intervals along
the street's perimeter, while the rest trotted into Baba Ila's compound, a modern three-story concrete building with a penthouse
on the top floor.

We abandoned our morning chores and gathered in alleys
and rooftops to catch a glimpse of the operation. Baba Ila—dark-

skinned, muscular, and middle-aged—was escorted out of his compound. He was clad in white cotton underwear, his wide, hairy chest naked. He looked weary and disoriented. Chin lowered, lips moving—as if in prayer.

The abongo men carted box-loads of imported stockfish, sardines, corned beef, and other dried goods from the house and stacked them in a pile out on the street. They broke into the storefronts of the building and emptied them of all their merchandise. There was a provision store, a textile retail outlet, and a rice wholesaler; and even though none of these businesses were Baba Ila's, he was still charged with "hoarding and smuggling."

The soldiers formed a ring around the merchant. One slapped him across the face, another kicked his groin, and a third, coming from behind, struck him on the head with a gun barrel. A gash on Baba Ila's head spewed blood, a dark bulb appeared around his left eye, shutting it completely. He was on all fours at this point, but that didn't stop his assailants from hitting him. "Get up, if you no wan' die!" a soldier shouted. Baba Ila made an attempt to stand, but swiftly fell on his back. His head hit the ground with a thud. "Kalabule man, we go kill you today!" they shouted with each kick of their boots.

Women clutched their bosoms and slapped their ample thighs and cried hysterically. The men just froze in frightful silence. We longed to approach the soldiers and vouch for Baba Ila's integrity. To say to them, Look, this Baba has never engaged in kalabule, and many of the poor folks on this street depend on him for their evening meals. But who were we to approach a red-eyed soldier during those hot days of the revolution?

Suddenly, what we had dreaded all along happened. A soldier smashed a Star beer bottle from which he had just finished drinking. Using a large piece of the broken glass, he began to scrape off Baba Ila's hair. They called it baban soja, the "designer" haircut the military gave to people in their custody. Blood was everywhere on the merchant's body. Next, the soldiers opened tins of sardine and corned beef and tore open boxes of raw stockfish. "Eat everything now, now," they barked. Baba Ila pushed the food into his mouth and ate until he began to choke. He coughed a guttural cough and vomited all over himself. That appeared to anger the soldiers, who started a fresh assault on him. They grabbed his lifeless-looking body and tossed it into one of the lorries as if he were a sack of rice. They formed a human chain, and within fifteen minutes they had filled their trucks with all the seized merchandise. Then, with a combination of dexterity and showmanship, the abongo men leaped onto the moving lorries, fired shots into the air, and sped off, leaving behind a cloud of red dust and a trail of sorrow and tears on Zongo Street.

3

Some say the owl is an animal of darkness. Others say it is an animal of vision. On the day following Baba Ila's abduction, a white owl appeared on Zongo Street. The bird sat comfortably for more than five minutes on a limb of the goji tree near the mosque, and not even once did it blink or turn its head in the usual shy manner of owls. Instead, the bird stared right back at those who accidentally caught its eye. Mallam Imran swore, this time by the grave of the Prophet himself, that the owl had revealed the destiny of the whole nation to him. "This time *he* is leaving us for sure," the boka said. "By Allah, we will not wake up with *him* next week."

"Keep talking nonsense," sneered BBC. "Far as I know, Sargey Leader is Allah's kwammander. And he here to stay."

As if what happened to Baba Ila wasn't enough to test our faith and scar our collective psyche, we woke up to more commotion one morning. We saw Hamda One, the latrine man, pacing up and down the street, with the usual bucket of feces on his head. He burst out into laughter any time he made eye contact with folks, breaking the unofficial taboo that had, for weeks, kept us from smiling. Mansa BBC remarked, "The carrion stew he been eating all these years at Mallam Bawa's pito bar done finally moved into his brain." Clearly there was something alarming, perhaps even sinister, in the way Hamda One carried himself that morning. The more we listened to the sound of his laughter, the more we became convinced that it didn't come from his body alone. Those nearby looked reproachfully at the latrine man, as if with his mirth he had committed a grave sin. These reproaches, however, did nothing to deter Hamda One. His laughter, a series of loud, high-pitched "hee-hee-hee" sounds, resembled the spotted hyena's, whose laughter carries dire meaning to its listeners. The latrine man seemed defiant—confrontational, even—as if provoking us to look at him. To smell our own excrement. He swayed his upper body, causing the feces to spill onto the ground. "Useless man, carry your shit, go somewhere else," several voices yelled at once. But he became even more animated and started a song in his Frafra language, a tongue none of us Hausa folks understood. His words and syllables, a litany of polyphonic phrases, sounded ominous. That morning, not a single heart on Zongo Street was unmoved. Even the book-long folks at Gado's barbershop, whose scorn for the latrine man was unsurpassed, showed some compassion toward him.

Eventually the spilled excrement found its way into Hamda One's mouth. The hysterical laughter gave way to a series of violent, ricocheting coughs. By now, almost all of the bucket's content was on the ground. With palm-covered mouths and noses we stared. Hamda One laughed and coughed until his body couldn't take it any longer. He collapsed in a heap and died instantly. His smeared face, mouth agape in mid-laughter, was the last we saw of the latrine man.

It was as if the spirits that had for several weeks stifled our laughter had suddenly decided to relieve us of our suffering; we could not make eye contact without bursting into teary laughter. Mallam Imran issued a fatwa for every adult to observe a three-day fast, "to ward off the evil forces that are bent on destroying this community." Nobody paid attention to the boka, not even the mendicants, who were, by this time, more preoccupied with finding something to eat than following an edict that could starve them to death.

With the owl's visit still on our minds, with the fear of hunger and the brutality of the soldiers overwhelming us, with the fate of Baba Ila still unknown, with the smoke from recently bombed houses choking our lungs, with the grotesque end of Hamda One unexplained, with the stench of feces still fresh in our noses, with the chants of "A luta continua!" and "Let the blood flow!" ruling the air in the town proper, we retreated to our compounds and reverted to our go-to mantra in times of crisis: Insha Allah!

Garments

FROM *Freeman's*

ONE DAY MALA lowers her mask and says to Jesmin, my boyfriend wants to marry you. Jesmin is six shirts behind so she doesn't look up. After the bell, Mala explains. For months now she's been telling the girls, ya, any day now me and Dulal are going to the Kazi. They don't believe her, they know her boyfriend works in an air-conditioned shop. No way he was going to marry a garments girl. Now she has a scheme and when Jesmin hears it, she thinks, it's not so bad.

Two days later Mala's sweating like it's July. He wants one more. Three wives. We have to find a girl. After the bell they look down the row of sewing machines and try to choose. Mala knows all the unmarried girls, which one needs a room, which one has hungry relatives, which one borrowed money against her wage and can't work enough overtime to pay it off. They squint down the line and consider Fatima, Keya, Komola, but for some reason or other they reject them all. There's a new girl at the end of the row, but when Mala takes a break and limps over to the toilet she comes back and says the girl has a milky eye.

There's a new order for panties. Jesmin picks up the sample. She's never seen a panty like it before. It's thick, with double seams on the front, back, and around the buttocks. The leg is just cut off without a stitch. Mala, she says, what's this? Mala says, the foreign ladies use them to hold in their fat and they call them Thanks. Thanks? Yep. Because they look so good, in the mirror they say to the panties, Thanks. Jesmin and Mala pull down their masks and trade a laugh when the morning supervisor, Jamal, isn't looking.

Jesmin decides it won't be so bad to share a husband. She doesn't have dreams of a love marriage, and if they have to divide the sex that's fine with her, and if he wants something, like he wants his rice the way his mother makes it, maybe one of them will know how to do it. Walking home as she did every evening with all the other factory workers, a line two girls thick and a mile long, snaking out of Tongi and all the way to Uttara, she spots a new girl. Sometimes Jesmin looks in front and behind her at that line, all the ribbons flapping and the song of sandals on the pavement, and she feels a swell in her chest. She catches up to the girl. Her name's Ruby. She's dark, but pretty. Small white teeth and filmy eyes. She's new and eager to make friends. I'm coming two, three hours from my village every morning, she complains. I know, Jesmin says. Finding a place to live is why I'm doing this.

The year Jesmin came to Dhaka she said to her father, ask Nasir chacha to give you his daughter's mobile contact. Nasir chacha's daughter Kulsum had a job in garments. Her father nodded, said she will help you. Her mother, drying mustard in front of their hut, put her face in the crook of her arm. Go, go, she said. I don't want to see you again. Jesmin left without looking back, knowing that, once, her mother had another dream for her, that she would marry and be treated like a queen, that all the village would tell her what a good forehead she had. But that was before Amin, before the punishing hut.

Kulsum did help her. Put in a good word when she heard they were looking. She has a place, a room in Korail she shares with her kid and her in-laws. Her husband works in foreign so she lets Jesmin sleep on the floor. She takes half of Jesmin's pay every month. You're lucky, she tells her, I didn't ask for the money up front. But now her husband's coming back and Jesmin has to find somewhere else. She has another relative, a cousin's cousin, but he lives all the way out in Mogbajar and Jesmin doesn't like the way he looks at her. There's a shanty not far from the factory and she heard there were rooms going, but when she went to look, the landlord said, I can't have so many girls in my building. What building? Just a row of tin, paper between the walls, sharing an outside tap. But still he told her he wasn't sure, had to think about it. If you had a husband, he said, that would be a different story.

When Jesmin joined the line, she started as Mala's helper. She tied her knots and clipped the threads from her shirt buttons. The

Rana strike was over and Mala's leg was broken and the bosses had their eye on her, always waiting to see if she'd make more trouble. Even now, Jamal gives her a look every time she walks by, waiting to see if she takes too long in the toilet. They would have got rid of her a long time ago if her hands weren't so good, always first in the line, seams straight as blades of grass, five, seven pieces ahead of everyone.

To make the Thanks you have to stretch the fabric tight against your left arm while running the stitch. Then you fold it, stretch again, run the stitch back up, till the whole thing is hard and tight. Jesmin trims the leg and takes a piece home. She pulls it up over her leg. Her thigh bulges in front and behind it. She doesn't understand. Maybe the legs of foreign ladies are different.

Jesmin and Mala know a foreign lady, Miss Bridgey. She came to the factory and asked them a few questions and wrote down what they said. How many minutes for lunch? Where is the toilet? If there's a fire, what will you do? In the morning before she came, Jamal lined everyone up. There's an inspector coming, he said. You want to make a good impression. Jamal liked to ask a question and supply the answer. Are we proud of the factory? Yes we are! What do we think of Sunny Textiles? We love SunnyTex! That day they opened all the windows and did the fire drill ten times. Then Miss Bridgey showed up and Jesmin could see the laugh behind Jamal's face. He thought it would be a man in a suit, and there was this little yellow-haired girl. Nothing to worry. Aren't we lucky? Yes we are.

When Miss Bridgey comes back Jesmin is going to ask her about the Thanks. But right now they have to explain the whole thing to Ruby. Mala's doing all the talking. We marry him, and that way we can tell people we are married. We give him a place to stay, we give him food, we give him all the things a wife gives. If he wants sex, we give him sex. When she mentions the sex, Jesmin feels her legs filling up with water. Why don't we get our own husbands? Ruby asks. She's green, she doesn't know. Ruby looks like she's going to cry. Then she bites her full lip with a line of those perfect little teeth and she says, okay, I'll do it.

When Jesmin was born, her mother took a piece of coal and drew a big black mark behind her ear. Jesmin went to school and learned the letters and the sums before any of the other children. The teacher, Amin, always asked her to sing the national anthem on Victory Day and stand first in the parade. Amin said she should go to secondary. He said, meet me after school. He taught her sums and a, b, c. He put his hand over her hand on the chalk.

Miss Bridgey comes a few days later and she takes Jesmin aside. I'm worried about the factory, she says. Has it always been this bad? Jesmin looks around. She takes in the fans in the ceiling, bars on the windows, rows and rows of girls bent over their machines. It's the same, she says. Always like this. This place good. This place okay. We love SunnyTex! But why, she asks Miss Bridgey, do the ladies in your country wear this? She holds up the Thanks. Miss Bridgey takes it from her hand, turns it around, then she laughs and laughs. Jesmin, you know how expensive these are?

On the wedding day Dulal comes to the factory. He's wearing a red shirt under the gray sleeveless sweater they made last year when the SunnyTex bosses decided to expand into knitwear. Jesmin and Mala and Ruby stand in front of him, and he looks at them with his head tilted to the side. Take a look at my prince! Mala says. He's got a narrow face and small black eyes and hair that sticks to his forehead. Now it's time to get married so they set off on two rickshaws, him and Mala in the front, Jesmin and Ruby following behind. They are all wearing red saris like brides do, except nobody's family has showed up to feed them sweets or paint their feet.

Jesmin watches the back of Mala and Dulal. She knows that Mala's brother died in Rana. That Mala had held up his photo for seven weeks, hoping he would come out from under the cement. That she was at the strike, shouting her brother's name. That her mother kept writing from the village asking for money, so Mala had to turn around and go back to the line. Mala's face was cracked, like a broken eggshell, until she found Dulal. Now she comes to the factory, works like magic, tells her jokes, does her overtime as if it never happened, but Jesmin knows that once you die like that, on the street or in the factory, your life isn't your life anymore.

This morning Jesmin went to the shanty to talk to the landlord. I'm getting married. Can I stay? He looked at her with one side of his face. Married? Show me the groom. I'll bring him next week, she said. He took one more drag and threw his cigarette into the drain and Jesmin thought for sure he was going to say no, but then he turned to her and said, what, I don't get any sweets? Then he slapped her on the back, and she shrank, but it was a friendly slap, as if she was a man, or his daughter. Next she went to Kulsum. I found a husband. Good, she said, you're getting old. Now I don't have to worry about you.

Jesmin sees marriage as a remedy. If you are a girl you have many problems, but all of them can be fixed if you have a husband. In the factory, if Jamal puts you in ironing, which is the easiest job, or if he says, take a few extra minutes for lunch, you can finish after hours and get overtime, you can say, but my husband is waiting, and then you won't have to feel his breath like a spider on your shoulder later that night when the current goes out and you're still in the factory finishing up a sleeve. Everything is better if you're married. Jesmin is giving Ruby all this good advice as their rickshaw passes the Mohakhali flyover but the girl's eyes are somewhere else. Bet she had some other idea about her life. Jesmin puts her arm around Ruby's shoulder and notices she smells very nice, like the biscuit factory she passes on the way to Sunny-Tex.

Jesmin is the only one who can sign her name on the wedding register. The others dip their thumbs into ink and press them into the big book. The kazi takes their money and gives them a piece of paper that has all their names on it. Jesmin reads it out loud to the others.

After, Dulal wants to stop at a chotpoti stall. Three men, friends of his, are waiting there. They look at the brides, up and down, and then they stick their elbows into Dulal's side and Dulal smiles like he's just opened a drawer full of cash. Who's first? they ask him. The old one, he replies, not bothering to whisper it. Then that one, he says, pointing to Jesmin. Next week Kulsum said she would let Jesmin string a blanket across and take half the bed. Her in-laws will be on the other half and she'll take the kid and sleep on the floor. Best for last, eh? his friend says. Dulal looks at Ruby like he's seeing her for the first time and he says, yeah, she's the cream.

The friends take off and then it's just the brides and groom. They sit on four stools along the pavement. Jesmin feels the winter air on her neck. Where's your village? Dulal asks, but before she can tell him, she hears Ruby's voice saying, Kurigram. Something in the sound of her voice makes Jesmin think maybe Ruby wants to be the favorite wife. She notices now that Ruby has tied a ribbon in her hair. They finish their plates and Mala holds hands with Dulal and they take off in the direction of her place. Jesmin and Ruby are taking the bus to Kulsum's. Ruby's giving Kulsum some of her pay so she can stay there too, just until they find her somewhere else.

Jesmin wants to say something to mark the fact that they are all married now. She can't think of anything so she asks Ruby if it gets cold in her village. Yes, she says, in winter sometimes people die. I'm from the south, Jesmin tells her, it's not so bad but still in winter, it bites. They hug their arms now as the sun sets. I wonder what they're doing, Ruby says. Do you think he's nice? He looks nice.

They're doing what people do, she tells Ruby, at night when no one is looking. They arrive at Kulsum's. She can share your blanket, Kulsum says, throwing a look at Ruby until Ruby takes the money out of her bag. They warm some leftover rice on the stove Kulsum shares with two other families at the back of the building. The gas is low and it takes half an hour to heat the rice, then they crush a few chilies into it. I have three younger sisters, Ruby says, even though Jesmin hasn't asked about her family. Where are they? Home and hungry, she says, and Jesmin gets a picture in her mind of three dark-skinned girls with perfect teeth, shivering together in the northern cold. What about you? Ruby asks. A snake took my brother, Jesmin says, remembering his face, gray and swollen, before they threw it in the ground. Hai Allah! Ruby rubs her hand up and down Jesmin's back. His forehead was unlucky, Jesmin says, pretending it wasn't so bad, like this wasn't the reason everything started to go sour, her parents with nothing to look forward to, just a daughter whose head was a curse and the hope that next year's rice would come up without a fight.

It's freezing on the floor. Jesmin is glad for Ruby's back spreading the warm into their blanket. You are kind, Ruby mumbles as she falls asleep, and Jesmin can see her breathing, her shoulders moving up and down. She lies awake for a long time imagining Mala with their husband. The watery feeling returns to her legs. Ruby shifts, moves closer, and her biscuit smell clouds up around them. Jesmin takes a strand of Ruby's hair and puts it into her mouth.

When she gets to SunnyTex the next morning Mala is already at her machine with her head down. Jesmin tries to catch her eye but she won't look up, and when they break for lunch she disappears and Jesmin doesn't see her until it's too late. Finally it's the end of the day and Mala is hurrying along in the going-home line. What d'you want? She squints as if she's looking from far away and when Jesmin asks her what the wedding night was like, she says, it wasn't so bad. That's all? You'll find out for yourself, don't let me go and spoil it, and then her face bends into a smile. She won't say anything else.

After their shift is over Jesmin tells Ruby, let's go to a shop. I don't have any money, Ruby says. Don't worry, we'll just look. They walk to the sandal shop at the end of the street. They stare at the wall of sandals. Ruby takes Jesmin's hand and squeezes her fingers. It's so nice, she can almost feel the sandals on her feet.

The week is over and finally it's Jesmin's turn. She scrubs her face till Kulsum scolds her for taking too long at the tap. She wears a red shalwar kameez. Ruby wants to do her hair. She makes a braid that begins at the top of Jesmin's head and runs all the way down her back. Her fingers move quickly and Jesmin feels a shiver that starts at her neck and disappears into her kameez. Ruby reaches back and takes the clip out of her own hair and puts it into Jesmin's. She feels it tense her hair together.

All day while they're sewing buttons onto check shirts, Jesmin can feel the clip pulling at her scalp. Mala, she says, I'm feeling scared. At first Mala looks like she's going to tell her something, but her eyes go back to her sewing machine and she says, all brides are scared. Don't worry, I tested him out for you. Equipment is working tip-top.

After work Dulal is standing outside the SunnyTex gate. He puts his finger under her chin and stares into her face like he's examining a leg of goat. His breathing is ragged and his cheeks are shining. She notices how dirty his shirt is under the sweater and she starts to wonder what sort of a man would want three wives all at once. She shakes her head to knock the thoughts out of it. She has a husband, that's what matters. The road unfolds in front of them as they walk home, his hand molded onto her waist. Kulsum is wearing lipstick and she tells her kid, look, your khalu has come to visit, give him foot-salaam, and her kid kneels in front of Dulal and touches his sandal. In the kitchen they pass around the food. Jesmin puts rice on Dulal's plate, and the bigger piece of meat. Kulsum gets a piece too and the rest of them do with gravy.

She's given him the mora from under the bed so he sits taller than everyone else. The gravy is watery but Jesmin watches Kulsum's kid run his tongue all across his plate. She thinks about Ruby. It's Thursday and she's gone home on the bus to spend the weekend with her brothers. Jesmin fingers the clip, still standing stiff on the side of her head.

Now it's time and they lie down together. The blanket is strung across but Jesmin can see the outline of Kulsum's mother-in-law, her elbow jutting into their side of the bed. Dulal turns his face to the wall and says, scratch my back. He squirms out of his shirt and she runs her fingers up and down his back and soon her nails are clogged with dirt. He takes her hand and pulls it over to the front of his body, and then he takes out his thing. His hand is over her hand, and she thinks of Amin and the chalk and the village, fog in the winter and the new season's molasses and everything smelling clean, the dung drying against the walls of her father's hut. Her arm is getting sore and Dulal's breath is slow and steady, his thing soft as a mouse. She thinks maybe he's fallen asleep but then he turns around and she feels the weight of him pressing down on her. He drags down her kameez and tries to push the mouse in. After a few minutes he gives up and turns back around. Scratch my back, he says, irritated, and finally he falls asleep with her hand trapped under his elbow.

The next day is Friday and Dulal says he's going to spend it with his sister, who lives in Uttara. Jesmin was hoping they could go to the market and look at the shops, but he leaves before she can ask. She takes the bus to Mohakhali. Mala's neighbor looks Jesmin up and down and says to her, so your friend is married now. Look at her, like a queen she is. Mala's wearing bright orange lipstick and acting like something good has happened to her. She's talking on her mobile and Jesmin waits for her to finish. Then she asks, is it supposed to be like that?

Mala looks up from the bed. You couldn't do it?

What, what was I supposed to do?

She grabs an arm. Did he put it in?

No.

She curses under her breath. But I told him you would be the one.

The one to what?

The one to cure his, you know, not being able to.

Jesmin struggles to understand. You told me his equipment was tip-top.

Mala shrinks from her. It occurs to Jesmin that she never asked the right question, the one that has been on everyone's mind. Why does a guy working in a shop, who doesn't get his hands dirty all day, want a garments girl, especially a broken one like Mala? Jesmin stares at her until Mala can't hold her eye anymore. Mala looks down at her hands. I paid him, she says.

You paid him?

Then he started asking for more, more money, and I didn't have it, so I told him you and Ruby would fix him. That's the only way he would stay.

She's got her head in her hands and she's crying. She rubs her broken leg, and Jesmin thinks of Rana, and Mala's brother, and her own brother, and she decides there's nothing to be done now but try and fix Dulal's problem, because now that they were married to him, his bad was their bad.

What next?

Try again, try everything. Mala hands her the tube of lipstick. Here, take this.

That night Jesmin asks Kulsum for a few sprays from the bottle of scent she keeps in a box under the bed and Kulsum takes it out reluctantly, eyeing her while she pats some of it onto her neck. Jesmin draws thick lines across her eyelids and smears the lipstick on hard. Dulal cleans his plate and goes outside to gargle into the drain. She stands with him at the edge of the drain and after he rinses and spits, he looks up at the night. There's all kinds of noise coming from the compound, kids screaming, dogs, a radio, but up there it looks quiet. Maybe Dulal's looking for a bit of quiet too. Fog's coming, she says. She asks about his sister. Alhamdulillah, he tells her, but doesn't say, I will take you to meet her. I hate winter, he says instead, makes my bones tired.

Winter makes her think of the sesame her mother had planted, years ago when she was a baby. The harvest was for selling, but after the first season the price at the market wasn't worth the water and the effort, so she gave it up. But still the branches came up, twisted and pointy every year, tearing the feet off anyone who dared walk across the field. Only Amin knew how to tread between the bushes, his feet unscarred, the soles of his feet always so soft. Jesmin ran them across her cheeks and it was like his palm was touching her, or the tip of his penis, rather than the underside of his big toe, that's how delicate his feet were. I'm only here to talk, he said, telling her the story of Laila and Majnu. From Amin she learned what it was to be swallowed by a man, like a snake swallowing a rat, whole and without effort. He pressed his feet against her face, showing her the difference between a schoolteacher and a farmer's daughter, and she licked the salt between his toes, and when she asked when they would get married, he laughed as if she had told him the funniest joke in the world. And then his wife went to the Salish, and the Salish decided she had tempted Amin, and they said, leave the village. But not before you are punished. And into the punishing hut she went, and when she came out, she looked exactly like she was meant to look, ugly and broken. Like a rat swallowed by a snake. Just like Mala looked after they told her the search was over and she would never see her brother again. Now Jesmin is wondering if something happened to Dulal that made him feel like the rest of them, like a small animal in a big, spiteful world.

Maybe that's why, she offers, speaking softly into the dark. He turns to her. What did you say?

Maybe that's why, you know, it's not—it's not your fault.

He comes close. His breath is eggy. That's when, out of nowhere, one side of her face explodes. When she opens her eyes she's on the ground and everyone is standing over her, Kulsum, her kid, her in-laws, and Dulal. The kid tugs at her kameez and she stands up, brushes herself off. No one says anything. Jesmin can taste lipstick and blood where she's bitten herself.

In the morning Jamal takes one look at her and runs her to the back of the line. You look like a bat, he says, you should've stayed home. What if that inspector comes nosing around? Her eye is swollen so she has to change the thread on the machine with her head tilted to one side. Ruby's back from her village and when she sees Jesmin she starts to cry. Don't worry, Jesmin says, it's nothing. She takes a toilet break, borrows a compact from Mala, and looks at herself. One side of her face is swallowing the other. When she comes out Ruby's holding a chocbar. She presses it against Jesmin's cheek and they wait for it to melt, then they tear open a corner and take turns pouring the ice cream into their mouths.

They go home. Dulal isn't there. Now look what you did, Kulsum says. They wait until the mosquitoes come in and finally eve-

ryone eats. When the kerosene lamp comes on and she's about
to bed on the floor with Ruby, Dulal bursts in and demands food.
She makes him a plate and watches him belch. The food's cold,
he says. After, it's the same, lying there facing his back, holding
his small, lifeless thing, except this time Ruby's on the floor next
to Kulsum and her kid. Scratch my head, Dulal mutters. He falls
asleep, and later, in the night, she hears him cry out, a sharp, bleating sound. She thinks she must have dreamed it because in the
moonlight his face is as mean as ever.

On the day of Ruby's turn, she looks so small. When she's cut
too much thread off her machine, Jamal scolds her and she spends
the rest of the day with her head down. But after lunch she goes
into the toilet and when she comes out she's got a new sari on and
the ribbon is twisted into her hair like a thread of happy running
all around the back of her head. Dulal comes to the gate and when
he sees Ruby his face is as bright as money. Ruby says something to
Dulal and he laughs. Jesmin watches them leave together, holding
hands, her heart breaking against her ribs.

Jesmin covers her ears against the sound of laughter.

In the punishing hut, the Salish gathered. The oldest one said,
take off your dress. When her clothes were on the ground he said,
walk. They sat in a circle and threw words like rotten fruit. She's
nothing but a piece of trash. Amin said: her pussy stinks like a
dead eel. She is the child of pigs. She's a slut. She's the shit of pigs.
Walk, walk. Move your hands. You want to cover it now? Where was
your shame when you seduced a married man? Get out now. Get
out and don't come back. Afterward, they laughed.

Jesmin covers her ears against the sound of laughter.

It's Friday. She packs her things and says goodbye to Kulsum.
The kid wraps his legs around her waist and bites into her shoulder. She hands money to the landlord and he waves her to the
room. There's a kerosene lamp in one corner and a cot pushed
up against another. Last year's calendar is tacked to the wall. The
roof is leaking and there's a large puddle on the floor. She sees her
face in the pool of water. She sees her eyes and the shape of her
head and Ruby's clip in her hair. She opens her trunk and finds
the pair of Thanks she stole from the factory. She holds it up. It
makes the silhouette of a piece of woman. She pulls the door shut
and the room darkens. She takes off her sandals, her shalwar. She
lies on the floor, the damp and the dirt under her back, and drags

the Thanks over her legs. When she stands up she straddles the pool of water and casts her eyes over her reflection. There is a body encased, legs and hips and buttocks. The body is hers but it is far away, unreachable. She looks at herself and hears the sound of laughter, but this time it is not the laughter of the Salish, but the laughter of the piece of herself that is closed. She knows now that Ruby will fix Dulal, that she will parade with him in the factory, spreading her small-toothed smile among the spools of thread that hang above their heads, and that Dulal will take Ruby to his air-conditioned shop, and her sisters will no longer be hungry, and Jesmin will be here, joined by the laughter of her own legs, no longer the girl of the punishing hut, but a garments girl with a room and a closed-up body that belongs only to herself.

The door opens. Jesmin turns to the smell of biscuits.

ANDREA BARRETT

Wonders of the Shore

FROM *Tin House*

I.

The sea-shore, with its stretches of sandy beach and rocks, seems, at first sight, nothing but a barren waste, merely the natural barrier of the ocean. But to the observant eye these apparently desolate reaches are not only teeming with life, they are also replete with suggestions of the past. They are the pages of a history full of fascination for one who has learned to read them.

THE COVER IS a faded olive, not flashy; not the first thing you'd pull from a bookshelf. *Wonders of the Shore.* Black type, black decorations: a small silhouette of a fiddler crab; a pair of stylized starfish bracketing the author's name. Coiled snails frame the "Wonder" while sea anemones frame the "Shore." Actually it *is* attractive, in a sober, subtle way. Someone labored over that design. And over the photographs too, reprinted from many sources but freshly labeled and crowded on thick, glossy paper, which makes the book heavy. The writing is old-fashioned, more detailed than we're used to now; it was published in 1889. The author, Daphne Bannister, thanks a long list of people at the end of her preface. Some are professors at places like Harvard and Barnard, others curators or —the women—assistants at the Smithsonian. Especially thanked are Celia Thaxter, "whose kind invitations to Thaxter Cottage made my working visits to the Hotel such a pleasure," and "my dear friend and stalwart companion, Miss Henrietta Atkins." Henrietta's great-niece, Suky Marburg, left the book behind with her other things, and for a long time no one looked at it.

II.

It is hoped that this book will suggest a new interest and pleasure to many, and that it will serve as a practical guide to this branch of natural history, without necessitating serious study. Marine organisms are interesting acquaintances when once introduced, and the real purpose of the author is to present, to the latent naturalist, friends whom he will enjoy.

Celia Thaxter is easy to trace; she wrote a book of poems, a collection of pieces about the beloved island where she was raised, a book about her garden. There are letters too, and portraits and photographs, and a couple of biographies. Among her well-known friends were Whittier, Sarah Orne Jewett, and the painters William Morris Hunt and Childe Hassam. Nathaniel Hawthorne visited her island cottage. Major Greely claimed her poems comforted him during his disastrous Arctic voyage. She met Dickens and Robert Browning.

Daphne, who wrote under two different names, is harder to classify, but she had her day as well, and people in Hammondsport noticed her: a woman, visiting repeatedly, traveling on her own. At the drugstore, at the theater. Walking along the lake with her friend, pale hair improbably thick above her sharp features and delicate neck, or skating—she had tiny feet, but was very fast—in a costume showing more leg than was usual in this part of upstate New York. Some were annoyed by her manners. After one visit, the *Crooked Lake Gazette* reported:

> Among those arriving last week by train from Bath was Miss Daphne Bannister, here for one of her frequent stays with our esteemed biology teacher, Miss Henrietta Atkins. A well-known authoress, Miss Bannister has written guides to the insect pests, the wildflowers of Massachusetts (where she makes her home), and the birds of the fields and farms. She traveled from the Cornell campus, where she presented a talk on parasitic nematodes.

That one, the gossips said. Henrietta's friend. All around Keuka Lake, people were aware of Henrietta. Mention of her in the *Gazette* goes back as far as grade school: "Winner of the Spelling Bee." "Student Fossil Collection Impresses Visitors." "Sisters Show Off Lake Trout Caught in Fishing Derby." Later articles note her departure for Oswego, where she went for her teacher training, and the grant she received when she finished. She met Daphne after she graduated, at a summer school for the study of natural history run by Louis Agassiz. After that she came back home to teach biology at the Hammondsport high school. She established the Natural History Club, the Fossil Collector's Club, an ice-skating group, a reading group. Several times she won teaching awards. Each year she pulled a few promising students into her investigations, which ranged from aiding the local farmers' experiments with breeding cows and corn, to studies of fish, the development of other uses for wine grapes during Prohibition, and a new method for producing the membrane used to make balloons and rigid airships impermeable to gas.

All of this is noted in the *Gazette*. Henrietta, so firmly rooted wherever she stands that she looks tall unless she's next to someone else, ages silently in the photographs; her skirts narrow, then rise, then give way to voluminous slacks. Her sleeves are always pushed back from her sturdy wrists and blunt-fingered hands, lines appearing as her hair grays and metamorphoses from a mass pinned at the back of her head to a neat crop just below her ears. Grateful students mention her as they in turn appear in the newspaper for one thing or another. Appreciative colleagues thank her as they retire. The tone is invariably kind—except for the notes about Daphne's visits, which are colored by something that wouldn't be there if either of the women had married. Now they seem to point at something. They might not have read that way then.

III.

Every coast-line shows the destructive effects of the sea, for the bays and coves, the caves at the bases of the cliffs, the buttresses and needles, are the work of the waves. And this work is constantly going on. The knotty sticks so commonly seen on the beach are often the hearts of oak or cedar trees from which the tiny crystals of sand have slowly cut away their less solid outer growth.

In August of 1885, Henrietta was thirty-three and had been teaching high school for twelve years. Although her sister, Hester, was almost a decade younger, she'd married two years earlier and left

Henrietta alone at home with their mother. This had suited Henrietta very well until her friend Mason Perrotte, an ambitious farmer whom she'd known for some time, began to court her attentively. Confusingly. Now, after seven months of thinking one way about this in the morning and another in the afternoon, she knew he was about to propose. She was fond of him, as was her mother. If she was going to change her life and start a family, it was surely time. But to leave her job, after all she'd put into it—no point to that unless she could do more work, not less, as Daphne had after leaving her own teaching job. And her mother's argument that Henrietta would be teaching her own children wasn't wholly convincing.

She and Daphne had shared a vacation every summer since they'd met, which didn't always mean Daphne visiting Henrietta: sometimes Henrietta went to the little town in western Massachusetts where Daphne, having pried herself free from her parents and her brothers, had bought herself a tiny white house. And twice they'd managed to stay at a resort. Once in the White Mountains, once in Rhode Island: what luxury, to have their meals cooked and their rooms cleaned! Henrietta had been Daphne's guest both times, which might have been awkward if instead of pointing out that the income she made from her books was much greater than Henrietta's small salary, Daphne had not insisted graciously that those books wouldn't exist without Henrietta's help, so the treat was simply Henrietta's due. This year, having done especially well, Daphne had offered three weeks at the hotel on Appledore Island, a few miles off the New Hampshire coast.

On the day before Henrietta began her journey to the island, Mason came from his farm in Pulteney with a tin of gingersnaps for the train ride and a big white canvas hat that tied with two strips of muslin under her chin. He was wearing the blue-checked shirt he knew she particularly liked. She could feel him trying to get her alone, but instead she sat steadfastly with her mother at the table, making lists of what she should bring and what she would read during this stretch of uninterrupted time. She'd been catching up with Darwin's work since Daphne first led her, years ago, to an acceptance of his great theory. Reading slowly and carefully as her interest deepened, filling pages with notes, repeating some of his experiments and adapting them for her students. But there was no catching up to Daphne.

Daphne wrote to Darwin, and was answered. Daphne wrote to Asa Gray. Daphne wrote about climbing plants and burrowing spiders, publishing more and more articles and then a book, and another and another, earning enough money from those (and also from the part of her writing life she kept quiet) to stop teaching at the academy where she'd been working when they met. Henrietta fell even further behind. Not giving up; but working more slowly than she wished. Only in the summers could she pursue her own investigations wholeheartedly, keeping the thread alive during the school year by stealing an hour or two at night, after her lessons were prepared.

Her "work"—what did she mean by that, exactly? In the libraries of central New York, you can find files of the horticultural and agricultural society bulletins so popular toward the end of the nineteenth century. *The New York Agricultural Experiment Station Bulletin. The Rural New Yorker. The Buffalo Naturalists' Field Club Bulletin. The Western New York Horticultural Society Bulletin. Transactions of the New-York State Agricultural Society.* In them are accounts of meetings and county fairs; brief observations about local growing conditions, new seeds and breeds, keeping a clean dairy; longer articles too, weaving multiple sources and reports into an overview for the farmer. Daphne was writing pieces like that when she and Henrietta met; now Henrietta wrote them. "The White Grub of the May Beetle." One or two a year, carefully observed, clearly written, thoughtfully and thoroughly referenced. Useful to students and farmers alike. Together they give a sense of her steady progress through the years, although they don't suggest the work she did with and for Daphne. There's a hint of that in a letter she wrote to Mason during the first week of her stay at Appledore Island:

> Already we've settled into a pleasant routine. Our rooms are on the third floor, mine a few doors down from Daphne's: hers larger than mine, of course, as she needs space for her specimens, but both very comfortable. In addition to my bed and dresser and wardrobe I have an armchair near a window that looks out over the tennis courts, and a sturdy desk. After breakfast in the dining hall downstairs (airy and well laid out, if a bit noisy; over two hundred people are staying here!) we take a walk along the shore and then return to our rooms to work. We meet again downstairs for lunch and then, depending on the tide and the weather, visit the tidal pools, or take out one of the hotel's rowboats,

or swim in the bathing area. The island is small (about half a mile wide, I think; and perhaps a bit longer) but so rugged and broken by the sea that we keep discovering new pools and crannies. After dinner we relax for a while on the huge porch, which stretches the length of the hotel and is lined with rocking chairs.

Daphne's working furiously on a book about the plants and creatures of the shore, collecting samples (I help her with this) and comparing them with the photos and descriptions in other books, writing up her own descriptions. I read what she writes each day and offer suggestions, but am also working through Darwin's book about insectivorous plants. Much of it is about the common sundew, which grows at home, so I can easily gather plants for my class.

Daphne knows the place already, from when she came here alone two years ago. She also met Mrs. Thaxter, who owns the big cottage near the hotel, then. But she hadn't really gotten to know her, and last night she announced, with much excitement, that she'd managed to get us an invitation to the evening's gathering at Mrs. Thaxter's cottage. Apparently this is a great coup! Only the most select of the hotel's guests are invited, writers and musicians and painters and so forth. Honestly I would rather have had a quiet night reading or watching the stars but Daphne was so pleased with herself (I think she tried and failed to get invited before) that I felt I had to go.

Some of this visit she describes in her next letter to Mason, noting especially the densely cluttered parlor. Chairs, tables, lamps, easels, every surface covered, and the walls obscured by paintings and sketches touching each other and rising from chair rail to ceiling. The mantels and windowsills packed with Mrs. Thaxter's famous flowers: poppies arranged by color and tea roses in matching bowls; sweet peas, wild cucumber, hop and morning-glory vines spilling from suspended shells and baskets; larkspurs and lilies in tall vases and stalks of timothy and other grasses rising above a massive vessel with a few red poppies interspersed.

She describes the olive-green upholstery on the sofas and chairs, the polished floor designed to enhance the sound of the piano being played by a man in a linen jacket, the loosely draped shawls on the women. But not the feeling she had after Daphne was pulled away by their hostess and introduced to a circle of literary men, which closed and left her partnered with a bookshelf. The linen man played Chopin, stroked his thin brown beard and played Mozart; she studied white water lilies floating in white bowls. Daphne's face pinked with pleasure as their hostess, who was very stout, said that her book on the insect pests had been of great use to her, really *enormous* use.

Then Mrs. Thaxter rested a plump hand on Daphne's arm and ranted about the island's dreadful slugs, her bolstered, comfortably bulging self making Daphne, short and even slimmer than she'd been a dozen years ago, look like a sea oat. Where Henrietta had softened and, she would have admitted, slowed, Daphne was still furiously energetic, her small hands scored by her determined work. She nodded vigorously as Mrs. Thaxter described waging war on the slugs each morning between four and five, when the dew still lay heavy in the garden. And the grubs, the vicious grubs destroying the carnations! Mrs. Thaxter stabbed with her free hand, emulating the long pin with which she dug the grubs from the stems. Daphne suggested importing toads to eat the slugs, answered questions about the grubs, acted the part of expert regarding all aspects of insect life, which in this context Henrietta supposed she was, and yet—

Yet still it was exasperating to be so thoroughly abandoned, to see her friend showing off so flamboyantly, and to know that Daphne would never admit to this artistic crowd that in fact she made much of her income writing cookery books under a different name. As Dorrie Bennett she had a separate and even more successful professional life, so absorbing that in the dining room she had to be careful not to draw her neighbors' attention to her judicious comments about the lobster or the biscuits. Here in Mrs. Thaxter's parlor, she might never have whipped egg whites and Cox's gelatin for her famous snow pudding, noting the time it took to raise the frothy white mass. Might never have worried over a bill or stayed up all night to meet a deadline.

At home, Henrietta kept Daphne's cookbooks shelved next to her more serious works, and when Mason asked about that juxtaposition, she had told him the truth; she'd wanted her two friends to understand each other. But their relationship was different now —and perhaps because of that, she hid from him her hurt feelings after that first visit, and also much about her second visit. She wrote:

> A smaller crowd last evening, four painters and a singer and a pianist, two writers from Boston, a doctor from Springfield, one of Mrs. Thaxter's brothers and one grown son (her husband passed away last year).

Mrs. Thaxter sat in her gray dress next to a table covered with roses and directed the conversation and the entertainments, which included Daphne's demonstration of mounting seaweed specimens. I brought over the metal trays, filled them with seawater, stood by with the sheets as Daphne floated the samples and teased apart the finest branches with a hatpin. A beautiful piece of Cystoclonium purpurascens mounted perfectly, after which all the gentlemen wanted to try their hands. Mrs. Thaxter, as one of the younger painters observed to me, likes being surrounded by men; women are sparser, which makes Daphne even more pleased about our invitations there.

What the younger painter, whose name was Sebby Quint, actually said was more cutting than that; and he said it to Henrietta not in the parlor but outside, on the cottage's porch, beneath the shelter of the vines with their densely crowded leaves. None of this, nor what followed from it, reached Mason.

IV.

We have to do, however, in this volume, not with the history of the past, nor with the action of physical forces, but with the life of the present, and to find this, in its abundance, one must go down near the margin of the water, where the sands are wet. There is no solitude here; the place is teeming with living things.

Out on the porch, where the candles cast confusing shadows, a warm breeze pushed through the leaves encasing the columns, muting the words and music easing through the open parlor windows—a surprisingly pleasant sensation, interrupted by footsteps behind her and the scratch of a match being lit. The man she'd noticed while Daphne did her hatpin trick (he was bulky, but with soft, intelligent eyes and a way of seeming to pay real attention) lit his pipe and said, "That dress suits you."

"Thank you," she said. She'd hoped, backing out of the room, that no one would see her. Twice she'd tried to insert herself into the conversation Mrs. Thaxter was orchestrating about the floating seaweeds; twice she'd been rebuffed. Bored and annoyed, she'd slipped off for a few minutes of quiet. She smoothed the tucks of her only good dress, glad now that Daphne had convinced her to bring it for evening events.

"The color," he continued. "The line of the neck. You can tell it's a success just by the way Mrs. Thaxter treats you. Your friend's in no such danger."

"What do you mean?"

He nodded at the circle, visible through the open windows. "Dear Mrs. Thaxter likes being the queen of the hive," he said. "She doesn't always welcome attractive women."

"Me?" Henrietta laughed. For years Daphne had been chasing suitors away, while she'd only had to deal with Mason. "She must like *you*, if you flatter her like that."

"She does like me," he said quietly. "And we all like her. She makes us welcome, she admires our paintings, she sells them to her hotel guests. I'd do anything for her. But these evenings—the same people, in the same room, saying the same things, pretending rapture over the same poems and flowers . . . it's not surprising you found it tiresome."

"I was mostly hot," Henrietta protested.

"But also bored, I think. And maybe feeling a little left out? I was watching your face. Your friend was treating you like an assistant."

He puffed out a little cloud, which hung between them. Daphne, she thought, had simply been focused on impressing Mrs. Thaxter. And why was he watching her face? From the other side of the tennis courts came the clack of something hitting a rock and then a man's quick bark of laughter.

"*Do* gather," Mrs. Thaxter called. "Everyone—Donald is going to play Beethoven for us now. Everyone come!"

Henrietta turned but couldn't force herself through the door. Behind her, the painter laughed. "Where are your manners?" he said.

"Where are yours?"

"Let's be rude together," he said. He brushed off a chair and waved her toward it, seizing another for himself. "Let's sit, and listen to the waves and the wind and Beethoven in the background, and relish the breeze instead of being suffocated by all the flowers and people crowded together inside. I haven't seen you here before. What's your name?"

She told him, and when he asked also told him where she lived, and how long she'd been friends with Daphne, and what they were doing there. He was from Newburyport, he said in return. A student of Appleton Brown's—"those pastels behind the row of vases are his"—kindly included in Mrs. Thaxter's invitation. He'd been sharing a small back room on the hotel's ground floor with two other students for the past three weeks. "So it's only fair I sing for my supper," he said wryly, "in return for a place to sleep on this fine island, three excellent meals a day, and plenty of time to paint. Some evenings Mrs. Thaxter prefers to have just her intimates; other times, if a particularly eminent guest is passing through, she'll put together a larger, more glittering group. If the guest list is more hit or miss, she'll ask me and the other students to round out the gathering and be jolly."

"Good thing Daphne doesn't know where she falls on the list," Henrietta said. He seemed to be in his late twenties: not so old that he'd object to sharing a room, but too old not to notice it. Aware of how Mrs. Thaxter calculated his value. Was Daphne aware of hers?

Sebby shrugged. "Your friend's interesting enough," he said. "I can see how she'd intrigue our hostess."

"It was good of her to invite us," Henrietta said. "And I don't mean to be ungrateful. But really"—she gestured at the scene framed by the windows—"*look* at them." Three middle-aged women were gravely painting flowers in painted vases, two men were bent over an album of poems, Mrs. Thaxter herself was examining the mounted seaweed through a hand lens while a group stood around an easel watching a young man, perhaps one of Sebby's roommates, render with gold and green pastels the moon's trail on the water. All trying to convey, by their attentive expressions and postures, that they were also listening to the pianist still playing his Beethoven. All of them, including Daphne.

"You feel left out," her new acquaintance repeated.

"I do *not*," she said, more loudly than she intended. Suddenly the music stopped.

Mrs. Thaxter moved toward the nearest window. "Whatever are you doing out there?" she said, clearly affronted. "Mr. Quint, is that you?"

"My apologies," Sebby said. "I stepped out for a smoke."

"Perhaps you can step back in again, then," she said. "Or at least not disturb our musical entertainment." In the dim light, all Henrietta could see of her was a mound of white hair above, the pleats of a white scarf below. Perhaps her own features were equally erased. Mrs. Thaxter waved vaguely in her direction. "You too," she added. Did she know whom she was waving at?

Sebby stepped through the parlor door but Henrietta, disliking that sense of being summoned, left both him and Daphne behind and headed back to the hotel. She slept poorly, woke when a big storm arrived and the wind shifted and the rain began to pound, and then lay sweating in her sheets before rising to drink more than she meant to of the bottle of brandy she'd brought along for emergencies. By morning the storm had blown away, leaving the shores littered with seaweeds and all kinds of creatures—exactly, Henrietta realized when she woke, what Daphne needed. She rose and dressed hurriedly, but still she was late to breakfast and Daphne, after greeting her coolly, said very little until she'd finished her creamed eggs. Henrietta, pushing her plate aside and signaling the waitress for coffee, said, "I'll bring extra boxes this morning, and extra mounting paper."

"No need," Daphne said. "I'll manage on my own; I want to concentrate on some particular groups so I can start writing the section introductions."

"Don't be angry," Henrietta said. "I'm sorry about last night."

Daphne buttered a roll without looking at her. "There's nothing to be sorry about," she said. "You seem not to have liked it there; no reason you should. But Mrs. Thaxter did ask me back this evening, and I'm going to go."

"I'm sorry," Henrietta repeated. If that young painter hadn't egged her on . . . why blame the painter, though, for her own feelings? "I'll behave better this time."

"Actually," Daphne said, tracing the cloth with the handle of the butter knife, "she asked if I'd mind not bringing you." The little scars netting her hands stood out in the morning light.

Beside them a large family rose, three girls in identical blue dresses watching fondly as their younger brother begged permission to go to the bathing area and their father at first resisted and then gave in. Beyond the open doors the water shimmered, the first boats were launched, the attendants opened the women's bathhouse and then the men's, a group of children ran down to the rocks, and the little boy, leaping from the last of the steps, ran toward them through the rinsed soft air. What a glorious day!

"You go, then," she said to Daphne. "I can entertain myself."

"There's a concert at eight," Daphne said, pointing with her knife to the announcements on the bulletin board.

Henrietta offered again to help with the morning's collections; Daphne refused again, more firmly, and then pushed back her chair and left. Outside, the three girls in their blue dresses formed a triangle on the rocks, and Henrietta, among the last to leave the dining room, fetched Mason's hat and after tying the muslin strips under her chin walked in the children's direction and for half an hour watched them at their sailing lessons in the cove. It was lovely, actually, to have a free day. When she went back upstairs she opened her windows wide, spread her books and papers on the desk, and settled into her own work, no hardship at all. Sailing lessons ended, bathers filled the pool, and she worked through Darwin's *Insectivorous Plants,* making notes for a set of experiments. *Drosera,* like the dew: the dew being the glistening, sticky droplets tipping the fine red hairs on the disks of the lollipop-shaped leaves. The chapters about what stimulated the hairs—tentacles, really, Darwin said—to bend and draw a possible bit of food into the cupped disk, and how the plant's secretions digested the bits, were the place to start. Each experiment offered a question posed correctly, to which an answer might be found.

Dead flies, bits of raw meat or boiled egg, specks of paper and wood and dried moss and cinders about the same weight as the flies, maybe some quills: that's all she'd need for her students to test a leaf's responses. After that, the problems weren't scientific but logistical—a huge part of teaching, as she'd slowly learned: in part from Daphne, and not just from the way she organized her scientific work. When Daphne tested recipes for her other work, substituting commonly found ingredients for tricky or uncommon ones, ordering the steps sensibly, and then scaling the result for a family dinner or a party for twenty or a wedding for eighty while working within a fixed budget, she was engaged in just the same sort of task.

They'd laughed over that many times, which Henrietta remembered when she sat down, Daphne-less, to a lunch of croquettes so nicely shaped and crisply fried, with such a savory sauce and garnish, that no one would have suspected Monday's roast turkey as their source. She ate alone, still thinking about the sequence of experiments, and then went to the lobby, where one of Mrs. Thaxter's brothers was swiftly sorting the letters and packages brought in the morning boat from Portsmouth. Among the crowd at the end of the long counter she waited for a view of her letterbox: empty, nothing. Why did she feel relieved? Sebby Quint, who was right behind her and bending to view his own box, bumped into her when she turned and then continued to stand so close that she couldn't avoid talking with him.

"You disappeared last night," he said. Quite gently, almost as if he weren't doing it, he rested two fingertips on her forearm.

"I was embarrassed," she said. "Weren't you? I couldn't face going back inside the parlor."

"I'm sure it would have been fine," he said.

"I don't think so," she said, and told him about her breakfast conversation with Daphne. "Apparently," she concluded, "I'm banished."

He frowned. "I'm sure Mrs. Thaxter didn't mean that. Your friend must have misinterpreted what she said."

Only a few minutes later, when Sebby left for his easel and she returned to her desk, did she realize that she might have implied that the incidents of the night before had caused a real rift. But as brusque as Daphne had been at breakfast, she was sure Daphne's disapproval wouldn't last; they'd had worse spats and misunderstandings over the past dozen years. Often Daphne pulled away when she was first offended, only to bounce back elastically, once she'd scared herself, across the gap she'd created. The best thing was not to argue but to wait quietly for a day or two.

Henrietta ate her lunch alone twice more and both times made excuses for Daphne's absence when she ran into Sebby at the letterboxes. Daphne, she explained, was working furiously on the short essays meant to introduce each phylum and class in her book, and taking her midday meal in her room.

"Busy woman," he said. He'd rolled up the sleeves of his white shirt, exposing his forearms and the little flecks of paint—carmine, cobalt, golden yellow—that dotted the tanned skin but not the burnished hairs. "Organizing the entertainments for Mrs. Thaxter's guests must take a lot of time too."

She shrugged, pretending that wasn't news. She knew Daphne continued to visit the cottage in the evenings, but they'd avoided talking about Mrs. Thaxter's gatherings during their quiet dinners together: simply, Henrietta thought, Daphne being discreet.

"The night before last, she arranged a little artificial pool and filled it with plants and creatures she'd gathered from the rock pools," he noted. "Last night"—was he summoned there every night?—"she brought more seaweeds to mount, enough so everyone could try their hand. I sketched those, and also some of the guests. She's good at knowing what will interest people."

"She is," Henrietta said. "She's very gifted that way."

"Gifted socially too," Sebby said. Was that admiration in his voice, or a sarcastic imitation? "She's making quite a friend of Mrs. Thaxter, and also some of her literary circle."

By the next day, when they met again, she'd begun to wonder if he timed his arrival to coincide with hers. They both had letters that day, and because he opened and read his little pile casually, at the counter, she did the same with her single envelope. A chatty, inconsequential letter from Mason: weather, news of a bicycling accident, a description of the agricultural society meeting in Ovid. *Dr. Sturtevant gave a good talk about corn and Professor Arnold some useful notes on butter-making in winter. The best was Law on contagious diseases in animals: he talked about bacteria in a way everyone in the room could understand.* Mason—balding, friendly, freckled; just a few years older than she was—being typically Mason. He'd gone to Cornell before returning to his family farm and was interested in the structure of soil and its microorganisms. He experimented with soil amendments and, when he could find the time, good-humoredly accompanied her class on field trips. Happily busy, he never begrudged her the time she needed for her work. Both her mother and Hester had hinted that this might change when he showed up with his grandmother's opal ring—but then some other life would appear, which at least part of her had thought she wanted.

Why, then, did she crumple the pages as Sebby looked up from his own? Why tighten her lips, stare blindly at the ground, let her eyes fill? Why, when Sebby touched her elbow and said, "What's happened? Is everything all right?," turn away as if she couldn't talk? And then turn back and say, "My friend at home, Mason, the man I thought—I thought we had an understanding. But it seems he has met someone else."

Sebby drew his breath in sharply. "He's breaking off your relationship?"

She nodded.

"In a *letter?*"

She nodded again, watching sympathy and affection flood his face. He seized her hand—by now they'd stepped away from the counter—and said, "That's terrible, what can I do?"

What was she doing? Her lips were trembling, her hands as well; the story she'd invented without thinking felt almost true and Sebby was as responsive as she'd somehow known he would be, his interest in her sharply fanned. That whiff of her needing help and leaning on him was hitting him like brandy.

"Nothing," she said. She ran a palm over both eyes.

"Nothing?"

"I don't know—maybe I could sit with you this afternoon and work on my notes while you paint? Daphne's busy and I don't want to brood by myself."

They spent the afternoon together, she in a chair drawn near the easel he'd set up on a flat rock overlooking the harbor, he moving between his canvas and her. Several times he rested his hand on her arm or her shoulder and once she reached her hand back to rest it on his. They parted at teatime, and, after Henrietta worked for a while, she answered the knock on her door to find Daphne holding a sheaf of pages, her expression cheerful and energetic.

"I did the overall introduction to the Coelenterata," she said. "And then smaller ones for the Hydrozoa, the Scyphozoa, and Actinozoa, and the Ctenophora—I got so much done! Will you read them for me and see how they strike you?"

"Of course," Henrietta said: her apology, as the pages were Daphne's. She read swiftly; she took notes. She suggested several cuts and a new opening for the piece about the ctenophores. Two hours later they went down to dinner together, Daphne by then asking Henrietta about her sundews and proposing an alteration in one of the experiments. In the lobby, they ran into Sebby.

"How are you feeling?" he asked Henrietta, looking at her intently. "I meant what I said, I am so sorry—"

Daphne froze. "What happened?"

"That wretched man," Sebby said.

"Mason," Henrietta clarified. Of course Sebby assumed she'd already told Daphne—and she'd meant to right away, to confess the impulsive lie and maybe even what was driving her to pull Sebby closer: but she and Daphne had been so caught up in the relief of working together again that she hadn't had time.

"What," Daphne said now, "did Mason do?"

"To dismiss her in a letter," Sebby said indignantly. "To tell her she's been *replaced . . .*"

Daphne's face reddened as Henrietta stumbled through a quick version of the story she'd told Sebby. "What an idiot!" Daphne said. "So stolid and unoriginal and slow, so—"

They'd met several times; when she and Henrietta had visited his farm last summer, she'd spoken admiringly of his ducks and his orchard and claimed to like him. "He doesn't hold a candle to you, I never knew what you saw in him. Really, you're well shed of him."

She put her arm around Henrietta's waist. "Just like him too, to tell you he's met someone else in a letter. Coward."

For a moment Henrietta felt properly put-upon—and then, as Daphne continued to rant, amazed to learn how much her friend had disliked Mason all along. Sebby listened, made sympathetic noises, fanned Daphne's indignation. He asked if he could join them for dinner and when Daphne encouraged him, offered his arm to Henrietta.

V.

As each wave retreats, little bubbles of air are plentiful in its wake. Underneath the sand, where each bubble rose, lives some creature. By the jet of water which spurts out of the sand, the common clam Mya arenaria reveals the secret of its abiding-place. Only the lifting of a shovelful of sand at the water's edge is needed to disclose the populous community of mollusks, worms, and crustaceans living at our feet, just out of sight.

Celia Thaxter died in 1894, nine years after the August day on which Henrietta and Daphne sailed from the island back to Portsmouth, and just a few months after she published the handsome volume about her gardens that we still read.

The other day, as I sat in the piazza which the vines shade with their broad green leaves and sweet white flowers climbing up to the eaves

and over the roof, I saw the humming-birds hovering over the whole
expanse of green, to and fro, and discovered that they were picking off
and devouring the large transparent aphides scattered, I am happy to
say but sparingly, over its surface . . .

That tangle of honeysuckle, hops, wild cucumber, and clematis,
impossible to separate, is where Henrietta and Sebby met—but
the vines are gone, and the piazza too; the hotel and Mrs. Thaxter's cottage burned in 1914, leaving only the foundations. A marine biological laboratory occupies most of the island now. College
students visit throughout the summer, studying the same creatures
Daphne and Henrietta collected, sampling the tidal pools and
each other. A group of ardent gardeners has rebuilt Mrs. Thaxter's
garden on its original site. Hollyhocks, sunflowers, poppies, roses,
the old-fashioned favorites of midsummer, which she surely would
have enjoyed.

Before she died, she apparently also enjoyed Daphne's *Wonders
of the Shore*. She kept copies in the hotel library, and a personal
copy, inscribed by Daphne, in her parlor; she gave others as gifts to
cherished visitors. The hotel declined after Mrs. Thaxter's death, as
other, more modern resorts and hotels sprang up along the Maine
and New Hampshire coasts, emulating and improving on the place
Henrietta and Daphne knew—but all of them stocked Daphne's
book for their guests. Many visitors bought copies; teachers used
it in their classes. Daphne built on that success with shorter books,
more richly illustrated and less technical: one specifically about
the seaweeds, another about the common shells. And when she
arrived once more in Hammondsport, on an August day in 1901,
she brought those, as well as copies of the most recent edition of
Wonders of the Shore, as gifts for Henrietta, her sister, and her nieces.
Marion, almost eight by then, tall and round-eyed and particularly
cherished after two stillbirths, took her copy as eagerly as a girl
from a different family might have taken a new doll. Caroline, who
was five, pointed at the title and said, "I can read!" Elaine, only a
few months old, kept her thoughts to herself.

Along with the books and the rest of her luggage, Daphne also
brought a large flat package wrapped in brown paper, which Henrietta noticed at the train station but then forgot to ask about.
They cooked and ate a simple meal in the kitchen that still, two
years after Henrietta's mother's death, seemed oddly empty; they

went to a meeting of the Fossil Collector's Club; they went to sleep early. The next day they had a pleasant excursion to the Grove Springs Hotel, lunch with some visitors from Elmira, and then a hectic dinner at Henrietta's sister's house. Nothing out of the ordinary—Elaine, a fussy baby, was distracted by the company and slow to nurse; Ambrose was out at a meeting; in their father's absence the older girls careened around the house as they vied for attention—but Henrietta, who came almost daily to help, was startled to see how uncomfortable this made Daphne. During earlier visits, before the baby was born, she'd been more relaxed and had even helped Henrietta put the girls to bed, but now she blushed at the sight of Hester's breast and flinched when Caroline knocked a cup from the table, a dark stream of coffee shooting from the pale china shattered on the floor.

They left immediately after dessert and when they reached Henrietta's house, Daphne collapsed in a chair on the porch. "Sorry to be so feeble," she said apologetically. "I'm not used to that much noise anymore."

"They were excited to see you," Henrietta said, taking a seat on the glider. The wisteria she'd planted years ago had climbed the pillars and fanned across the scrollwork, filtering the glow from the streetlights through the leaves. For a few minutes they sat and said nothing. Then Daphne went inside and returned with the parcel, which she handed to Henrietta.

"This came last month," Daphne said, fiddling with the edge where she'd torn the paper open. "But it was meant for you, and you should have it."

She stood with one hand on the railing. Still slight, still very erect: the resilient, resourceful person who, when Henrietta had first known her, taught herds of little boys. Her hair still golden in the leafy light and not half gray (Henrietta's by then was completely gray) and her crushed-paper skin returned to youthful smoothness.

"Do you envy your sister her life?" Daphne said. "Even when they're squabbling, they look like what everyone seems to think a family should look like. And you're so good with your nieces, it makes me wonder . . ."

Henrietta shrugged. "That's because they're my nieces," she said. "I'm not responsible for them all the time, just when I choose —it's easy to be good when you just dip in now and then. But no: I love those girls, but I wouldn't want Hester's life. I'm glad I avoided it."

"Me too," Daphne said. Did that mean, *I too am glad you avoided that life*? Or *I'm glad I avoided that life myself*? Neither of them mentioned Mason. Daphne retreated to the room that had once been Hester's, which was where she always stayed, and Henrietta went to her own room and unpacked the parcel. First she looked at the letter addressed to Daphne.

It is not likely you will remember me but we met some years ago on Appledore Island, where over the course of several weeks we were both welcomed into Mrs. Thaxter's parlor for her evening entertainments. I hope you will not think me vain if I say I was the painter of the watercolors you claimed to admire—Mrs. Thaxter's garden, the roses and sunflowers and so on. You were there with a friend but she came only once or twice to the evenings and I confess I can no longer recall her name. She is actually the one I am trying to find.

I was there with a friend too—one of my roommates, another painter—whose name was Sebby Quint. Sadly, he passed away earlier this year after a peculiar accident. Disposing of his few belongings has been complicated (he was estranged from his family, and never married) and as the contents of his studio passed to me I am presently trying to find homes for the work that mattered so much to him. Hence this package. There are a number of sketchbooks, but the contents date this one to the summer we all met. A few pages are of such a personal nature that I felt the entire book should go to your friend. I am hoping that you two are still in touch, and that you can convey this to her along with my best wishes and hopes that she is well.

May I just say here that I have enjoyed your *Wonders of the Shore* very much, and that I remember some of what you so generously showed our motley crowd during those happy evenings? The place is, sadly, very much changed since Mrs. Thaxter's death but I hope you too remember it fondly.

Henrietta couldn't read the signature—a short first name, a last name beginning with a *P*? Sebby had had two roommates; she couldn't picture either one: Why should this person know about Sebby's death, when she did not? Although they'd not stayed in touch, for sixteen years he'd been as present to her imagination as Daphne, leaping to mind unexpectedly when a wave lapped at a hull with a particular sound, or a cedar branch shook off the raindrops beading up on its needles.

For a minute she tried to absorb the enormous fact of Sebby's death: hopeless. He was gone, yet the image of him in her mind remained the same, his voice still humming in her ear, his touch still warming her skin. The sketchbook, opened, smelled of him and of the sea. There were the cliffs, waves foaming through the trap dike. Rock pools, landing dock, breakwater protecting the bathing pool from the rougher sea; within the pool, some children on a raft. Three girls dressed alike in blue, regarding a little boy. A mass of vines enfolding a porch, the vine leaves themselves, some small white flowers and twisted stems. A man—she remembered that man!—frowning intently as he drew a bow over his violin strings. A blank page and then . . .

A woman's hand, wrist, and forearm. A woman's naked back, rising in a powerful curve from the skirts heaped around it. On a ledge deeply cut into the cliffs, a woman with her face hidden by her raised arms, the rest of her exposed to the sun. A pair of woman's legs dangling over the edge of a rowboat. Did she want those to be hers, or did she not? She looked again at the penciled lines, the deft light strokes, the delicate shading. On one of the bare calves, a scar curved where hers did: her legs, then. Her arms, her back. Her self. As Sebby's friend had realized. And as Daphne must have realized too.

How little, after all, she'd kept secret from Daphne. Only the letter, perhaps; perhaps not even that.

After she lied about Mason's letter, she and Daphne had spent their evenings apart. Daphne continued to visit Mrs. Thaxter's cottage—pushing forward, she admitted, with her conquest of that circle of painters, literary men, and musicians; no one but Henrietta understood how much she depended on such connections for the success of her work. Henrietta was less frank about her pursuit of Sebby, but no less determined. When Mason's letters continued to arrive, she ostentatiously threw them out unread. She cut up Mason's hat. She pretended grief and let Sebby comfort her. She pretended confusion and let Sebby seduce her when in fact, and despite her ignorance, she seduced him. Soon he stopped going to Mrs. Thaxter's cottage, telling his friends that he was making a set of night paintings but instead spending the hours after dinner with Henrietta. On that tiny island, smaller than Henrietta's village and densely populated by summer guests and the staff who looked after them, she and Sebby still found secret spots where they curled into each other. On a pile of kapok life-vests, in the corner of a boathouse. In the nooks of the northern headlands. During the day, as they worked together, Henrietta listened to Daphne disparage Mason, congratulate her for shedding him, reiterate (she herself had already shed several suitors) the enormous advantages of the single life. Then at night Henrietta undid Sebby's buttons with fingers so deft they seemed to have practiced without her knowledge.

Did Daphne know what she and Sebby were doing? Roughly, at least; probably: Henrietta had sometimes sensed (almost instantly denying this to herself) an intensity to Daphne's gaze that might have come from her sorting and weighing bits of evidence, speculating with her usual fierce intelligence as to their cause. So perhaps Daphne had known what she was doing and, since Sebby was headed soon for a studio in Rome, judged the risk acceptable —as Henrietta herself had known, without knowing the details, how intently Daphne was campaigning to win over Mrs. Thaxter's friends. The unspoken details of their night lives were, along with the work they'd returned to sharing, part of the sturdy thread that continued to bind them. Only the lie that had started it all, and the difficult scene during which, when she finally returned to Hammondsport, she'd broken things off with Mason, remained her secret.

She forgot it herself, sometimes: forgot what she'd done, forgot that she and not Mason had ended their relationship. She forgot, when she saw Mason and his pleasant wife and their four boys at a holiday gathering or a fair, that she'd been the one to walk away from that life—not so she could take Daphne's firm advice that remaining single was the better path (Daphne, across the hall, crackled the page of a book just enough to signal that she was awake if Henrietta wanted to talk, but busy if Henrietta needed her privacy)—but so that, for barely more than a week, she could feel Sebby's hair against her lips.

The Bears

FROM *Glimmer Train*

ONCE, WHEN I was convalescing, I was sent to a farmhouse in the country. No one there knew I had been sick. A woman came to cook in the evenings, and her daughter would appear at odd hours with a mop and bucket, keeping the place clean. There were many kinds of tea to be found in the kitchen, and a woven tray on which you could arrange the tea things. Also there were deep old wooden chairs lined up along the front porch, so you could sit as long as you liked, looking out over the fields, the trees, and sometimes even the mountains if the sky was truly clear. Because of the porch and the tray and the slow way the day ended, I felt, in this place, though no one knew of my miscarriage, as if I were being gently attended to, as if all the demands of the world had been softly lifted away, and that I should rest.

I had been invited there to finish a chapter on William James. I was to do so in the company of eight other people working on interesting, improbable projects. The invitation had come as a great surprise to me and had a magical effect on my confidence. As soon as I set foot in the farmhouse, however, every thought and hope I had about William James flew out of my head, like a bit of charred paper up a chimney. He had been my companion for several months, and now he turned into a man I barely knew. His sudden disappearance made the days seem long. Soon I discovered that the pastimes I had always imagined I'd enjoy—such as dipping into newly published novels, and drifting off to sleep in the middle of the afternoon—left me with a stiff neck, as well as a feeling of dread.

My only relief was to walk along the sides of the highway and the roads. Though they were country roads, they were not laid out in a haphazard way, and I decided that if I were to set out, and turn left, and then left again, turning and turning until I found my way back again, I would be all right. I walked slowly, but for distances that surprised me. I walked without my wallet or my glasses, and felt my life was far away. The city I lived in, the appointments I made, the students I taught, my dog, my friend—it seemed as if what held me to them had loosened and let go. When I thought of home, all I remembered was a route I would sometimes follow as I walked to the bus stop, a route that took me past an empty parking lot, where long grasses and weeds had been allowed to grow in profusion. Even though it wasn't strictly on my way, I liked walking past this empty lot because of the wild, sweet smell it sent out into the world. No other lot or overgrown yard I knew of had managed to achieve the right alchemy of grass and clover and tall spindly wildflowers, and no other place could secrete this same smell. But here, along the side of the highway, it was everywhere, the smell.

Reading the signs that appeared on the road, I learned I was walking through a part of the countryside that had yet to be discovered and made over in a sentimental way. This area remained practical and suspicious. At frequent intervals, sometimes only two or three trees apart, the signs were posted: PRIVATE PROPERTY, they said. Then came a list of numerous activities, followed by the words STRICTLY FORBIDDEN, and for final emphasis, the phrase SHALL BE PROSECUTED. As if these yellow signs left room for doubt and interpretation, some people had gone to the trouble of making their own: NO VISITORS, said one. NO TRESPASSING, said another. And even the cornfields were wrapped around with barbed wire. But not once did I see another person walking along the road. It was hard to imagine who the trespassers might be.

Other than me, of course. The pickup trucks wouldn't slow down when they passed me on the road. They hadn't slowed down for other things either. Along the highway's edge I saw a rabbit, its remains vanishing, its bits of fur lifting up from the pavement as dreamily as thistledown; I saw a small black songbird, throbbing with larvae, and a freshly dead chipmunk, curled up on its side as if in sleep. There were also many beautiful horses, heraldic and fully alive. I wanted to watch them gallop across the fields with their ravishing black manes streaming behind them, but it seemed when left alone they had little reason to do so. They chose to stand still, in mysterious silence. The cows, in contrast, were full of spirit, but maybe only when being pushed into a trailer. I happened to be walking by while this process was underway. The cows already inside the trailer made an alarming sound, a truly unhappy and outraged sound, the sort of hoarse trumpeting you might hear from an elephant. It could not be described as either mooing or lowing. I wondered where the cows were being taken, whether their misery was mindless and fleeting, as they were simply being driven to another pasture; or whether the truth was darker and the animals sensed the sure approach of death. So I studied the cows, and I noted that these were black, and large, with heavy brows and small eyes, and that their boulder-like bodies hung low to the ground. But what did this mean? I had no idea. I had no way of knowing just where they were off to.

The list of things I did not know was getting longer. I could name only two of the plants that grew in abundance on the side of the road. If there had been a child walking alongside me, its hand in my own, and if this child had shown any curiosity about the world, I would have been able only to say, That is goldenrod. And that, Queen Anne's lace. It would have been a poor display of knowledge. Pale starry blue flowers and velvety purses of orange and gold, whole swamps of tawdry purple tapers and creeping vines that spread their fingers out into the road—all of it as common as day, and all of it inscrutable to me. I had also been forced to admit, while trying to write a postcard, that I wasn't completely sure which mountains I was looking at. The cows, the flowers, the mountain range; why William James had seen fit to abandon me; whether I would ever get well; how to relieve the sorrow of my friend.

That I continued to call him my friend probably added to his unhappiness. But the other names sounded antiseptic to me. Sometimes he would identify himself lightheartedly on phone messages as *the father of your unborn child*. After a certain point, though, this no longer applied. I believed *friend* to be a true honorific, but he said he felt differently, and so what to call him was among the many unknown things that troubled me as I made my slow way around the fields.

But there was always the white house of Jerry Roth, which I did come to know. And, in fact, the house seemed such a reflection of him, I sometimes felt as if I knew him, the man. His house was set back slightly from the road, sitting upon a soft rise in the land; it looked out over the acres of a horse farm, and nearer than that a fishing pond, edged with cattails, shadowed by willow trees, a row-boat resting on its grassy bank. Perfect as in a painting or a dream; as if all the charm and sentiment the countryside had been coolly withholding could now, at last, express itself, could gloriously un-furl, in one long exhalation of white clapboard and dappled shade and undulating lawn. A colonial house, but without stiffness or symmetry: a wing rambled off to the right, toward a glassed-in porch, and on the left stood a new addition, a sort of studio or guest quarters, its face yawning open in a wide cathedral window, and its entrance marked by a great glass lantern, which echoed, in wittily enormous proportions, the quaint, black-leaded lights that hung beside the front door of the original house.

I did not apprehend all of this graciousness at once. It revealed itself to me in a slow unfolding of surprises. One afternoon, the wind stirred the leaves of Jerry Roth's old maple, and only then did I see how beautifully it spread its canopy across the front lawn, and how thickly the plantings grew beneath it, their dark green leaves polished and aglow, the white flowers floating above their long stems like candle flames. Another day, hearing a window shut, I turned and saw the kaleidoscopic horse standing calmly in the garden. The same size, the same stillness as the creatures across the road, but its coat glistened with blue sky and yellow stars, with tempera paint and varnish, with winding streams and hills of violet and umber and red. And in this backward glance I also found the apple tree, crooked with age, its lowest branch dipping only a few feet from the ground, extended as if in invitation for a child to take a seat.

What else. There was a plaque attached to the mailbox post, its delicate Roman capitals spelling out JEROME ROTH, and be-neath that a picture of a pheasant, wings spread, like something you might find on a piece of porcelain. And opposite the mailbox, a square of white-and-blue tin announcing that this little stretch of road should be known as RUE JERRY ROTH (MARIN EMERITÉ). The street sign was displayed on a dully red barn, now turned into a garage for three wonderful cars: a wood-paneled station wagon, a Volkswagen van, and a sleek silver two-seater, Japanese and new. One evening, while walking along the highway, I was passed from behind by the wood-paneled station wagon, and my heart quickened involuntarily, as though I'd seen a star.

I guess it shouldn't have surprised me that my heart beat the way it did. For having walked by his house so many times, and gleaned with such pleasure all the small and large details of the world he had made, I admired him. I would have liked him for a friend. Even more, I would have liked him to gather me into his family, a family I imagined as manifesting the same humor and whimsy and discernment that was evident everywhere in his house and on his land. For I knew there must be a family, moving through the clean rooms of the house, laughing and groaning, just beyond the reach of what I could see.

That same evening I returned to the farmhouse, still elated by the sight of the station wagon, to find that there was swordfish for dinner. And tired of my own reticence, I decided I wanted to talk about Jerry Roth. Not to the woman who had cooked the swordfish, with whom I usually talked, but to the people who were eating it with me. I think I would have liked the farmhouse much more if it hadn't been for those eight other people, who would emerge from their rooms at the end of the afternoon, looking dazed and replete. They took turns walking to the village to buy bottles of wine that were opened and poured at dinner. I had to wait for a pause in the conversation; the wine made them talkative, and they had hit again upon a favorite subject: the other farmhouses, castles, villas, and cottages where they had been guests in the past.

Potatoes. At every meal, said Laszlo. Boiled or fried. Or cold, cut up in little chunks and mixed together with an herb I couldn't identify.

But it's Italy! Anna cried.

My point, Laszlo said irritably, and jiggled the wine in his glass. Not what one would expect.

Mary spoke: The first week with the baronessa, I could barely eat, she made me so nervous. And all those little dogs underfoot. I was sure I was going to step on one and cripple it. But the food was good; there were no potatoes.

Ah, so you've been to Santa Maddalena, Laszlo said with a small sigh of resentment.

The platter of swordfish was heaved up into the air and then made its precarious way around the table for a second time.

They are fattening me up here, Cesar said, helping himself.

Haven't you seen that great big oven there in the back? Behind the barn? Erga said. We're going to be plump and delicious when we're done.

She was looking at her plate as she said this, and without eye contact, I could not tell how merrily she intended it. We ate in silence, and for a fleeting moment it seemed possible that we had all been tricked, that this gift of quietude was in fact a term of captivity and terror.

Have you tried walking? I asked them finally. I find that walking helps.

Mary wiped her mouth and gently pushed back her chair.

I just run, she said, I run as fast as I can.

And so it was that I was running the next time I saw the house of Jerry Roth. By that point the running had become painful and strange to me. At first, when I began to run, I felt surprised by my lightness, I felt young and strong, I felt like a child running ecstatically, for no reason at all. But soon that feeling changed and my breath started to disappear. I had to pause to hitch up my jeans and wipe the fog from my glasses. Then, out of perversity, I began running again. Just to that tree, I told myself. And after the tree, an electrical pole, a mailbox, a NO TRESPASSING sign. I kept promising that upon reaching these landmarks I would stop, yet I didn't stop, I continued to run, trying to be swift, becoming more damp and anguished as I passed each marker and found another just a little farther on. I must have been bleeding for some time before I noticed it. I suppose I thought the wetness slipping down my legs was sweat. So what made me notice? Maybe the smell, the faint animal smell, a smell that has always made me think of wounded prey in the underbrush, or a mother licking afterbirth off her young. Foolishly, I had not been expecting it. In the deepest part of me, I had not believed that my body would return to normal, or that one day I would be well again.

I'm not sure if it was the thought of being well or the memory of getting sick that affected me. But either way, I bent over and started to cry. For the first time I wanted help, but predictably no one was near; there was a detached humming in the air, coming from the hidden insects or the electrical lines overhead. The horses and cows were absent from the fields. The sun burned indistinctly behind a thin screen of clouds. I limped out to the middle of the road, but I couldn't see any trucks in the distance, approaching me at dangerous speeds. I was at a loss. I didn't even know what to call the place where I had stopped. There was a route number posted on a sign a few hundred yards ahead, but that number had no meaning for me.

Standing there in the road, I was visited by an idea, startling and clear. It was the idea of crisis; the idea that I was in the midst of having one. And with this idea, my earlier sense of lightness returned, and though my face was burning and my chest hurt and sharp pains were rocketing up my shins, I wanted to run again. I wanted to get there fast. For I knew now exactly where I was going.

I knew too what I was going to tell him. Why I had come, a stranger running down the road, and knocked on his door. Doubled over on the threshold of his old house, beneath the black-leaded lights, breathless and red-faced, dark stains growing on the legs of my pants. And it wasn't completely untrue. It had been true only two months before, but then I had been in the restroom on the third floor of my department, inside a stall where the metal was beginning to show through the gray-green paint, as a slender graduate student I had once taught was energetically brushing her teeth at the sink. She had probably just finished eating one of the frugal, grainy meals she brought with her to campus in a cloudy plastic container.

So I ran as best as I could until at last the white house appeared before me; climbed the steps at the base of the slope, followed the flagstone path, passed beneath the branches of the magnificent tree, all the while ushered along by the profound sense of permission that the word *crisis* had given me. In fact I'd come to feel that I was seeking help for someone other than myself. As if under a spell, I lifted the knocker, and when the brass hammer dropped down on its plate, the force of its fall eased open the door, which was, of course, unlocked. Jerry Roth shared none of his neighbors' suspicions. No bolts, no barbed wire, just a half-lit entryway with a good Turkish carpet and a bowl of summer roses, and beyond that a bright kitchen smelling of coffee and slightly burnt toast. And the table! The table was even better than I'd imagined: huge, rough-hewn, radiant with age, practically seaworthy; surely salvaged from a tumbledown farm nearby and then refurbished at some expense. The kitchen chairs looked rescued too, mismatched as they were, some with spindles, others slatted, one with a little painting of grapes and fruit fading on its back, all of them gathered in expectation around the table, as charming and different as children. The chair I sat in had narrow armrests, and I could feel the shallow dip in the wood where hundreds of other elbows had rested, or maybe only a few chosen elbows repeatedly over the course of a hundred years. The newspaper was close at hand, not the local paper but the *Times,* whose presence I so missed that I almost started crying again, already opened to the film section, my favorite, and a review of an Iranian movie that my friend and I planned to see together.

The review was admiring, not to anyone's surprise, and full of the sort of empty reverential phrases—*a master of world cinema,* etc.—that made my friend particularly impatient. My friend had little patience with a number of things: dog owners, pigeons, overcooked food, fatuous reviews, ATM fees, antiques, and people's mispronunciation of his name. Yet he had been unfailingly patient with me. Opening the windows wide, reading to me from William James, walking my dog, taking my clothes and sheets to the laundromat. Why something that not only ended but began in an accident should have so undone me—but, well, it did. And he had been undone too, which moved me. It made me realize that he'd been serious all along.

As I was finishing the review, an orange cat wandered into the kitchen and promptly jumped up onto the table, and for the first time I experienced a pang of disapproval: Jerry Roth was not a great disciplinarian with his animals, and the cat settled itself right on top of the newspapers. I moved a dish out of the way so the cat wouldn't lick the butter from the toast, deciding as I did so that I might as well eat the rest of the toast myself, since it was already cold.

Did I call out at any point? Make myself known? I think I said hello when I stepped inside his house; I must have done that. But I felt quite sure, quite quickly, that no one was home, despite the cups and dishes still scattered on the table, despite the smell of breakfast in the air. The house had the quality of being recently and hurriedly evacuated, but not for any sinister reason—maybe the kids were late for swim practice, or the milk had run out. They had left the house in a rush, they would be back soon; but for now, it was mine.

All of my senses opened in recognition. The mixed scent of newsprint and butter, the muted ticking of the modern cuckoo clock on the wall, the enamel tea kettle gleaming atop the immense stove, the marmalade still sharp in my mouth: home. Here it was. Or something like it. Something homelike. *Heimlich.* How would the Germans say it? *Gemütlich.* Touchingly, where the soul or spirit belongs. To put it another way, cozy. Which did not describe my overheated apartment in the city, or the dim, chaotic ranch house I'd grown up in, places that were home but not home, not the home I wished to have, might one day have, if time or means or aptitude ever allowed it. A home I'd have to make. Sitting at Jerry Roth's table, I felt suddenly that I'd spent my adult life engaged in the most impoverished kind of making. What did I have to show but lecture notes, a short book on other books, comments in the margins of seminar papers, an occasional terrarium? It occurred to me then that to make a kitchen like this required a breadth of imagination I might not be able to summon.

Back at the farmhouse there was a pedestal in the corner of the sitting room, and on the pedestal sat a large guestbook that held the names of past visitors, a book I had already leafed through many times, trying to kill the afternoon. Most of the names meant little to me, but once in a while a name would leap from the page and spread its light over the room—a moment both exhilarating and deeply shameful for me as I was reminded that I had no business being there. The guestbook adhered to a formula, full name followed by discipline and date of residency, and one of the earlier entries stopped me, because instead of putting down *architect* or *composer* or *essayist*, the visitor had written, in pretty capital letters, *HOMEMAKER.* But she was a poet, I knew—a poet of such importance that even I, who almost never read poetry, perked up at the sight of her name. She had written this in 1976, long enough ago that it was hard for me to interpret the word. Was it a political act to write that, a reclamation? A gesture of defiance? Or could it be modesty. Self-doubt. A wry critique of taxonomy and titles? Maybe, more simply, she felt it the most apt description of how she spent her days. I couldn't tell; though the writing itself looked black and fresh, her intent remained distant and unreadable to me. Nevertheless this entry in the guestbook made me happy. In the years since she wrote it, her genius as a poet had been named and rewarded, and I liked how the word she chose early for herself now had the glamour of genius attached to it; how *HOMEMAKER* reached forward through time and lightly claimed that.

The orange cat shifted peaceably on the newspaper. I considered fixing myself another piece of toast, or finding a guest room and lying down to rest for a few minutes. My body was still tired and weird from all the running, and when I stood up from my chair, my knees buckled and I nearly lost my balance. I laid my palm on the knotted surface of the table. Through the wide kitchen windows I could see the rainbow horse waiting in the garden, and beyond that, the crooked apple tree. A fringe of young trees grew along the property line, weakly shielding the back lawn from the shaggier woods that rose up behind them, and while I was staring at the saplings, trying to figure out what kind they were, I saw a large body emerge from the forest and start lumbering toward the house. It took me a second to realize that the body belonged to a man. It was so pale and slow and enormous, and wearing such a short and colorful bathrobe, I thought unfairly at first that I must be seeing a woman, a morbidly obese woman in a swimming cap. But what I mistook for a swimming cap was actually a bald head. And as the man drew closer, I understood more and more clearly the size of him. He moved laboriously, shuffling more than walking, halting every few steps to catch his breath. His head shone and his shoulders heaved. The hem of his bathrobe fluttered above legs that looked at once curdled and bloated, swollen to the point of bursting. His leg flesh drooped over his knees.

I knew but did not accept that this man approaching the house was Jerry Roth. He made his slow, huffing way across the lawn in the unthinking manner of someone who had done so a thousand times before. Upon noticing something in the grass, he kicked at it briefly, but didn't, probably couldn't, bend over to pick it up. It seemed impossible that the man responsible for this house was the same as the huge, repellent person kicking at his lawn. I was too inexperienced to understand how the two were not at all irreconcilable.

Jerry Roth then lifted his eyes and blindly took in the whole of his house, or at least the back view of it, a view I had never seen, and I must have forgotten that I was as fully apparent to him as he was to me, because I continued to gaze at my ease from the kitchen, and felt truly shocked when his blank stare narrowed into a hard look, pointed in my direction like a gun. He stopped short and raised a heavy arm to block the glare from his eyes. I could see now that his bright bathrobe was covered in flocks of flying cranes, wings and necks outstretched. Suddenly he dropped his arm and began moving toward me at a pace I didn't think possible for him.

In that moment I thought meaningfully, for the first time in several weeks, about William James; in this case, about William James and his bear. To explain, James published an influential paper in 1884, a paper titled "What Is an Emotion?," and in this paper James put forth the theory that standard emotions such as sadness or rage or fear are not antecedent to the physiological responses we associate with them, but rather the product of these bodily changes. This was a radical notion at the time, a reversal of the usual way of seeing things. Common sense, according to James, tells us that when we lose our fortune, we are sorry and weep; we meet a bear, are frightened and run; we are insulted by a rival, are angry and strike. Yet this order of sequence is incorrect, James asserted: the more rational statement is that we feel sorry because we cry; angry because we strike; afraid because we tremble. Coming between the stimulus (bear) and the feeling (fear) is the body: quickened heartbeat, shallow breathing, trembling lips, weakened limbs. And that collection of responses is what lets you know that you're afraid.

My own research had very little to do with his theory of emotion, and I confess to feeling somewhat irritated when the bear would be brought up almost immediately upon my mentioning an interest in William James. Why did it loom so large in people's memory, and why did it seem to be the only aspect of James's work that they retained? It needled me, enough so that at some point I went back and reread the paper, only to discover that the famous bear made the most minor of appearances, invoked only twice and amid a series of instances. Much more remarkable to me was the story James tells of being a child of seven or eight years old and seeing a horse bled. The blood was in a bucket, with a stick in it; James stirred the blood around and, his childish curiosity aroused, lifted the stick to watch the blood drip from it. Then, without warning, he fell over in a dead faint. James recalls feeling, even at such a young age, astonished that the mere presence of a pailful of red liquid could provoke *such formidable bodily effects*. The child and his bucket of blood—now why didn't anyone remember that?

But as I stood there frozen in the kitchen of Jerry Roth's house, I felt in my every muscle the indelibleness of James's oft-cited example. It was simple. When you meet a bear in the woods, you run. And of course that is what I did: I ran.

In another version of the story, I jump out the nearest window and break my neck in the fall. Otherwise I am devoured, or thrown into a fire, or drowned. Barring that, I am dropped from a church steeple as punishment. In the version first recorded by Robert Southey, I manage to get away but am taken up by the constable and sent to the House of Corrections for being the vagrant that I am. It takes almost no effort to dig up these variations; over time, the trespasser turns from curious fox to bad old woman to bold little girl: a girl who is at the start called Silver Hair but who eventually gets saddled with the cloying name she hasn't been able to shake since. Given the possibilities, it's clearly best to be young, blond, and impertinent, because then you do not suffer any retribution for what you've done. Your escape is assured. As for me, I am over thirty-five, soft-spoken, brown-skinned—yet I too seem to have gotten off scot-free.

It can be difficult, however, to sift out retribution from reward, to really tell the two apart, commingled as they often are. For instance, after I left the farmhouse, having never touched my chapter on William James, my friend and I decided to have another go at it, this time more solemnly and deliberately than before, and to our indescribable relief, it stuck. My body grew larger and larger, unrecognizably larger, until suddenly one morning our daughter was born. We rigged up a sort of three-sided crib at the edge of the bed that allowed me to reach for her in the middle of the night and to nurse, without ever having to sit up or even raise my head from the pillow, and when she was done, I'd just slide her back on her special shelf and fall asleep again. Which is all to say that though she slept beside me I never worried, in those blurry months, about rolling over on my child and smothering her; among the many possibilities I worried over, this was not one of them, this was one of the few I could lay to rest. Strangely, though, my body remained convinced that I had to stay very still as I was sleeping, that I couldn't toss about or sprawl, that I needed to contain myself to a sliver of the bed, as if to avoid the risk of something terrible happening. It was an odd compulsion, and my hand or arm would often go numb as the result of sleeping in this anxious, unmoving way. Then one night my daughter's voice punctured my dreaming so cleanly that I was able to hold the shape of dream before it vanished, and the shape was the shape of Jerry Roth, the monstrous bulk of him, heaving softly beside me in the bed, and I knew, I knew, that I couldn't move, because to wake him would be—to what? To die? My heart raced, my breath was shallow. I brought my hands to my chest and they were damp with sweat. In the darkness this felt like fear. But I lifted the elastic band on my underwear and put a hand between my legs, and I understood then that my rigid, dreaming body hadn't been afraid. After wiping my fingers on the sheets, I reached out and found my daughter on her shelf.

As if not to be stopped, I became pregnant again, sooner than expected, and the apartment soon revealed itself as too expensive and too small, making the once unimaginable choice appear to us natural, attractive, inescapable, imminent: we moved to a house in the country. Our town is less than two hours away from the city by train; the backyards peter out into forests or fields; the houses are for the most part rundown, but with a lot of original detail, as the agent liked to say. A specialty food shop has bravely opened up, and there is a drive-in movie theater that still operates in the summer. At dusk, we flick the insects from our eyes and turn blankly to the wide, transparent sky, something like calm sliding over us.

But the days can be long, which I remember from my first stay in the country, and I often catch myself calculating the hours and little activities until dusk falls and the train comes in and the babies are put to sleep. The stretch between the morning nap and the afternoon nap always has a particular endlessness to it. My children are just different enough in age to be impossible to entertain simultaneously; what mesmerizes one infuriates the other; their developmental stages appear mortally opposed. I shuttle between the two of them to neither's satisfaction. Like a bad employee I tend to hang back and dawdle, taking longer than necessary in the bathroom, surreptitiously checking my email, drawn helplessly to any window to watch the smooth, indifferent functioning of the seductive world outside. There's usually not that much to see. A couple of guys from the power company checking the lines, or the older husband and wife from down the road, walking in single file and not talking, intent on their exercise. The mailman, of course; or in our case, the mailwoman. More rarely, the brown UPS truck. But every once in a while I'll look out the window and see someone who doesn't belong there, like an overweight girl wearing enormous headphones and jogging miserably, or a woman dressed in city clothes who tramps along the side of the road with a faint frown on her face. I have no way of knowing who she is and where she's off to, but she looks so unlikely out there among the gravel and the weeds, and so impractically dressed, that I briefly wonder if her car has broken down. I think to open the door and call out to her, asking if she needs help, if everything's all right, but to do so seems altogether impossible, as impossible as one of those huge prehistoric fish half-hibernating at the bottom of the tank knocking on the glass and mouthing *hello!* to a bright, quickly moving visitor on the other side. To our mutual embarrassment, though, she sees me, our eyes meet, and after automatically glancing away she looks back at me again and lifts her hand in a tentative wave. I wave back at her, electrified and sad. And then my daughter, in the far distance somewhere, lets out a long howl of frustration, and by the time I've gotten down on my hands and knees, rescued the wooden mixing spoon from under the stove, rinsed it off in hot water, hurried back to the window—the woman walking down the highway has already moved on, innocent of what waits for her, and passed out of sight.

The Great Silence

FROM *e-flux journal*

THE HUMANS USE Arecibo to look for extraterrestrial intelligence. Their desire to make a connection is so strong that they've created an ear capable of hearing across the universe.

But I and my fellow parrots are right here. Why aren't they interested in listening to our voices?

We're a nonhuman species capable of communicating with them. Aren't we exactly what humans are looking for?

The universe is so vast that intelligent life must surely have arisen many times. The universe is also so old that even one technological species would have had time to expand and fill the galaxy. Yet there is no sign of life anywhere except on Earth. Humans call this the Fermi paradox.

One proposed solution to the Fermi paradox is that intelligent species actively try to conceal their presence, to avoid being targeted by hostile invaders.

Speaking as a member of a species that has been driven nearly to extinction by humans, I can attest that this is a wise strategy.

It makes sense to remain quiet and avoid attracting attention.

The Fermi paradox is sometimes known as the Great Silence. The universe ought to be a cacophony of voices, but instead it's disconcertingly quiet.

Some humans theorize that intelligent species go extinct before they can expand into outer space. If they're correct, then the hush of the night sky is the silence of a graveyard.

Hundreds of years ago, my kind was so plentiful that the Río Abajo Forest resounded with our voices. Now we're almost gone. Soon this rainforest may be as silent as the rest of the universe.

There was an African grey parrot named Alex. He was famous for his cognitive abilities. Famous among humans, that is.

A human researcher named Irene Pepperberg spent thirty years studying Alex. She found that not only did Alex know the words for shapes and colors, he actually understood the concepts of shape and color.

Many scientists were skeptical that a bird could grasp abstract concepts. Humans like to think they're unique. But eventually Pepperberg convinced them that Alex wasn't just repeating words, that he understood what he was saying.

Out of all my cousins, Alex was the one who came closest to being taken seriously as a communication partner by humans.

Alex died suddenly, when he was still relatively young. The evening before he died, Alex said to Pepperberg, "You be good. I love you."

If humans are looking for a connection with a nonhuman intelligence, what more can they ask for than that?

Every parrot has a unique call that it uses to identify itself; biologists refer to this as the parrot's "contact call."

In 1974, astronomers used Arecibo to broadcast a message into outer space intended to demonstrate human intelligence. That was humanity's contact call.

In the wild, parrots address each other by name. One bird imitates another's contact call to get the other bird's attention.

If humans ever detect the Arecibo message being sent back to Earth, they will know someone is trying to get their attention.

Parrots are vocal learners: we can learn to make new sounds after we've heard them. It's an ability that few animals possess. A dog may understand dozens of commands, but it will never do anything but bark.

Humans are vocal learners too. We have that in common. So humans and parrots share a special relationship with sound. We don't simply cry out. We pronounce. We enunciate.

Perhaps that's why humans built Arecibo the way they did. A

receiver doesn't have to be a transmitter, but Arecibo is both. It's an ear for listening, and a mouth for speaking.

Humans have lived alongside parrots for thousands of years, and only recently have they considered the possibility that we might be intelligent.

I suppose I can't blame them. We parrots used to think humans weren't very bright. It's hard to make sense of behavior that's so different from your own.

But parrots are more similar to humans than any extraterrestrial species will be, and humans can observe us up close; they can look us in the eye. How do they expect to recognize an alien intelligence if all they can do is eavesdrop from a hundred light-years away?

It's no coincidence that "aspiration" means both hope and the act of breathing.

When we speak, we use the breath in our lungs to give our thoughts a physical form. The sounds we make are simultaneously our intentions and our life force.

I speak, therefore I am. Vocal learners, like parrots and humans, are perhaps the only ones who fully comprehend the truth of this.

There's a pleasure that comes with shaping sounds with your mouth. It's so primal and visceral that throughout their history, humans have considered the activity a pathway to the divine.

Pythagorean mystics believed that vowels represented the music of the spheres, and chanted to draw power from them.

Pentecostal Christians believe that when they speak in tongues, they're speaking the language used by angels in Heaven.

Brahmin Hindus believe that by reciting mantras, they're strengthening the building blocks of reality.

Only a species of vocal learners would ascribe such importance to sound in their mythologies. We parrots can appreciate that.

According to Hindu mythology, the universe was created with a sound: "Om." It's a syllable that contains within it everything that ever was and everything that will be.

When the Arecibo telescope is pointed at the space between stars, it hears a faint hum.

Astronomers call that the "cosmic microwave background." It's the residual radiation of the Big Bang, the explosion that created the universe fourteen billion years ago.

But you can also think of it as a barely audible reverberation of that original "Om." That syllable was so resonant that the night sky will keep vibrating for as long as the universe exists.

When Arecibo is not listening to anything else, it hears the voice of creation.

We Puerto Rican parrots have our own myths. They're simpler than human mythology, but I think humans would take pleasure from them.

Alas, our myths are being lost as my species dies out. I doubt the humans will have deciphered our language before we're gone.

So the extinction of my species doesn't just mean the loss of a group of birds. It's also the disappearance of our language, our rituals, our traditions. It's the silencing of our voice.

Human activity has brought my kind to the brink of extinction, but I don't blame them for it. They didn't do it maliciously. They just weren't paying attention.

And humans create such beautiful myths; what imaginations they have. Perhaps that's why their aspirations are so immense. Look at Arecibo. Any species that can build such a thing must have greatness within it.

My species probably won't be here for much longer; it's likely that we'll die before our time and join the Great Silence. But before we go, we are sending a message to humanity. We just hope the telescope at Arecibo will enable them to hear it.

The message is this:

You be good. I love you.

LOUISE ERDRICH

The Flower

FROM *The New Yorker*

OUTSIDE AN ISOLATED Ojibwe country trading post in the
year 1839, Mink was making an incessant racket. She wanted what
Mackinnon had, trader's milk—a mixture of raw distilled spirits,
rum, red pepper, and tobacco. She had bawled and screeched her
way to possession of a keg before. The noise pared at Mackinnon's
nerves, but he wouldn't beat her into silence. Mink was from a
family of powerful healers. She had been the beautiful daughter
of Shingobii, a supplier of rich furs. She had also been the beautiful wife of Mashkiig, until he destroyed her face and stabbed her
younger brothers to death. Their eleven-year-old daughter hud-
dled with her now, under the same greasy blanket, trying to hide.
Inside the post, Mackinnon's clerk, Wolfred Roberts, had swathed
his head in a fox pelt to muffle the sound, fastening the desiccated
paws beneath his chin. He wrote in an elegant, sloping hand, three
items between lines. Out there in the bush, they were always afraid
of running out of paper.

Wolfred had left his home in Portsmouth, New Hampshire,
because he was the youngest of four brothers and there was no
room for him in the family business—a bakery. His mother was the
daughter of a schoolteacher, and she had educated him. He was
just seventeen. He missed her, and he missed the books. He had
taken only two with him when he was sent to clerk with Mackinnon: a pocket dictionary and Xenophon's *Anabasis and Memora-
bilia,* which had belonged to his grandfather, and which his mother
hadn't known contained lewd descriptions.

Even with the fox on his head, the screeching rattled him. He tried to clean up around the fireplace and threw a pile of scraps out for the dogs. As soon as he walked back inside, there was pandemonium. Mink and her daughter were fighting the dogs off. The noise was hideous.

Don't go out there. I forbid you, Mackinnon said. If the dogs kill and eat them, there will be less trouble.

The humans eventually won the fight, but the noise continued into darkness.

Mink started hollering again before sunup. Her high-pitched wailing was even louder now. The men were scratchy-eyed and tired. Mackinnon kicked her, or kicked one of them, as he passed. She went hoarse that afternoon, which only made her voice more irritating. Something in it had changed, Wolfred thought. He didn't understand the language very well.

That rough old bitch wants to sell me her daughter, Mackinnon said.

Mink's voice was horrid—intimate with filth—as she described the things the girl could do if Mackinnon would only give over the milk. She was directing the full force of her shrieks at the closed door. Part of Wolfred's job was to catch and clean fish if Mackinnon asked. He went down to the hole he kept open in the icy river, crossing himself as he walked past Mink. Although of course he wasn't Catholic, the gesture had cachet where Jesuits had been. When he returned, Mink was gone and the girl was inside the post, crouching in the corner underneath a new blanket, her head down, still as death.

I couldn't stand it another minute, Mackinnon said.

Wolfred stared at the blanketed lump of girl. Mackinnon had always been honest, for a trader. Fair, for a trader, and showed no signs of moral corruption beyond the usual—selling rum to Indians was outlawed. Wolfred could not take in what had happened, so again he went fishing. When he came back with another stringer of whitefish, his mind was clear. Mackinnon was a rescuer, he decided. He had saved the girl from Mink, and from a slave's fate elsewhere. Wolfred chopped some kindling and built a small cooking fire beside the post. He roasted the fish whole, and Mackinnon ate them with last week's tough bread. Tomorrow Wolfred would bake. When he went back into the cabin, the girl was exactly where she'd been before. She hadn't moved a hair. Which also meant that Mackinnon hadn't touched her.

Wolfred put a plate of bread and fish on the dirt floor where she could reach it. She devoured both and gasped for breath. He set a tankard of water near her. She gulped it all down, her throat clucking like a baby's as she drained the cup.

After Mackinnon had eaten, he crawled into his slat-and-bear-skin bed, where it was his habit to drink himself to sleep. Wolfred cleaned up the cabin. Then he heated a pail of water and crouched near the girl. He wet a rag and dabbed at her face. As the caked dirt came off, he discovered her features, one by one, and saw that they were very fine. Her lips were small and full. Her eyes hauntingly sweet. Her eyebrows perfectly flared. When her face was uncovered, he stared at her in dismay. She was exquisite. Did Mackinnon know?

Gimiikwaadiz, Wolfred whispered. He knew the word for how she looked.

Carefully, reaching into the corner of the cabin for what he needed, he mixed mud. He held her chin and spread the muck back onto her face, blotting over the startling line of her brows, the perfect symmetry of her eyes and nose, the devastating curve of her lips.

Mackinnon spoke to the girl in her language, and she hid her muddy face.

All I did was ask her name, he said, throwing up his hands. She refuses to tell me her name. Give her some work to do, Roberts. I can't stand that lump in the corner.

Wolfred made her help him chop wood. But her movements displayed the fluid grace of her limbs. He showed her how to bake bread. But the fire lit up her face and the heat melted away some of the mud. He reapplied it. When Mackinnon was out, he tried to teach her to write. She learned the alphabet easily. But writing displayed her hand, marvelously formed. Finally—at her suggestion—she went off to set snares and a trapline. She made herself well enough understood. She planned to buy herself back from Mackinnon by selling the furs. He hadn't paid that much for her. It would not take long, she implied.

All this time, because she knew exactly why Wolfred had replaced the grime on her face, she slouched and grimaced, tousled her hair, and smeared her features.

She picked up another written letter every day, then words, phrases. She began to sprinkle them in her talk. For a wild savage, she was certainly intelligent, Wolfred thought. Pretty soon she's going to take my job. Ha-ha. There was nobody to joke with but himself.

The daughter of Mink brooded on the endlessly shifting snow. *I will make a fire myself, as the stinking chimookoman won't let me near his fire at night. Then I can pick the lice from my dress and my blanket. His lice will crawl on me again if he does the old stinking chimookoman thing he does.* She saw herself lifting the knife from his belt and slipping it between his ribs.

The other one, the young one, was kind but had no power. He didn't understand what the crafty old chimookoman was doing. Her struggles seemed only to give the drooling dog strength, and he knew exactly how to pin her, how to make her helpless.

The birds were silent. She had scrubbed her body red with snow. She threw off everything and lay naked in the snow asking to be dead. She tried not to move, but the cold was bitter and she began to suffer intensely. A person from the other world came. The being was pale blue, without definite form. It took care of her, dressed her, tied on her makizin, blew the lice off, and wrapped her in a new blanket, saying, Call upon me when this happens, and you shall live.

Wolfred hacked off a piece of weasel-gnawed moose. He carried it into the cabin and put it in a pot heaped with snow. He built up the fire just right and hung the pot to boil. He had learned from the girl to harvest red-gold berries, withered a bit in winter, which gave the meat a slightly skunky but pleasant flavor. She had taught him how to make tea from leathery swamp leaves. She had shown him rock lichen, edible but bland. The day was half gone.

Mashkiig, the girl's father, walked in, lean and fearsome, with two slinking minions. He glanced at the girl, then looked away. He traded his furs for rum and guns. Mackinnon told him to get drunk far from the trading post. The day he'd killed the girl's uncles, Mashkiig had also stabbed everyone else in the vicinity. He'd slit Mink's nose and ears. Now he tried to claim the girl, then to buy her, but Mackinnon wouldn't take back any of the guns.

After Mashkiig left, Mackinnon and Wolfred each took a piss, hauled some wood in, then locked the inside shutters and loaded their guns. About a week later, they heard that he'd killed Mink. The girl put her head down and wept.

Wolfred was a clerk of greater value than he knew. He cooked well and could make bread from practically nothing. He'd kept his father's yeast going halfway across North America, and he was always seeking new sources of provender. He was using up the milled flour that Mackinnon had brought to trade. The Indians hadn't got a taste for it yet. Wolfred had ground wild rice to powder and added it to the stuff they had. Last summer, he had mounded up clay and hollowed it out into an earthen oven. That was where he baked his weekly loaves. As the loaves were browning, Mackinnon came outside. The scent of the bread so moved him, there in the dark of winter, that he opened a keg of wine. They'd had six kegs and were down to five. Mackinnon had packed the good wine in himself, over innumerable portages. Ordinarily, he partook of the trader's rum that the voyageurs humped in to supply and resupply the Indians. Now he and Wolfred drank together, sitting on two stumps by the heated oven and a leaping fire.

Outside the circle of warmth, the snow squeaked and the stars pulsed in the impenetrable heavens. The girl sat between them, not drinking. She thought her own burdensome thoughts. From time to time, both of the men glanced at her profile in the firelight. Her dirty face was brushed with raw gold. When the wine was drunk, the bread was baked. Reverently, they removed the loaves and put them, hot, inside their coats. The girl opened her blanket to accept a loaf from Wolfred. As he gave it to her, he realized that her dress was torn down the middle. He looked into her eyes and her eyes slid to Mackinnon. Then she ducked her head and held the dress together with her elbow while she bit into the loaf.

Inside, they sat on small stumps, around a bigger stump, to eat. The cabin had been built around the large stump so that it could serve as a table.

Wolfred looked so searchingly at Mackinnon that the trader finally said, What?

Mackinnon had a flaccid bladder belly, crab legs, a snoose-stained beard, pig-mad red eyes, red sprouts of dandered hair, wormish lips, pitchy teeth, breath that knocked you sideways, and nose hairs that dripped snot on and spoiled Wolfred's perfectly inked numbers. Mackinnon was also a dead shot, and hell with his claw hammer. Wolfred had seen him use it on one of the very minions who'd shadowed Mashkiig that day. He was dangerous. Yet. Wolfred chewed and stared. He was seized with sharp emotion. For the first time in his life, Wolfred began to see the things of which he was capable.

Wolfred sorted through the options: They could run away, but Mackinnon would not only pursue them but pay Mashkiig to get to them first. They could stick together at all times so that Wolfred could watch over her, but that would make it obvious that Wolfred knew and they would lose the element of surprise. Xenophon had lain awake in the night, asking himself this question: What age am I waiting for to come to myself? This age, Wolfred thought. Because they had to kill Mackinnon, of course. Really, it was the first thing Wolfred had thought of doing, and the only way. To feel better about it, however, he had examined all the options.

How to do it?

Shooting him was out. There might be justice. Killing him by ax, hatchet, knife, or rock, or tying him up and stuffing him under the ice were also risky that way. As he lay in the faltering dark imagining each scenario, Wolfred remembered how he'd walked the woods with her. She knew everything there was to eat in the woods. She probably knew everything not to eat as well. She probably knew poisons.

Alone with her the next day, he saw that she'd managed to sew her dress together with a length of sinew. He pointed to the dress, pointed in the general direction of Mackinnon, then proceeded to mime out picking something, cooking it, Mackinnon eating it, holding his belly, and pitching over dead. It made her laugh behind her hand. He convinced her that it was not a joke, and she began to wash her hands in the air, biting her lip, darting glances all around, as though even the needles on the pines knew what they were planning. Then she signaled him to follow.

She searched the woods until she found a stand of oaks, then put a cloth on her hand and plunged it into the snow near a cracked-off stump, rotted down to almost nothing. From beneath the snow she pulled out some dark-gray strands that might once have been mushrooms.

That night Wolfred used the breast meat of six partridges, the tenders of three rabbits, wild onions, a shriveled blue potato, and the girl's offering to make a highly salted and strongly flavored stew. He unplugged a keg of high wine and made sure that Mackinnon drained it half down before he ate. The stew did not seem to affect him. They all went to their corners, and Mackinnon kept on drinking the way he usually did until the fire burned out.

In the middle of the night, his thrashing, grunting, and high squeals of pain woke them. Wolfred lit a lantern. Mackinnon's entire head had turned purple and had swollen to a grotesque size. His eyes had vanished in the bloated flesh. His tongue, a mottled fish, bulged from what must have been his mouth. He seemed to be trying to throw himself out of his body. He cast himself violently at the log walls, into the fireplace, upon the mounds of furs and blankets, rattling guns off their wooden hooks. Ammunition, ribbons, and hawksbells rained off the shelves. His belly popped from his vest, round and hard as a boulder. His hands and feet filled like bladders. Wolfred had never witnessed anything remotely as terrifying, but he had the presence of mind not to club Mackinnon or in any way molest his monstrous presence. As for the girl, she seemed pleased at his condition, though she did not smile.

Trying to disregard the chaotic death occurring to his left, now to his right, now underfoot, Wolfred prepared to leave. He grabbed snowshoes and two packs, moving clumsily. In the packs he put two fire steels, ammunition, bannocks he had made in advance. He doubled up two blankets and another to cut for leggings, and outfitted himself and the girl with four knives apiece. He took two guns, wadding, and a large flask of gunpowder. He took salt, tobacco, Mackinnon's precious coffee, and one of the remaining kegs of wine. He did not take overmuch coin, though he knew which hollowed log hid the trader's tiny stash.

Mackinnon's puffed mitts of hands fretted at his clothing and the threads burst. As Wolfred and the girl slipped out, they could hear him fighting the poison, his breath coming in sonorous gasps. He could barely draw air past his swelled tongue into his gigantic purpled head. Yet he managed to call feebly out to them, My children! Why are you leaving me?

From the other side of the door they could hear his legs drumming on the packed earth floor. They could hear his fat paws wildly pattering for water on the empty wooden bucket.

On snowshoes of ash wood and sinew, Wolfred and the girl made their way south. They would be easy to follow. Wolfred's story was that they'd decided to travel toward Grand Portage for help. They had left Mackinnon ill in the cabin with plenty of supplies. If they got lost, wandered, found themselves even farther south, chances were nobody would know or care who Mackinnon was. And so they trekked, making good time, and set up their camp at night. The girl tested the currents of the air with her face and hands, then showed Wolfred where to build a lean-to, how to place it just so, how to find dry wood in snow, snapping dead branches out of trees, and where to pile it so that they could easily keep the fire going all night and direct its heat their way. They slept peacefully, curled in their separate blankets, and woke to the wintertime scolding of chickadees. The girl tuned up the fire, they ate, and were back on their way south when suddenly they heard the awful gasping voice of Mackinnon behind them. They could hear him blundering toward them, cracking twigs, calling out to them, Wait, my children, wait a moment, do not abandon me!

They started forward in terror. Soon a dog drew near them, one of the trading post's pathetic curs; it ran alongside them, bounding effortfully through the snow. At first they thought that Mackinnon had sent it to find them, but then the girl stopped and looked hard at the dog. It whined to her. She nodded and pointed the way through the trees to a frozen river, where they would move more quickly. On the river ice they slid along with a dreamlike velocity. The girl gave the dog a piece of bannock from her pocket, and that night, when they made camp, she set her snares out all around them. She built their fire and the lean-to so that they had to pass through a narrow space between two trees. Here too she set a snare. Its loop was large enough for a man's head, even a horribly swollen one. They fed themselves and the dog, and slept with their knives out, packs and snowshoes close by.

Near morning, when the fire was down to coals, Wolfred woke. He heard Mackinnon's rasping breath very close. The dog barked. The girl got up and signaled that Wolfred should fasten on his snowshoes and gather their packs and blankets. As the light came up, Wolfred saw that the sinew snare set for Mackinnon was jigging, pulled tight. The dog worried and tore at some invisible shape. The girl showed Wolfred how to climb over the lean-to another way, and made him understand that he should check the snares she'd set, retrieve anything they'd caught, and not forget to remove the sinews so that she could reset them at their next camp.

Mackinnon's breathing resounded through the clearing around the fire. As Wolfred left, he saw that the girl was preparing a stick with pine pitch and birch bark. He saw her thrust it at the air again and again. There were muffled grunts of pain. Wolfred was so frightened that he had trouble finding all the snares, and he had to cut the sinew that had choked a frozen rabbit. Eventually, the girl joined him and they slid back down to the river with the dog. Behind them, unearthly caterwauls began. To Wolfred's relief, the girl smiled and skimmed forward, calm, full of confidence. Though she was still a child.

Wolfred asked the girl to tell him her name. He asked in words, he asked in signs, but she wouldn't speak. Each time they stopped, he asked. But though she smiled at him, and understood exactly what he wanted, she wouldn't answer. She looked into the distance.

The next morning, after they had slept soundly, she knelt near the fire to blow it back to life. All of a sudden, she went still and stared into the trees. She jutted her chin forward, then pulled back her hair and narrowed her eyes. Wolfred followed her gaze and saw it too. Mackinnon's head, rolling laboriously over the snow, its hair on fire, flames cheerfully flickering. Sometimes it banged into a tree and whimpered. Sometimes it propelled itself along with its tongue, its slight stump of neck, or its comically paddling ears. Sometimes it whizzed along for a few feet, then quit, sobbing in frustration at its awkward, interminable progress.

Fighting, outwitting, burning, even leaving food behind for the head to gobble, just to slow it down, the girl, Wolfred, and the dog traveled. They wore out their snowshoes, and the girl repaired them. Their moccasins shredded. She layered the bottoms with skin and lined them with rabbit fur. Every time they tried to rest, the head would appear, bawling at night, fiery at dawn. So they moved on and on, until, at last, starved and frozen, they gave out.

The small bark hut took most of a day to bind together. As they prepared to sleep, Wolfred arranged a log on the fire and then fell back as if struck. The simple action had dizzied him. His strength had flowed right out through his fingers into the fire. The fire now sank quickly from his sight, as if over some invisible cliff. He began to shiver, hard, and then a black wall fell. He was confined in a temple of branching halls. All that night he groped his way through narrow passages, along doorless walls. He crept around corners, stayed low. Standing was impossible, even in his dreams. When he opened his eyes at first light, he saw that the vague dome of the hut was spinning so savagely that it blurred and sickened him. He did not dare to open his eyes again that day, but lay as still as possible, lifting his head only to sip the water the girl dripped between his lips from a piece of folded bark.

He told her to leave him behind. She pretended not to understand him.

All day she cared for him, hauling wood, boiling broth, keeping him warm. That night the dog growled ferociously at the door, and Wolfred opened one eye briefly to see infinitely duplicated images of the girl heating the blade of the ax red hot and gripping the handle with rags. He felt her slip out the door, and then there began a great babble of howling, cursing, shrieking, desperate groaning and thumping, as if trees were being felled. This went on all night. At first light, he sensed that she'd crept inside again. He felt the warmth and weight of her curled against his back, smelled the singed fur of the dog or maybe her hair. Hours into the day, she woke, and he heard her tuning a drum in the warmth of the fire. Surprised, he asked her, in Ojibwe, how she'd got the drum.

It flew to me, she told him. This drum belonged to my mother. With this drum, she brought people to life.

He must have heard wrong, or misunderstood. Drums cannot fly. He was not dead. Or was he? The world behind his closed eyes was ever stranger. From the many-roomed black temple, he had stepped into a universe of fractured patterns. There was no relief from their implacable mathematics. Designs formed and re-formed. Hard-edged triangles joined and split in an endless geometry. If this was death, it was visually exhausting. Only when she started drumming did the patterns gradually lose their intensity. Their movement diminished as she sang in an off-key, high-pitched, nasal whine that rose and fell in calming repetition.

The drum corrected some interior rhythm, a delicious relaxation painted his thoughts, and he slept.

Again, that night, he heard the battle outside, anguished, desperate. Again, at first light, he felt her curl against him and smelled the scorched dog. Again, when she woke, she tuned and beat the drum. The same song transported him. He put his hand to his head. She'd cut up her blanket, crowned him with a warm woolen turban. That night, he opened his eyes and saw the world rock to a halt. Joyously, he whispered, I am back. I have returned.

You shall go on one more journey with me, she said, smiling, and began to sing.

Her song lulled and relaxed him so that when he stepped out of his body he was not afraid to lift off the ground alongside her. They traveled into vast air. Over the dense woods, they flew so fast that no cold could reach them. Below them, fires burned, a village only two days' walk from their hut. Satisfied, she turned them back and Wolfred drifted down into the body that he would not leave again until he had completed half a century of bone-breaking work.

Two days later, they left the deep wilderness and entered a town. Ojibwe bark houses, a hundred or more, were set up along the lakeshore. On a street of beaten snow, several wooden houses were neatly rooted in an incongruous row. They were so like the houses that Wolfred had left behind out east that, for a disoriented moment, he believed they had traversed the Great Lakes. He knocked at the door of the largest house. Not until he had introduced himself in English did the young woman who answered recognize him as a white man.

She and her husband, missionaries, brought the pair into a warm kitchen. They were given water and rags to wash with, and then a tasteless porridge of boiled wild rice. They were allowed to sleep with blankets, on the floor behind the woodstove. The dog, left outside, sniffed the missionaries' dog and followed it to the barn, where the two coupled in the steam of the cow's great body. The next morning, speaking earnestly to the girl, whose clean face was too beautiful to look at, Wolfred asked if she would marry him.

When you grow up, he said.

She smiled and nodded.

Again, he asked her name.

She laughed, not wanting him to own her, and drew a flower.

The missionary was sending a few young Ojibwe to a Presbyterian boarding school, in Michigan, that was for Indians only, and he offered to send the girl there too, if she wanted to become educated. She agreed to do it.

At the school, everything was taken from her. Losing her mother's drum was like losing Mink all over again. At night, she asked the drum to fly back to her again. But there was no answer. She soon learned how to fall asleep. Or let the part of myself they call hateful fall asleep, she thought. But that was all of herself. Her whole being was Anishinaabe. She was Illusion. She was Mirage. Ombanitemagad. Or what they called her now—Indian. As in, Do not speak Indian, when she had been speaking her own language. It was hard to divide off parts of herself and let them go. At night, she flew up through the ceiling and soared as she had been taught. She stored pieces of her being in the tops of the trees. She'd retrieve them later, when the bells stopped. But the bells would never stop. There were so many bells. Her head ached, at first, because of the bells. My thoughts are all tangled up, she said out loud to herself, inbiimiskwendam. However, there was very little time to consider what was happening.

The other children smelled like old people. Soon she did too. Her woolen dress and corset pinched, and the woolen underwear made her itch like mad. Her feet were shot through with pain, and stank from sweating in hard leather. Her hands chapped. She was always cold, but she was already used to that. The food was usually salt pork and cabbage, which cooked foul and turned the dormitory rank with farts, as did the milk they were forced to drink. But no matter how raw, or rotten, or strange, she had to eat, so she got used to it. It was hard to understand the teachers or say what she needed in their language, but she learned. The crying up and down the rows of beds at night kept her awake, but soon she cried and farted herself to sleep with everyone else.

She missed her mother, even though Mink had sold her. She missed Wolfred, the only person left for her. She kept his finely written letters. When she was weak or tired, she read them over. That he called her Flower made her uneasy. Girls were not named for flowers, as flowers died so quickly. Girls were named for deathless things—forms of light, forms of clouds, shapes of stars, that which appears and disappears like an island on the horizon. Sometimes the school seemed like a dream that could not be true, and she fell asleep hoping to wake in another world.

She never got used to the bells, but she got used to other children coming and going. They died of measles, scarlet fever, flu, diphtheria, tuberculosis, and other diseases that did not have a name. But she was already accustomed to everybody around her dying. Once, she got a fever and thought that she would also die. But in the night her pale-blue spirit came, sat on the bed, spoke to her kindly, and told her that she would live.

Nobody got drunk. Nobody slashed her mother's face and nose, ruining her. Nobody took a knife and stabbed an uncle who held her foot and died as the blood gushed from his mouth. Another good thing she thought of while the other children wept was that the journey to the school had been arduous and far. Much too far for a head to roll.

YALITZA FERRERAS

The Letician Age

FROM *Colorado Review*

LETICIA'S MOTHER SPOTTED the glint in between the cobble-stones, near the statue of Christopher Columbus in Parque Colón, across the edge of her stomach like a tiny sun on the horizon. She bent down sideways, careful not to fold on the fetus that would soon be her baby girl. The ring was tiny, sized for a rich child's finger. A pronged crown nestling a ruby intercepted the gold band.

I hope it's a girl.

Once home, she led her husband to the backyard, past her sister crouched down cooking on coals, over to the avocado tree that would shield them from family and neighbors, and unfurled her hand under a sliver of sunlight, the ruby instantly peacocking its brilliant red facets.

"For the baby."

He reached for it, but Leticia's mother enclosed the ring in a fist. As he shook his head and moved his two fingers in unison with it, she pictured Leticia wearing the ring, her hair in ribboned, tubular ringlets, clad in a satiny tiered dress, inexplicably atop a prize goat, in a velvet-draped, gilded room. She wedged the fist in the deep triangle formed by the intersection of her engorged breasts and the top of her stomach.

The appraiser in Zona Colonial, not far from where she found the ring, affirmed its authenticity, the thing that Leticia's mother had felt in her heart. It had been a few years since she found the ring, and the lure of where that statue of Columbus pointed to (new horizons, the North) was pulling heavily on her family. Turned out that a child's trinket could buy only so much, but shady loans were secured, and decisions about who would stay and who would go were made.

Off to the New World.

Leticia's mother bought her a tiny fish tank with a tiny fish in it, which she named Pedro. They stared at the fish together and talked about his iridescence, litheness, ease of movement, and the impossibility of his breathing underwater. At the bottom of the tank was a small treasure chest like the ones that were sunken off the coast of Boca Chica, the ones her father had told her about as they sat in the sand, waves washing over their legs. He had told her there were jewels in the treasure chest like the one in the ring she'd once had, and that those jewels came from the earth and were excavated to give to good girls like her. She liked to be re-minded of home. Leticia hoped that Pedro's sort of beauty and wonder would be present in their lives, even though she had expe-rienced only cold, filth, and restrictions since arriving in New York. Back home she had played and run around with her cousins and neighbors in the dirt surrounding their houses. She wanted her father to make up fantastic stories about shiny things born out of the earth, but he never had any time to dream with her anymore.

She imagined Pedro was from an island too, and that he had many feelings and needs just like her own. She placed little rocks she picked up on her way home from school in his tank and fed him potato chips from her lunch because that was the only part of her lunch she liked to eat and thought Pedro would think the same. When he died, she stared as the white, gooey substance be-gan appearing on him, and on the rocks after he started decom-posing. He returned her stare with his marbled, milky eyes as he undulated in the current of the tank filter, the white wisps growing off his body, longer each day, billowing like ship sails. She had made her own foraminiferan—a sediment builder made out of fossilized fish, which drop to the ocean floor to become foraminif-eran ooze. It took her mother two weeks to notice that Pedro was dead. She was too busy sweating at a sweatshop, coming home to not one but two babies, and Leticia. Her mother wouldn't let her touch the ooze before she flushed Pedro down the toilet.

Louis Agassiz (1807–1873, Swiss) became one of the best-known scien-tists in the world (several animal species, lakes, mountains, and a crater on Mars were named after him) for his study and classification of fossil fish, and was the first to propose that the earth had been subject to a great "Ice Age." His *Etudes sur les glaciers* discussed the movements of the glaciers and their influence in grooving and rounding the rocks over which they traveled and in producing striations that would shape the surface of the earth for millennia.

When she was eight years old, she began her rock collection in shoeboxes in a crowded Washington Heights apartment shared with her aunt, uncle, and their four children. A few more family members lived two floors down from them; her family formed conglomerates—accumulations in shallow coastal waters—and their housing project was stacked up too, overflowing with people from everywhere, plus Mrs. Nussbaum, the lone white holdout.

All the children slept in bunk beds, two bunk beds to a room and one or two kids to a bunk. She slept on a top bunk by herself (all the top bunkers slept by themselves for safety), and Gabriel and Adriana, the twins, slept on a bottom bunk together with pillows on the floor beside them in case they fell out. Her parents slept on the sofa bed in the living room.

And out of her entire extended family, it was the twins who held everyone's attention. They were a creamy, caramel color that was a perfect mixture of their father's dark and their mother's lighter skin, topped with undulating curls that were somewhere in between her father's coarse Afro and her mother's soft waves. Leticia was one hundred percent her father's daughter—dark skin, kinky hair, and although it was too early to tell, it seemed as if she would also have a boyish figure instead of her mother's show-stopping curves. Everyone was amazed by the similarity of the twins' features and synchronization of their gestures. Leticia gave them a wide berth, imagining they would devise a silent signal, suddenly look up from their toys, and connect together like living, breathing puzzle things to cause the world's destruction.

Occasionally she would come home and find her collection scattered from its hiding place in her bunk. She longed for the time when she was an only child, when her family looked like the one in the picture—just her, her mother and father, and the ruby. She'd once been a rare, precious gem.

"Your toys are not fun at all," all the children said.

Leticia hid. She didn't frolic in front of the open fire hydrant, or spread out on the pavement to play jacks, or dart in and out of the jump rope for double dutch. She folded herself inside the corners of the apartment, wedged herself under the kitchen table in between the chair legs, built forts out of sheets and open umbrellas, and gathered the rocks in her hands, pushed them around on her palm.

She looked at her favorite library book, a glossy explosion of color, which showed rocks in their unpolished and polished forms side by side. There was a picture of dark men with shiny foreheads and sweat-stained shirts and pants tied together with rope, holding pickaxes, one of them in the foreground with a big, white, toothy grin, holding up a piece of craggy earth to a white man in a wide-brimmed safari hat, pleased with his worker's discovery. She had seen dark, sweaty men like these back home—men resembling her father—hanging off the sides of trucks, yelling in everyone's faces, selling plátanos and mangos.

In Cibao, her father's birthplace, amber was sometimes mined through bell pitting, a process that required the miners to dig foxholes, which often collapsed. Some men perished like the animals and insects trapped in the amber and were dug out of their tombs by dusty-faced men like themselves, who delivered their bodies to their loved ones wrapped in the burlap sacks they used to carry away the earth's treasures.

Leticia would talk to her rocks about how they came into being, where they lived, and what composed them; she honored the places and minerals they came from and praised the rocks they had become. She enjoyed classifying and reclassifying them and going on geological expeditions around the projects. She referred to their pictures in the books and then painted them with felt markers to mimic mineral content, and in this way the cement chunk of the sidewalk became azurite (blue marker), limonite (red marker), zippeite (yellow marker), and so on. Then she put them in different boxes according to the region in which they belonged, where she wished she had found them.

> In his *De natura fossilium* (1546), Georgius Agricola (1494–1555, German) presented the first scientific classification of minerals and ponders whether amber is the "unctuous sweat of the Earth."

Geological changes that took thousands or millions of years to occur looped in Leticia's head like a never-ending movie: mountain

ranges pushing out of the earth, minerals being formed from fluids that solidified and turned into beautiful crystals, rocks being
compressed by heat and pressure, and the tiny scream of a mos-
quito as its life was pressed away. In volcanoes, the slow processes
were sped up like the cataclysmic changes she wanted in her own
life, but most people were like rocks—shaped by circumstances
and time. Yet once in a while a person explodes out of her bedrock
and becomes something else. When she was twelve, she told her
parents about her plans—to be the first famous Dominican geologist and perhaps volcanologist. The conversation:

"Where will you live? I don't see any volcanoes here."

"Do something practical. If you apply yourself you can become
a secretary or maybe an accountant."

"She's going to leave and get married and have kids and then
we wasted our money."

"I don't want you working in factories like us. You have to work
in an office like a professional."

And, quieter, when they thought she wasn't paying attention:

"We'll see what Gabriel wants to do."

When her father came over, rubbed her cheek, and said, "Your
rocks will be a nice pastime," Leticia thought of a city-sized, burning globule of a millipede snaking its way through the 125th Street
fault line, pushing up through manhole covers, softly searing anyone and everything it touched, the screams and crushing sounds
muted in her mind.

She looked over at Adriana—perpetually clad in pink, with
her long, wavy hair clasped in plastic bow-shaped barrettes—
as she played with her dolls. In contrast, there was Leticia with
her shlubby self, always wearing things that were too tight in the
wrong areas and too loose in the right areas; it turned out that she
would be shaped like her father and such was the way that clothing
would always fit her. Her hair was matted down to her head, as her
mother had already begun chemically relaxing it in an effort to
make her look somehow neater, less unwieldy.

She had hoped maybe getting older would move her out of her
awkward stage, that she could start talking to someone about college; maybe someone could suggest the right classes to take, or
there would be some sort of program that would identify her as
special in some way. Only the pregnant girls received special treatment at her school.

She wanted special treatment too, or maybe just a place in history.

George Barrow (1853–1932, English) discovered that different temperatures produce different metamorphic rocks from the same ingredients. The index mineral (determined by the composition of the parent rock) forms under specific pressure and temperature conditions.

Gabriel liked to swim at the community pool or chase cats into traffic, and there wasn't much more to him as far as Leticia knew, but that seemed to be enough for her parents because he was a boy. Adriana liked to stick stickers on things, and let boys stick their hands down her pants, but the family found out about that only later, and also she was the other half of Gabriel and that was enough too. But they were still young and there was time and hope—this they had. When they were together, they kicked each other's feet for hours while they watched TV after school. If one of them left the room, the foot of the remaining twin would stop moving, but as soon as the foot from the other twin came back, they would start up again. They were unaware that they did this, but Leticia was aware, because she stared at them, wishing she had been fused to someone too. The few times she tried to interest them in a volcano documentary on PBS, Gabriel would answer, *Only if there's lava and people burning and screaming,* and then Adriana would laugh and say, *Yeah. Duh.*

Leticia had some friends she barely talked to at school, so mostly she ditched to take the subway to Central Park and climbed up on the slabs of metamorphic schist (part of the Manhattan Cambrian Formation) that were scattered throughout the park. The schist was corrugated with striations carved out by rocks embedded in the base of the North American ice sheet that moved over the schist during the last ice age in the Wisconsin Glacial Episode. She lay down on the slab, running her hands slowly over the striations, looking up at the sky, and imagining riding the ice sheet as it moved southward toward melting.

The tenants of the building told them what had happened: people screaming, doors flung open, yelling out of windows, running toward the street—and running toward them. One could hear *those goddamn boys* and *the cliff* and *Gabriel* and *jumping* and finally, *not breathing.*

Leticia pictured Gabriel, a carefree, careless boy soaring through the air, then plummeting down, layers of millions of years of Earth's history speeding by his beautiful face.

Interspersed between her mother's screams, she heard her father say, "My boy," over and over again. Adriana had tears running down her face as she made a low, continuous rumbling sound like gears of machinery winding down. She sat on the couch, kicking her feet out in front of her, kicking the air she breathed.

Leticia drifted out of the apartment and made her way to Marble Hill, to the place the three of them had loved, where she would be alone, her brother and sister with their friends. The boys would jump into the dirty waters of the Harlem River and pretend like they lived in Ohio, or Iowa, or something, where people frolicked in swimming holes like it was nothing (something their parents talked about doing back on the island). The cops usually chased them away, occasionally arresting one or two of them as a show of force. Everyone would ignore her as usual while she studied the low-grade metamorphic marble that was formed when continents collided against each other during the breakup of Pangaea. She'd watch her siblings pirouette—Gabriel off the cliff, Adriana off the wet hands of the boys who waited their turn. When the cops showed up Leticia ran away too, alongside all the wet boys, exhilarated at being so close to their bodies, their pulsating muscles dripping with river water—so alive.

> William Morris Davis (1850–1934, American). A founder of geomorphology (scientific landform studies) who developed a theory of the cycle of erosion. (Is it really a cycle when you are ground down to nothing? Then what?)

Among many jobs, Leticia worked at a clothing store, folding jeans and shirts over and over. No small talk, only answering questions about colors and sizes, the inventory of which she memorized as she replaced and restocked. None of this school and geology nonsense. Fit in like everyone else. Fold and tuck yourself small.

Her father worked when he wasn't getting fired from the factories, depending on how much rum had been brought back by someone from the bodega or Cibao. Her mother had developed a "nervous condition," discovered "the system," and had her disability payments extended.

Adriana became obnoxious and loud enough for two people. No one in the family could pin her down long enough to make her get a job, so Leticia toiled for all of them and tried hard not to upset her parents. Adriana tried to upset them at every chance. On the mineral hardness scale of one (talc) to ten (diamond) —each mineral is able to scratch all those softer than itself—Leticia estimated her sister was a nine, like corundum, the mineral that ruby is derived from. Adriana cried, screamed, ran, stole, and fucked her way through her teenage years, but she never got a reaction out of their parents. And she didn't get a reaction out of Leticia when Adriana would wait until Leticia was snuggled in bed, exhausted from a full day of work, and Adriana would ask her things like *Hey, have you ever been fingered?* Or *Have you had a dick in your mouth?* The answer was no, but Leticia kept that answer to herself.

At some point, the questions stopped and the crying began, softly in the middle of the night. Leticia paid for Adriana's abortion with money she had saved up for school, for one day when she had the time. Leticia folded herself around her sister's body, snuggling her arm around her waist and burying her face in her hair in order to protect her sister from her own sharp crags, and Adriana let her—every mineral can also scratch itself.

As time passed, like compasses, they all began pointing more or less in the same directions they had been pointing before Gabriel's death. Leticia took a part-time job at a crystal store and enrolled in community college while she sold crystals and geodes to people looking for something sparkly to put on their desks, kooky New Agers searching for their energy, and more serious types like the guy who had a piece of the San Andreas fault in all its scratched glory.

Mark walked in looking for something he saw in a magazine ad —geodes cut in half into bookends. Leticia thought those were a travesty but didn't tell him that.

"What color bookends are you interested in?" She hated asking this question. People had no idea what they were buying even after she told them.

"My sister likes pink."

He was wearing a Columbia T-shirt, so she asked him what he

studied there as she pulled out the dissected Brazilian pink-agate geode. He said he was working toward a master's in astrophysics. "Oh," she said. She was instantly jealous. "What interested you?"

"When I was a kid, I saw a PBS documentary about stars that explained that humans are partly made out of stardust, like the carbon in our bodies and the iron in our blood. So of course I went outside and proceeded to name every star. You know—my mom, dad, sister, uncles, aunts, anyone else I could think of." He paused, seemed to make sure she was listening. "I guess that's when I started looking at them all the time."

As she noticed his beautiful eyes, the color of translucent brown eulytite crystals, she said, "Wow."

"I know, I know. It's silly, but I was five or six or something."

She fidgeted with the geode, poking her finger into its crags. "So . . . umm . . . do you spend all your time looking through telescopes?"

"No, these days I spend very little time looking at actual stars. It's mostly looking at hard data."

"Oh, I'm sorry. Yeah, of course, it's more complicated than just looking up at the sky. I do that a lot. Just look up." She couldn't believe she said that. She put the geode down and picked up a long piece of jagged citrine quartz off the counter, jamming it into her palm.

He smiled. He said, "Well, I still stare up at stars when I'm not at school. I still name them after people I know. Only difference is I know their scientific names too."

She considered this and thought about naming a star after Gabriel. Maybe Mark could help her choose the right one.

He continued, "Now I know that my Uncle Charles is actually Gorgonea Tertia."

She laughed and then told him what she had never told anyone before. "When I was little, I used to paint rocks different colors to classify them according to mineral content and pretend they were the real thing. They became kind of elaborate after a while."

"Cool! Do you still have your collection? Have you compared it to real samples?"

"No, it's gone." She didn't tell him that throwing it out after Gabriel died had felt like the right thing to do. It had felt like the end of a lot of things.

Mark looked down at the geode and picked up the half she wasn't holding. "That's too bad. My parents still pull out the drawings I made of stars with people's faces on them. Maybe your parents kept some. You know, to embarrass you later."

"No. You're talking about, like, regular parents. My parents are mostly tired all the time."

He nodded his head. "Yeah. I guess kids are hard . . . especially if you have more than one. Do you have siblings?"

"Yes, two. But now one."

"Oh. I'm sorry."

She didn't want to ruin the moment. All she could think of saying was "Yeah. He was the star." She smiled.

Each time Mark came back, he asked her increasingly detailed questions about the crystals. If she was busy, Mark would wander around the store until Leticia was available to help him. Whenever she didn't understand his question, she spat out random rock properties, and he would just look, smile, and then ask more questions. She felt he was testing her but wasn't sure to what end. He waited for her after work one night and walked her to the subway.

When they reached the subway entrance, he looked up, pointed at a star, and said, "See the one next to Alpha Cassiopeiae, the double star I told you about? That one is called Zeta Cas." He paused and looked into her eyes before he continued, and pointed up again. "There you are. There's Leticia."

That's when her poles reversed. The earth has experienced many polarity reversals, lasting from hundreds to thousands of years. Paleomagnetists can study sedimentary deposits on the ocean floor to date when these polarity reversals occurred. The anomaly can be observed as a stripe in the sedimentary rock layer. One thing was clear to her as she stared up at her twinkling star: nothing would ever be the same. Leticia believed that when she was dug up one day, there would be a visible stripe in her bones marking the moment she fell in love.

Mark didn't seem to be as afraid to meet her parents as she was to meet his. And her parents were afraid of him too. As soon as he stepped through the door they sat down and stared at the TV, which they had turned to an English-speaking channel, a show that she knew they didn't watch because they didn't understand it. Adriana took the time only to say a quick hi to Mark and then motioned for Leticia to meet her in the kitchen. She whispered, "Dang, Leti. You brought home—the—whitest—guy." She laughed as she walked out of the apartment.

When Mark spoke, her mother lifted a tray of chips with dip —an American appetizer that she had bought at a store, and not the tostones with mojo she usually made, and her father asked him if he wanted a beer by pointing back and forth between the one he was holding in his hand and Mark. Watching them with him made her realize that she was the same way with Mark, always nervous, but she felt there was nothing she could do to lessen the magnetic force of fear.

She didn't know what she was doing, didn't know how to be his girlfriend. He was a real scientist and she was taking intro to trigonometry at Borough of Manhattan Community College. She was afraid to meet his friends, afraid to be asked, *So what do you do?* She was afraid—no, she would have fantasies—that when his parents asked her what her parents did, she would feel backed into a corner and scream, *The North American plate is slipping under the Caribbean plate right now, and we're gonna be on top of you one day!* She was afraid she would never have the courage to say this. When she did meet his parents, she found them to be adorable, well-meaning people who were intrigued by her, charmed by the implausibility of a girl from the projects with such interests and that their son met her in the first place. His mother said things like "You have the most beautiful smooth brown skin," which made Leticia feel as if she were about to be eaten. But she knew they were decent people, and at least they tried.

This was the best thing that had ever happened to her, and she didn't want to ruin it. She was so grateful to have found someone who called her *his twin ball of hydrogen gas,* because stars are formed when enough hydrogen gas is pulled together into one spot.

No one in the family had ever moved in with anyone out of wedlock. Her parents had approved of Mark, had appreciated the fact that he wasn't one of what her father called *the charlatans* from around their neighborhood, but her mother screamed so loud the earth shook.

Georges Lemaître (1894–1966, Belgian). Proposed the Big Bang theory for the origin of the universe. Some scientists believe that there was never an explosion, but rather an expansion of matter. Both camps, however, believe that there is expansion and that it is still happening, distant galaxies moving farther away from us at great speeds.

Leticia was excited like an expectant parent—the earth was having a baby and she wanted to be there to see its fiery newborn. They were visiting Hawaii so Mark could conduct research at the Gemini Telescope on the Mauna Kea volcano on the Big Island. She was thrilled to be on her first volcano but was really awaiting their visit to Kilauea, where Hawaiian legend says Pele now lives after creating each of the Hawaiian Islands, starting with Kauai, and where she was now throwing her tantrums on the newest volcano. Leticia admired Pele's ability to spark both fear and awe.

On their way to Hawaii Volcanoes National Park, they passed the town of Kalapana, which was buried in lava flows from a 1990 eruption—just a few years earlier. They stopped and took pictures of each other pretending their feet were stuck in the partially lava-covered sections of highway that were once part of the town. When they reached the observatory, Mark got down on one knee and pulled an engagement ring with a brilliant ruby out of his pocket.

When she said yes, Mark hugged her and whispered in her ear, "I love you. Let's go see some lava."

She cried as she held on to him tightly. She felt like they were harnessing the forces that forged the ruby's fiery, molten, isomorphic mixture of corundum and aluminum oxide, and together they would be beautiful.

Outside the observatory, a ranger pointed to distant lava flows oozing out of Pu'u 'Ō'ō Crater. The lava flows were actually coming out of lava tubes on the sides of the crater, but because they were slow-moving, they cooled quickly and crusted over, so they didn't look like the bright orange river that she had expected. As they walked past the sign that said DON'T GO PAST THIS SIGN, the ranger told them that he couldn't stop them from continuing, but then added that in the previous month, a man had fallen to his death when an acre-sized section of the lava field collapsed and fell into the ocean. Leticia giggled as Mark told the ranger that they had just gotten engaged and that this was how they were going to start their lives together and that they would be careful. They stayed away from the coast, which sporadically steamed from hot lava meeting the cool ocean. Leticia tripped a few times while staring at her ring.

A few miles later, the ground became warmer and bouncier, strands of dried, ropey pahoehoe lava snapping under their feet. Mark wanted to stop; he felt the air around them getting hotter and hotter, and he was concerned that maybe the lava was closer to the surface than they realized. She knew that the lava was close and that it was moving beneath them, flowing—alive. She was giddy with the thought that they were walking on the newest land on earth. She would keep walking ahead, and Mark would turn around and threaten to go back to the ranger station, but he always remained by her side. She knew he was mad, and probably scared, but she hoped he admired her, that he felt proud to be marrying a brave girl.

Then she saw it. It was moving slowly and belching sizzling, molten material. There was smooth pahoehoe lava on one side and walls of chunky a'a lava on the other. She crouched down and waited for the lava to reach her. Heat caressed her face.

Mark screamed, "What are you doing? No!"

She was not sure how long the moment lasted, but she tried very hard to resist the urge to reach out to the lava, as the earth's core reached out to her. The movie from her childhood dreams was playing out in front of her; she wanted to be a part of it, affect the process in some way. The increasingly searing heat reminded her that she was mortal and small and weak. She heard Mark call out to her again. She finally stood up, turned around, and said, "I know. I'm sorry. I just can't believe I'm finally here," and started walking back toward him.

Something popped, out onto her foot, her thigh. The feeling was surprisingly heavy, like she was being pushed. She bent down to take off her melting hiking boot, but the lava hit her hand. She made a fist from the agony, her hand encrusted with tiny, sizzling rocks that cracked into her skin. She couldn't dig herself out of the pain.

The last thing she remembers is being pulled away, leaving skin mixed with earth.

Walther Penck (1888–1923, Austrian). His erosion theory argued that different hill slopes reflected variations in the balance between rates of land uplift and denudation. An increase in fortitude can occur only in response to tectonic processes of crustal thickening (such as love and courage), changes in the density distribution of the crust and underlying self-doubt, and flexural support due to the bending of years of accumulated cultural and gender expectations. Uplift relates to denudation in that it brings buried sediment—that is—sentiment closer to the surface.

2.0—She felt as though she had been sucked into a cave, wedged into a dark, airless space all by herself. *One way of looking at Charles Francis Richter's (1900–1985, American) scale is as a measure of displacement.*

4.0, 4.2, 3.7, 2.9, 5.8—No, it wasn't the end of the world. Yes, she could re-form her life, make neat stacks out of the pieces. The aftershocks were relentless. Was it really an accident? Did it have to take a piece of her? Was the earth (and maybe the universe) out to get her?

5.9—Skin. Scabs. Fluids. Bone. Pain.

6.0—Wait. Stop. She requested that her mother bring her pictures, the ones where she was wearing her ruby ring. She stared at her perfect baby body, pondered what was going on in her unclouded baby mind, and wished she had never existed past that moment. She hadn't seen her engagement ring since it was cut off her.

6.4—"You never told me if you finished your research at the telescope."

"No. I'll have to go back at some point."

"Because of me? Because of what happened?"

"Don't put it like that, Leticia."

8.0—He suggested that they leave the house to go somewhere other than the hospital, that they go to the park and sit on some slabs, that she cover this stratum of her life with hope and optimism and good . . . well . . . better feelings and such—and that they have sex. Could they please have sex? *It's okay, we'll go slow, I won't look . . .*

She would never let him see her again. He became frustrated when she remained a monolith. *This can't go on forever,* he would say, as she felt the layers of forever crushing her down.

8.5—The coddling of a mother who had never coddled, the guilt magnifying the swaddling and care taken to shield her daughter—herself—from pain. She had lost one and she wasn't going to lose another one. She was going to hold her close and protect her from her silly ideas. All this scientific pondering to explain what? *It couldn't explain why bad things happen to good people.* Leticia had begun to believe her.

9.1—It came down to the big difference between them. No, not the science thing. Not the money, or the skin color, or the privilege thing. Not even the condescension thing. Yes, he *had* made judgments, general sweeping comments about her lack of confidence, about her family's lack of everything. The cleave, *the thing,* was that he thought that every single thing would be all right. He had smiled and told her, "I found your list. You need to find your place on it. Finish school."

As he smiled, pleased he had figured out the narrative that would make sense of the senseless, all she could think was *You have hope.*

9.2—About that list. She had listed forty-something of her favorite geologists in alphabetical order, hoping she could someday insert herself last: Leticia Maria Zamora. A few months before Hawaii, Leticia had considered removing Agassiz (the second one on her alphabetical list, the rock star of geologists) after she found out that he believed in a form of polygenism, the idea that races came from separate origins, accordingly endowed with unequal attributes.

9.3—She and Mark were completely mismatched and she finally knew it.

10.0—It was decided that her family could take better care of her while she recovered. She retreated back to her life with her parents and Adriana.

The apartment was on a transform fault (a boundary that occurs when two plates grind past each other), with everyone grinding past Leticia. Her mother said things: *Who has a volcano accident?* and *If she had just stayed home like she was supposed to, none of this would've happened.* Her father was silent. He flinched when she tried to grab a mug with her missing fingers. Phantom limb is for real.

Adriana walked into the bedroom she shared with Leticia, which had always been small but was now overcrowded with medical supplies stacked on every surface. As Leticia watched TV in bed, Adriana placed a box by her feet. She said, "My boss gave these to everybody for Christmas—sorry for re-gifting," then walked out of the room and shut the door behind her.

Adriana was working as an administrative assistant in an advertising agency and having an affair with her boss, which their parents kept quiet about, hoping it would result in a marriage, but all she ever brought home were discarded executive gifts and kinky lingerie only Leticia got to see. Adriana had been an ambitious girl after all, going after what she wanted, and this would be her way out. She had moved on to more suitable types as she matured and would probably keep working hard at it (not for too long, though, since there was her youth to think about).

Leticia put down the remote control and grabbed the box. She pulled the box next to her leg with her good hand and read its description: *Zen gardening helps clear the mind of the chaos associated with everyday life. The rocks represent mountains and the sand represents water. The patterns you create by raking the sand around the rocks will provide you with serenity. Includes a Book of Meditations to give you a complete set of stress-relief tools. The Deluxe Zen Garden makes a perfect gift for an executive or a client.*

She slipped the box under her bed and picked up the remote control. She had been dormant for some time.

John Tuzo Wilson (1908–1993, Canadian). Contributed to plate tectonics theory and coined the geological terms "plates" and "transform faults" to refer to the moving pieces of the earth. A restless puzzle—abutting, diverging, colliding.

From inside a shoebox in her closet, Leticia pulled out the rock she had brought home a year earlier from Hawaii. The rock was rhyolite or andesite, both rich in feldspar and mica. She had picked it up when they went to Mauna Kea the day before the accident and gently snuggled it into a sock in her luggage without telling Mark. Visitors are warned not to remove any rocks from the volcano because Pele will curse you for taking her children. There was a display of letters at the post office in the town of Volcano from tourists who had mailed back their rock souvenirs, describing the bad luck and tragedies that had befallen them upon their return home. Some of the letters begged the goddess Pele to have mercy on them, to reverse their bad fortune.

She put the rock under her pillow, then walked out of the bedroom, into the bathroom. She grabbed Adriana's bright-red glitter nail polish that she had been eyeing since it appeared in the bathroom a few days earlier.

Her mother saw her walking out of the bathroom with the nail polish tucked under her armpit and asked, "Do you need help with that? Are you going out?"

"Of course not," she answered, closing the door behind her.

She considered painting the rock as she had done with her collection, but this rock was the real thing, an artifact from her failed expedition. Further, she could extract its information about the earth's history, and even its provenance within the universe (according to Mark's studies).

Her mother cried in between yelling, "Leticia, you need to go out into the world! You cannot live like this!" She repeated over and over, "This is not what I want for my daughter."

She looked down at the striations, the scarring, the stretching and pulling of healing, the foreign skins metamorphosed onto her hand—the missing parts and their replacements. She had once been grafted to her mother, her father even, a long time ago, when they had all been hopeful.

She discarded the nail polish and started scratching the rock, felt as if she could get some answers from it even if she wasn't sure of the questions. Brown, powder-fine material accumulated under her fingernail as she scratched harder, her nail snagging on the uneven surface over and over again. She dabbed a drop of blood onto the rock with the pad of her index finger, where it was quickly absorbed, the iron and calcium bonding with their counterparts in the rock. She worked through the pain. She thought of the painting of Pele that hung in the post office in Volcano, her hair flowing, forming the slopes of Kilauea. Mark had said Leticia looked like her—a goddess who moves the earth.

For the God of Love, for the Love of God

FROM *American Short Fiction*

STONE HOUSE DOWN a gully of grapevines. Under the roof, a great pale room.

Night had been drawn out by the way the house eclipsed the dawn. Morning came when the sun flared against the hill and suddenly shone in. What had begun in the dark of the room came clear to the man in the fields who was riding a strange sort of tractor that straddled the vines. He idled, parallel to the window, to watch.

Amanda's face flushed: her idea for waking Grant up had come from the tractor's first squatting pass in the window ten minutes earlier. She slapped her husband's stomach below and said, Finish.

A minute later she strode off the bed and went to the window, and, leaning for the curtains on each side, pressed her chest against the glass, to tease. The man on the tractor wasn't a man, but a young boy. He was laughing.

In dark again, they heard the tractor moving off, then the flurries of roosters down in the village.

That was nice, Grant said, sliding his hand down her thigh. Hope we didn't wake them. He stretched, lazy. Amanda imagined their hosts in the room below: Manfred staring blankly at the wall. Drooling. Genevieve with her passive-aggressive buzzing beneath the duvet.

Who cares, Amanda said.

Well, Grant said. There's Leo too.

I forgot, she said.

Poor kid, Grant said. Everyone always forgets about Leo.

Amanda went down the stairs in her running clothes. She passed the boy's room, then doubled back.

Leo stood on the high window ledge, his wisp of a body pressed against the glass. Here, the frames rattled if you breathed on them wrong. There was rot in the wood older than Amanda herself. But Leo was such an intense child, and so purposeful, that she watched him until she remembered hearing once that glass was just a very slow liquid. Then she ran.

He was so light for four years old. He turned in her arms and squeezed her neck furiously and whispered, It's *you*.

Leo, she said. That is so dangerous. You could have died.

I was looking at the bird, he said. He pressed a finger to the glass and she saw, down on the white rocks, some sort of raptor with a short beak. Huge and dangerous, even dead.

It fell out of the sky, he said. I was watching the black go blue. And the bird fell. I saw it. Boom. The bad thing, I thought, but actually it's just a bird.

The bad thing? she said, but Leo didn't answer. She said, Leo, you are one eerie mammerjammer.

My mom says that, he said. She says I give her the wet willies. But I need my breakfast now, he said, and wiped his nose on the strap of her sports bra.

Leo bit carefully into his toast and Nutella, watching Amanda. She'd never met a child with beady eyes before. Beadiness arrives after long slow ekes of disappointment, usually in middle age. She had to turn away from him and watched the light spread into the pool and set it aglow.

You're not somebody's mom, Leo said.

Jesus, kid, she said. Not yet.

Why not? he said.

She didn't believe in lying to children. This she might reconsider if she had one. Grant and I've been too poor, she said.

Why? he said.

She shrugged. Student loans. I work with homeless people. His company is getting off the ground. The usual. But we're trying. I may be someone's mom soon. Maybe next year.

So you're not poor anymore? he said.

You practice radical bluntness, I see, she said. We are, yes. But I can't wait forever.

Leo looked at the giraffe tattoo that ran up from her elbow to nibble on her ear. It made him vaguely excited. He looked at the goose bumps between her sports bra and running shorts. My mom says only Americans jog. She says they have no sense of dignity.

Ha! Amanda said. I know your mom from back when her name was Jennifer. She's as American as they come.

As they come? As who comes? Genevieve said from the doorway. So much coming this morning! she said, showing her large white teeth.

Sorry about that, Amanda said. She didn't mean it.

Genevieve walked lightly across the flagstone floor and kissed her son on his pale cowlick. Her tunic was see-through silk, the bikini beneath, black. She wore sunglasses inside.

Hi, Jennifer, Leo said slyly.

Too much wine last night? Amanda said. Was the restaurant worth all of its stars?

But Genevieve was looking at her son. Did you just call me Jennifer? she said.

Aunt Manda told me, he said. And someone *is* coming today. The girl. The one that's taking care of me until we can go home.

Genevieve propped her sunglasses on her crown and made a face. Amanda closed her eyes and said, Jesus, Genevieve. Mina's coming. My niece.

Oh my God, Genevieve said. Oh, that's right. What time's her flight? Three. She did some calculations and groaned and said, Whole day shot to hell.

Because you had some extremely important business, Amanda said. Pilates. Flower arranging. Yet another trip to yet another cave to taste yet another champagne. Such a sacrifice to take a few hours to pick up Mina, who's basically my sister, the person who will be watching your child for the rest of the summer for the price of a plane ticket—

I get it, Genevieve said.

—a ticket, Amanda was saying, that Grant and I bought so that we could go out to dinner at least once on our only vacation in four years, instead of babysitting for Leo while you go out.

The women both looked at Leo, flinching.

Whom I love very much, Amanda said. But, still.

Do you feel better? Genevieve said. Some people just don't mellow with age, she said to her son.

Leo slid off his stool and went out the veranda doors, down the long slope toward the pool.

If I didn't love you like a sister, I'd throttle the shit out of you, Amanda said.

Her boy gone, Genevieve's smile was too. The skin of her face was silk that had been clenched in a hand. I guess you have the right to be upset, she said. I've been using you. But you know that food's the only thing that wakes Manfred up, and Leo can't go to those restaurants.

Amanda breathed. Her anger was always quick to flare itself out. She came slowly over the distance and hugged her friend, always so tiny, but so skinny these days, her bones as if made of chalk. Somewhere within this sleek new woman was a redheaded girl who was quiet and cool, who opened the window many nights so Amanda could climb in and sleep in peace. I'm just frustrated, she said into Genevieve's hair. You know we're mostly fine with it, especially since you're letting us drink all of your champagne.

Genevieve leaned against Amanda and rested for some time there.

Oh, my. Well, hello ladies, Grant said, having come down the stairs silently. His lanky arms suspended him in the doorway, his eyes lovelier for the sleep still in them. So beautiful, her husband, Amanda thought. Scruffy, the flecks of white at his temples. Unfair how men got better-looking as they aged. He'd been only a little more beautiful than Amanda when they had met; but maybe he masked his beauty under all the hemp and idealism then.

When the women stepped apart, Grant said, Even better idea. Let's take it all upstairs, and he winked.

Big fat perv, Amanda said, and kissed him, her hands briefly in his curls, and went out into the driveway, walking a circle around the dead bird before setting off on a run down the hill toward the village.

Genevieve and Grant listened to Amanda's footsteps until they were gone. Grant smiled, and after a moment, Genevieve smiled back. He came close, touched the curve her hip outlined in the fabric of her tunic. Genevieve looked down the lawn; Leo was all the way past the pool, in the cherry orchard, huddling over something in the grass, and Amanda was gone. She looked at Grant wryly. She nodded, touched his smooth stomach under his shirt.

They heard a step, heavy on the stairs. Manfred.

Fuck, Grant mouthed.

Later, Genevieve mouthed. She clicked the gas on the stovetop, pulled eggs from the refrigerator. The flush had already faded from her cheeks when she cracked them in the pan.

Grant set the espresso maker on the stove; Manfred entered the room. His hair was silvery and swept back, and he carried himself like a man a foot taller and a hundred pounds lighter.

The old swelling in Genevieve's chest to see him in his crisp white shirt and moccasins. He sat at the scrubbed pine table in its block of sun and lifted his fine face to the warmth like a cat.

Darling, she said. How do you feel today?

I'm having difficulty, he said softly. Things aren't coming back.

She measured out his pills into her hand and poured sparkling water into a glass. It hasn't been three weeks yet, she said. Last time you got it all back at around three weeks. She handed him the pills, the glass. She pressed her cheek to the top of his head, breathing him in.

Eggs are burning, Grant said.

Then flip them, she said without looking up.

The bees above Leo were loud already. Grass cold with dew. Leo was careful with the twigs. He wouldn't look at the vines beyond; they were too much like columns of men with their arms over one another's shoulders. Beyond were tractors and the Frenchmen in the fields, too far to pluck meaning out of their words: zhazhazhazhazha. There was a time before Manda came, and after his father returned from the hospital looking like a boiled potato, when there had been a nice old lady from the village who had cooked their dinners for them. She'd let Leo stay some nights with her when his mother couldn't stop crying. Her pantry had been long and cold and lined with shining jars and tins of cookies. She'd had hens in her yard and a fig tree and got cream from her son. That's where he'd go if Manda didn't take him when she left. With the thought, his body buzzed with worry as if also filled with bees. Manda was his beautiful giraffe. He'd set all the rest of them on fire if he could. When he was finished with his work, he went back up the hill. In the kitchen, Grant was drinking coffee and reading a novel, and Leo's father was slowly cutting a plate of eggs to bleed their yellow on a slab of ham. There was yolk on his chin. Leo took the poker and shovel from the great stone hearth. There was a tiny cube of cheese in the corner that Leo looked at for a long time and imagined popping in his mouth, his molars sinking through the hard skin into the soft interior. He resisted. Outside, the falcon was heavier than he imagined it'd be. He had to rest three times even before he passed his mother doing cat pose beside the pool. She always tried to get him to do it with her, but he didn't see the point. Corpse pose was the position he preferred to do himself. In the orchard again, he put the bird on the pile of twigs that he'd built. He stood back, holding his breath. The wind came and the bird's feathers ruffled, and he watched, feeling the miracle about to bloom. But the wind died again, and the bird remained stiff on the nest he'd made it, and it, like everything, was still dead.

As soon as they were in the car, Amanda felt lighter. She didn't like to think this way, but there was something oppressive about Manfred. A reverse star, sucking in all light.

We may as well get lunch in the city, Genevieve said as they wound through the village.

I can't believe we're going to Paris, Amanda said. She thought of pâté, of crêpes, neither of which she'd ever had served by an actual French person. Her wet hair filled the car with the scent of rosemary. Leo in the backseat flared it, eyes closed.

You've never been to Paris? Genevieve said. But you were a French major in college.

Those were the years their friendship had gone dark. Genevieve had been shipped up to her fancy New England college, had forgotten her old friends among her new ones. Amanda had been stuck at UF, pretending she hadn't grown up down the street. They reconnected a few years after graduation, when Genevieve took a job in Florida, though Sarasota barely qualified.

Never made it to France at all, Amanda said. I had to have three jobs just to survive.

But that's what student loans are for, Genevieve said. When Amanda said nothing, Genevieve sighed and made a circular gesture with her hand and said, Aha. I did it again. Sorry.

After a little time Amanda said, My mom once quit smoking

and saved the money so I could go. But my dad found her little stash. You know how it goes with my family.

Sure do. Yikes. How is that hot mess?

Better, Amanda said. Dad got put into a VA home, and Mom's wandering around the house. My brothers lost the forklift business last year but they're okay. And my sister's in Oregon, we think. Nobody's heard from her in three years.

Even Mina? Genevieve said. You said she was in college. She hasn't heard from her mom in three years?

Even Mina, Amanda said. She's been living in our spare room to save money. It's fantastic to have her around, she's like a beam of light, does all the dishes, takes care of the garden. But then again I basically raised her, even when I was pretty much a baby myself. You remember. I had to change so many fucking diapers that I couldn't even try out for soccer. Sophie was such a whore.

Genevieve laughed, and then saw Leo watching them in the mirror and stopped, blowing her cheeks out. Mine are the same as ever, she said. Marching clenched and seething toward eternity.

Remember that Frost poem we used to say when we were wondering which of our families would kill us first? Amanda said. *Some say the world will end in fire, some say in ice.* Et cetera. I would have given anything for a little ice.

At least you had some joy in your family. At least there was love, Genevieve said. She blinked fast behind her sunglasses. Amanda squeezed her knee.

At least your family never made you bleed, Amanda said. All the time.

Forgotten from the backseat, Leo's little voice: I thought you were sisters.

God, no! Genevieve said, then looked at Amanda and said, Sorry.

Amanda smiled and said, I wouldn't mind sharing some of your mom's genes. Her pretty face. At the very least, her cheekbones. What I could have done if I'd just had those cheekbones. Ruled the world.

You have your own beauty, Genevieve said.

Privilege speaking, Amanda said, making the circular gesture with her hand.

Leo thought about this through two whole villages. There was a field full of caravans, kids running and a roil of dogs that made him shiver with longing. Why would Amanda want to look like his mom when Amanda was so very, very lovely? But when he started to ask, the women were already talking about other things.

The sun moved. Manfred moved his chair with it. He thought of nothing, time the consistency of water. Energy was being conserved until there was enough to let it blow bright and blow itself out. He couldn't see it coming yet but could sense the build. Silence, nothing. The songbirds were holding their songs; all outside was still. The tall man the women had left behind flittered from place to place without settling. Manfred didn't bother to listen when he spoke. At noon the sun was overhead and the last slip of warmth fled. Manfred was left in the cold. Soon, he would stand; he thought of the dinner he would make tonight, planned every bite. His energy was finite, after all, and he must save it. He opened his fingers to find that the pills had dissolved into a paste in his palm, the way they had the day before and the day before.

The women had taken a table in a plaza framed with plane trees. The empty carousel spun. Amanda once saw a mother who had lost her children in a grocery store who had had the same hysterical brightness.

Monoprix? Amanda said. Her first Parisian food and it was from a five-and-dime.

Honey, we only have an hour and the café's not terrible. Also, Leo loves the carousel, Genevieve said.

The backs of Amanda's eyelids felt sanded.

Lunch is on me! Genevieve said.

Well, then: Amanda ordered the lobster salad and a whole bottle of cold white wine. The waitress frowned at her French and answered in English. Genevieve was driving but motioned for a glass for herself.

Leo gazed at the carousel without touching his steak-frites, until Genevieve loosed him with a handful of euros and he ran off. He spoke in each animal's ear until he settled on a flying monkey. The man operating the carousel boosted him up, and Leo clung to the monkey's neck, and the music began, and the monkey moved up and down on its pole. Amanda watched Leo go around three times. He was serious, unsmiling. She ate his fries before they went cold.

I'm sorry this isn't nicer, Genevieve said. You'll have time to eat well before you fly home next week.

I hope so, Amanda said.

Truth is, we're cutting costs a bit, Genevieve said wearily.

Amanda laughed until her eyes were damp. So ludicrous. Where are you cutting costs? she said when she caught her breath. Your 15,000-square-foot house in Sarasota? The castle in the Alps?

A flicker of irritation over Genevieve's face; but this too she quelled. Sarasota is being rented to a rapper for the year, she said. And the castle has been sold.

But. Wait. I thought that was Manfred's family place, Amanda said.

Three centuries, Genevieve said. It couldn't be helped.

Amanda picked up her full glass and drank and drank and put her glass down when it was empty. You really are broke, she said.

No joke, Genevieve said. Bankrupt. Manfred's mania went international this time. The rapper's rent is what's keeping us afloat. What is it they say? It's all about the Benjamins.

That's what they said when we were young. Well, in our twenties. I thought the house where we're staying was yours.

No. Manfred's sister's. The poor one, until about six months ago.

Ha! Amanda said. It was so unexpected, this grief for her friend. She'd become used to seeing Genevieve as her own dumb daydream. The better her.

Don't cry for me, Genevieve said lightly, squeezing Amanda's arm. We'll be okay.

I'm crying for *me*, Amanda said. I don't even know who to envy anymore.

Genevieve studied her friend, leaned forward, opened her mouth. But whatever was about to emerge withdrew itself, because Leo was running toward them across the plaza, his head down. The carousel had stopped. The air had stilled and there was a sudden silence, like wool packed in the ears. Darling! Genevieve called out, half-standing, upsetting the last of the bottle of wine.

And then the blanket covering the sky ripped open, and Leo, still running, vanished in the downpour. Leo! they both shouted. In a moment, the boy appeared on Amanda's side of the table, and he put his cold face on her bare legs. Then there was the blind run through the rain, holding the little boy by the hand between them. They reached the parking garage, a wall of dryness. They laughed with relief and turned to look at the curtain of rain a foot beyond them, at the wet dusk that had descended so swiftly in midday.

But as they watched, shivering, there was a great crack, and a bolt of light split the plaza wide open, and the lightning doubled itself on the wet ground, the carousel in sudden grayscale and all the animals bulge-eyed and fleeing in terror. The others crowded into Amanda, put their faces on her shoulder and her hip. She held them and watched the tumult through the sear of red that faded from her vision. Something in her had risen with the rain, was exulting.

They were still wet when they arrived at the airport. Genevieve's dress was soaked at the shoulders and back, her hair frizzed in a great red pouf. Leo looked molded of wax.

Mina, on the other hand, was fresh even off the plane. Stunning. Red lipstick, high heels, miniskirt, one-shoulder shirt. Earbuds in her ears, accompanied by her own soundtrack. Even in Paris, the men melted from her path as she walked. Amanda watched her approach, her throat thick with pride.

One more year of college, and the world would blow up wherever Mina touched it. Smart, strong, gorgeous, everything. Amanda could hardly believe they were related and found herself saying the silent prayer she said whenever she saw her niece. The girl hugged her aunt hard and long, then turned to Leo and Genevieve.

Leo was looking up the long stretch of Mina, his mouth open.

Genevieve said, But you can't be Mina.

I can't? Mina laughed. I am.

Genevieve turned to Amanda, distressed. But I was there when she was born, she said. I was in the hospital with you, I saw the baby before her mother did because Sophie had lost so much blood, she was passed out. I left for college when Mina was five. She looked just like your sister. She was fair.

Oh, said Mina, leaning against Amanda. I see. She means I can't be me because I'm black.

Amanda held her laugh until it passed, then said, Her father was apparently African American, Genevieve.

I'm sorry? Genevieve said.

I grew up and everything got darker, Mina said. It happens sometimes. No big deal. Hi, she said, bending to Leo. You must be my very own kiddo. I'm beyond pleased to make your acquaintance, Mr. Leo.

You, he breathed.

We're going to be friends, Mina said.

I'm so sorry. It's just that you're so beautiful, Genevieve said. I can't believe you're all grown up and so gorgeous.

Mina said, You're pretty too.

Oh, God! The condescension in her voice: Amanda wanted to squeeze her.

Let's get a move on, Amanda said. We have to speed home if we're going to get to the shops down in the village and buy some dinner before they close.

Amanda knew that in the car Genevieve would tell too much about herself, confide to Mina about Manfred's electroshock therapy, about Leo's enuresis, about her own gut issues whenever she eats too much bread. Amanda would sit in the front seat, ostentatiously withholding judgment. In the backseat, Mina and Leo would be playing a silent game of handsies, cementing their alliance. Out in the parking garage, the day felt fresh, newly cold after the rainstorm. As soon as they left the city, the washed fields shone gold and green in the afternoon sun.

It was time. Manfred rose from his chair. Grant nearly choked on his apple. All morning, he'd swum in the pool and pretended to work on the website he was designing—the very last he'd ever design, no more jobs lined up—and all afternoon he'd played solitaire on his computer. He'd come to believe that he'd been left alone in the house. The other man had been so still that he had become furniture. It had been easier when Grant believed himself alone. He had all day in silence to defend himself against the thought of Mina: the kiss he'd taken in the laundry room, the chug of machine and smell of softener, the punch so hard he'd had a contusion on his temple for a week afterward. He could be forgiven. It was all over soon enough, in any event.

The women will be back presently. We should make our preparations, Manfred said, walking out to the Fiat that Grant and Amanda had rented.

Crazy motherfucker, Grant said to himself, but reached for his keys and wallet. He started the car and almost pulled out onto the road, but there was a line of tractors heading up the hill homeward. They had to wait for the spindly things to pass. Where are we going? Grant said, watching the tractors trail around the bend.

The village, of course, Manfred said, his hands tightly clenching his knees.

Of course, said Grant.

The bakery was out of boules, so Manfred selected baguettes reluctantly. He bought a napoleon for dessert, he bought a pastel assortment of macarons. Leo loves these, he said to Grant, but before they reached the greengrocer's he'd already eaten the pistachio and the rose.

He bought eggplants, he bought leeks, he bought endives and grapes; he bought butter and cream and crème fraîche, he bought six different cheeses all wrapped in brown paper.

At the wine store, he bought a case of a nice Bourgogne. We have enough champagne at the house, I think, he said.

Grant thought of the full crates stacked in the corner of the kitchen. I'm not sure, he said.

Manfred looked at Grant's face for the first time, worry passing over his own, then relaxed. Ah, he said. You are joking.

At the butcher's, lurid flesh under glass. Manfred bought sausages, veal, terrine in its slab of fat, he bought thin ham. Grant, who was carrying nearly all the crates and bags, could barely straighten his arms when they reached the car. Manfred looked to the sky and whistled through his front teeth at something he saw there, but Grant couldn't see what he did.

We shall have a feast tonight, Manfred said, once they'd gotten in and closed the doors. We shall, Grant said. The little car felt overloaded starting up the hill.

From behind, from the east, there came a whistling noise, and Grant looked in the rearview mirror to see a wall of water climbing the hill much more swiftly than the car could go. He flipped on the wipers and lights just as the hard rain began to pound on the roof. Grant couldn't see to drive. He pulled into the culvert, leaving two wheels in the road. If anybody sped up the hill behind him, the Fiat would be crushed.

Manfred watched the sheets of water dreamily, and Grant let the silence grow between them. It wasn't unpleasant to sit like this with another man. All at once, Manfred said, his voice almost too soft under the percussive rain, I like your wife.

Grant couldn't think quite what to say to this. The silence became edged, and Manfred said with a small smile, More than you do, perhaps.

Oh, no, Grant said. Amanda's great.

Manfred waited, and Grant said, feeling as if he should have more enthusiasm, I mean, she's so kind. And so smart too. She's the best.

But, Manfred said.

No. No, Grant said. No buts. She is. It's just that I got into law school in Ann Arbor and she doesn't know yet. That I'm going.

He did not say that Amanda would never go with him, couldn't leave her insane battered mother behind in Florida. Or that as soon as he'd realized he would go up to Michigan alone, leaving behind the incontinent old cat he hated, the shitty linoleum, the scrimping, the buying of bad toilet paper with coupons, Florida and its soul-sucking heat, he felt light. A week ago when they drove up to the ancient stone house framed in all of those grapevines, he knew that this was what he wanted: history, old linen and crystal, Europe, beauty. Amanda didn't fit. By now, she was so far away from him, he could barely see her.

He felt a pain somewhere around his lungs: dismay. What he did say was so small but still a betrayal of its kind.

I'm waiting for the right time to tell Amanda, so don't say anything, please, he said.

Manfred's hands held one another. His face was blank. He was watching the wall of rain out the windshield.

Grant took a breath and said, I'm sorry. You weren't even listening.

Manfred flicked his eyes in Grant's direction. So, leave. What does it matter. Everyone leaves. It is not the big story in the end.

Like that, the stone that had pressed on his shoulders had been lifted. Grant began to smile. Grade-A wisdom there, buddy, he said. Lightning sizzled far off in the sky. They watched.

Except there is one thing you must tell me, Manfred said suddenly. Who is this Ann Arbor woman? And, when Grant looked startled, Manfred gave another small smile and said, That was also a joke, and Grant laughed in relief and said, Seriously, please don't tell Amanda, and Manfred inclined his head.

Grant felt uncomfortably intimate with Manfred so close in the tiny car. There had been something he'd wanted to say since Genevieve's wedding in Sarasota ten years ago, during what was in retrospect clearly a manic swing of Manfred's pendulum. There had been peacocks running around the gardens; the guest favors were silver bowls. Grant had watched, making little comments about the excess that Amanda lobbed back with bitter spin. He saw things differently now.

Forgive me for saying this, Grant said. But sometimes, you even look like an Austrian count. You have a certain nobility to you.

But I am only a Swiss baron, Manfred said. It means nothing.

It means something to me, Grant said.

It would, Manfred said. You are very American. You are all secretly royalists.

In the distance, the clouds cracked and the sky showed blue through them. Manfred sighed. He said, We have had a pleasant talk. But I believe you may drive.

Grant turned the car on and pushed up the hill, home.

The women gave out little yodels of surprise when they arrived to find the men in the kitchen in aprons, chopping vegetables. The men looked at Mina when she came out of the car, and Leo felt power turning and beginning to flow in her direction, like the stream at the bottom of the hillside when he shifted rocks in its bed. Outside smelled like rich earth, like cows. Manfred had poured them all champagne and brought the flutes out on a platter, and they drank it on the wet white gravel, looking at the way the vines sparked with late light, the green and purple tinge to the edge of sky. *To Mina*, they all said. Even Leo got an inch of champagne, which he had always loved like cola. He downed it. His mother was watching his father carefully over her drink, and it was true his father had a dangerous pink in his cheeks. Badness moved in Leo. He stole into the kitchen, now dim with dusk, and to the fireplace, the small ceramic box that had ALLUMETTE written on it, or so Manda had said a few days earlier with her shy French. Leo had to wait for Grant to come in, bouncing Mina's suitcases up the stairs. His mother and Mina followed behind, his mother explaining the wonky shower, Leo's schedule, how Leo couldn't swim yet so everyone had to be careful with the pool. Leo's father gravely handed him a purple macaron and turned back to cook, and Leo put the sweet thing up the chimney for the pigeons to eat. He hated macarons. He came out on the grass, past the pool, down into the cool orchard with its sticky smell. It appeared that the hawk had grown while he'd gone. It was huge with the shadows that had fallen on it. He stood over the bird on its nest and said words in German, then English, then French. He made some magic words up and said them. In one of his father's old books, back at home in the castle in the Alps, there had been a drawing of an old bird set aflame and in the next illustration it turned into a glorious new bird. Leo thought with longing of his own bed there, his own books and his own toys and the mountain in his window when he awoke. He struck the match on a stone. The flame sizzled then took. The sticks were wet, but not right under the bird, and those dry twigs caught just before the flame touched his hand. The bird's feathers, burning, let off a reek that he hadn't foreseen. He stepped back, crouching on his heels, to watch. Black roil of smoke. When he looked up again it was much later, shadows around him deepened. The bird was a charred, ugly thing now, half-feathered, half-flesh. The fire had gone out entirely, and there was no more red in the embers. A voice was calling for him, *Leo, Leo!* He stood and ran up the hill, feeling weariness in his legs and all along the back of his neck. It was Mina, with the sunset bright in her hair, with another glass of champagne shining in her hand. Someone is burning something awful, she said, sniffing. An orange-faced boy rode by on a tractor that looked like a leggy animal; he stood up and shouted gleeful words that neither of them caught over the noise. Mina waved, smiled with her teeth. She looked at Leo's dirty face, his dirty hands. She said, laughing, Wash yourself, eat your dinner fast, and I'll give you a bath and put you to bed. His heart could hardly bear all that he was feeling. It was either expanding to the sky or contracting to a pin, hard to say. Leo, his mother called, come give me a kiss. *Die*, he thought, but kissed her anyway on her soft and powdery cheek. He kissed Manda up the giraffe's neck on her neck, and she blushed and laughed. His father, he would not. Let the boy be, his father murmured to his mother. The gleam on Mina's legs up the stairs. He would eat her if he could. He let her wash him with warm water, and she put him in clean pajamas, and he petted her soft cheek and smelled her while she sang him to sleep.

It was chilly outside on the veranda. Amanda wore a fleece, Genevieve wore a brocaded shawl. They waited for the food to cook and ate terrine on baguettes and drank champagne, listening in the monitor to Leo's little piping voice and Mina's gravelly one answering him. There was light coming from the kitchen and on the table one candle in a pewter candlestick that looked ancient. Manfred had put on *Peter and the Wolf,* which was Leo's CD, but all of the other music in the house was his sister's, and all of it was 1990s grunge. There was some kind of newborn glitter in Manfred's eyes that Amanda was having a difficult time looking at directly. Something had shifted between Grant and Manfred; there was a humming line between them there had never been before.

Yesterday, Manfred said suddenly, I poisoned the rats in the kitchen. I forgot to say. Do not eat the cheese you will find in the corners.

Poor little rats, said Genevieve. I wish you had told me. I would have found a humane trap somewhere. It's an awful thing to die of thirst. She pulled the shawl tighter to her.

Oh! That explains the falcon, Amanda said. The others looked at her.

Leo saw a falcon fall dead out of the sky this morning, she said. It was huge. It was in the driveway. I don't know how you all missed it. I bet it ate a poisoned rat and croaked midair.

No, Genevieve said, too quickly.

It seems likely, doesn't it, Manfred said. Oh dear. It is terrible luck to kill a raptor. It signifies the end of things.

I mean, the thing probably just had a heart attack, Amanda said, but rested her head on her husband's shoulder, and it took him a moment to slide his chair over and put his arm around her.

The wind restrained itself, the treetops shushed. The moon came from behind a cloud and looked at itself in the pool.

Now Mina was singing in the monitor, and Amanda said, Listen! "Au Clair de la Lune." She sang along for a stanza, then had to stop.

Why are you crying, silly? Genevieve said gently, touching Amanda's hair. Twice in a day and you never used to cry. I once saw all four of your big old brothers sitting on you, one of them bouncing on your head, and you didn't cry. You just fought like a wild thing.

Hormones, I think, Amanda said. I don't know. It's just that all those nights when Sophie would go out and leave Mina at our house, I would sing this to her until she went to sleep. For hours and hours. Everybody would be screaming downstairs, just awful things, and once in a while the cops would show up, and there would be flashing lights in the window. But in my bed there'd be this sweet baby girl, sucking her thumb and saying, Sing it again. And so I'd sing it again and it was all I could do.

They listened to Mina's beautiful, raspy voice over the monitor . . . *Il dit à son tour—Ouvrez votre porte, pour le Dieu d'amour.*

Well, thank God for Madame Dupont, Genevieve said. Forcing us to learn it in seventh grade. She made us sing at school assembly, remember? God, I wanted to die.

Manfred gave a dry cough, and the clammy ghost of his attempt in the spring, how Genevieve had found him, brushed by. Nobody looked at him; they studied the knives, the bread. The moment passed.

Grant said, What's she saying? Genevieve turned to him, a softness in her face.

Amanda saw tears in her husband's eyes; she squeezed the back of his neck. She was moved. It had been so long since she had seen the side of him that would weep during movies about dolphin harvests. A different Grant had grown up over him, a harder one.

Manfred didn't seem inclined to translate. Amanda listened for a minute to gather herself. It's a story, she said. Harlequin wants to write a letter, but he doesn't have a pen and his fire went out, and so he goes to his buddy Pierrot to borrow them. But Pierrot is in bed and won't open the door, and he tells Harlequin to go to the neighbor's to ask because he can hear someone making a fire in her kitchen. And then Harlequin and the neighbor fall in love. It's silly, she said. A pretty lullaby.

But Manfred was looking at her from the shadows. He leaned forward. Dear Amanda, he said. The world must be hard for you. All substance, no nuance. Harlequin is on the prowl. He wants sex, *pour l'amour de Dieu.* When Pierrot turns him away, he goes to the neighbor to *battre le briquet.* Double-entendre, you see. He is, in the end, fucking the neighbor.

Genevieve sat back slowly in the darkness.

Manfred smiled at Amanda, and there was a strange new electricity in the air; there was something here, announcing itself to Amanda, in the very back of her head. It had almost arrived, the understanding; it was almost here. She held her breath to let it step shyly forward into the light.

*

Mina watched the couples from the doorway, feeling as if she were still flying over the Atlantic, the ground distant and swift beneath. Nobody was speaking; they were not looking at one another. Something had soured since she'd left them a half hour ago. She had come from a house of conflict. She knew just by looking there would be an argument breaking out in a moment and that it would be bad.

She took a step out to distract them, smiling. The other four snapped their eyes up at her. She felt herself expanding into her body as she always did when she was watched. She was new tonight, strange. The champagne was all she'd consumed since leaving Orlando, and it made her feel languorous, like a cat.

Sometime after arriving she'd come to a decision that she'd been mulling over for the past few days; and now what she knew and what they didn't filled her with a secret lift of joy. Internal helium. She wouldn't board the plane at the end of the summer. School was so gray and useless compared to what waited for her in Paris; her life on hold in that hot place where she'd lived out her terrible childhood. Florida. Well. She was finished with all of that. A whole continent in the past. She would go toward the glamour. She was only twenty-one. She was beautiful. She could do whatever she wanted. She felt herself on the exhilarating upward climb. As she walked toward them, she saw how these people at the table had stopped climbing, how they were teetering on the precipice (even Amanda; poor tired Amanda). That Manfred man was already hurtling down. He was a mere breath from the rocks, it was clear.

This sky huge with stars. Glorious, Mina thought, as she walked toward them. The cold in the air, the smell of cherries wafting up from the trees, the veal and endives cooking in the kitchen, the pool with its own moon, the stone house, the vines, the country full of velvet-eyed Frenchmen. Even the flicks of candlelight on those angry faces at the table were romantic. Everything was beautiful. Anything was possible. The whole world had been split open like a peach. And these poor people, these poor fucking people. Why couldn't they see? All they had to do is reach out and pluck it and raise it to their lips, and they would taste it too.

MERON HADERO

The Suitcase

FROM *Missouri Review*

ON SABA'S LAST day in Addis Ababa, she had just one un-
checked to-do left on her long and varied list, which was to explore the neighborhood on her own, even though she'd promised
her relatives that she would always take someone with her when
she left the house. But she was twenty, a grownup, and wanted
to know that on her first-ever trip to this city of her birth, she'd
gained at least some degree of independence and assimilation.
So it happened that Saba had no one to turn to when she got to
the intersection around Meskel Square and realized she had seen
only one functioning traffic light in all of Addis Ababa, population four million people by official counts, though no one there
seemed to trust official counts, and everyone assumed it was much
more crowded, certainly too crowded for just one traffic light.
That single, solitary, lonely little traffic light in this mushrooming
metropolis was near the old National Theater, not too far from the
UN offices, the presidential palace, the former African Union—a
known, respected part of the city located an unfortunate mile (a
disobliging 1.6 kilometers) away from where Saba stood before a
sea of cars, contemplating a difficult crossing.

Small, nimble vehicles, Fiats and VW Bugs, skimmed the pe-
riphery of the traffic, then seemed to be flung off centrifugally,
almost gleefully, in some random direction. The center was a tangled cluster of cars slowly crawling along paths that might take
an automobile backward, forward, sideward. In the middle of this
jam was a sometimes visible traffic cop whose tense job seemed
to be avoiding getting hit while keeping one hand slightly in the

air. He was battered by curses, car horns, diesel exhaust as he nervously shifted his body weight and tried to avoid these assaults.
Saba quickly saw she couldn't rely on him to help her get across.
She dipped her foot from the curb onto the street, and a car raced
by, so she retreated. A man walked up next to her and said in English, "True story, I know a guy who crossed the street halfway and
gave up."

Saba looked at the stranger. "Pardon, what was that?"

"He had been abroad for many years and came back expecting
too much," the man said, now speaking as slowly as Saba. "That
sad man lives on the median at the ring road. I bring him books
sometimes," he said slyly, taking one out of his messenger bag and
holding it up. "A little local wisdom: don't start what you can't finish." Saba watched the stranger dangle his toes off the curb, lean
forward, backward, forward and back, and then, as if becoming
one with the flow of the city, lunge into the traffic and disappear
from her sight until he reemerged on the opposite sidewalk. "Mi-
raculous," Saba said to herself as he turned, pointed at her, then
held up the book again. Saba tried to follow his lead and set her
body to the rhythm of the cars, swaying forward and back, but
couldn't find the beat.

As she was running through her options, a line of idling taxis
became suddenly visible when a city bus turned the corner. She
realized that, as impractical as it seemed, she could hail a cab to
get her across the busy street. The trip took ten minutes; the fare
cost 15 USD, for she was unable to negotiate a better rate, though
at least she'd found a way to the other side. She turned back to
see the taxi driver leaning out the window talking to a few people, gesturing at her, laughing, and she knew just how badly she'd
fumbled yet another attempt to fit in. All month Saba had failed
almost every test she'd faced, and though she'd seized one last
chance to see if this trip had changed her, had taught her at least
a little of how to live in this culture, she'd only ended up proving
her relatives right: she wasn't even equipped to go for a walk on
her own. What she thought would be a romantic, monumental
reunion with her home country had turned out to be a fiasco; she
didn't belong here.

She was late getting back to her uncle Fassil's house, where
family and friends of family were waiting for her to say goodbye,
to chat and eat and see her one last time, departures being even

more momentous than arrivals. Twelve chairs had been moved into the cramped living room. Along with the three couches, they transformed the space into a theater packed with guests, each of whom sat with his or her elbows pulled in toward the torso to make space for all. They came, they said, to offer help, but she sensed it was the kind of help that gave—and took.

It was time to go, and she was relieved when Fassil said—in English, for her benefit—"We are running out of time, so we have already started to fill this one for you." He pointed past the suitcase that Saba had packed before her walk and gestured to a second, stuffed with items and emitting the faint scent of a kitchen after mealtime. At her mother's insistence, Saba had brought one suitcase for her own clothes and personal items and a second that for the trip there was full of gifts from America—new and used clothes, old books, magazines, medicine—to give to family she had never met. For her return, it would be full of gifts to bring to America from those same relatives and family friends.

Saba knew this suitcase wasn't just a suitcase. She'd heard there was no DHL here, no UPS. Someone thought there was FedEx, but that was just for extremely wealthy businessmen. People didn't trust the government post. So Saba's suitcase offered coveted prime real estate on a vessel traveling between here and there. Everyone wanted a piece; everyone fought to stake a claim to their own space. If they couldn't secure a little spot in some luggage belonging to a traveling friend, they'd not send their things at all. The only reasonable alternative would be to have the items sent as freight on a cargo ship, and how reasonable was that? The shipping container would sail from Djibouti on the Red Sea (and with all the talk of Somali pirates, this seemed almost as risky as hurling a box into the ocean and waiting for the fickle tides). After the Red Sea, a cargo ship that made it through the Gulf of Aden would go south on the Indian Ocean, around the Cape of Good Hope, across the Atlantic, through the Panama Canal, to the Pacific, up the American coast to Seattle. An empty suitcase opened up a rare direct link between two worlds, so Saba understood why relatives and friends wanted to fill her bag with carefully wrapped food things, gifts, sundry items, making space, taking space, moving and shifting the bulging contents of the bag.

Fassil placed a scale in front of Saba and set to zeroing it. She leaned over the scale as he nudged the dial to the right. The red needle moved ever so slightly, so incredibly slightly that Saba doubted it worked at all, but then Fassil's hand slipped, the needle flew too far, to the other side of zero. He pushed the dial just a hair to the left now, and the red needle swung back by a full millimeter. He nudged the dial again; now it stuck.

"Fassil, Saba has to go," Lula said, shaking her hands like she was flicking them dry. "Let's get going. Her flight leaves in three hours, and with the traffic at Meskel Square and Bole Road . . ."

Saba leaned toward that wobbly needle as Fassil used his fingernail to gently coax the dial a breath closer. A tap, nearly there. A gentle pull.

"Looks good, Fassil," Saba said kindly but impatiently.

"It has to be precise," Fassil replied, then turned to the gathered crowd. "Look what you're making the poor girl carry." He pointed to that second suitcase.

Saba tried to lift it, but it was as heavy as an ox. Fassil rushed over and helped her pick it up, and when he felt its weight, he said, "There's no way they'll let her take this." The crowd was unhappy to hear that, and so was Saba. The room hummed with disapproval, punctuated with *tsk*s and clicked tongues. "I can just pay the fee," Saba quickly said, but Lula stood again, put up her hands, and boomed, "You will not pay a fee. It's too much money. You are *our* guest, and *our* guest will pay no fee!"

"It's okay," Saba said. "If we must, we must." But now the resistance came from everyone. Saba looked helplessly at Fassil. "Let me pay. I have to go. What else can I do?" she asked. She looked at the others and wondered if this was one of those times when a "No" was supposed to be followed by a "Please, yes!" "No, no." "Really, I insist." "No, we couldn't." "Really, yes, you must." "Okay." "Okay." Was it that kind of conversation? That call and response? Or was it the other kind, the "No, no!" "Really, I insist!" "No, we just couldn't." "Okay, no, then."

"Of course you can't pay. They will never let you," Fassil said, ending Saba's deliberation. He announced, "I'll weigh the suitcase," and there was a general sigh of approval. "But," Fassil continued, "if it's overweight, which it is, we are going to have to make some tough choices." He turned to Saba. "You are going to have to make some tough choices." She nodded and hoped silently that it would come in at weight, please. If she could be granted one earthly wish in this moment, that was what she would wish for. She watched Fassil heave the suitcase onto the scale and winced as the needle that hovered, almost vibrated, above zero shot to the right. Thirty kilos—ten kilos too heavy.

The crowd began to murmur anxiously, and a few shouted out sounds of frustration. Then one by one, the guests began to speak in turns, as if pleading their cases before a judge.

Konjit was the first up. She was old, at least seventy, a verified elder who settled disputes and brokered weddings and divorces, part of that council of respected persons that held a neighborhood together. As Konjit walked toward Saba, Saba bowed a little.

"Norr," Saba said, a sign of respect.

"Bugzer," Konjit replied, acknowledging that the order of things hadn't been completely turned on its head. Konjit lifted the edge of her shawl, flung it around her shoulder, and walked slowly right up to the suitcase and unzipped it. She took out a package of chickpeas and tossed it on the ground, and though someone grumbled at this, Konjit just smoothed her pressed hair behind her ears as if she were calming herself before an important announcement, an orator about to make a speech, an actress set to perform. Konjit held a hand up to the others who sat on the couches and chairs, and waited for total silence. Then she turned to Saba, put her hands on both her hips, which swayed as she stepped closer to Saba, and said in a low voice that filled the small space, "Please, Sabayaye, I haven't seen my grandchildren since they were two years old. How old are you?"

"Twenty," Saba said apologetically.

"Twenty? Ah, in all the time you've been alive in this world I have not seen them. Imagine! I'm old now. Who can even say how old I am? I'm too old to count and getting older. I want to send this bread so they know people here love them."

Most of the others in the room nodded in agreement, but not Rahel. Rahel shook her head as she stood from the couch and walked right up to Konjit, putting a hand on Konjit's arm. "Who can say how old you are, Konjit? Me, I can say how old you are. Not the number of years of course, but I can say for sure that I am older than you. One month, remember."

Rahel brought up that one-month position of seniority often, and Saba had come to expect it. Within just her first week there, Saba learned that Rahel and Konjit had grown up and grown old fighting often about things like which church had the most blessed holy water, Ledeta (Rahel) or Giorgis (Konjit), or whether it was better to use white teff flour (Konjit) or brown teff flour (Rahel), or where you could get the best deals on textiles, Mercato (Konjit) or Sheromeda (Rahel). Without fail, each argument ended with Rahel staking out a win by virtue of being slightly elder.

Rahel bent down and removed one of the three loaves of bread from the suitcase and tried to hand it back to Konjit, who refused to take it. Saba, wanting to hurry things along, reached out for the loaf, but Rahel placed the bread on the floor by her feet. "You can bake a loaf, Konjit, I give you that, but it takes you three hours to make that bread? Eh? I spent two days—two *days*—making this beautiful doro wat for my nephew. The power kept switching off. I had to go to Bole to freeze it in Sintayu's freezer, and she has all those kids and all those in-laws and hardly any space in her house, let alone her freezer, but still, that's what it took to make this beautiful wat. Then I had to wrap the container so tight that, should any melt in transit, it will stay safe and secure—and with these old old old fingers," she said, putting up her index, middle, and ring fingers. "Can you believe it? These old old fingers," she said, now raising her pinky and thumb. "These fingers a month older than yours, Konjit." She pulled Saba over and put her fanned fingers on Saba's left shoulder, leaning on her. "Just take this beautiful wat for me. It will be no problem, right?"

Before Saba could say that this seemed reasonable, Wurro walked up to Saba, and Saba shifted her attention again. "I may not be the oldest, and my hands don't ache like Rahel's, but please, think about this objectively, Saba," said Wurro, whose utilitarian views led her to make obviously questionable decisions, like employing fifteen workers in her small grocery so that fifteen more paychecks went out each month and fifteen more families would be happy, even if it put her one family on the verge of ruin. Wurro never argued her utilitarian views as forcefully, though, as when they matched her own purposes. She cleared her throat, and Saba waited for what she feared would be another well-argued plea. Wurro began, "If you don't send this bread, Konjit, your family will still eat bread. If you don't send this wat, Rahel, your family will still eat wat." Wurro took Saba's hand and said, "My niece had a difficult pregnancy. You have to take this gunfo because if you don't take it, well, there is no way to get gunfo in America, and who has ever heard of a woman not eating gunfo after labor? If you don't bring it, she won't have it. Milk for the baby, gunfo for the mother. It's natural logic. You can't deny it."

"But American women don't eat gunfo. Do they eat gunfo, Saba?" asked Lula.

"She's never been pregnant in America, right? How would she know?" asked Wurro.

"She's never been pregnant here. Does she even know gunfo?" Konjit asked.

Saba said, "I know gunfo," and was met with whispered words of approval, so she refrained from adding how hard she had to swallow to get a spoonful down of the thick paste made from (she'd heard) corn, wheat, barley, or banana root, she wasn't even sure. Whatever gunfo was, she'd rather not bring it, if it was up to her, but she wasn't actually sure of that either. Was it up to her?

"Saba is a smart girl," Lula said. "She probably read *at least* ten books in the four weeks she was here." Saba felt guilty then, because it was true that she had declined as many invitations as she accepted, choosing sometimes to read alone at home. "She must know Americans have high-tech things for women after their pregnancies. They don't need gunfo," Lula said, rearranging the contents of the suitcase to make room for her own package. "But you know what they do need in America? Have you ever tasted American butter?"

Lula looked at the others as if this would end the discussion. She stood up, opened her arms. "Have you had American butter?" No one spoke. Saba kept quiet, for of course she had eaten American butter, but what good would it do to mention that now? Besides, few had the courage to challenge strong-willed Lula, even with the truth.

"No one here has ever had American butter, so then that settles it." Lula took out another of Konjit's loaves of bread and a bag of roasted grains. "*I* have eaten American butter. *I* have tasted it with my own tongue. *I* can say with certainty that American butter is only the milk part, no spices, no flavor. It just tastes like fat. Please bring this butter to my best friend for her wedding banquet," Lula said with her hands now pressed over her heart and looking pleadingly at Saba. "Ahwe, her wedding! And what a feat to get that man to the altar. His gambling and staying out late and—"

"Aye aye aye," Konjit interrupted, shaking her head and removing Lula's butter and putting a second loaf back into the suitcase.

"You want her to bring butter so your friend can marry a bad man? Have you ever heard such nonsense?" Konjit asked Saba. Saba shrugged, and Konjit said, "See, she has never heard such nonsense," and Saba didn't have the heart to correct her and didn't have the heart not to correct her, and she didn't know which would have helped her bring this to the right resolution, so she just made a vague gesture and let them finish.

"He is not a bad man, just a *man* man," Lula said.

"Well, my son is a *good* man raising *good* grandchildren. Lula, my son brought you the stretchy pants you asked for from America when he visited. Wurro, my son brought you a laptop last time he came. Rahel, he brought you cereal with raisins, the kind you always ask for. Fassil, he brought you books, since you have long gone through everything at every library here, I assume. Saba, one day if you live in Ethiopia, he will bring you something too, anything you ask. Name something you miss here."

"Too much talk, Konjit!" Rahel yelled. "The traffic, she has to go!"

Konjit swatted away Rahel's interruption and gestured to Saba.

Saba tried to think of what to say. She didn't want to offend them by making them believe she had lacked for anything. She remembered how hurt Konjit had been when Saba visited after lunchtime, only to find a full meal waiting for her. When Saba refused, Konjit insisted that the dishes were very clean and the food fresh. That wasn't as bad, though, as sitting down to eat "just a little" and passing on the salad, the water, the cheese, the fruit, eating only the lentils and bread, accepting some coffee but not even the milk. "You have all been so kind to me," Saba said, bowing respectfully, pronouncing all her syllables perfectly, precisely, as quickly as she could. "I have not missed a thing. But it's late, and it's true, the traffic is bad . . ."

Konjit dismissed Saba. "She has learned the Ethiopian way. Good girl. Too polite to say you need anything here," Konjit replied, putting an arm on Saba's shoulder. Konjit continued, "Okay, don't tell us, that's okay. But if you visit again to stay a while, and if you find you are homesick for something you grew accustomed to there in America, my son will bring it. He is a good son. I am asking you to take two loaves of bread. Okay, forget about the third, I don't want to ask too much of you, even though I am an old lady who has not seen her grandchildren in, oh, who knows how long.

But these two loaves must stay in the suitcase, two loaves for my three grandchildren so they know I am thinking about them. That I have not forgotten them.'" Saba could see that Konjit was too proud to say what she really meant: she didn't want her grandchildren to forget about her, a fear she must bear, living so far away for so many years with only limited lines of connection.

Konjit's argument hung there in the air until Fikru stood hesitantly and walked over to the suitcase, finding his bags of spices on the floor beside it. He reached into the suitcase and took out three Amharic-English dictionaries and tossed them onto the coffee table. Hanna shouted out, "Aye! Why, Fikru, would you do that?" She ran over and picked up the books, then threw them back in, but Konjit took them out, for they crushed her bread.

Fikru, who kept opening his mouth to speak but found himself overpowered by the more forceful voices, seized his opportunity like a fourth-chair orchestral musician stealing a flourish at the end of a number. He stood next to an overwhelmed Saba and said, "Everyone here has a relative in Seattle, yes? Then why is it that only my son is going to pick Saba up from the airport?" He turned to the others. "You talk about what so-and-so needs or has done, but my son, without asking for anything, has volunteered to get her. He will be carrying this heavy suitcase to his car. Then he will take her to her dorm and bring this heavy suitcase up the stairs, if there are stairs, or down the hall, should there be a hall. What can it hurt to bring a few items for him?" Fikru showed Saba his items. "Just a few bags of spices: corrorima, grain of paradise, berbere. Please, Saba, a humble parcel for my humble son."

Saba turned to her uncle Fassil and discreetly pointed to her watch. "Okay, you all have something to say," Fassil offered, cutting off the remaining guests who gathered around the suitcase, eager to make their appeals. "But the traffic!"

"Yes, the traffic," said Fikru.

"The traffic," Rahel and Konjit said in unison, and Lula nodded.

Fassil turned to Saba. She asked him, "What do you want to do?"

"What do *you* want to do?" Fassil asked her. Though each person in that room had his or her body turned to the suitcase, all eyes were on Saba, who was trying to figure out how to navigate this scene. They looked her over and imagined she looked so . . . what? Different? Just . . . apart with her woven bag, which intermittently glowed with the light from her iPhone or beeped and pinged and vibrated from the sound of her other gadgetry, her American jeans tucked into tall leather boots, a white button-down shirt and gold earrings, while they wore modest clothes and hand-me-downs, some of which she had brought herself.

She had been in the country one whole month and had tried, they must know, to learn the culture, to reacquaint herself with her first home and fit in. And now, here she stood, on the last moments of her last day, still not sure what to do, while they looked at her lovingly and with curiosity too. Saba felt the weight of choosing what should be taken and what should be left behind. She was looking for a way out and a way in, but she realized there really were no shortcuts here.

"You have all been so kind," Saba said. "Rahel, you took me to listen to the Azmaris sing," she said, omitting that she had been too shy to dance such unfamiliar dances no matter how encouraging Rahel had been. A few days later, Rahel came back to take her to one of the fancy new hotels where an American cover band played to a foreign crowd, and Saba pretended to like being there. She imagined Rahel had pretended too.

"Wurro, you took me to the holiday dinner, and we ate that delicious raw meat," Saba said, of course not mentioning that Fassil had to take her to the clinic the next day to get Cipro for her stomach cramps.

"Fikru, you brought me to Mercato to buy a dress," Saba said. But what she most remembered was spending the trip chasing after him through the labyrinthine alleyways; every so often, when Fikru looked back at her, she would wave and smile, and he'd keep going, losing her twice.

She remembered the man with the messenger bag that morning, the one who had crossed the street, and his warning about starting things you can't finish or giving up too soon. Saba walked to the suitcase she had packed herself, filled with her own things, and in one quick gesture opened it, emptied the contents. Her best clothes fell to the floor: her favorite old jeans, most sophisticated dresses, her one polished blazer, a new pair of rain boots, T-shirts collected from concerts and trips and old relationships. She pushed this empty suitcase to the center of the room.

"Dear friends, neighbors, and relatives," she said in forced Amharic, looking at the confused expressions that confronted her, "please, now there is room for it all."

There were gasps, whispers, whistles, an inexplicable loud thud, but no laughter.

"Are you sure?" Fikru asked.

"This is the least I can do," Saba said slowly. "It is the least I can do."

"What about your belongings?" Fassil asked.

"We'll keep them safe for her in case she returns," Konjit said, her voice commanding the space.

"*Until* she returns," Rahel corrected.

"Until you return?" Konjit asked, and Saba said yes.

Fassil got a bag, put Saba's things in, and told her he would store it in his own closet. The two suitcases were packed, weighed (the room applauded when both came in just under the limit), and thrown into the trunk of Fassil's car, which sagged a little in the rear. There were three cars in their little caravan that headed to the airport. The ride was slow. The weight of the overfull cars possibly complicated the trip, as did the rocky side streets and, of course, the congestion at the difficult intersections. They pressed on, and they reached the airport with absolutely no time to spare. Saba said quick, heartfelt goodbyes, thank-yous, made fresh promises, then pulled the two big suitcases onto a luggage cart. Her family and friends of family watched from the waiting area as she moved quickly through the line to get her boarding pass. They looked on as the two suitcases were weighed and thrown on the screening belt, and they saw her pass the main checkpoint. Every time she looked back to the lobby, she could catch glimpses of them on tiptoe, waiting to see if they might connect with her one more time.

Treasure State

FROM *Tin House*

JOHN WENT TO VISIT his father in the prison hospital. The old man sat up against a pile of gray pillows. There were dark half-moons under his eyes, and the skin around his mouth was purple and yellow like he'd been hit there. He breathed heavily through cracked and bloody lips. "Lookit you," the old man said. "You're all growed and swole up." He looked at John's arms.

"You can't come live with us," John said.

His father fixed him with an expressionless gaze that conveyed nothing but the monstrous obstinacy that had landed him in prison in the first place. It was supposed to be for life.

"You tell your mother?" he said.

"She knows I'm here."

The son of a bitch pushed himself up, and it took something out of him to do so. He panted slowly for a moment.

"She agreed to it already, don't you know," his father croaked.

John looked off, away from his emaciated father, the bruised face, the cracked lips, and the hairline crossing the high crown of the older man's head. What all cancer had done to his once handsome features.

"You better get used to it," his father said, his lips drawing back in a dry grin. "I'm awn die in that house a mine."

John and his brother, Daniel, left the next day. They pulled out of their little place in Gnaw Bone, Indiana, and drove through the hills they'd coursed as boys, farther, to woods they knew less well, and then they were on a plain country road through abject farmland, foreign odors blowing through the windows. John said they were better off traveling the back roads.

Outside of Adolf, Indiana, they stopped for lunch in a diner choked with senior citizens.

"What can I get?" Daniel asked. He was fifteen and had been suspended from school for fighting.

"Anything."

"Anything?"

"Yeah."

"But you said we don't got more'n eighty dollars to make it the whole way."

"I said we weren't making it the whole way on eighty dollars. You got to listen."

Daniel looked at the menu and then at his brother, who was reading through the local paper, the *Adolf Announcement*. He asked John what he was reading for. Daniel wouldn't even open a book unless it looked like it might have pictures in it.

"Just order," John said, nodding toward the waitress who was standing there. She was pretty, given the town. She had close-set eyes and a wreckage of teeth, but still looked okay to a kid from Gnaw Bone. Daniel ordered a Denver omelet with no peppers or onions, a side of bacon, and a chocolate shake. John said he'd have black coffee and pancakes.

"She's awful cute," Daniel offered, as she went to get John's coffee. "Can we take her with us?" He wiggled his eyebrows like an idiot.

"Why'd you order a Denver omelet if you were just going to have them make a ham and cheese?"

"We're going to Denver, ain't we?"

"No."

"Well, it's in Montana, ain't it?"

"No. It *ain't*. Jesus. How dumb are you?"

"Pretty goddamn dumb," Daniel said.

"Well, see if you can at least wrap your mind around this," John said, pointing at an obituary. "Says here the service is in about an hour."

People being the way they are, few realized that their dead had been robbed. They returned from the funeral and set out the cold cuts on the silver trays, the faceted glasses, and the punch. They stocked bottles of beer and cans of Coke in buckets of ice, smoked a quick cigarette out back, and met the grief-stricken, the condolers, and the well-wishers at the door. The furniture smelled of the person they'd just praised to heaven and commended to the dirt. The mourners assembled along the walls in grim or conversant clusters, depending on their affinity with the dead and the yet living. Then they stole away to the upstairs bedroom or the chest in the basement or the desk in the study, only to discover the particular heirloom missing. And the surprise turned hot, and they tiptoed out of the room, slowly pinched closed the door, went up or down the stairs, and took their spot along the wall. They glowered at their kin, wondering which one had got there first.

A few days later, John and Daniel were pressing on to Long Creek to fence the things in the backseat. A fur coat, a sword, three crystal glass cats, and a variety of other finds that might have been worth something or nothing at all, it was hard to tell.

John asked how much they had and Daniel opened the glove box and pulled out the transparent bank-tube canister. They put money in it now, but when they'd found the canister in a bottom drawer back in Weston, it was full of empty prescription bottles. There was a lot of weird shit in bottom drawers. Daniel twisted open the canister and counted the bills.

"Not great. About a hundred-twenty-something."

"Let's just see what we get for this stuff in Long Creek," John said.

"I dunno," Daniel said.

"Don't know what?"

"We're doing this, then? We're not going back?"

"You wanna live with that piece of shit?"

"I ain't afraid of him."

"Lookit you, big man. You wanna go back and kill him, then?" Daniel sighed at the endless farmland ahead of them.

"There's no speed limit in Montana, you know," said John.

"You already said."

"Marijuana is legal there." John adjusted the rearview mirror. "We have to, we can sleep in the car."

"But you said we shouldn't sleep on the road. That was a rule, you said."

"Let's just see what we get for this stuff in Long Creek."

They chose Montana because of the way the word sounded and because they'd been to Chicago and had formed opinions about cities. A city was a terrible thing, but Montana sounded romantic and open, the opposite of Gnaw Bone, which sounded like something a dog was doing.

In a town called Oscarville they took too long. Or else the funeral was shorter than normal. A car door closed. Footsteps on the porch, voices downstairs. They waited until it was quiet, then slunk to a rear window. But after they jumped off the sloping roof of the back porch and landed in the yard, a woman came out the back door and started at the sight of them standing there. Then she collected herself and said everyone was gathering in the living room. She held open the door for them, and they were obliged to go into the house they had been burgling just moments before.

"And how did you know Gary?" the woman asked, almost greedily, as might one who had just lost a loved one and wanted to savor every last instance of the dead person's intimacies, however slight.

John looked at Daniel and then coughed into his hand.

"From the youth center, I'll bet," she said.

"Yes, ma'am," John said. "The youth center."

Daniel grinned helpfully.

"That man," she said, squeezing their forearms.

They went down a narrow hall, past a rolltop desk that had nothing of value in it, and a bedroom where a teenage girl now sat on a bed. Daniel paused at her door and winked at his brother, but John pulled him along.

In the living room congregated about fifteen people of approximately the same age as the woman—John guessed seventy—some of whom rose slowly from their chairs, asked John and Daniel their names, shook their hands, and said nice things about the youth center over in Benton County, wherever that was. John and Daniel said they weren't hungry, but someone brought John a plate of cake and baby carrots anyway. Daniel said again that he didn't want anything to eat, and for a moment they were alone along the wall.

"I'monna hit the head, John."

"Just hold it. We're getting out of here in a minute."

"I gotta go," Daniel said, slipping John's reach.

Daniel stopped at the room where the girl was still sitting on the bed, and leaned against the jamb. She didn't notice him right away. She wore a plain black dress, but her hair had green streaks in it. Her cowboy boots were shiny as wet tar. Eyes within dark makeup flashed when she noticed him there. He was neither especially handsome nor dynamic, but now had an aura of freedom and outlawry about him.

"Hey," he said.

She sat up straight. He could see her black bra strap where it separated from the strap of her dress.

"I'm Dan."

"Hi, Dan."

"Hi."

"I'm Gwen."

"Well, hi, Gwen."

They smiled at each other.

"You wanna go outside?" he asked.

"Only if I never come back in," she said.

She reached under her bed and drug out an olive duffel that had things written all over it in black marker.

"Do you have a car?" she asked.

"Uh-huh."

"Take me somewhere."

Daniel turned around to get a view of the front room and his brother, but he couldn't see through the throng. It appeared that a lot of kids from the outlying towns who'd gone to the youth center had arrived. The bedroom window was open and she'd thrown her bag through it.

"Hold up," Daniel said, and climbed out after her.

She was originally from Baltimore, but the Treasure State sounded just fine to her. She said no funny business, she didn't put out, and that she'd give him money for the ride. She seemed almost expert at negotiations of this sort. Daniel could not believe this was in fact happening. The overwhelming actuality of a girl. He let her into the backseat of the car, put her bag in next to her, and jumped into the passenger seat.

"What's all this stuff?"

"Our things."

"A menorah?"

"A what?"

She held up the brass menorah. He shrugged.

"Why are you in the passenger seat?" she asked.

"My brother'll be here in a minute."

He yearned toward the front door for his brother to come out.

"How'd you know my uncle?"

"I didn't."

"What do you mean you didn't?"

"Just never mind. Here comes John."

Daniel could see John mouthing *Hell no.*

He got in. "Hell no," he said. "Sorry hon, but no."

"Why not?" Daniel asked.

"Are you stupid?" He turned all the way around in the seat. "You need to exit this vehicle. Now."

"Come on, John. We already busted into the pl—"

"Dan! Jesus. Shut up."

Her eyes pinged between the two of them. "Were you two robbing our house?"

John took off his sunglasses and squeezed the bridge of his nose. Then he got out, opened the back door, yanked her bag into the street, and reached in for her. She slid to the other side and kicked at him.

"I'll tell!" she said. John stopped trying to get her. He stood and looked out over the car to the house, where the people were gathered inside, and then up the block, where no one was ever about in any of these towns. Everyone was at a funeral or a wake. He knew immediately why the girl was running away. He ducked back down.

"You'll do what you'll do. But you're coming out of there one way or the other."

"You're a fuckin' dick, man," she said.

"You'll see I'm worse than that. You got two seconds before I pull you out by that green hair. I shit you not, girl."

She glared at him, and when he grabbed at her, she knocked

his hand away and let herself out the passenger side. John got in, started the car, and pulled out. Daniel watched her gather her bag and the things that had spilled from it into the road.

There was a night when John had a hammer in his bed and promised himself that he would kill the old man if he came into their room again. He was about twelve years old and there wasn't anything he wanted more than his father's death.

It was Daniel who always got the brunt of it. Something about Daniel's softness and curiosity just enraged the old man. Even things that weren't his fault. Things John had done. Left a toy in the yard or forgot to turn off the sprinkler. Their father would go after Daniel even if John tried to take the blame.

Times, he wished his father would come after him instead. It was so much worse to be afraid for Daniel than for himself.

So he'd taken the hammer from the shed. Practiced hitting the pumpkins in Cartwright's field, the peen chopping into the shell, ripping out the stringy orange meat and seeds. Tore up a half acre.

The next day his mother cleaned up while they were at school. Sheets changed, toys put away. When they got home, the hammer was gone, not in the shed, nowhere.

In Juniper they sold a Polaroid camera and several box sets of VCR tapes. It was wet but not presently raining and they perched on a wet stone bench in front of the courthouse. A cop came out of the building, descended the marble steps, and nodded at them. When he was out of sight, they went to their car and left town.

They found a KOA and set up a moldering tent they'd stolen from a garage in a small town called Wellington. They cooked pilfered hot dogs over a campfire and ate them rolled in slices of white bread they'd also stolen and drank water from the nearby spigot. They didn't even have a cup.

"I thought we'd be in Montana by now," Daniel said.

"We need to get a little more money to make a run at it."

"Can't we just do this all the way out there?"

"The towns get farther apart out west."

"Oh."

The fire snapped out a small red coal near John's foot.

"We're still going to Littleton tomorrow."

"Yup."

John put out the coal with his heel.

"I wonder if that girl is okay," Daniel said.

"You're wondering if her tits are okay."

"She didn't turn us in."

"You don't know that."

"We'd of been arrested by now.

John studied the fire. Daniel stood.

"Not everybody is a son of a bitch, John."

"I'm just trying to protect you."

"I'd like to know what the hell from."

Daniel stomped off to the tent, and John sat by the fire, feeding it for a few hours until he ran out of sticks. He went in to sleep, but only turned on the ground and listened to Daniel's untroubled breathing. It was pure luck that the old man had been caught red-handed and went down. Though it galled John that a broken tail-light saved them. And even though John had seen with his own eyes that their father was in no condition to come after them, nor really had a reason to, the fear of the man kept him awake just the same.

He went out in the brush for more firewood and brooded over the fire until morning.

John found a pawnshop in Littleton to sell a sword, *The American History of Folk Music,* and several rings. The man slowly counted out five twenties, and over his glasses watched John, who was pacing off his nerves. John could see small alarms going off in the pawn-broker's eyes, could sense it coming.

"These things are yours to sell, right?"

John strode over to the counter.

"You want them or not?"

"Well, now I'm sure I don't know."

John swept the rings into his hand and stuffed them into his jeans, tucked the LPs under his arm, and gathered up the sword and scabbard, all the while glaring at the clerk, expecting the man to stop him. But he didn't.

"Asshole," John said.

"Get on out of here before I call the cops."

The sun quaked overhead and the light flashing off the worn white roadway was too much to even look around. He made straight for the car. He tossed the sword and the records into the trunk and slid into the front seat, but Daniel was not inside and nowhere about. He pulled his sunglasses from behind the visor and went to look for his goddamn brother.

He walked up the block past the pawnshop onto a main street that was nearly abandoned, save a few cars parked on the main drag, one of which was a squad car with a policeman in it. He nodded at the policeman and crossed the street and felt the cop's eyes on him the whole way as he passed the closed-up storefronts and peered uselessly into the tinted opaque windows of the bars for his brother. This was pointless. He stopped in the middle of the sidewalk and immediately started walking back to the car, patting his pockets and pantomiming that he'd forgotten his wallet.

The girl, Gwen, was sitting on the hood of the car, her legs crossed behind Daniel, who stood between them. The skin on the back of John's head tingled at the sight of her. Daniel turned around.

"Now look, John. You might as well know right now that she comes with us or I want half my money and we'll go our separate ways."

John ignored him and went around and got into the driver's seat. Daniel opened the passenger door. The squad car slid past, the cop looking in their direction, and Daniel's voice was lost in John's ears. This was real trouble, you could see how it would go down, right here in Littleton: the runaway with seaweed streaks in her hair, the suspicious pawnbroker, the squad car slowing to stop, red-and-blues lit up. Just like the old man.

"Get in," John said.

"I mean it, John. I'm not gonna let you leave her here—"

"Just get in!"

Daniel and Gwen hopped in the back together with her bag. John pulled out of the lot and went up the street. Nothing happened. He took to the highway and nothing happened. They drove for two hours, nothing happened. They weren't pulled over, they weren't surrounded as he filled the tank in Ballinger, and they weren't dragged from the tent in the night. Their father didn't materialize out of the dark, fumy and distorted with rage. But John did not sleep, such was his dread.

John could hear them kiss with glacial quiet so as not to wake him, and when they could take it no longer, they snuck out to the car to do it. But the rear window was cracked open and he could hear their moans as the car gently rocked like a boat in a wake, and when they were finished, John could hear her quietly crying and Daniel saying things in a slow, sad way, how a person might talk to a wounded animal or a child who was stuck in a well. Somehow Daniel was good, a good person. And John felt terrifically alone and strained to hear exactly what they communed, but it wasn't for him however much he might want, deserve, or need it, people don't get what they deserve, everything oh every last thing is given out at random.

They were nearing a town called Casper that John said might be promising when Daniel asked why they weren't going west. Gwen had taken the map and was having Daniel pose her questions.

"We are going west."

"I don't think so," Daniel said, looking at the place she pointed to on the map.

"Casper is east of us," Gwen said. "It's not even a day away from Indiana."

John turned on the radio, panned the dial for something to listen to.

"We're going in circles," Gwen said.

The house in Casper was locked, but John got on a milk crate and pried open the bathroom window with a crowbar. He squirmed through the hole and peeked back out at his brother below. He told him to go wait in the car.

"What? Fuck that."

"Honk twice if you see anything."

John closed the window on his brother's protests and strode briskly down the hall. At the end were two bedrooms. One was a child's room. A small table. Bunk beds. Vases, flowers, scrapbooks. There were balls of tissue, and pictures of the children were fanned out over the floor next to a half glass of wine.

John didn't understand until he went into the other room. On the bed were two black dresses, and shoes spilled out of the closet. When he realized what had happened to the children he couldn't seem to get enough air and the inside of his chest felt like a twisted bed sheet. He sat on the floor, his vision pinholed, taking big lungfuls of air.

When he felt okay again, he stood. His head was a heavy gourd and he was very tired. He looked inside the closet and the dresser and saw no clothes for a man. He sat on the bed and dropped back onto the dresses and bedclothes. The air was cool and still and no sound punctured the air's dull nothing hum. His heartbeat slowed. He was very tired.

There had been two sharp honks, but he remembered the sound of them only when he heard the front door opening. The pad of feet on the runner in the hall. He rolled off the bed and scuttled under it just as a woman came in, pulling off her pumps. She unzipped, and her dress fell smartly to the floor. She left the room, and he started to slide out from under the bed, but she immediately returned and he wriggled back underneath. She sat down and opened a drawer in the bedside table. She got all the way onto the bed and was at something, but he could not tell what. In a few moments, he heard a lighter and smelled marijuana. She moved against the headboard and smoked. There was a knock at the front door, but she was still and he was still. He wondered how she couldn't sense him under there, hear him breathing, feel his body heat. He could tell everything she was doing and she had no idea he was down there. Another knock. He wondered if it was Daniel. *Go away,* he thought, even though he wanted to escape. *Leave her alone.*

She lit the joint again and smoked and for long minutes it was quiet. He couldn't think of a way to reveal himself that wouldn't scare the hell out of her. He would've liked to explain. Apologize, even commiserate. But it would be unbearably cruel to scare her now.

A long, thin sound as through reed without an instrument escaped her and turned into a slow moan and then outright sobbing. Heaving. The covers churned up as she must have been clutching and writhing in them. By the way the bed sometimes bounced under her, the mattress sagging and just kissing his chest when she did so, he imagined her pelvis high up and then dropping.

For minutes she was still, and then she would remember or want to cry some more and she would start up again. Hours it went like this. The house would go still for so long that he thought she might be asleep, and he would be about to slide out from under the bed, and she would begin sobbing again. So often that he quit feeling bad for her. So often that it was now dusk, now dark, now the bottomless night.

He woke to her breathing, slow and steady, the sleeper's breathing. He moved out from under the bed, crouched where he could see the back of her head. He wanted to pet her brown hair, to see her face. He bear-crawled to the door. In the hall he stood. A truck somewhere outside shifted gears and he waited until it passed, then unlocked the front door, closed it softly behind him, and strode out into the naked day.

He went up the street, refreshed from the sleep that'd been forced on him, the first good sleep in a long time. He felt okay.

He spotted the car in front of a café. They wanted to know where he'd been, what had happened to him. He looked like shit, they said. He told them to order him a coffee and went to the bathroom to wash his face.

He drove all day and through the night, his brother and Gwen curled up in the backseat asleep. He pulled into town, got a local paper, and scanned the obituaries. The day was dawning. He took the county road and stopped by the field.

Daniel woke up, got out to pee, and then sat on the rear bumper with his brother.

"What the fuck are we doing?" Daniel asked.

"You remember when I busted up all those pumpkins?"

"With the hammer?"

"The old man beat the hell out of you for it. Even though I did it."

The patch had already been harvested, Cartwright's pickup in the field, the trailer full of pumpkins. Daniel's sigh steamed out into the cold air.

"So you're going over there," he said.

John nodded.

"You don't need to."

"You two can just drop me off."

"We can just keep going."

John looked over at his brother. "He has it coming, Dan."

*

John went inside, where his father lay on the couch in the throes of his last fever. The sound of the screen door clapping shut and the sight of his son startled him.

"What in the hell are you at?" he rasped. "Sneaking in here like this."

His father reached under the cushions and drew out an old revolver, but it promptly slipped from his hand onto the hardwood floor, thudding harmless as a hammer. The old man didn't reach for it, he was too winded even from this effort. The air rattled in and out of him, his eyes watered from an undisclosed agony. When John stepped forward to pick up the gun, his father's eyes raced about for something to defend himself against this inevitability.

But John noticed how little his father's fear or this profound reversal pleased him and he just stood there, waiting for rage as one might a train on a platform.

"Do what you come to do!" his father hissed.

John went out onto the porch, the old man coughing terribly. He waved at Daniel and Gwen to go on. Daniel scowled and then backed out and drove away, and John realized how he must've looked to them with the pistol, like all kinds of trouble, but the old man was well killed already and there was nothing to be afraid of, nothing to do but see him off.

Pat + Sam

FROM *Copper Nickel*

I

BEFORE THE PARTY Pat spent an hour crying in her bedroom
—her and Harry's room, their old room—and used up a stick of
concealer trying to hide the crinkled half-moons under her eyes.
She left the girls with the neighbors. She put on lipstick. At the
party she asked Sam Kwan for a light.

It was a cold October night in 1974. They smoked back then,
everybody did. This was before Pat's two children became Sam's
and before there were three children, before they grounded the
oldest when Pat found a pack of Newports in her room. By then
they would have forgotten their own youth, or rather, they would
hold their children to higher standards. The children would be
confident and happy—they'd feel entitled to happiness—and for
that Pat and Sam would resent them.

Pat told Sam she used to live in the city, but now she lived in
Jersey. Some friends had invited her to the party, so she'd driven
out to her old neighborhood in Queens. "Where I live," she said,
"it's like the country, but there's a train to the city."

Sam told Pat he lived in Brooklyn and never went to New Jersey.
"It must be nice to have trees and grass."

The apartment was a dump, the room too hot and crowded,
the moss-green carpet balding in patches, like a neglected lawn.
To the right of the sunken couch was a folding table with a paper
plate of pretzel crumbs, a six-pack of beer, and a plastic jug of
deli gin.

"What's the guy's name that lives here?" Pat asked in Cantonese.

Sam recognized the words and said, "I have no idea. My friend Ben invited me."

Sam's laugh was a joyful bark, and Pat thought she saw, through his thick eyeglasses, the glint of a troublemaker.

The music surged. Annabelle Uy leaped off the couch and started shaking her hips, rear end plump and wide like a bakery bun. "Dance, Pat, dance," Annabelle shouted, pointing to Pat, and Pat looked at Sam and he shrugged—why not.

Even if she didn't care that much about dancing, Sam's willingness to do so made him more appealing. They danced, not terribly, but not particularly well. Their shoulders remained hunched, feet rooted to the floor. Their arms swung slowly but they moved closer to each other.

The next day Pat's mother called and said, "I don't know how you do it, all alone in that big house with two little children. All alone and nobody to help you. I don't see why you can't move back to Chicago already."

"All right, Ma," Pat said. "I met someone."

"Who?"

"He's Chinese. We're going out next Saturday."

"Oh?"

"He has a good job. And he knows all about the kids and Harry."

"And he's still talking to you? There must be something wrong with him."

"Nothing's wrong with him!"

"But he'll want his own house."

"He likes New Jersey. He thinks it's nice."

Her mother made a pleased, cooing sound.

2

He had never been with a woman longer than four months, and that was years ago, in Hong Kong, with a girl named Helen whose voice could peel the skin off babies. Sam was just her type; locked up, quiet-angry, a kid who had lived in ten different homes after his father left and his mother went to find work in Singapore. In Hong Kong he had wanted to be a musician. He put on his one good outfit and went to the Sunday afternoon tea dances when he could afford it, screamed and danced to The Lotus belting out *I'll be waiting I'll be waiting I'll be waiting*, the chorus pressing into him like a thumb against a vein. He could strum a guitar and keep a beat but that's as far as his music dreams went. His high school teachers said engineering was the way to get a student visa, so he put engineering on his application and Nebraska gave him a full scholarship. After four long years in Omaha he boarded a bus for New York, watched the flat fields of the Midwest bump by as if they were unspooling toilet paper, ready to flush down the drain.

New York was a platter of girls: towering blonds with custard tits, smooth-skinned babes with sultry lips. When Sam talked it felt like his words were crisscrossing in the air, scrambled before they landed. Things that sounded fine in his mind left his mouth and entered women's ears in some garbled syntax. "Nice dress," he said, and they looked at him like he'd groped them on the subway. "Buy you a drink?" They'd recoil like he'd spit in theirs.

He went to record stores and jazz clubs and sat alone in the back. What they saw: a scrawny Chinese guy, barely any meat on his bones, five-foot-seven on a good day, Coke-bottle glasses, cheap clothes, an underfed accountant's underfed accountant loser brother. They saw a man who couldn't dance. They heard a man who couldn't sing. But in his leaky water-balloon heart, Sam could sing and dance. In the apartment he shared with a rotating cast of roommates, he locked the door to his room and played records on his turntable, James Brown and Maceo Parker, Sly Stone. It felt like being unraveled.

I lost someone, my love
Someone who's greater than the stars above
I wanna hear you scream!

He hadn't lost a love like that. His father—that was a loss, but not of a real person, only the idea of father. Yet there was always a feeling of incompleteness, a reaching for, a wanting of. Some thread left unstitched. The missing chunk. Late at night in his room, he dreamed of meeting a woman who would understand all of that, who'd be able to listen to music and feel the notes crawl up her spine, who would sing along, who would dance with him, who would leave him alone.

His buddy Ben lived with a girl named Lily in a studio apartment in Chinatown that smelled like overcooked eggs, both of them skinny enough that they'd sometimes share clothes. The idea of living with a girl seemed as improbable to Sam as waking up on the moon. Shacking up, Ben called it. He cheated on Lily with a college girl who wore matching dresses, shoes, and panties and a rich jook-sing with a Pomeranian that slept in her bed and woke him up by licking his toes. "We're too young to be tied down," Ben told Sam, and Sam pictured himself splayed out on his back, limbs spread, hands and feet tied snugly to four posts in the ground, Helen from Hong Kong triple knotting the ropes.

Pat was a woman with very little curve to her, smooth hips and flat ass, dark hair permed into a frizzy halo. Behind rounded red frames, her eyes were wet and giant, her nose and mouth miniature. She had the look of a doll owl. Doll owl, Sam thought, turning the words around in his mouth.

"Fire me up." Those were the first words she said to him, the sentence he would later see as the spark; or, on worse days, the culprit.

She wanted a light—she wanted to be *fired up*.

3

On the night of her and Sam's first official date, Pat had already spoken on the phone to her mother and Annabelle Uy.

"Make sure you look good for once," her mother said. "It wouldn't kill you to put on a little makeup and wear a dress. Wear heels because you're such a little shrimp. But not too-high heels. Remember, you don't want to be taller than the man. You haven't gained any weight, have you?"

Annabelle said, "I asked Jack Ng who asked Ben Chan who said that Sam was quiet but a stand-up guy. But really? You gotta watch out for those quiet ones. He must like you if he's going all the way out to New Jersey. Watch out!"

Pat was dressed in red slacks and a cream-colored, V-neck blouse, curls sprayed tight, mascara and eyeliner carefully applied. Sam was arriving on the six o'clock train. Lynette and Cynthia were wearing corduroys and turtlenecks, hair pulled into long pigtails. The Mulligans up the block were out of town, the Antonicellis already had plans for the night, and Pat didn't know anyone else in Warwick, so she told the girls they were going out for dinner with a friend.

When Sam asked her out, she thought they could see each other just this one time, and then she'd never have to tell him about Harry and the girls.

"Can we have pizza?" Cynthia asked.

"We'll see," said Pat. "Behave yourselves, we're the guests."

At Romeo's they got looks. The barn-shaped pizzeria was noisy, the air heavy with grease. There were a few empty tables but the waitress told Sam and Pat to wait, and they stood in a small corner space by the door, the girls droopy and shivering with their backs pressed against a cigarette machine. Each time the door opened, it brought in more cold air. Family after family came in, spoke to the waitress, waited until their names were called, and sat down. Sam and Pat watched as those families flipped through menus and placed orders. When the waitress brought out a pepperoni pie and a pitcher of soda, Cynthia tugged at Pat's coat and said, "Why aren't we eating yet?"

Twenty minutes had passed and her stomach was growling. Sam's face was creased and tight. He shook his head and pushed his way to the waitress. "Why are we still waiting?" He pointed to Cynthia and Lynette. "Children are waiting." It sounded like he was shouting.

The waitress had a nose like a soft banana, a small pouch of fat under her otherwise thin face. She was taller than Sam, and as he shouted at her, she took a step back.

"We haven't been seated. You seated those families first, and they came in after us." Sam pointed to the family eating the pepperoni pie, then back at the waitress, jabbing a finger.

The waitress looked at him as if he was speaking in another language. "Pardon me?"

Pat wanted Sam to punch the waitress. She wanted to punch the waitress herself. Sam stood there, glaring, his hands shoved into his coat pockets.

"Say something," Pat whispered.

Sam said nothing. She felt relieved that he didn't make a scene. How would she have explained it to the girls? Maybe they had imagined everything, maybe there really weren't any tables available, maybe all the families that came in after them were close relatives of the waitress and they were just being paranoid.

"Let's go," Sam said. It was a command, a bark. Without looking back, he kicked the door open and walked out. Pat waited to see if he'd return or open the door for her, but he didn't. She took the girls' hands and pushed the door open herself.

Sam stood in the parking lot with his fists balled. "Those fuckers."

"Don't yell. You're scaring the girls."

"They think they can walk all over us!"

Pat took out her car keys and wondered if she could ever return to Romeo's. "They're not all that bad."

He took out a pack of cigarettes. "Want one?"

"I don't smoke around the girls."

Sam put the pack back into his pocket. The girls climbed into the backseat and stared at him. Pat wanted to give them a hug.

Cynthia said, "I'm hungry."

4

Trees were different in New Jersey, bigger, more colorful. The train had rolled past houses with single-car garages, three-block downtowns, stores with awnings, even an official town clock. Pat had said on the phone to look out for the green Beetle, and he spotted it when he got off in Warwick, the only car in the lonely parking lot with its lights on. Two little girls sat in the backseat, watching him.

"These are my daughters. Lynette and Cynthia. Say hello to Sam."

"Hello," the children chorused.

Sam's brain was flipping through the possibilities. Who were these children? Was this a setup? Pat didn't wear a wedding ring; she had agreed to the date. Should he get out of the car before her husband returned and kicked his ass all the way back to Brooklyn?

She put her hand on top of his. It was small and warm, clammy with sweat.

"I'm sorry I didn't say anything earlier. I didn't know how. My husband, Harry, well, my ex-husband, he passed away."

"I'm so sorry."

The girls were silent.

"It was almost a year ago."

Only? Almost? "I'm sorry."

Pat clapped her hands together and turned on the ignition. "I couldn't get a sitter for tonight," she said in Cantonese.

Sam looked at her, then toward the backseat.

"They don't understand," Pat said. "Their father was jook-sing, Chinese but born in America."

"Oh?"

"We met in Queens."

"Oh."

"Are we going for pizza?" one of girls asked. "Do you like pizza?"

"I love pizza," Sam said, switching back to English, even though eating cheese gave him stomach cramps.

At Romeo's he wished they were in the city, where there were other Chinese, and later he would feel that he had backed down too easily, that he should've gone back inside and let the waitress know they couldn't mess with him. He wondered if, in not doing so, he had let Pat down.

Pat drove them to another pizzeria and they ordered a pie to go, brought it back to the house, and ate it at the kitchen table. The girls drank sodas, Pat and Sam beers. The scene at Romeo's receded, somewhat. Sam was surprised at how large the house was on the inside. The ceilings were tall, and the fluffy shag carpet clean and warm. The kitchen was twice the size of his rented room, and the windows faced a tree-filled backyard. He walked around the living room full of hanging plants and children's toys and looked at framed photos on the fireplace mantel. The jook-sing husband was in some of them, and Sam noted that he wasn't too tall, although he was good-looking, with hard, chiseled features and wiry hair. The girls took after him.

There was a picture of Pat and the jook-sing husband smiling in front of a small Christmas tree strung with so much tinsel, it was if the tree had metallic hair. They wore matching red plaid pants. Had this been the jook-sing husband's last Christmas? He didn't look sick. Sam looked at his deceased competition—for now he had put himself into the running—and Pat began to take on a new shape, that of a steely, vulnerable survivor. Someone who'd been wanted, before.

Then she was standing next to him. "I'm sorry," she said. "This isn't much of a date."

Sam wanted to scoop her into his chest. "It's okay." He reached over and put an arm around her shoulders, patting her at regular intervals.

"His name was Harry," she said, "and he died in a car accident."

5

Sam washed the dishes as Pat put the girls to bed. In the bathroom mirror, dark circles beneath her eyes were emerging like storm clouds, and she decided he had asked her out only because he was being kind. She brushed her tongue with her toothbrush to scrub off the cheese taste and walked downstairs. She would drop Sam off at the train station and go to sleep and wake up at six-thirty, get the girls off to Warwick Elementary and get herself to the lawyers' office on Route 17 where she worked as a paralegal —two exits south of where Harry had died—and pick the girls up from school, fix dinner, mediate when Cynthia pinched Lynette and Lynette cried, plant them in front of the television, hug them when they said they missed Daddy, and fall asleep in her work clothes at nine o'clock. She would think again about selling the house and moving back to Queens.

The kitchen was empty and the back door open. Sam was in the middle of the yard, looking at the sky. The shadows lent him solidity. His zip-up jacket was old and cheap-looking but it gave him the appearance of heft. For a moment she wondered who this man was and what he was doing in her yard. Pat walked toward him, the leaves damp beneath her boots. She would have to rake them; she had never raked leaves in her life.

"I'm smelling the sky," he said. "It smells good, the fresh air."

"Maybe you're not a city type after all. Maybe you belong in New Jersey."

"Maybe," he said, and as they studied each other through their glasses he leaned down an inch, she up an inch, and they made out like teenagers. He felt less flimsy than he looked, his hands gripping her waist, and when her mouth opened and closed she was surprised by how promptly she was turned on, how acutely she wanted more.

6

When you start to hope, then comes the danger. You begin to think that love is like song lyrics, and then you're in trouble.

He listened to too much music and he wanted too much—a deep gnawing, a terrible hunger, an uppercut to the heart. He pictured himself standing at Pat's doorway holding flowers in one hand and a bundle of records in the other. They could save each other from all the lonely days after lonely days.

He went to work at the drafting job he hated, marked up the Help Wanted ads, and slept fitfully in his room, thinking of dark backyards and big trees. In Pat's backyard he had seen stars, shining so hard it was as if they were vibrating, quivering from the effort of producing all that light.

Riding the subway into Manhattan, Sam imagined being a father. He had no idea how to deal with children, never mind girls, the girls of the woman he was dating and a dead man. Walking through midtown, he wondered if he was ready for the challenge —was he being challenged?—and his walk grew faster and stronger. Hadn't he traveled across the world by himself? If the jook-sing husband could be a father, he could. In New Jersey there were no Chinese but the air was so clean. Not like Omaha, where open space was like strangling.

They fell into a routine. Pat picked him up at the train station on Sundays. Sam brought Lynette and Cynthia coloring books and asked them questions about their favorite TV shows. Pat told him about the accident and Sam said nothing because it scared him. He was simply listening to her, being supportive. He wondered if he could be satisfied being her second choice, if the jook-sing husband would have gone back inside the pizzeria, yet sometimes he thought that being second was better than not being a choice at all.

It would be easier if she didn't have kids.

Pat had yet to visit him in Brooklyn, and he didn't want to ask her, knowing it would be hard with the girls. But he wanted her to spend the night with him, to prove she was interested.

"I think you should come stay with me one night," he said, after almost two months of Sunday visits. "I really think you need to."

7

"So, did you make it with him yet?"

"What? Annabelle!"

"Did you, or didn't you?"

"No!" Then Pat added, "Not yet."

"Come on," said Annabelle. "There's no need to play the prude."

"He's come by six Sundays in a row," Pat said.

Annabelle laughed. "Now it's serious."

Pat thought of the way her heart beat after she and Sam made out in the yard each Sunday, how they took their glasses off and looked at each other as if they were seeing new people. He looked bare, slippery, different.

"Maybe I'm falling in love?" she said. Annabelle screeched and dropped the phone.

Her mother called and said, "Don't push him away. You can't be so picky at your age."

Contrary to what her mother thought, Pat was still young, but she didn't feel young. Still, Sam would be content with not knowing all the details that came before him. He wouldn't ask.

He was still coming into focus for her. The lens would adjust, and on some days she would see him shaped into the same type of man as Harry, slim hips and swagger, all muscle, ready to fire. Harry and Pat had worked next door to each other in Queens. He did taxes. She did filing. It seemed like before she knew it, she had married him, given birth to two children, and moved out to New Jersey, envisioning life as a whimsical crapshoot, a leisurely canoe ride down a river on an endless summer afternoon, floating on a current that would take her wherever it pleased. She played along, believing that she didn't have much of a choice, but she had chosen Harry, she had chosen him hard. There had been boyfriends before, mild-mannered boys that Pat neither loved nor hated. But they had judged her passiveness to be lack of interest and eventually backed away. Only Harry had seen it for what it was. An invitation. A cracked door.

She used to try to catch Harry in unguarded moments, look at him across the room as he ironed shirts in his boxer shorts, had to sit on her hands to stop herself from pushing herself into him. He had made her feel crazy and out of control, as if she'd wanted him until there was no want left in her.

Whoever came next would get the crumbs.

On other days, the lens would adjust and Sam's shape would recede, the lines of his body redrawn into another man, the illusion of cockiness fine-tuned into a shape Pat couldn't yet read.

The first time he saw her car in the daylight, he asked her about the dent in the fender. She explained that it was a new car, the old one had been wrecked in the accident. The dented fender was from Pat's own accident.

"After he died I was so scared I couldn't drive on the highway. Then one day I took the car out and drove it into the pond in Warwick."

"Why?" he asked.

"I don't know. Maybe because he died, I was safe. Superstitious, you know?"

They were sitting at the kitchen table, their feet rubbing against each other's. Pat put her hand against her mouth. Her breath wet her palm. She wanted to rewind and snatch back everything she'd just revealed.

Sam looked at her with confusion and pity. The minutes ticked by and he said nothing. He said nothing.

Pat removed her feet from his. Finally, he said, "Then what happened?"

"The car was a little banged up, but I wasn't hurt. I told everyone it was an accident, and they believed me." He put his arm around her and she felt so relieved, she said, "I can get a sitter for next weekend."

At dinner in Manhattan Chinatown, Pat ate quickly and greedily. Afterward, as they walked to Sam's apartment, she felt like a schoolgirl swinging hands with her boy. She belonged here! She was in love! She was so lucky to feel this way twice!

Don't be too proud, her mother used to tell her. A little proud is okay. Too much is not okay.

All Pat wanted was a less busy heart.

In Sam's apartment the floorboards slanted dramatically to the right, and the tiny living room held only a television set on a plastic crate and several plastic chairs. She imagined picking up his dirty beer bottles and dishes every night after work. His room was similarly small and bare, a twin mattress lying resigned in the corner, the floor coated in so much dirt that Pat was afraid to take off her shoes.

They sat on the mattress and kissed. Sam's mouth tasted like dinner. They kissed for a long time.

He got up and pulled a record from a stack of albums in the corner, placed it on the turntable that sat on an overturned cardboard box, and gently lowered the needle. The music began. It was strange music, some song she'd never heard before. It sounded like a man yelping, screaming words about losing someone.

"What do you think? Do you like it?" Sam's glasses were off, his face expectant.

"I don't know," Pat said. "It's so loud. So much screaming."

He looked disappointed, so she said, "Okay, then let's dance." They got up and danced in the space between the mattress and the wall. Pat giggled at how silly the scene was, the loud music, the sad room. Sam didn't laugh back. His face was still and serious.

No humor.

What was so serious about this shrieking music, anyway? What was the big deal?

8

It was time to do it. It was over too soon. He was embarrassed.

She didn't understand his music. She hated his apartment. He'd seen the way her mouth pinched when she saw his room.

He hated her for that, and he hated himself for caring that the jook-sing husband had been able to buy her that huge house. Pat acted like she was too good for the city.

"Sam?"

She lay beside him, naked. He pulled the sheets over her, not wanting to see the paunch on her stomach, the floppy, ridiculous skin.

"Sam?" Pat asked again. He felt like he was being drowned. "Do you have a cigarette? Sam?"

Sam thought he was too young to be tied down, but that morning Ben had called from a pay phone in Lake Tahoe, where he was on a skiing trip. "We're moving to California," Ben announced. "I asked Lily to marry me and she said yes."

Ben said it was time to make his real life start, and Sam said he hadn't realized that what he'd been living wasn't real life. When he put the phone down he realized that his early days in New York were over.

9

Pat exhaled smoke. The record player spun static. Sam was quiet, his hair sticking up in a cowlick. He curled away from her, breathing. Was he sleeping or only pretending to?

"You know, women sometimes take longer."

She said it and knew she shouldn't have. It was only their first time. It could get better. She said his name again, and he said nothing.

Outside, it was dark already. Pat heard a bus screech on the street, footsteps and voices in the next room. Four roommates, all single men. She had to use the bathroom, but she was trapped here until the roommates left.

The room was cold and she missed her girls. There were nights, alone with them in the house, when she thought she could do this life solo. It wasn't so bad, just the three of them. On other nights, she felt like she was the only person left in the world, with two girls and a dead husband and nowhere to go, and she was so angry she wanted to smash the walls with an ax, throw chairs through the windows.

She dragged deeper on the cigarette, trying to outrun the sinking feeling. Her mother had said, "I'm so happy, I'm so relieved. I'm so happy you met a nice man."

"Are you awake?" Pat asked now, in a last effort, and Sam didn't respond. The space between them, imperceptible at first, became a sudden tear, threads popping from seams in one sure stroke.

But he was nice enough, she thought. He was a nice man.

Cold Little Bird

FROM *The New Yorker*

IT STARTED WITH bedtime. A coldness.

A formality.

Martin and Rachel tucked the boy in, as was their habit, then stooped to kiss him good night.

"Please don't do that," he said, turning to face the wall.

They took it as teasing, flopped onto his bed to nuzzle and tickle him.

The boy turned rigid, endured the cuddle, then barked out at them, "I really don't like that!"

"Jonah?" Martin said, sitting up.

"I don't want your help at bedtime anymore," he said. "I'm not a baby. You have Lester. Go cuddle with him."

"Sweetheart," Rachel said. "We're not helping you. We're just saying good night. You like kisses, right? Don't you like kisses and cuddles? You big silly."

Jonah hid under the blankets. A classic pout. Except that he wasn't a pouter, he wasn't a hider. He was a reserved boy who generally took a scientific interest in the tantrums and emotional extravagances of other children, marveling at them as though they were some strange form of street theater.

Martin tried to tickle the blanketed lump of person that was his son. He didn't know what part of Jonah he was touching. He just dug at him with a stiff hand, thinking a laugh would come out, some sound of pleasure. It used to work. One stab of the finger and the kid exploded with giggles. But Jonah didn't speak, didn't move.

"We love you so much. You know?" Martin said. "So we like to show it. It feels good."

"Not to me. I don't feel that way."

"What way? What do you mean?"

They sat with him, perplexed, and tried to rub his back, but he'd rolled to the edge of the bed, nearly flattening himself against the wall.

"I don't love you," Jonah said.

"Oh, now," Martin said. "You're just tired. No need to say that sort of stuff. Get some rest."

"You told me to tell the truth, and I'm telling the truth. I. Don't. Love. You."

This happened. Kids tested their attachments. They tried to push you away to see just how much it would take to really lose you. As a parent, you took the blow, even sharpened the knife yourself before handing it to the little fiends, who stepped right up and plunged. Or so Martin had heard.

They hovered by Jonah's bed, assuring him that it had been a long day—although the day had been entirely unremarkable—and he would feel better in the morning.

Martin felt like a robot saying these things. He felt like a robot thinking them. There was nothing to do but leave the boy there, let him sleep it off.

Downstairs, they cleaned the kitchen in silence. Rachel was troubled or not, he couldn't tell, and it was better not to check. In some way, Martin was captivated. If he were Jonah, ten years old and reasonably smart, starting to sniff out the world and find his angle, this might be something worth exploring. Getting rid of the soft, warm, dumb providers who spun opportunity around you relentlessly, answering your every need. Good play, Jonah. But how do you follow such a strong, definitive opening move? What now?

Over the next few weeks, Jonah stuck by his statement, wandering through their lives like some prisoner of war who'd been trained not to talk. He endured his parents, leaving for school in the morning with scarcely a goodbye. Upon coming home, he put away his coat and shoes, did his homework without prompting. He helped himself to snacks, dragging a chair into the kitchen so that he could climb on the counter. He got his own glass, filling it with water at the sink. When he was done eating, he loaded his dishes in the dishwasher. Martin, working from home in the afternoons, watched all this, impressed but bothered. He kept offering to help, but Jonah always said that he was fine, he could handle it. At bedtime, Martin and Rachel still fussed over Lester, who, at six years old, regressed and babified himself in order to drink up the extra attention. Jonah insisted on saying good night with no kiss, no hug. He shut his door and disappeared every night at eight p.m.

When Martin or Rachel caught Jonah's eye, the boy forced a smile at them. But it was so obviously fake. Could a boy his age do that?

"Of course," Rachel said. "You think he doesn't know how to pretend?"

"No, I know he can pretend. But this seems different. I mean, to have to pretend that he's happy to see us. First of all, what the fuck is he so upset about? And second, it just seems so kind of . . . grown-up. In the worst possible way. A fake smile. It's a tool one uses with strangers."

"Well, I don't know. He's ten. He has social skills. He can hide his feelings. That's not such an advanced thing to do."

Martin studied his wife.

"Okay, so you think everything's fine?"

"I think maybe he's growing up and you don't like it."

"And you like it? That's what you're saying? You like this?"

His voice had gone up. He had lost control for a minute there, and, as per motherfucking usual, it was a deal-breaker. Rachel put up her hand, and she was gone. From the other room, he heard her say, "I'm not going to talk to you when you're like this."

Okay, he thought. Goodbye. We'll talk some other time when I'm not like this, AKA never.

Jonah, it turned out, reserved this behavior solely for his parents. A probing note to his teacher revealed nothing. He was fine in school, did not act withdrawn, had successfully led a team project on Antarctica, and seemed to run and play with his friends during recess. Run and play? What animal were they discussing here? Everybody loved Jonah was the verdict, along with some bullshit about how happy he seemed. "Seemed" was just the thing. Seemed! If you were an idiot who didn't know the boy, who had no grasp of human behavior.

At home, Jonah doted on his brother, read to him, played with him, even let Lester climb on his back for rides around the house, all fairly verboten in the old days, when Jonah's interest in Lester had only ever been theoretical. Lester was thrilled by it all. He suddenly had a new friend, the older brother he worshiped, who used to ignore him. Life was good. But to Martin it felt like a calculated display. With this performance of tenderness toward his brother, Jonah seemed to be saying, "Look, this is what you no longer get. See? It's over for you. Go fuck yourself."

Martin took it too personally, he knew. Maybe because it was personal.

One night, when Jonah hadn't touched his dinner, they were asking him if he would like something else to eat, and, because he wasn't answering, and really had not been answering for some weeks now, other than in one-word responses, curt and formal, Martin and Rachel abandoned their usual rules, the guideposts of parenting they'd clung to, and moved through a list of bribes. They dangled the promise of ice cream, and then those monstrosities passing for Popsicles, shaped like animals with chocolate faces or hats, which used to turn Jonah craven and desperate. When Jonah remained silent and sort of washed-out-looking, Martin offered his son candy. He could have some right now. If only he'd fucking say something.

"It's just that you're all in his face," Rachel said to him later. "How's he supposed to breathe?"

"You think my desire for him to speak is making him silent?"

"It's probably not helping."

"Whereas your approach is so amazing."

"My approach? You mean being his mother? Loving him for who he is? Keeping him safe? Yeah, it is pretty amazing."

He turned over to sleep while Rachel clipped on her book light.

They'd ride this one out in silence, apparently.

Yes, well. They'd written their own vows, promising to be "intensely honest" with each other. They had not specifically said that they would hold up each other's flaws to the most rigorous scrutiny, calling out each other's smallest mistakes, like fact checkers, believing, perhaps, that the marriage would thrive only if all personal errors and misdeeds were rooted out of it. This mission had gone unstated.

*

In the morning, when Martin got up, Jonah sat reading while Lester played soldiers on the rug. Lester was fully dressed, his backpack near the door. There was no possible way that Lester had done this on his own. Obviously, Jonah had dressed his brother, emptied the boy's backpack of yesterday's crap art from the first-grade praise farm he attended, and readied it for a new day. Months ago, they'd asked Jonah to perform this role in the morning, to dress and prepare his brother, so that they could sleep in, and Jonah had complied a few times, but halfheartedly, with a certain mysterious cost to little Lester, who was often speechless and tear-streaked by the time they found him. The chore had quickly lapsed, and usually Martin awoke to a hungry, half-naked Lester, waiting for his help.

Today, Lester seemed happy. There was no sign of crying.

"Good morning, Daddy," he said.

"Hello there, Les, my friend. Sleep okay?"

"Jonah made me breakfast. I had juice and Cheerios. I brought in my own dishes."

"Way to go! Thank you."

Martin figured he'd just play it casual, not draw too much attention to anything.

"Good morning, champ," he said to Jonah. "What are you reading?"

Martin braced himself for silence, for stillness, for a child who hadn't heard or who didn't want to answer. But Jonah looked at him.

"It's a book called *The Short*. It's a novel," he said, and then he resumed reading.

A fat bolt of lightning filled the cover. A boy ran beneath it. The title lettering was achieved graphically with one long wire, a plug trailing off the cover.

"Oh, yeah?" Martin said. "What's it about? Tell me about it."

There was a long pause this time. Martin went into the kitchen to get his coffee started. He popped back out to the living room and snapped his fingers.

"Jonah, hello. Your book. What's it about?"

Jonah spoke quietly. His little flannel shirt was buttoned up to the collar, as if he were headed out into a blizzard. Martin almost heard a kind of apology in his voice.

"Since I have to leave for school in fifteen minutes, and since I was hoping to get to page 100 this morning, would it be okay if I didn't describe it to you? You can look it up on Amazon."

He told Rachel about this later in the morning, the boy's unsettling calm, his odd response.

"Yeah, I don't know," she said. "I mean, good for him, right? He just wanted to read, and he told you that. So what?"

"Huh," Martin said.

Rachel was busy cleaning. She hadn't looked at him. Their argument last night had either been forgotten or stored for later activation. He'd find out. She seemed engrossed by a panicked effort at tidying, as if guests were arriving any second, as if their house were going to be inspected by the fucking UN. Martin followed her around while they talked, because if he didn't she'd roam out of earshot and the conversation would expire.

"He just seems like a stranger to me," Martin said, trying to add a lightness to his voice so she wouldn't hear it as a complaint.

Rachel stopped cleaning. "Yeah."

For a moment, it seemed that she might agree with him and they'd see this thing similarly.

"But he's not a stranger. I don't know. He's growing up. You should be happy that he's reading. At least he wasn't begging to be on the stupid iPad, and it seems like he's talking again. He wanted to read, and you're freaking out. Honestly."

Yes, well. You had these creatures in your house. You fed them. You cleaned them. And here was the person you'd made them with. She was beautiful, probably. She was smart, probably. It was impossible to know anymore. He looked at her through an unclean filter, for sure. He could indulge a great anger toward her that would suddenly vanish if she touched his hand. What was wrong? He'd done something or he hadn't done something. Figure it the fuck out, Martin thought. Root out the resentment. Apologize so hard it leaks from her body. Then drink the liquid. Or use it in a soup. Whatever.

Jonah came and went, such a weird bird of a boy, so serious. Martin tried to tread lightly. He tried not to tread at all. Better to float overhead, to allow the cold remoteness of his elder son to freeze their home. He studied Rachel's caution, her distance-giving, her respect, the confidence she possessed that he clearly lacked, even as he saw the toll it took on her, what had become of this person who needed to touch her young son and just couldn't.

Then, one afternoon, he forgot himself. He came home with groceries and saw Jonah down on the rug with Lester, setting up his Lego figures for him, such an impossibly small person, dressed so carefully by his own hand, his son—it still seemed ridiculous and a miracle to Martin that there'd be such a thing as a son, that a little creature in this world would be his to protect and befriend. Without thinking about it, he sat down next to Jonah and took the whole of the boy in his arms. He didn't want to scare him, and he didn't want to hurt him, but he needed this boy to feel what it was like to be held, to really be swallowed up in a father's arms. Maybe he could squeeze all the aloofness out of the boy, just choke it out until it was gone.

Jonah gave nothing back. He went limp, and the hug didn't work the way Martin had hoped. You couldn't do it alone. The person being hugged had to do something, to be something. The person being hugged had to fucking exist. And whoever this was, whoever he was holding, felt like nothing.

Finally, Martin released him, and Jonah straightened his hair. He did not look happy.

"I know that you and Mom are in charge and you make the rules," Jonah said. "But even though I'm only ten, don't I have a right not to be touched?"

The boy sounded so reasonable.

"You do," Martin said. "I apologize."

"I keep asking, but you don't listen."

"I listen."

"You don't. Because you keep doing it. So does Mom. You want to treat me like a stuffed animal, and I don't want to be treated like that."

"No, I don't, buddy."

"I don't want to be called buddy. Or mister. Or champ. I don't do that to you. You wouldn't want me always inventing some new ridiculous name for you."

"Okay." Martin put up his hands in surrender. "No more nicknames. I promise. It's just that you're my son and I like to hug you. We like to hug you."

"I don't want you to anymore. And I've said that."

"Well, too bad," Martin said, laughing, and as if to prove he was right, he grabbed Lester, and Lester squealed with delight, squirming in his father's arms.

Do you see how this used to work? Martin wanted to say to Jonah. This was you once, this was us.

Jonah seemed genuinely puzzled. "It doesn't matter to you that I don't like it?"

"It matters, but you're wrong. You can be wrong, you know. You'll die, without affection. I'm not kidding. You will actually dry up and die."

Again, he found he had to explain love to this boy, to detail what it was like when you felt a desperate connection with someone else, how you wanted to hold that person and just crush him with hugs. But as Martin fought through the difficult and ridiculous discussion, he felt as if he were having a conversation with a lawyer. A lawyer, a scold, a little prick of a person. Whom he wanted to hug less and less. Maybe it'd be simpler just to give Jonah what he wanted. What he thought he wanted.

Jonah seemed pensive, concerned.

"Does any of that make sense to you?" Martin asked.

"It's just that I'd rather not say things that could hurt someone," Jonah said.

"Well . . . that's good. That's how you should feel."

"I'd rather not have to say anything about you and Mom. At school. To Mr. Fourenay."

Mr. Fourenay was what they called a "feelings doctor." He was paid, certainly not very much, to take the kids and their feelings very, very seriously. Martin and Rachel had trouble taking *him* seriously. He looked like a man who had subsisted, for a very long time, on a strict diet of the feelings of children. Gutted, wasted, and soft.

"Jonah, what are you talking about?"

"About you touching me when I don't want you to. I don't want to have to mention that to anyone at school. I really don't."

Martin stood up. It was as if a hand had moved inside him.

He stared at Jonah, who held his gaze patiently, waiting for an answer. "Message received. I'll discuss it with Mom."

"Thank you."

Without really thinking about it, Martin had crafted an adulthood that was essentially friendless. There were, of course, the friends of the marriage, who knew him only as part of a couple—the dour, rotten part—and thus they were ruled out for anything remotely candid, like a confession of what the fuck had just gone down in his own home. Before the children came, he'd managed, sometimes erratically, to maintain preposterous phone relationships with several male friends. Deep, searching, facially sweaty conversations on the phone with other semi-articulate, vaguely unhappy men. In general, these friendships had heated up and found their purpose around a courtship or a breakup, when an aria of complaint or desire could be harmonized by some pathetic accomplice. But after Jonah was born, and then Lester, phone calls with friends had become out of the question. There was just never a time when it was okay, or even appealing, to talk on the phone. When he was home, he was in shark mode, cruising slowly and brutally through the house, cleaning and clearing, scrubbing food from rugs, folding and storing tiny items of clothing, and, if no one was looking, occasionally stopping at his laptop to see if his prospects had suddenly been lifted by some piece of tremendous fortune, delivered via email. When he finally came to rest, in a barf-covered chair, he was done for the night. He poured several beers, in succession, right onto his pleasure center, which could remain dry and withered no matter what came soaking down.

The gamble of a friendless adulthood, whether by accident or design, was that your partner would step up to the role. She for you, and you for her.

But when Martin thought about Jonah's threat—blackmail, really—he knew he couldn't tell Rachel. In a certain light, the only light that mattered, he was in the wrong. The instructions were already out that they were not to get all huggy with Jonah, and here he'd gone and done it anyway. Rachel would just ask him what he had expected and why he was surprised that Jonah had lashed out at him for not respecting his boundaries.

So, yeah, maybe, maybe that was all true. But there was the other part. The threat that came out of the boy. The quiet force of it. To even mention that Jonah had threatened to report them for touching him ghosted an irreversible suspicion into people's minds. You couldn't talk about it. You couldn't mention it. It seemed better to not even think it, to do the work that would begin to block such an event from memory.

*

The boys were talking quietly on the couch one afternoon a few days later. Martin was in the next room, and he caught the sweet tones, the two voices he loved, that he couldn't even bear. For a minute he forgot what was going on and listened to the life he'd helped make. They were speaking like little people, not kids, back and forth, a real discussion. Jonah was explaining something to Lester, and Lester was asking questions, listening patiently. It was heartbreaking.

He snuck out to see the boys on the couch, Lester cuddled up against his older brother, who had a big book in his hands. A grown-up one. On the cover, instead of a boy dashing beneath a bolt of lightning, were the good old Twin Towers. The title, *Lies,* was glazed in blood, which dripped down the towers themselves.

Oh, motherfucking hell.

"What's this?" Martin asked. "What are you reading there?"

"A book about 9/11. Who caused it."

Martin grabbed it, thumbed the pages. "Where'd you get it?"

"From Amazon. With my birthday gift card."

"Hmm. Do you believe it?"

"What do you mean? It's true."

"What's true?"

"That the Jews caused 9/11 and they all stayed home that day so they wouldn't get killed."

Martin excused Lester. Told him to skedaddle and, yes, it was okay to watch TV, even though watching time hadn't started yet. Just go, go.

"Okay, Jonah," he whispered. "Jonah, stop. This is not okay. Not at all okay. First of all, Jonah, you have to listen to me. This is insane. This is a book by an insane person."

"You know him?"

"No, I don't know him. I don't have to. Listen to me, you know that we're Jewish, right? You, me, Mom, Lester. We're Jewish."

"Not really."

"What do you mean, not really?"

"You don't go to synagogue. You don't seem to worship. You never talk about it."

"That's not all that matters."

"Last month was Yom Kippur and you didn't fast. You didn't go to services. You don't ever say Happy New Year on Rosh Hashanah."

"Those are rituals. You don't need to observe them to be part of the faith."

"But do you know anything about it?"

"9/11?"

"No, being Jewish. Do you know what it means and what you're supposed to believe and how you're supposed to act?"

"I do, yes. I have a pretty good idea."

"Then tell me."

"Jonah."

"What? I'm just wondering how you can call yourself Jewish."

"How? Are you fucking kidding me?"

He needed to walk away before he did something.

"Okay, Jonah, it's actually really simple. I'll tell you how. Because everyone else in the world would call me Jewish. With no debate. None. Because of my parents and their parents, and their parents, including whoever got turned to dust in the war. Zayde Anshel's whole family. You walk by their picture every day in the hall. Do you think you're not related to them? And because I was called a kike in junior high school, and high school, and college, and probably beyond that, right up to this fucking day. And because if they started rounding up Jews again they'd take one look at our name and they'd know. And that's you too, mister. They would come for us and kill us. Okay? You."

He was shaking his fist in his son's face. Just old-school shouting. He wanted to do more. He wanted to tear something apart. There was no safe way to behave right now.

"They would kill you. And you'd be dead. You'd die."

"Martin?" Rachel said. "What's going on?"

Of course. There she was. Lurking. He had no idea how long she'd been standing there, what she'd heard.

Martin wasn't done. Jonah seemed fascinated, his eyes wide as his father ranted.

"Even if you said that you hated Jews too, and that Jews were evil and caused all the suffering in the world, they would look at you and know for sure that you were Jewish, for sure! Buddy, champ, mister"—just spitting these names at his son—"because only a Jew, they would say, only a Jew would betray his own people like that."

Jonah looked at him. "I understand," he said. He didn't seem shaken. He didn't seem disturbed. Had he heard? How could he really understand?

The boy picked up the book and thumbed through it.

"This is just a different point of view. You always say that I should have an open mind, that I should think for myself. You say that to me all the time."

"Yes, I do. You're right." Martin was trembling.

"Then do I have your permission to keep reading it?"

"No, you absolutely don't. Not this time. Permission denied."

Rachel was shaking her head.

"Do you see what he's reading? Do you see it?" he shouted.

He waved the book at her, and she just looked at him with no expression at all.

After the kids were in bed, and the house had been quietly put back together, Rachel said they needed to talk.

Yes, we do, he thought, and about fucking time.

"Honestly," she said. "It's upsetting that he had that book, but the way you spoke to him? I don't want you going anywhere near him."

"Yeah, well, that's not for you to say. You're his mom, not mine. You want to file papers? You want to seek custody? Good luck, Mrs. Freeze. I'm his father. And you didn't hear it. You didn't hear it all. You have no fucking idea."

"I heard it, and I heard you. Martin, you need help. You're, I don't know, depressed. You're self-pitying. You think everything is some concerted attack on you. For the record, I am worried about Jonah. Really worried. Something is seriously wrong. There is no debate there. But you're just the worst possible partner in that worry—the fucking worst—because you make everything harder, and we can't discuss it without analyzing your bullshit feelings. You act wounded and hurt, and we're all supposed to feel sorry for you. For you! This isn't about you. So shut down the pity party already."

When this kind of talk came on, Martin knew to listen. This was the scold she'd been winding up for, and if he could endure it, and cop to it, there might be some release and clarity at the other end. A part of him found these outbursts from Rachel thrilling, and in some ways it was possible that he co-engineered them, without really thinking about it. Performed the sullen and narcissistic dance moves that, over time, would yield this kind of eruption from her. His wife was alive. She cared. Even if it seemed that she might sort of hate him.

He circled the house for a while, cooling off, letting the attack —no, no, the truth—settle. Any argument or even discussion to the contrary would just feed her point and read as the defensive bleating of a cornered man. Any speech, that is, except admission, contrition, and apology, the three horsemen.

Which was who he brought back into the room with him.

Rachel was in bed reading, eyes burned onto the page. She didn't seem even remotely ready to surrender her anger.

"Hey, listen," Martin said. "So I know you're mad, but I just want to say that I agree with everything you said. I'm scared and I'm worried and I'm sorry."

He let this settle. It needed to spread, to sink in. She needed to realize that he was agreeing with her.

It was hard to tell, but it seemed that some of her anger, with nothing to meet it, was draining out.

"And," he continued. He waited for her to look up, which she finally did. "You'll think I'm kidding, and I know you don't even want to hear this right now, but it's true, and I have to say it. It made me a little bit horny to hear all that."

She shook her head at the bad joke, which at least meant there was room to move here.

"Shut up," she said.

This was the way in. He took it.

"You shut up."

"Sorry to yell, Martin. I am. I just—this is so hard. I'm sorry."

She probably wasn't. This was simply the script back in, to the two of them united, and they both knew it. One day, one of them would choose not to play. It would be so easy not to say their lines.

"No, it's okay," he said to her, climbing onto the bed. "I get it. Listen, let's take the little motherfucker to the shop. Get him fixed. I'll call some doctors in the morning."

They hugged. An actual hug, between two consenting people. A novelty in this house.

"Okay," she said. "I'm terrified. I don't know what's happening. I look at him and want so much to just grab him, but he's not there anymore. What has he done to himself?"

"Maybe he just needs minor surgery. Does that work on 9/11 truthers?"

"Oh, look," she said to him softly. "You're back. The real you. We missed you."

They talked a little and got up close to each other in bed. For a moment, their good feeling came on them—a version of it, anyway. It felt mild and transitory, but he would take it. It was nice. He was in bed with his wife, and they would figure this out.

"Listen," he said to her. "Do you want to just shag a pony right now, get back on track?"

"I don't know," she said. "I feel gross. I feel depressed."

"I feel gross too. Let's do it. Two gross people licking each other's buttons."

She went to the bathroom and got the jar of enabler. They took their positions on the bed.

He hoped he could. He hoped he could. He hoped he could.

He was cold and insecure, so he left his shirt on. And his socks.

They used a cream. They used their hands. They used an object or two. During the brief strain of actual fornication they persisted with casual conversation about the next day's errands. In the early days of their marriage, this had seemed wicked and sexy, some ironic ballast against the animal greed. Now it just seemed efficient, and the animal greed no longer appeared. Minus the wet spot at the end, and the minor glow one occasionally felt, their sex wasn't so different from riding the subway.

It turned out that there was a deep arsenal of medical professionals who would be delighted to consult on the problem of a disturbed child. Angry, depressed, anxious, remote, bizarre. Even a Jew-hating Jewish child who might very well be dead inside. Only when his parents looked at him, though. Only when his parents spoke to him. Important parameter for the differential.

They zeroed in on recommendations with the help of a high-level participant in this world, a friend named Maureen, whose three exquisitely exceptional children had consumed, and spat back out, various kinds of psych services ever since they could walk. Each of the kids seemed to romance a different diagnosis every month, so Maureen had a pretty good idea of who fixed what and for how much goddamn moolah.

When they told her, in pale terms, about Jonah, she, as a connoisseur of alienating behavior from the young, got excited.

"This is so *The Fifth Child*," she said. "Did you guys read that? I mean, you probably shouldn't read that. But did you? It's like a fiction novel. I don't think it really happened. But it's still fascinating."

Rachel had read it. Happy couple with four children and perfect life have fifth child, leading to less perfect life. Much, much, much, much less perfect. Sorrow, sorrow, sorrow, grief, and sorrow. Not really life at all.

"Yeah, but the kid in that book is a monster," Rachel said. "So heartless. He's not real. And he just wants to inflict pain. Jonah wouldn't hurt anyone. He wants to be alone. Or, not that, but. I don't know what Jonah wants. He's not violent, though. Or even mad. I don't think."

"All right, but he is hurting you, right?" Maureen said. "I mean, it seems like this is really causing you guys a lot of pain and suffering."

"I haven't read the book," Martin said. "But this isn't about us. This is about Jonah. His pain, his suffering. We just want to get to the bottom of it. To help him. To give him support."

In Rachel's silence he could feel her agreement and, maybe, her surprise that he would, or even could, think this way. He knew what to say now. He wasn't going to get burned again. But did he believe it? Was it true? He honestly didn't even know, and he wasn't so sure it mattered.

The doctor wanted to see them alone first. He said that it was his job to listen. So they talked, just dumped the thing out on the floor. It was ugly, Martin thought, but it was a rough picture of what was going down. The doctor scribbled away, stopping occasionally to look at them, to really deeply look at them, and nod. Since when had the act of listening turned into such a strange charade?

Then the doctor met with Jonah, to see for himself, pull evidence right from the culprit's mouth. Martin and Rachel sat in the waiting room and stared at the door. What would the doctor see? Which kid would he get? Were they crazy and was this all just some preteen freak-out?

Finally, the whole gang of them—doctor, parents, and child—gathered to go over the plan, Jonah sitting polite and alert while the future of his brain was discussed. They told him the proposal: a slow ramp of antidepressants, along with weekly therapy, and then, depending, some group work, if that all sounded good to Jonah.

Jonah didn't respond.

"What do you think?" the doctor said. "So you can feel better? And things can maybe go back to normal?"

"I told you, I feel fine," Jonah said.

"Yes, good! But sometimes when we're sick we think we're not. That can be a symptom of being sick—to think we are well."

"So all the healthy people are just lying to themselves?"

"Well, no, of course not," the doctor said.

"Right now I never think about hurting myself, but you want to give me a medicine that might make me think about hurting myself?"

The doctor seemed uneasy.

"It's called suicidal ideation," Jonah said.

"And how do you know about that?" the doctor asked.

"The Internet."

The adults all looked at one another.

"How come people are so surprised when someone knows something?" Jonah asked. "Your generation had better get used to how completely unspecial it is that a kid can look up a medicine online and learn about the side effects. That's not me being precocious. It's just me using my stupid computer."

"Okay, good. Well, you're right, you should be informed, and I want to congratulate you on finding that out for yourself. That's great work, Jonah."

Martin watched Jonah. He found himself hoping that the real Jonah would appear, scathing and cold, to show the doctor what they were dealing with.

"Thank you," Jonah said. "I'm really proud of myself. I didn't think I could do it, but I just really stuck with it and I kept trying until I succeeded."

Martin could not tell if the doctor caught the tone of this response.

"But you might have also read that that's a very uncommon symptom. It hardly ever happens. We just have to warn you and your parents about it, to be on the lookout for it."

"Maybe. But I have none of the symptoms of depression, either. So why would you risk making me feel like I want to kill myself if I'm not depressed and feel fine?"

"Okay, Jonah. You know what? I'm going to talk to your parents alone now. Does that sound all right? You can wait outside in the play area. There are books and games."

"Okay," Jonah said. "I'll just run and play now."

"There," Martin said. "There," after Jonah had closed the door. "That was it. That's what he does."

"Sarcasm? Maybe you don't much like it, but we don't treat sarcasm in young people. I think it's too virulent a strain." The doctor chuckled.

"No offense," Martin said to the doctor, "and I'm sure you know your job and this is your specialty, but I think that way of speaking to him—"

"What way?"

"Just, you know, as if he were much younger. He's just—I don't think that works with him."

"And how do you speak to him?"

"Excuse me?"

"How do you speak to him? I'm curious."

Rachel coughed and seemed uncomfortable. They'd agreed to be open, to let each other have ideas and opinions without feeling mad or threatened.

"It's true," she said. "I mean, Martin, I think you have been surprised lately that Jonah is as mature as he is. That seems to have really almost upset you. You know, you really have yelled at him a lot. We can't just pretend that hasn't happened." She looked at him apologetically. "Aside," she added, "from the scary things that he's been saying."

"Is it maturity? I don't think so. Have I been upset? Fucking hell, yes. And so have you, Rachel. And not because he thinks the Jews caused 9/11 or because he threatened to report us for sexual abuse for trying to hug him, which, for what it's worth, I spared you from, Rachel. I spared you. Because I didn't think you could bear it."

Rachel just stared at him.

"What you're seeing is a very, very bright boy," the doctor said.

"Too smart to treat?" Martin asked.

"I think family therapy would be productive. Very challenging, but worthwhile, in my opinion. I could get you a referral. What you're upset about, in relation to your son, may not fall under the purview of medicine, though."

"The purview? Really?"

"To be honest, I was on the fence about medication. Whatever is going on with Jonah, it does not present as depression. In my opinion, Jonah does not have a medical condition."

Martin stood up.

"He's not sick, he's just an asshole, is what you're saying?"

"I think that's a very dangerous way for a parent to feel," the doctor said.

"Yeah?" Martin said, standing over the doctor now. "You're right. You got that one right. Because all of a parent's feelings are dangerous, you motherfucker."

At home that night, Martin stuffed a chicken with lemon halves, drenched it in olive oil, scattered a handful of salt over it, and blasted it in the oven until it emerged deeply burnished, with skin as crisp as glass. Rachel poured drinks for the two of them, and they cooked in silence. To Martin, it was a harmless silence. He could trust it, and if he couldn't, then to hell with it. He wasn't going to chase down everything unsaid and shout it into their home, as if all important messages on the planet needed to be shared. He'd said enough, things he believed, things he didn't. Quota achieved. Quota surpassed.

Rachel looked small and tired. Beyond that, he wasn't sure. He was more aware than ever, as she set the table and put out Lester's cup and Jonah's big-kid glass, how impossibly unknowable she would always be—what she thought, what she felt—how what was most special about her was the careful way she guarded it all.

No matter their theories—about Jonah or each other or the larger world—their job was to watch over Jonah on his cold voyage. He had to come back. This kind of controlled solitude was unsustainable. No one could pull it off, especially not someone so young. Except that his reasoning on this, he knew, was wishful parental bullshit. Of course a child could do it. Who else but children to lead the fucking species into darkness? Which meant what for the old-timers left behind?

Dinner was brief, destroyed by the savage appetite of Lester, who engulfed his meal before Rachel had even taken a bite, and begged, begged to be excused so that he could return to the platoon of small plastic men he'd deployed on the rug. According to Lester, his men were waiting to be told what to do. "I need to tell my guys who to kill!" he shouted. "I'm in charge!"

At the height of this tantrum, Jonah, silent since they'd returned from the doctor's office, leaned over to Lester, put a hand on his shoulder, and calmly told him not to whine.

"Don't use that tone of voice," he said. "Mom and Dad will excuse you when they're ready."

"Okay," Lester said, looking up at his brother with a kind of awe, and for the rest of their wordless dinner he sat there waiting, as patiently as a boy his age ever could, his hands folded in his lap.

At bedtime, Rachel asked Martin if he wouldn't mind letting her sleep alone. She was just very tired. She didn't think she could manage otherwise. She gave him a sort of smile, and he saw the effort behind it. She dragged her pillow and a blanket into a corner of the TV room and made herself a little nest there. He had the bedroom to himself. He crawled onto Rachel's side of the mattress, which was higher, softer, less abused, and fell asleep.

In the morning, Jonah did not say goodbye on his way to school, nor did he greet Martin upon his return home. When Martin asked after his day, Jonah, without looking up, said that it had been fine. Maybe that was all there was to say, and why, really, would you ever shit on such an answer?

Jonah took up his spot on the couch and opened a book, reading quietly until dinner, while Lester played at his feet. Martin watched Jonah. Was that a grin or a grimace on the boy's face? he wondered. And what, finally, was the difference? Why have a face at all if what was inside you was so perfectly hidden? The book Jonah was reading was nothing, some silliness. Make-believe and colorful and harmless. It looked like it belonged to a series, along with that book *The Short*. On the cover a boy, arms outspread, was gripping wires in each hand, and his whole body was glowing.

The Politics of the Quotidian

FROM ZYZZYVA

THE COMMITTEE WANTS to have a word with her.

The temperature is just below freezing on the morning of her exit interview. As soon as she wakes, winking into the cold, she grapples for the unseen knob of the radiator. It chugs to life as she swings her feet from the bed to the ground. The whitewashed floorboards groan awake beneath her weight.

Shuddering, she scurries to her closet. She lives in a tiny railroad flat on the outer ring of the city's public transit system. The closet stands in the path of the apartment's sole window, where she lets the gray light tickle her back until she's warm enough to think. Then she closes her eyes and breathes up the committee room behind the skin of her eyelids.

Mikael Sbocniak (department chair) will take the seat in the middle. Tomas Ulrikson (selection committee head for her post-doc interview) will be on his left, with Ernst Lichtenberg (faculty mentor whom she's met only once) on his right. She'll sit on the other side of the table, facing them. A triptych of white beards, deep voices, cashmere sport coats. The same look from brewing for decades in the same stock of misanthropic contempt.

Pity. The study of philosophy should have done something for them—made them kinder or more thoughtful—but she's not sure what it's done for her, either. Years ago, when she was just starting graduate school, she'd have loved to critique the power dynamics of a meeting like this one. She'd be spouting Hegel and Foucault. Now she no longer wants to say anything at all.

Now she's just relieved that her side of the table will be next to the committee room's window. She'll be able to feel the sun's weak warmth while she's telling lies.

Chuckling, she pulls a pair of wool tights out of her closet and frog-leaps into them. They'll ask her if she has any idea about the academic job market. They'll nod at one another with satisfaction about there having been only three ethical philosophy positions in the country last year.

After they've finished telling her what they think are hard truths, she'll tell them that her metaphysics were misplaced and her ideals were out of proportion. She slips a dress over her head, considering. Maybe she had wildly optimistic expectations about a life of the mind, instead of managed calculations about debt and paperwork. Such tales would soothe them, would appeal to the kind of young men they'd once been. Perfect. Then she wouldn't have to try and explain the kind of young woman she was now.

Best to keep them away from that subject, she thought as she walked to her window. The truth of why she was leaving was that she could no longer hear what was being said in the rooms they all shared. Now she could listen only to the wind that blew around them, the rain that fell on the windowpanes, and the birds that floated above them. This shift had been a long time coming, but at last she'd embraced it. She'd had no other choice this fall.

Among other classes, she'd taught an undergraduate seminar about the politics of the quotidian. She'd been talking about Kantian aesthetics, a subject that so many hated but that she loved because Kant had appreciated such ordinary things. Wallpaper and weather—things she could understand, even when she first read him as an eighteen-year-old college freshman. Kant didn't care that she hadn't grown up going to museums. It was a revelation to find one of the most important philosophers in history speaking a language she could recognize.

Kant's aesthetics had locked her into philosophy, but few of her undergraduates were having the same revelation. They seemed confused as usual, so she'd brought someone more accessible into her talk: Roland Barthes. It was a digression, since Barthes wasn't a proper philosopher. But Barthes was readable, so there was a chance some of the students might know him, and he made arguments about banal objects. As she began to talk about Barthes, the student interrupted her. He happened to believe that he knew more about Barthes than she ever would.

"That's not what he meant," the student called out.

He was loud and defiant and his voice was aggressive. All heads swiveled his way.

"I read *Mythologies*," he said.

He said it with determination, as if it were the only book he'd ever read. Maybe it was.

"He didn't think any of these things were quotidian at all," he shouted. His face was pinching and puckering now. "That was the whole point."

She pitched backward to regain her balance. Without thinking, she'd leaned toward his words.

"No, the whole point was that we believe these things are quotidian, and they're actually charged with significance," she said.

At least her voice was calm and strong. She uncurled her fingers from the table at which they were all sitting. She'd have preferred a lectern and rowed seating, but the university wanted to make classrooms feel less hierarchical. The result was disrespectful crap like this. "He's quite clear about this, in the last long essay in the book—"

"You don't know what you're talking about," the student said. A slight gasp skipped around the room, a flutter of eyebrows and excitement. Folding his laptop closed, the student stood up and pointed at her. "You've never known what you were talking about since the beginning of this class."

"You don't belong here right now," she said, and he left.

It was only a brief scene—a few noisy sounds as he gathered his laptop and his books and stomped out the door.

But she felt its poison slide in. Now the other students would be asking themselves, *Is he right? Does she know what she's talking about?* They'd wonder why he chose her to pick on, whether it was because she didn't look like his other teachers, in which case he had no point, or whether it was because she was incompetent, which meant that he had a point.

"Please excuse the interruption," she said in a cold voice after the door slammed behind him.

They were impressed by her decisiveness. She could see it from the way that their faces relaxed. Murmuring for a moment was okay—it wasn't every day that they saw open confrontation—so she let them do that, and then she began to speak again. A magisterial tone was the right one for the rest of the class, she decided, in case anyone else got ideas.

No one else got ideas. She kept it up until the class period ended and they all filed out. Only then did she collapse on her chair, arms quivering.

She gulped in air and thought about the student. All she could envision was his smug face; his name wasn't memorable. He had written a couple of short papers for her. They were full of scrawled thoughts, disordered footnotes, off-syllabus references. She needed to review his work and to reassure herself that he was dumber than she was.

Until she started graduate school she'd been the smartest person in every room. No one, least of all her parents, knew where her gifts had come from. Her scores on standardized tests were hair-raising; her excellent grades had won her scholarships to boarding school and college. Her decision to become a philosophy professor made sense to her family only because they never understood what she was talking about anyway.

Recent years had brought on her first niggling hints of self-doubt. In college, she'd gotten a mere magna cum laude distinction—not a big enough deal in an age of Ritalin and grade inflation. That had meant a graduate school of a slightly lower tier than she'd expected. After graduate school had come her current existence—endlessly postdoc, never tenure-track. Once again, not unusual these days, but not what she'd planned on either.

Now there was this scene with the student. She hadn't experienced this nasty sort of business since she was a new arrival at boarding school. She'd been patient with all of that foolishness then, choosing to bide her time. She looked different from the other kids, came from a different kind of family, didn't have the money to go on their kinds of vacations. Fine. All she could do was what she did best—study—and sure enough, after the first semester's results came in, all of the offensive behavior and snide comments fell away. The other students asked her for help with their papers, their notes, their test answers. She'd had a kind of power then. But she'd come to the end of her testing days.

Looking at that student's papers would make her feel better. She rolled her chair over to the classroom computer and shook the mouse like a maraca. Sighing, the screen bloomed alive. Widgets, lists, unfoldered documents—the desktop was such a mess that it took a while to find the proper application. Impatiently, she tore the mouse down its pad. The number of students in the course was at the top of her registration document: eleven.

All semester long there had been twelve.

Each student's name was listed on the document. Galakov, Misha. O'Connor, Patricia. Their flat, unsmiling faces flashed before her eyes as she clicked down the list. This is how she remembers everything and this was how she'd remember the name of that awful student. When she came to the end of the list she felt a mild panic—his name had disappeared. Normally it took days, not minutes, to complete a registration withdrawal.

Not this time. That day's incident passed without so much as a digital ripple. It was as if he'd never taken her class at all.

Confused, she turned her head to the window. Beyond the computer screen glowed the stained purple sky and ruined quads of late fall. The trees were balding and the leaves that still clung were pockmarked and thin. Most of the foliage stretched over the earth in a golden carpet. Rusted gold—mud-stained, sodden after days of rain. Soon the snow would come and bury them under the blackening land. In the spring they'd be reborn—black, silver, worn through. The torn strips of a resurrected body.

She glanced at the jacket she'd thrown over the back of her chair. It'd be too light for the days and weeks ahead. Better to go home now, to pull out her winter clothes, and to have a glass of wine to take her mind off today's humiliations.

But when she got home she wound up drinking not one but three glasses of wine. As her weekday excesses went, this one was so rare and luxurious that it made her feel wild and irresponsible. By the third glass she was dancing in her underwear, all alone in her apartment. She exhausted her commute playlist, then queued up the old songs she'd loved in boarding school. They blasted through her cheap computer speakers. Singing along, chugging the wine, she felt comforted by the dull blue swell of the screen.

It was only when she woke in the middle of the night, hair askew and mouth athrob, that she felt sheepish and ashamed. The overhead lights were still blazing. She could feel their pulse in her head.

She fumbled into the bathroom. While she swabbed makeup remover over her eyelids, which were webbed shut by smeared mascara, she realized that she hadn't unpacked her winter coats. Her fall jacket, worn and faded from the season, was still slung over the entryway chair by the front door. In the morning she wore it again, hunched and headachy from her pity party.

She needed to talk to someone, but she wasn't sure who that person might be. Her faculty mentor was always at a foreign conference or faraway archive. The philosophy department's other instructors grunted at each other in gnomic phrases. When she stood up in meetings to give her class reports, they stared at her with bewilderment. The initial shock on their faces when she spoke wasn't encouraging, nor was the fact that none of them could remember her name. She'd grown used to saying her missing mentor's name as a way to identify herself.

So she emailed Matt. (Or Mike? M. something.) They'd gone to graduate school together and now shared the same postdoc fellowship.

In graduate school they'd taken the same first-year seminar and several second-year sections. He was studying the riskier conjunction of philosophy and linguistics; she was trodding the well-worn path of ethics and political philosophy. She'd been told by their professors that her path was more employable, whatever that meant these days, but here they were at the same program.

Maybe his enthusiasm had helped him in the interview. He was one of those young men with a Talmudic knowledge of not just semiotics but also ambient electronic music, manual camera lenses, and lots of other tiny cultural niches cramped by tribal adherents. She remembered—as soon as she hit "send" on the email—that their past interactions had made her feel tired. His idea of conversation was a circle jerk of references and small fights and even pettier victories. But then came his reply:

"Hey, fantastic to hear from you! Of course we can get together to talk; it's been way too long. I've been so busy hacking together MIDI controllers for my DJ sets that I haven't seen anyone from our program in ages. Hit me back with some possible dates, and don't let those idiots bother you."

It made her smile, though she wasn't sure if he was flirting with her. She had no expectations, of course.

They agreed to meet on an evening that arrived soggy with rain. Great gusts of water whipped around the streets. It felt like the last storm of fall—when the storm was over the trees would be stripped, and there would be nothing to do but greet winter.

She'd finally unpacked her coats, and she was happy to wrap herself in one as the wind blew her into their meeting place. He'd picked the bar—a fashionable place downtown that was once frequented by the men who worked in the city's factory. When the factory shut down, the men disappeared, but their traces remained. These were their pool cues, that was their coin-operated jukebox. The newcomers just added lighting and microbrews and shuffled the contemporary country songs off the playlist.

Women came to this bar now too, and she studied them as she walked in. All of their clothing looked as if it was vintage, and expensive—not thrift. Though their hair was tousled for an appearance of effortlessness, their eyes were clouded with anxiety. They spoke to each other endlessly, probably about the source of that anxiety—nut allergies, or the books they weren't reading, or the sexual encounters they were pretending to enjoy. She's not one of these women and normally this doesn't bother her, but for some reason she felt bothered when she saw them in the bar. They were the kinds of women that she imagined M. would date. Suddenly she felt foolish about asking him to meet her.

She sat down on a stool and ordered a vodka and soda. Sipping her drink, she gazed numbly in front of her, the way she looks numbly ahead while taking a public bus. Just like the experience of riding a public bus, a strange man read her refusal to make eye contact as an invitation to speak. In this case, it was the bartender.

"Have you tried our new vodka yet?" He brandished a tall glass bottle near her face. The label was on heavy white stock; the font looked imperial. "We just got it in from Poland," the bartender said. "I'll pour a sample in your next drink."

From his excitement she guessed that she should be excited too.

"Thanks," she said.

M. chose that moment to be beaten into the room by the wind. His coat was furry with rain and she could see bits and pieces of his hair where they'd splintered out of his knit cap. He pounded his boots against the floor mat. She waved hello with an arc of her arm and hated herself for it.

"Hey," he called across the room. "Order me a beer, will you?"

She tried, but the bartender wasn't interested in just a beer. Even her second guess, "whatever's on tap," wasn't specific enough.

There were six different beers on tap and each of them had special qualities; by the time he was finished explaining each one, M. had shook out his hair, hung up his coat, taken a seat, and asked to hear it all again.

She felt as though she'd hailed the last train to Dunkirk and they hadn't even spoken yet. The two men parried hops and malts while she sucked her drink to the dregs. Though she couldn't fathom what it might be, she must have done something right because at least the bartender mixed her another drink with no more demands about the new vodka.

When M. had his beer at last he turned to her. "So how's it going?"

There was a cautious note in his casual tone, and he kept an arm on the bar between them.

"Good," she said. "I mean things are good, just a little weird sometimes."

"Huh."

"How are things with you?"

"Great."

"Oh?"

"Yeah. I've been working on this paper with Professor Niemeyer —you know him?"

Naturally, she knew Professor Niemeyer, he was only the foremost linguistics expert on this side of the country. Everyone knew him; many grad students saw the slim chance of getting to work with him as the only reason to apply for this postdoc.

"He liked my work on Husserlian bracketing. You remember that paper I did? Anyway, we're doing a piece together. It's kind of like a precursor to my bracketing work, a textual study on this ancient Greek story for *The Journal of Linguistics*. I mean, I can't even speak ancient Greek but that's kind of the point, creating your own meaning, right?"

"Wow, that's great. You're doing it for *The Journal of Linguistics*?"

"Yeah. I wasn't sure if I was ready, but Niemeyer thinks I am."

"That's . . . amazing. I didn't know you were working with him."

"If you haven't seen me around, that's why. He's keeping me pretty busy. Between that and my DJ gigs I'm barely sleeping. And I haven't had time to catch up with anyone, including you. How're you doing? You're doing something with ethnic studies, right?"

"No. No. I studied philosophical theory. With you."

"Of course. We were in those tedious sections with Hubel, oh my God, I'll never forget, they turned me off of Kant for life."

"Then why would you assume—?"

She stopped asking her question because M. was going red, like an iron poker gathering heat from a fireplace. Besides, he was talking over her, going on and on about the sections they'd taken together. Instead of listening to him she tilted her head to the side, so she could hear the noises in the bar. A pool game had started up behind them. She focused on the *thwack* of balls hitting balls, and the grunts of men achieving their own small victories.

She listened for so long that even M. fell silent, and it took only a few of those silent moments for him to get nervous again.

"So you said you wanted to talk to me about something."

"Right." She shook her head back in his direction. "No big deal. Something weird happened in one of my undergrad seminars, I wondered if you'd ever experienced anything like it."

"Hmm."

"I was giving a lecture and some kid got up in the middle of it. He said I didn't know what I was talking about, in a really loud voice. So I threw him out of class and he withdrew the same day."

"Wow."

"Weird, right?"

"Well . . . yeah. What were you talking about?"

"Barthes. Has anything like that ever happened to you?"

"Barthes? He got angry with you over Barthes? I mean, even a kindergartner can understand Barthes"—he was laughing, and it took her a long moment to locate the name of the emotion that she was feeling.

Anger. That was it. M. was making her angry.

It took her a long time to understand Barthes, not in a superficial way but down to the soul, because she didn't think that there was anything simple about Barthes's direct approach or his furious clarity. If M. had any sense he'd know that. But M. didn't know he was insulting her and he wasn't kind enough to care.

"So I take it nothing like that has ever happened to you."

The ice in her voice surprised both of them. M. stopped laughing and shifted around on his stool. "No," he said without looking at her. "It hasn't."

There was silence for a moment, and then they spoke of other things. M. mentioned a girl he'd been dating. She hadn't asked, so it felt like he brought her up on purpose. He sounded smug. It left her feeling even angrier than the crack about Barthes.

When she got home that evening, she was drunk, but not drunk enough to forget the evening. Instead of falling right to sleep she stretched across her bed, fully clothed, and stared at the ceiling until she was too tired to go through the motions of washing her face and brushing her teeth. While she dozed, she felt the overhead lights twitching behind her eyes.

Days passed. The first frost was late. She rejoiced in the dry crispness of the air and the velvety dark of longer nights. Even the rain, with its icepick sharpness, seemed like a glorious way to stretch out the autumn. When the snow came, smothering the rust and gold, there would be no more mossy smells from the earth and no more ink-line paintings in the sky. Though she'd always loved the snow, with each passing day she loved the autumn more. With every thought that arose unbidden she remembered what she was missing outside.

Two weeks after meeting M. she went to the department office to drop off some paperwork on a new data-privacy policy. The secretary, whose nameplate read JANET, was banging away on her keyboard. Janet didn't look up when she walked in; she was hunched over with her hands clawed atop the keys. Janet hit them with the audible noise of a puncture wound. The keyboard popped around her desk like a firecracker.

Janet remained oblivious so she kept watching, wondering why the bizarre scene seemed familiar. The keyboard, the claws, the noise — after a few fruitless moments a memory sprang to the front of her mind. Janet typed on a computer like her mother did. Even though her mother knew, as Janet must know, that computer keys liked softer strokes.

She'd explained this to her mother seventeen years ago and the lesson hadn't stuck. Maybe it was because she was only fifteen at the time; her mother had trouble believing that there were things she knew better than her mother ever would. It turned out to be the last year she spent in her parents' house, the last year she was nothing more than her mother's bright, beloved kid.

They were having an adventure that day. Her mother was always up for an adventure. So they'd set off for the public library, giggly with excitement. Her mother had gazed at her with pride:

her daughter was going to show her how to use one of those new desktop computers.

She'd turned on the monitor and pointed out the mouse. Her mother liked the mouse. Her mother had oohed and aahed as she sketched over the foam pad with it, making tipsy circles on the screen. Then her mother began to type as if the keyboard were a typewriter: with hard, emphatic strokes.

She'd pulled the keyboard away from her mother.

"Mom," she'd said. "You don't have to slam each key. Watch me."

Her mother had been offended. She'd snatched the keyboard back.

"You can be soft if you want to," her mother had said. "Maybe that works for you. But the keys won't listen to me unless I'm strong with them."

It was such a strange thing to say that it flash-froze in her memory. All of the philosophy in the world couldn't explain her mother's reaction to her in that moment. She must have had an odd look on her face when Janet finally looked up at her.

"Yes?" Janet said. "What do you need?"

"Here's my data-privacy form." She passed it to Janet, who studied it with raised eyebrows. "And while I'm here. Would you mind checking the number of students I have in my Thursday seminar? Class number is A316. I've had a little trouble with the computer in that classroom."

"That's strange," the secretary said. "Can I see your ID?"

The university issued an ID to everyone who studied or worked on campus. Every door of every building had been activated to open at their touch. It was like the plastic-card bodies were filigreed not with raised type but magic. She carried her ID everywhere, so that she might open all of the doors, but she was unused to having strangers demand it from her. She gathered her patience and fumbled in her bag.

While she was rooting around, she tried to remember if she'd seen Janet before. Most of the others had grown accustomed to her face; maybe Janet was new or a recent transfer from a different department. That could also explain the childish typing. Perhaps Janet wasn't familiar with the office equipment.

When she found her ID she passed it to Janet, who glanced back and forth between the card and her face.

"You look different now," Janet said.

"Hmm," she said.

"But we were all younger when they took these pictures," said Janet, marveling at her ID under the light of the desk lamp. "We all looked different."

If she looked different in her ID picture, it wasn't because she was so much younger last year, it was because the photographer didn't have the proper lighting. She knew this only because he'd told her as much. It was his way of apologizing for the fact that her face on the ID was an orange smudge.

"These color filters," the photographer had said. "They're designed for lighter skin. I hope that's not a weird thing to say. I don't see color, myself. But the camera does, and if I had known I'd have brought different ones."

"If you had known what?" she'd asked him.

"I mean, they said philosophy department," he'd said, laughing. She didn't like his joke.

She cleared her throat and said to Janet, "So, those numbers for my class?"

"Right." Janet handed back her ID, pushed her chair over to the computer, and proceeded to bang away with such agonizing slowness that she was tempted to wrestle the keyboard from Janet's claws and do it herself. Centuries passed. Empires rose and fell. Then Janet turned with a bright smile and said, "Twelve."

Her knees wobbled. She grabbed the desk ledge before the sudden sway in her back tipped her over.

"Really? Twelve?"

"The seminar on the politics of the quo-quo—"

"The quotidian."

"Yeah, that. Twelve enrollees."

Janet tilted the computer screen so that she could see it. The number winked from the bottom of the nest of spreadsheet boxes. Twelve.

"That's . . . interesting. Can I see the names?"

"Sorry, miss. Those are in a separate file that I don't have the authority to access. New privacy policy. You should have access, though, since you're supposedly the teacher."

Supposedly. "Yes, but I've been having computer problems in that classroom."

"That's too bad."

"Aren't you going to offer to contact the computer technician?"

The secretary blinked twice. "Is that what you want?"

"Is that what I want?" she sputtered. "What I want is for things to work. What I want is students who know how to behave . . ."

"Me too, honey," Janet said. "Me too."

The secretary was looking right at her, and since she felt like her outburst was inappropriate, she backed out of the office and made her way down the hall. When she got inside the seminar classroom she sat down in the chair and leaned back as far as she could without smashing her brains across the floor.

Then she whiplashed herself upright and confronted the computer. It was an ancient beast; it'd probably arrived with a dot-matrix printer. The hard drive churned rigorously, grunting as it pulled up her class list. She tore the mouse to the bottom of the pad. Eleven enrollees.

She stood up, marched down the hall, shoved open the department office door, and threw herself into the room. The brass door-knob hit the wall with a bang that echoed down the corridor.

"You again?" said Janet.

"Me again," she said. "I checked the computer. There's no way it can be twelve students."

"Huh," said Janet, lifting her eyebrows with the exquisite slowness that now seemed familiar. "I thought you said that computer didn't work."

"I don't know what's going on with it. I only know that it was showing a different number of students in that course and that the discrepancy is important."

"You'll have to email the tech folks and set up a repair appointment," Janet said.

"That'll take a week," she said. "Will you pull up the file again?"

"I'm working on something else right now," Janet said. "Maybe you can come back?"

"Look, this is important"—the exhaustion in her voice made her cringe—"I wouldn't be asking if it wasn't important."

Janet kept banging on her keyboard.

She glanced over at the window. The gray flesh of the sky. Against it the sleet jumped out in steel-bright daggers. With no more leaves to marvel at, this would be the only color she would see for the rest of fall. She was still watching the gray when Janet realized that she hadn't gone away.

"Hey," Janet said.

"Excuse me?" she said.

"You wanted your class file. I pulled it up again."

She peered over Janet's shoulder at the computer screen. By squinting hard she could just make out the number before the blinking cursor—that absolutely wrong number of twelve.

"Can you pull up the names of the students?" she said.

"That's now outside my jurisdiction. Only the course instructor, which is what you say you are, and the department head and the dean have the authorization to see those names. Privacy."

"I know what the new policy is," she said to Janet, and the exhausted whininess was gone from her voice. In its place were coldness and anger, and a sort of detached hatred so deep it wasn't fathomable to her.

It was a voice for taking a hostage, she realized, but who was being taken?

"As I mentioned earlier," she said, "there are some problems with the computer in my classroom. So how can we solve this problem?"

"Maybe you could come back when you've calmed down," Janet said. "You seem angry right now, and it's making me uncomfortable."

"I think my question to you was quite clear," she said to Janet.

Janet stared at her in silence.

The identity of the hostage was also quite clear. She felt a certain lightness at the revelation of her fate.

"What are you going to do?" she said to Janet.

"I think I need to call someone," Janet said.

"That's a great idea, Janet, calling someone who can help me get the class list."

"That's not what I meant. I meant calling someone about your behavior in this office. You don't belong in here right now."

She laughed. She threw her head back, opening her throat. It was a vulnerable thing to do, giving someone like Janet access to her softest part, and if Janet could do anything to physically harm her she would have been afraid. But Janet had already harmed her in all of the ways that Janet could harm her, and it had only shown her what she already knew to be true.

"Call the department head," she said. "Call the dean."

Her voice was still low and furious. Janet wanted to call security, not the department head or the dean, so she backed out of Janet's office in order to call Chair Mikael Sbocniak herself. Janet, picking up the phone, was staring at her as she backed into the hallway, and into the embrace of her big laughter.

She turned as she stepped out. She started to run, and those last words of Janet's—*you don't belong here you don't belong here you don't belong here*—jangled in her mind, taunting her with their truth.

Unfortunately, Mikael Sbocniak and Ernst Lichtenberg and Tomas Ulriksen won't understand why those words are true.

So she must tell them something else.

Standing at her apartment window, she can see a bird plucking at the mud hole next to her building. A tree had fallen there in the spring, so the mud hole was still raw and jagged and new, and the snow last week had turned it black. When those first flurries fell, the temperature was too high for them to freeze on the ground. That snowfall was a victim of circumstance, like so much of the avant-garde.

But those flakes prepared the way for the next ones, which are supposed to arrive today. It's a good five degrees colder than it was a week ago, and tomorrow will be cold, as well. This time the snow should stay.

She's been waiting for it all autumn. Now the expectation is exhilarating. The calm of snow, its quiet, its cold stroke on her skin.

At the window, she mouths the lines she's going to say at her exit interview, but she is thinking about whether or not she'll see the snowfall from the committee room. Next to that window, she should be able to see something, even if it's just a slow white blur. As it falls it'll bring a gathering silence to everything outside. Covering the gold, the red, the black, the gray. If she listens closely, she'll hear it happen.

DANIEL J. O'MALLEY

Bridge

FROM *Alaska Quarterly Review*

HE SAW THE old couple twice, once when they stopped halfway across to pose for a picture, and again a year later when they came back, this time without a camera, and for a while all they did was stand there.

Both times he watched from the window, which was not what he was supposed to be doing, he knew that, he knew well what he was supposed to be doing, which was studying. In the mornings, his mother would tell him things—he would follow her around the house while she did her inside work, then outside where she did her garden work and her chicken work—and he would listen and take notes in his notebook while she talked about the histories of their state and their country and their family—his mother's family, plus his father's family, and then their own family, the family they made when they made him—but also about the flood and locusts and frogs and other plagues that had happened before and could happen again, and he would take notes so that in the afternoon he could sit in his bedroom and study, and then in the evening, after the supper dishes were done, he could stand and recite for his father what all he'd learned from his mother in the morning.

But his memory was strong. His mother's words found a home in his mind the moment they left her mouth. So most days he passed his afternoon study time staring out the window and down at the bridge, which was the only thing he could see between the trees.

On the other side of the bridge, he knew, was an enormous building built to look like a log cabin where people came to live for a few days at a time and eat fried fish. This was something people did, his father had told him, because they weren't satisfied with the lives they'd made for themselves back home. And the fish, his father had said, did not come from the river beneath the bridge, they came from somewhere else. But he knew that part without his father saying, because almost always the water was low enough to see dirt and rocks at the river's bottom. As for where the fish actually did come from, he wasn't sure. Because once his father had said that they came from a farm in Arkansas, and he had believed his father, but then another time his father told him that the fish came not from Arkansas but from Asia, first by boat and then by train and then by truck, frozen.

The bridge had been built for trains, but trains did not cross it anymore. People crossed it now, walking, and usually only halfway before they turned around and walked back. They would stop and stare sometimes, either over the edge or straight down between the boards. Sometimes they took pictures, balancing their cameras on the bridge's side rail.

He recognized the old couple because of their hats. They both wore straw hats with wide brims and red-and-yellow bands. The first time they came, they held hands and waited for their camera to flash, and then held hands again as they walked back. The second time, they wore the same hats, but they didn't have a camera, they just stood there, not smiling, not holding hands, not even speaking, at least not that he could hear all the way up the hill.

Minutes passed that way before the couple began untucking and unbuttoning their shirts, then stepping out of their sandals and unbuckling their belts and their pants and taking off those things, as well as the things underneath, and pushing the clothes all into a pile that the man picked up and dropped over the rail. They threw their hats too, and then they just stood there again, only now they were both naked and—he squinted—it looked like they were both bald. He blinked several times, then held his eyes closed, and when he opened his eyes the couple was still there, still naked. He glanced at his bedroom door, which was closed. He could hear his mother whistling, water splashing in the kitchen. When he turned back to the window, he pressed his nose to the screen and watched the old couple take a step closer and hold their faces together in a way that may have meant kissing. And then he watched as they turned and gripped the rail and eased themselves over one leg at a time, and even as they fell, they never made a sound.

Remembering it, he had to remind himself that a whole year had passed between these sightings. Because in his mind they blurred together, and for moments he would wonder what happened to the camera that they'd balanced on the rail—was it still there? could it be his now?

But then he would remember that there was no camera, not the second time. The second time it was just the man and the woman, and then they were gone, over the rail and down without a sound.

His father told him it wasn't possible, just not possible, that it happened that way. His father said that there must have been a sound, if not of voices then at least of impact, humans being as heavy as they are. And he wanted to believe his father, because he knew that what his father said was true. But at the same time, he also knew that what he himself had said was true, because he'd seen it, and, standing there in the living room after supper, as his mother folded towels and his father re-folded the newspaper, he struggled to see how everything could be true all at once.

When his mother finally spoke, she agreed with his father. She agreed that it was not possible for her son to have seen what he said he'd seen, her reason being that for him to have seen what he said he'd seen, he would have had to have been standing and staring out the window and not studying that morning's notes, as he knew he should have been, sitting at his desk, which was a good wooden desk, made by hand by his father and facing the wall all the way on the other side of the room.

And so he said he agreed with his mother. He said he hadn't seen anything at all, he must have imagined it. Or maybe it was a hallucination, an illusion, such as people experienced in the desert, though he had not been in a desert, he had been in his room, but maybe he needed to drink more water, he said, and his mother agreed, she said more water certainly couldn't hurt.

But what he saw on the bridge had not been an illusion, he knew that, and back in his room he tried to see the whole thing again. It was nighttime now and the house was quiet. He got out of his bed and crawled underneath. Under his bed he could pretend that he was in a cave, or that he was a turtle and the bed was his shell, and he found it easier to think this way, easier to concentrate. When he closed his eyes, he could see it—the bridge, the couple standing there in their hats, staring, holding hands then not holding hands, then undressing, now naked, over the rail and down. And then nothing. No, not nothing, he thought. It couldn't be nothing. He kept thinking and thinking until finally he thought, *Birds.* The old couple were birds, or rather they had become birds. He closed his eyes and saw it all again—the couple, the undressing, everything as before, but this time before they hit the ground, their bodies shrank and their arms turned flat and wide, flapping. He saw it again and again, each time a little clearer. Their mouths became beaks. They sprouted feathers. Their eyes turned shiny and small and black, and their toes curled and sharpened like talons—they looked like hawks—and they dipped their talons down in the water, but there weren't any fish there. So the old couple flew on, they circled back under the bridge and up into the woods where there were mice and worms and rabbits, because to a bird these things would taste good, and actually he himself had eaten a rabbit before, though he hadn't realized this at the time. He didn't know that what he'd eaten was a rabbit until afterward, when his father told him. He hadn't been happy about that. But then his father told him that rabbits were meant for eating, and his mother had agreed, and he thought about it and decided that he wasn't upset anymore. He'd felt bad because he'd known that rabbit since it was the size of a mouse, but he decided that his father was right, the rabbit was just doing its job, which was to feed their family, and then he felt fine. He did, mostly. But now, under his bed, thinking about the old couple and the bridge and about flying and birds, he did not feel fine. He couldn't help wondering now what if the rabbit hadn't really been a rabbit at all.

The Prospectors

FROM *The New Yorker*

THE ENTIRE RIDE would take eleven minutes. That was what the boy had promised us, the boy who never showed.

To be honest, I hadn't expected to find the chairlift. Not through the maze of old-growth firs and not in the dwindling light. Not without our escort. A minute earlier, I'd been on the brink of suggesting that we give up and hike back to the logging road. But at the peak of our despondency we saw it: the lift, rising like a mirage out of the timber woods, its four dark cables striping the red sunset. Chairs were floating up the mountainside, forty feet above our heads. Empty chairs, upholstered in ice, swaying lightly in the wind. Sailing beside them, just as swiftly and serenely, a hundred chairs came down the mountain. As if a mirror were malfunctioning, each chair separating from a buckle-bright double. Nobody was manning the loading station; if we wanted to take the lift we'd have to do it alone. I squeezed Clara's hand.

A party awaited us at the peak. Or so we'd been told by Mr. No-Show, Mr. Nowhere, a French boy named Eugene de La Rochefoucauld.

"I bet his real name is Burt," Clara said angrily. We had never been stood up before. "I bet he's actually from Tennessee."

Well, he had certainly seemed European, when we met him coming down the mountain road on horseback, one week ago this night. He'd had that hat! Such a convincingly stupid goatee! He'd pronounced his name as if he were coughing up a jewel. Eugene de La Rochefoucauld had proffered a nasally invitation: would we be his guests next Saturday night, at the gala opening of the Evergreen Lodge? We'd ride the new chairlift with him to the top of the mountain and be among the first visitors to the marvelous new ski resort. The president himself might be in attendance.

Clara, unintimidated, had flirted back. "Two dates—is that not being a little greedy, Eugene?"

"No less would be acceptable," he'd said, smiling, "for a man of my stature." (Eugene was five foot four; we'd assumed he meant education, wealth.) The party was to be held seven thousand feet above Lucerne, Oregon, the mountain town where we had marooned ourselves, at nineteen and twenty-two; still pretty (Clara was beautiful), still young enough to attract notice, but penniless, living week to week in a "historic" boarding house. "Historic" had turned out to be the landlady's synonym for "haunted." "Turn-of-the-century sash windows," we'd discovered, meant "pneumonia holes."

We'd waited for Eugene for close to an hour, while Time went slinking around the forest, slyly rearranging its shadows; now a red glow clung to the huge branches of the Douglas firs. When I finally spoke, the bony snap in my voice startled us both.

"We don't need him, Clara."

"We don't?"

"No. We can get there on our own."

Clara turned to me with blue lips and flakes daggering her lashes. I felt a pang: I could see both that she was afraid of my proposal and that she could be persuaded. This is a terrible knowledge to possess about a friend. Nervously, I counted my silver and gold bracelets, meting out reasons for making the journey. If we did not make the trip, I would have to pawn them. I argued that it was riskier *not* to take this risk. (For me, at least; Clara had her wealthy parents waiting back in Florida. As much as we dared together, we never risked our friendship by bringing up that gulf.) I touched the fake red flower pinned to my black bun. What had we gone to all this effort for? We owed our landlady twelve dollars for January's rent. Did Clara prefer to wait in the drifts for our prince, that fake frog, Eugene, to arrive?

For months, all anybody in Lucerne had been able to talk about was this lodge, the centerpiece of a new ski resort on Mount Joy. Another New Deal miracle. In his Fireside Chats, Roosevelt had promised us that these construction projects would lift us out of the Depression. Sometimes I caught myself squinting hungrily at the peak, as if the government money might be visible, falling from the actual clouds. Out-of-work artisans had flocked to northern Oregon: carpenters, masons, weavers, engineers. The Evergreen Lodge, we'd heard, had original stonework, carved from five thousand pounds of native granite. Its doors were cathedral huge, made of hand-cut ponderosa pine. Murals had been commissioned from local artists: scenes of mountain wildflowers, rearing bears. Quilts covered the beds, hand-crocheted by the New Deal men. I loved to picture their callused black thumbs on the bridally white muslin. Architecturally, what was said to stun every visitor was the main hall: a huge hexagonal chamber, with a band platform and "acres for dancing, at the top of the world!"

W.P.A. workers cut trails into the side of Mount Joy, assisted by the Civilian Conservation Corps boys from Camp Thistle and Camp Bountiful. I'd seen these young men around town, on leave from the woods, in their mud-caked boots and khaki shirts with the government logo. Their greasy faces clumped together like olives in a jar. They were the young mechanics who had wrenched the lift out of a snowy void and into skeletal, functioning existence. To raise bodies from the base of the mountain to the summit in eleven minutes! It sounded like one of Jules Verne's visions.

"See that platform?" I said to Clara. "Stand there, and fall back into the next chair. I'll be right behind you."

At first, the climb was beautiful. An evergreen army held its position in the whipping winds. Soon the woods were replaced by fields of white. Icy outcroppings rose like fangs out of a pink-rimmed sky. We rose too, our voices swallowed by the cables' groaning. Clara was singing something that I strained to hear and failed to comprehend.

Clara and I called ourselves the Prospectors. Our fathers, two very different kinds of gambler, had been obsessed with the Gold Rush, and we grew up hearing stories about Yukon fever and the Klondike stampeders. We knew the legend of the farmer who had panned out $130,000, the clerk who dug up $85,000, the blacksmith who discovered a haul of the magic metal on Rabbit Creek and made himself a hundred grand richer in a single hour. This period of American history held a special appeal for Clara's father, Mr. Finisterre, a bony-faced Portuguese immigrant to southwestern Florida who had wrung his modest fortune out of the sea-damp wallets of tourists. My own father had killed himself outside the dog track in the spring of 1931, and I'd been fortunate to find a job as a maid at the Hotel Finisterre.

Clara Finisterre was the only other maid on staff—a summer job. Her parents were strict and oblivious people. Their thousand rules went unenforced. They were very busy with their guests. A sea serpent, it was rumored, haunted the coastline beside the hotel, and 90 percent of our tourism was serpent-driven. Amateur teratologists in Panama hats read the newspaper on the veranda, drinking orange juice and idly scanning the horizon for fins.

"Thank you," Mr. Finisterre whispered to me once, too sozzled to remember my name, "for keeping the secret that there is no secret." The black Atlantic rippled emptily in his eyeglasses.

Every night, Mrs. Finisterre hosted a cocktail hour: cubing green and orange melon, cranking songs out of the ivory gramophone, pouring bright malice into the fruit punch in the form of a mentally deranging Portuguese rum. She'd apprenticed her three beautiful daughters in the Light Arts, the Party Arts. Clara was her eldest. Together, the Finisterre women smoothed arguments and linens. They concocted banter, gab, palaver, patter—every sugary variety of small talk that dissolves into the night. I hated the cocktail hour, and whenever I could, I escaped to beat rugs and sweep leaves on the hotel roof. One Monday, however, I heard footsteps ringing on the ladder. It was Clara. She saw me and froze.

Bruises were thickening all over her arms. They were that brilliant pansy-blue, the beautiful color that belies its origins. Automatically, I crossed the roof to her. We clacked skeletons; to call it an "embrace" would misrepresent the violence of our first collision. To soothe her, I heard myself making stupid jokes, babbling inanities about the weather, asking in my vague and meandering way what could be done to help her; I could not bring myself to say, plainly, *Who did this to you?* Choking on my only real question, I offered her my cardigan—the way you'd hand a sick person a tissue. She put it on. She buttoned all the buttons. You couldn't tell that anything was wrong now. This amazed me, that a covering so thin could erase her bruises. I'd half-expected them to bore holes through the wool.

"Don't worry, okay?" she said. "I promise, it's nothing."

"I won't tell," I blurted out—although of course I had nothing to tell beyond what I'd glimpsed. Night fell, and I was shivering

now, so Clara held me. Something subtle and real shifted inside
our embrace—nothing detectable to an observer, but a change I
registered in my bones. For the duration of our friendship, we'd
trade off roles like this: anchor and boat, beholder and beheld. We
must have looked like some Janus-faced statue, our chins pointing
east and west. An unembarrassed silence seemed to be on loan to
us from the distant future, where we were already friends. Then
I heard her say, staring over my shoulder at the darkening sea:
"What would you be, Aubby, if you lived somewhere else?"

"I'd be a prospector," I told her, without batting an eye. "I'd be
a prospector of the prospectors. I'd wait for luck to strike them,
and then I'd take their gold."

Clara laughed and I joined in, amazed—until this moment, I
hadn't considered that my days at the hotel might be eclipsing
other sorts of lives. Clara Finisterre was someone whom I thought
of as having a fate to escape, but I wouldn't have dignified my own
prospects that way, by calling them "a fate."

A week later, Clara took me to a debutante ball at a tacky mansion that looked rabid to me, frothy with white marble balconies.
She introduced me as "my best friend, Aubergine." Thus began
our secret life. We sifted through the closets and the jewelry boxes
of our hosts. Clara tutored me in the social graces, and I taught
Clara what to take, and how to get away with it.

One night, Clara came to find me on the roof. She was blinking
muddily out of two black eyes. Who was doing this—Mr. Finisterre?
Someone from the hotel? She refused to say. I made a deal with
Clara: she never had to tell me who, but we had to leave Florida.

The next day, we found ourselves at the train station, with all
our clothes and savings.

Those first weeks alone were an education. The West was very
poor at that moment, owing to the Depression. But it was still
home to many aspiring and expiring millionaires, and we made it
our job to make their acquaintance. One aging oil speculator paid
for our meals and our transit and required only that we absorb his
memories; Clara nicknamed him the "allegedly legendary wit." He
had three genres of tale: business victories; sporting adventures
that ended in the death of mammals; and eulogies for his former
virility.

We met mining captains and fishing captains, whose whiskers

quivered like those of orphaned seals. The freckled heirs to timber fortunes. Glazy baronial types, with portentous and misguided
names: Romulus and Creon, who were pleased to invite us to gala
dinners and to use us as their gloating mirrors. In exchange for
this service, Clara and I helped ourselves to many fine items from
their houses. Clara had a magic satchel that seemed to expand
with our greed, and we stole everything it could swallow. Dessert
spoons, candlesticks, a poodle's jeweled collar. We strode out of
parties wearing our hostess's two-toned heels, woozy with adrena-
line. Crutched along by Clara's sturdy charm, I was swung through
doors that led to marmoreal courtyards and curtained salons and,
in many cases, master bedrooms, where my skin glowed under the
warm reefs of artificial lighting.

But winter hit, and our mining prospects dimmed consider-
ably. The Oregon coastline was laced with ghost towns; two paper
mills had closed, and whole counties had gone bankrupt. Men
were flocking inland to the mountains, where the rumor was that
the W.P.A. had work for construction teams. I told Clara that we
needed to follow them. So we thumbed a ride with a group of
work-starved Astoria teenagers who had heard about the Evergreen Lodge. Gold dust had drawn the first prospectors to these
mountains; those boys were after the weekly three-dollar salary.
But if government money was snowing onto Mount Joy, it had yet
to reach the town below. I'd made a bad miscalculation, suggesting
Lucerne. Our first night in town, Clara and I stared at our faces
superimposed over the dark storefront windows. In the boarding
house, we lay awake in the dark, pretending to believe in each
other's theatrical sleep; only our bellies were honest, growling at
each other. *Why did you bring us here?* Clara never dreamed of asking me. With her generous amnesia, she seemed already to have
forgotten that leaving home had been my idea.

Day after day, I told Clara not to worry: "We just need one good
night." We kept lying to each other, pretending that our hunger
was part of the game. Social graces get you meager results in a
shuttered town. We started haunting the bars around the C.C.C.
camps. The gaunt men there had next to nothing, and I felt a
pang lifting anything from them. Back in the boarding house, our
fingers spidering through wallets, we barely spoke to each other.
Clara and I began to disappear into adjacent rooms with strang-

ers. *She was better off before,* my mind whispered. For the first time since we'd left Florida, it occurred to me that our expedition might fail.

The chairlift ascended 7,250 feet—I remembered this figure from the newspapers. It had meant very little to me in the abstract. But now I felt our height in the soles of my feet. For whole minutes, we lost sight of the mountain in an onrush of mist. Finally, hands were waiting to catch us. They shot out of the darkness, gripping me under the arms, swinging me free of the lift. Our empty chairs were whipped around by the huge bull wheel before starting the long flight downhill. Hands, wonderfully warm hands, were supporting my back.

"Eugene?" I called, my lips numb.

"Who's *You-Jean?*" a strange voice chuckled.

The man who was not Eugene turned out to be an ursine mountaineer. With his lantern held high, he peered into our faces. I recognized the drab green C.C.C. uniform. He looked about our age to me, although his face kept blurring in the snow. The lantern, battery powered, turned us all jaundiced shades of gold. He had no clue, he said, about any *Eugene.* But he'd been stationed here to escort guests to the lodge.

Out of the corner of my eye, I saw tears freezing onto Clara's cheeks. Already she was fluffing her hair, asking this government employee how he'd gotten the enviable job of escorting beautiful women across the snows. How quickly she was able to snap back into character! I could barely move my frozen tongue, and I trudged along behind them.

"How old are you girls?" the C.C.C. man asked, and "Where are you from?," and every lie that we told him made me feel safer in his company.

The lodge was a true palace. Its shadow alone seemed to cover fifty acres of snow. Electricity raised a yellowish aura around it, so that the resort loomed like a bubble pitched against the mountain sky. Its A-frame reared out of the woods with the insensate authority of any redwood tree. Lights blazed in every window. As we drew closer, we saw faces peering down at us from several of these.

The terror was still with us. The speed of the ascent. My blood felt carbonated. Six feet ahead of us, Not-Eugene, whose name we'd failed to catch, swung the battery-powered lamp above his head and guided us through a whale-gray tunnel made of ice. "Quite the runway to a party, eh?"

Two enormous polished doors blew inward, and we found ourselves in a rustic ballroom, with fireplaces in each corner shooting heat at us. Amethyst chandeliers sent lakes of light rippling across the dance floor; the stone chimneys looked like indoor caves. Over the bar, a mounted boar grinned tuskily down at us. Men mobbed us, handing us fizzing drinks, taking our coats. Deluged by introductions, we started giggling, handing our hands around: "Nilson, Pauley, Villanueva, Obadiah, Acker . . ." Proudly, each identified himself to us as one of the C.C.C. "tree soldiers" who had built this fantasy resort: masons and blacksmiths and painters and foresters. They were boys, I couldn't help but think, boys our age. More faces rose out of the shadows, beaming hard. I guessed that, like us, they'd been waiting for this night to come for some time. Someone lit two cigarettes, passed them our way.

I shivered now with expectation. Clara threaded her hand through mine and squeezed down hard—time to dive into the sea. We'd plunged into stranger waters, socially. How many nights had we spent together, listening to tourists speak in tongues, relieved of their senses by Mrs. Finisterre's rum punch? Most of the boys were already drunk—I could smell that. Some rocked on their heels, desperate to start dancing.

They led us toward the bar. Feeling came flooding back into my skin, and I kept laughing at everything these young men were saying, elated to be indoors with them. Clara had to pinch me through the puffed sleeve of my dress:

"Aubby? Are we the only girls here?" Clara was right: where were the socialites we'd expected to see? The Oregon state forester, with his sullen red-lipped wife? The governor, the bank presidents? The ski experts from the Swiss Alps? Fifty-two paying guests, selected by lottery, had rooms waiting for them—we'd seen the list of names in Sunday's Oregon *Gazette*.

I turned to a man with wise amber eyes. He had unlined skin and a wispy blond mustache, but he smiled at us with the mellow despair of an old goat. "Excuse me, sir. When does the celebration start?"

Clara flanked him on the left, smiling just as politely.

"Are we the first guests to arrive?"

But now the goat's eyes flamed: "Whadda you talkin' about? This party is *under way*, lady. You got twenty-six dancing partners to choose from out there—that ain't enough?"

The strength of his fury surprised us; backing up, I bumped my hip against a bannister. My hand closed on what turned out to be a tiny beaver, a carved ornament. Each cedar newel post had one.

"The woodwork is beautiful."

He grinned, soothed by the compliment.

"My supervisor is none other than O. B. Dawson."

"And your name?"

The thought appeared unbidden: *Later, you'll want to know what to scream.*

"Mickey Loatch. Got a wife, girls, I'm chagrined to say. Got three kids already, back in Osprey. I'm here so they can eat." Casually, he explained to us the intensity of his loneliness, the loneliness of the entire corps. They'd been driven by truck, eight miles each day, from Camp Thistle to the deep woods. For months at a time, they lived away from their families. Drinking water came from Lister bags; the latrines were saddle trenches. Everyone was glad, glad, glad, he said, to have the work. "There wasn't anything for us, until the Emerald Lodge project came along."

Mr. Loatch, I'd been noticing, had the strangest eyes I'd ever seen. They were a brilliant dark yellow, the color of that magic metal, gold.

Swallowing, I asked the man, "Excuse me, but I'm a bit confused. Isn't this the *Evergreen* Lodge?"

"The Evergreen Lodge?" the man said, exposing a mouthful of chewed pink sausage. "Where's dat, gurrls?" He laughed at his own cartoony voice.

A suspicion was coming into focus, a dreadful theory; I tried to talk it away, but the harder I looked, the keener it became. A quick scan of the room confirmed what I must have registered and ignored when I first walked through those doors. Were all of the boys' eyes this same hue? Trying to stay calm, I gripped Clara's hand and spun her around like a weathervane: gold, gold, gold, gold.

"Oh my God, Clara."

"Aubby? What's wrong with you?"

"Clara," I murmured, "I think we may have taken the wrong lift."

Two lodges existed on Mount Joy. There was the Evergreen Lodge, which would be unveiled tonight, in a ceremony of extraordinary opulence, attended by the state forester and the president. Where Eugene was likely standing, on the balcony level, raising a flute for the champagne toast. There had once been, however, on the southeastern side of this same mountain, a second structure. This place lived on in local memory as demolished hope, as unconsummated blueprint. It was the failed original, crushed by an avalanche two years earlier, the graveyard of twenty-six workers from Company 609 of the Oregon Civilian Conservation Corps.

"Unwittingly," our landlady, who loved a bloody and unjust story, had told us over a pancake breakfast, "those workers were building their own casket." With tobogganing runs and a movie theater, and more windows than Versailles, it was to have been even more impressive than the Evergreen Lodge. But the unfinished lodge had been completely covered in the collapse.

Mickey Loatch was still steering us around, showing off the stonework.

"Have you gals been to the Cloud Cap Inn? That's hitched to the mountain with wire cables. See, what we done is—"

"Mr. Loatch?" Swilling a drink, I steadied my voice. "How late does the chairlift run?"

"Oh dear." He pursed his lips. "You girls gotta be somewhere? I'm afraid you're stuck with us, at least until morning. You're the last we let up. They shut that lift down until dawn."

Next to me, I heard Clara in my ear: "Are you crazy? We just got here, and you're talking about leaving? Do you know how rude you sound?"

"They're dead."

"What are you talking about? Who's dead?"

"Everyone. Everyone but us."

Clara turned from me, her jaw tensing. At a nearby table, five green-clad boys were watching our conversation play out with detached interest, as if it were a sport they rarely followed. Clara wet her lips and smiled down at them, drumming her red nails on their table's glossy surface.

"This is so beautiful!" she cooed.

All five of the dead boys blushed.

"Excuse us," she fluttered. "Is there a powder room? My friend here is just a mess!"

THE LADIES ROOM read a bronzed sign posted on an otherwise undistinguished door. At other parties, this room had always been our sanctuary. Once the door was shut, we stared at each other in the mirror, transferring knowledge across the glass. Her eyes were still brown, I noted with relief, and mine were blue. I worried that I might start screaming, but I bit back my panic, and I watched Clara do the same for me. "Your nose," I finally murmured. Blood poured in bright bars down her upper lip.

"I guess we must be really high up," she said, and started to cry.

"Shh, shh, shh . . ."

I wiped at the blood with a tissue.

"See?" I showed it to her. "At least we *are,* ah, at least we can still . . ."

Clara sneezed violently, and we stared at the reddish globules on the glass, which stood out with terrifying lucidity against the flat, unreal world of the mirror.

"What are we going to do, Aubby?"

I shook my head; a horror flooded through me until I could barely breathe.

Ordinarily, I would have handled the logistics of our escape —picked locks, counterfeited tickets. Clara would have corrected my lipstick and my posture, encouraging me to look more like a willowy seductress and less like a baseball umpire. But tonight it was Clara who formulated the plan. We had to tiptoe around the Emerald Lodge. We had to dim our own lights. And, most critical to our survival here, according to Clara: we had to persuade our dead hosts that we believed they were alive.

At first, I objected; I thought these workers deserved to know the truth about themselves.

"Oh?" Clara said. "How principled of you."

And what did I think was going to happen, she asked, if we told the men what we knew?

"I don't know. They'll let us go?"

Clara shook her head.

"Think about it, Aubby—what's keeping this place together?"

We had to be very cautious, very *amenable,* she argued. We couldn't challenge our hosts on any of their convictions. The Emerald Lodge was a real place, and they were breathing safely inside it. We had to admire their handiwork, she said. Continue to exclaim over the lintel arches and the wrought-iron grates, the beams and posts. As if they were real, as if they were solid. Clara begged me to do this. Who knew what might happen if we roused them from their dreaming? The C.C.C. workers' ghosts had built this place, Clara said; we were at their mercy. If the men discovered they were dead, we'd die with them. We needed to believe in their rooms until dawn—just long enough to escape them.

"Same plan as ever," Clara said. "How many hundreds of nights have we staked a claim at a party like this?"

Zero, I told her. On no occasion had we been the only living people.

"We'll charm them. We'll drink a little, dance a little. And then, come dawn, we'll escape down the mountain."

Somebody started pounding on the door: "Hey! What's the holdup, huh? Somebody fall in? You girls wanna dance or what?"

"Almost ready!" Clara shouted brightly.

On the dance floor, the amber-eyed ghosts were as awkward and as touching, as unconvincingly brash as any boys in history on the threshold of a party. Innocent hopefuls with their hats pressed to their chests.

"I feel sorry for them, Clara! They have no idea."

"Yes. It's terribly sad."

Her face hardened into a stony expression I'd seen on her only a handful of times in our career as prospectors.

"When we get back down the mountain, we can feel sad," she said. "Right now, we are going to laugh at all their jokes. We are going to celebrate this stupendous American landmark, the Emerald Lodge."

Clara's mother owned an etiquette book for women, the first chapter of which advises, *Make Your Date Feel Like He Is the Life of the Party!* People often mistake laughing girls for foolish creatures. They mistake our merriment for nerves or weakness, or the hysterical looning of desire. Sometimes, it is that. But not tonight. We could hold our wardens hostage too in this careful way. Everybody needs an audience.

At other parties, our hosts had always been very willing to believe us when we feigned interest in their endless rehearsals of the
past. They used our black pupils to polish up their antique tri-
umphs. Even an ogre-ish salmon-boat captain, a bachelor again at
eighty-seven, was convinced that we were both in love with him.
Nobody ever invited Clara and me to a gala to hear our honest
opinions.

At the bar, a calliope of tiny glasses was waiting for me: honey
and cherry and lemon. Flavored liquors, imported from Italy, the
bartender smiled shyly. "Delicious!" I exclaimed, touching each to
my lips. Clara, meanwhile, had been swept onto the dance floor.
With her mauve lipstick in place and her glossy hair smoothed, she
was shooting colors all around the room. Could you scare a dead
boy with the vibrancy of your life? "Be careful," I mouthed, motioning her into the shadows. Boys in green beanies kept sidling
up to her, vying for her attention. It hurt my heart to see them
trying. Of course, news of their own death had not reached them
—how could that news get up the mountain, to where the workers
were buried under snow?

Perched on the barstool, I plaited my hair. I tried to think up
some good jokes.

"Hullo. Care if I join you?"

This dead boy introduced himself as Lee Covey. Black bangs
flopped onto his brow. He had the small, recessed, comically de-
spondent face of a pug dog. I liked him immediately. And he was
so funny that I did not have to theatricalize my laughter. Lee's
voluble eyes made conversation feel almost unnecessary; his con-
viction that he was alive was contagious.

"I'm not much of a dancer," Lee apologized abruptly. As if to
prove his point, he sent a glass crashing off the bar.

"Oh, that's okay. I'm not, either. See my friend out there?" I
asked. "In the green dress? She's the graceful one."

But Lee kept his golden eyes fixed on me, and soon it became
difficult to say who was the mesmerist and who was succumbing to
hypnosis. His Camp Thistle stories made me laugh so hard that I
worried about falling off the barstool. Lee had a rippling laugh,
like summer thunder; by this point I was very drunk. Lee started in
on his family's sorry history: "Daddy the Dwindler, he spent it all,
he lost everything we had, he turned me out of the house. It fell to
me to support the family . . ."

I nodded, recognizing his story's contours. How had the other workers washed up here? I wondered. Did they remember their childhoods, their lives before the avalanche? Or had those memories been buried inside them?

It was the loneliest feeling, to watch the group of dead boys dancing. Coupled off, they held on to each other's shoulders. "For practice," Lee explained. They steered each other uncertainly around the hexagonal floor, swaying on currents of song.

"Say, how about it?" Lee said suddenly. "Let's give it a whirl—you only live once."

Seconds later, we were on the floor, jitterbugging in the center of the hall.

"Oh, oh, oh," he crooned.

When Lee and I kissed, it felt no different from kissing a living mouth. We sank into the rhythms of horns and strings and harmonicas, performed by a live band of five dead mountain brothers. With the naive joy of all these ghosts, they tootled their glittery instruments at us.

A hand grabbed my shoulder.

"May I cut in?"

Clara dragged me off the floor.

Back in the powder room, Clara's eyes looked shiny, raccoon-beady. She was exhausted, I realized. Some grins are only reflexes, but others are courageous acts—Clara's was the latter. The clock had just chimed ten-thirty. The party showed no signs of slowing. At least the clock is moving, I pointed out. We tried to conjure a picture of the risen sun, piercing the thousand windows of the Emerald Lodge.

"You doing okay?"

"I have certainly been better."

"We're going to make it down the mountain."

"Of course we are."

Near the western staircase, Lee waited with a drink in hand. Shadows pooled unnaturally around his feet; they reminded me of peeling paint. If you stared too long, they seemed to curl slightly up from the floorboards.

"Jean! There you are!"

At the sound of my real name, I felt electrified—hadn't I introduced myself by a pseudonym? Clara and I had a telephone book of false names. It was how we dressed for parties. We chose alter egos for each other, like jewelry.

"It's Candy, actually." I smiled politely. "Short for Candace."

"Whatever you say, *Jean*," Lee said, playing lightly with my brace-let.

"Who told you that? Did my friend tell you that?"

"You did."

I blinked slowly at Lee, watching his grinning face come in and out of focus.

I'd had plenty more to drink, and I realized that I didn't re-member half the things we'd talked about. What else, I wondered, had I let slip?

"How did you get that name, huh? It's a really pretty name, Jeannie."

I was unused to being asked personal questions. Lee put his arms around me, and then, unbelievably, I heard my voice in the darkness, telling the ghost a true story.

Jean, I told him, is what I prefer to go by. In Florida, most eve-rybody called me Aubby.

My parents named me Aubergine. They wanted me to have a glamorous name. It was a luxury they could afford to give me, a spell of protection. "Aubergine" was a word that my father had learned during his wartime service, the French word for "dawn," he said. A name like that, they felt, would envelop me in an aura of mystery, from swaddling to shroud. One night, on a rare trip to a restaurant, we learned the truth from a fellow diner, a bald, genteel eavesdropper.

"Aubergine," he said thoughtfully. "What an *interesting* name."

We beamed at him eagerly, my whole family.

"It is, of course, the French word for 'eggplant.'"

"Oh, darn!" my mother said, unable to contain her sorrow.

"Of course!" roared old Dad.

But we were a family long accustomed to reversals of fortune; in fact, my father had gone bankrupt misapprehending various facts about the dog track and his own competencies.

"It suits you," the bald diner said, smiling and turning the pages of his newspaper. "You are a little fat, yes? Like an eggplant!"

"We call her Jean for short," my mother had smoothly replied.

*

Clara was always teasing me. "Don't fall in love with anybody," she'd say, and then we'd laugh for longer than the joke really warranted, because this scenario struck us both as so unlikely. But as I leaned against this ghost I felt my life falling into place. It was the spotlight of his eyes, those radiant beams, that gently drew motes from the past out of me—and I loved this. He had got me talking, and now I didn't want to shut up. His eyes grew wider and wider, golden nets woven with golden fibers. I told him about my father's suicide, my mother's death. At the last second, I bit my tongue, but I'd been on the verge of telling him about Clara's bruises, those mute blue coordinates. Not to solicit Lee's help—what could this phantom do? No, merely to keep him looking at me.

Hush, Aubby, I heard in Clara's tiny, moth-fluttery voice, which was immediately incinerated by the hot pleasure of Lee's gaze.

We kissed a second time. I felt our teeth click together; two warm hands cupped my cheeks. But when he lifted his face, his anguish leaped out at me. His wild eyes were like bees trapped on the wrong side of a window, bouncing along the glass. "You . . ." he began. He stroked at my cheek. "You feel . . ." Very delicately, he tried kissing me again. "You taste . . ." Some bewildered comment trailed off into silence. One hand smoothed over my dress, while the other rose to claw at his pale throat.

"How's that?" he whispered hoarsely in my ear. "Does that feel all right?"

Lee was so much in the dark. I had no idea how to help him. I wondered how honest I would have wanted Lee to be with me, if he were in my shoes. *Put him out of his misery,* country people say of sick dogs. But Lee looked very happy. Excited, even, about the future.

"Should we go upstairs, Jean?"

"But where did Clara go?" I kept murmuring.

It took great effort to remember her name.

"Did she disappear on you?" Lee said, and winked. "Do you think she's found her way upstairs too?"

Crossing the room, we spotted her. Her hands were clasped around the hog stubble of a large boy's neck, and they were swaying in the center of the hexagon. I waved at her, trying to get her attention, and she stared right through me. A smile played on her face, while the chandeliers plucked up the red in her hair, strumming even the subtlest colors out of her.

Grinning, Lee lifted a hand to his black eyebrow in a mock salute. His bloodless hand looked thin as paper. I had a sharp memory of standing at a bay window, in Florida, and feeling the night sky change direction on me—no longer lapping at the horizon but rolling inland. Something was pouring toward me now, a nothingness exhaled through the floury membrane of the boy. If Lee could see the difference in the transparency of our splayed hands, he wasn't letting on.

Now Clara was kissing her boy's plush lips. Her fingers were still knitted around his tawny neck. *Clara, Clara, we have abandoned our posts.* We shouldn't have kissed them; we shouldn't have taken that black water onboard. Lee may not have known that he was dead, but my body did; it seemed to be having some kind of stupefied reaction to the kiss. I felt myself sinking fast, sinking far below thought. The two boys swept us toward the stairs with a courtly synchronicity, their uniformed bodies tugging us into the shadows, where our hair and our skin and our purple and emerald party dresses turned suddenly blue, like two candles blown out.

And now I watched as Clara flowed up the stairs after her stocky dancing partner, laughing with genuine abandon, her neck flung back and her throat exposed. I followed right behind her, but I could not close the gap. I watched her ascent, just as I had on the lift. Groggily, I saw them moving down a posy-wallpapered corridor. Even squinting, I could not make out the watery digits on the doors. All these doors were, of course, identical. One swung open, then shut, swallowing Clara. I doubted we would find each other again. By now, however, I felt very calm. I let Lee lead me by the wrist, like a child, only my bracelets shaking.

Room 409 had natural wood walls, glowing with a piney shine in the low light. Lee sat down on a chair and tugged off his work boots, flushed with the yellow avarice of four a.m. Darkness flooded steadily out of him, and I absorbed it. "Jean," he kept saying, a word that sounded so familiar, although its meaning now escaped me. I covered his mouth with my mouth. I sat on the ghost boy's lap, kissing his neck, pretending to feel a pulse. Eventually, grumbling an apology, Lee stood and disappeared into the bathroom. I heard a faucet turn on; Lord knows what came pouring out of it. The room had a queen bed, and I pulled back a corner of the soft cotton quilt. It was so beautiful, edelweiss white. I slid in with my dress still pinned to me. I could not stop yawning; seconds from now, I'd drop off. I never wanted to go back out there, I decided. Why lie about this? There was no longer any chairlift waiting to carry us home, was there? No mountain, no fool's-gold moon. The earth we'd left felt like a photograph. And was it such a terrible thing, to live at the lodge?

Something was descending slowly, like a heavy theater curtain, inside my body; I felt my will to know the truth ebbing into a happy, warm insanity. We could all be dead—why not? We could be in love, me and a dead boy. We could be sisters here, Clara and I, equally poor and equally beautiful.

Lee had come back and was stroking my hair onto the pillow. "Want to take a little nap?" he asked.

I had never wanted anything more. But then I looked down at my red fingernails and noticed a tiny chip in the polish, exposing the translucent blue enamel. Clara had painted them for me yesterday morning, before the party—eons ago. *Clara,* I remembered. *What was happening to Clara?* I dug out of the heavy coverlet, struggling up. At precisely that moment, the door began to rattle in its frame; outside, a man was calling for Lee.

"He's here! He's here! He's here!" a baritone voice growled happily. "Goddamn it, Lee, button up and get downstairs!"

Lee rubbed his golden eyes and palmed his curls. I stared at him uncomprehendingly.

"I regret the interruption, my dear. But this we cannot miss." He grinned at me, exposing a mouthful of holes. "You wanna have your picture taken, don'tcha?"

Clara and I found each other on the staircase. What had happened to her, in her room? That's a lock I can't pick. Even on ordinary nights, we often split up, and afterward in the boarding house we never discussed those unreal intervals. On our prospecting expeditions, whatever doors we closed stayed shut. Clara had her arm around her date, who looked doughier than I recalled, his round face almost featureless, his eyebrows vanished; even the point of his green toothpick seemed blurred. Lee ran up to greet him, and we hung back while the two men continued downstairs, racing each other to reach the photographer. This time we did not try to disguise our relief.

"I was falling asleep!" Clara said. "And I wanted to sleep so badly, Aubby, but then I remembered you were here somewhere too."

"I was falling asleep," I said, "but then I remembered your face."

Clara redid my bun, and I straightened her hem. We were fine, we promised each other.

"I didn't get anything," Clara said. "But I'm not leaving empty-handed."

I gaped at her. Was she still talking about prospecting?

"You can't steal from this place."

Clara had turned to inspect a sculpted flower blooming from an iron railing; she tugged at it experimentally, as if she thought she might free it from the bannister.

"Clara, wake up. That's not—"

"No? That's not why you brought me here?"

She flicked her eyes up at me, her gaze limpid and accusatory. And I felt I'd become fluent in the language of eyes; now I saw what she'd known all along. What she'd been swallowing back on our prospecting trips, what she'd never once screamed at me, in the freezing boarding house: *You use me. Every party, you bait the hook, and I dangle. I let them, I am eaten, and what do I get? Some scrap metal?*

"I'm sorry, Clara . . ."

My apology opened outward, a blossoming horror. I'd used her bruises to justify leaving Florida. I'd used her face to open doors. Greed had convinced me I could take care of her up here, and then I'd disappeared on her. How long had Clara known what I was doing? I'd barely known myself.

But Clara, still holding my hand, pointed at the clock. It was five a.m.

"Dawn is coming." She gave me a wide, genuine smile. "We are going to get home."

Downstairs, the C.C.C. boys were shuffling around the dance floor, positioning themselves in a triangular arrangement. The tallest men knelt down, and the shorter men filed behind them. When they saw us watching from the staircase, they waved.

"Where you girls been? The photographer is *here*."

The fires were still burning, the huge logs unconsumed. Even the walls, it seemed, were trembling in anticipation. This place wanted to go on shining in our living eyes, was that it? The dead boys feasted on our attention, but so did the entire structure.

Several of the dead boys grabbed us and hustled us toward the posed and grinning rows of uniformed workers. We spotted a tripod in the corner of the lodge, a man doubled over, his head swallowed by the black cover. He was wearing a flamboyant costume: a ragged black cape, made from the same smocky material as the camera cover, and bright-red satin trousers.

"Picture time!" his voice boomed.

Now the true light of the Emerald Lodge began to erupt in rhythmic bursts. We winced at the metallic flash, the sun above his neck. The workers stiffened, their lean faces plumped by grins. It was an inversion of the standard firing squad: two dozen men hunched before the photographer and his mounted cannon. "*Cheese!*" the C.C.C. boys cried.

We squinted against the radiant detonations. These blasts were much brighter and louder than any shutter click on earth.

With each flash, the men grew more definite: their chins sharpening, cheeks ripening around their smiles. Dim brows darkened to black arcs; the gold of their eyes deepened, as if each face were receiving a generous pour of whiskey. Was it life that these ghosts were drawing from the camera's light? No, these flashes—they imbued the ghosts with something else.

"Do not let him shoot you," I hissed, grabbing Clara by the elbow. We ran for cover. Every time the flashbulb illuminated the room, I flinched. "Did he get you? Did he get me?"

With an animal instinct, we knew to avoid that light. We could not let the photographer fix us in the frame, we could not let him capture us on whatever film still held them here, dancing jerkily on the hexagonal floor. *If that happens, we are done for,* I thought. *We are here forever.*

With his unlidded eye, the photographer spotted us where we had crouched behind the piano. Bent at the waist, his head cloaked by the wrinkling purple-black cover, he rotated the camera. Then he waggled his fingers at us, motioning us into the frame.

"Smile, ladies," Mickey Loatch ordered, as we darted around the cedar tables.

We never saw his face, but he was hunting us. This devil—excuse me, let us continue to call him "the party photographer," as I do not want to frighten anyone unduly—spun the tripod on its rolling wheels, his hairy hands gripping its sides, the cover flapping onto his shoulders like a strange pleated wig. His single blue

lens kept fixing on our bodies. Clara dove low behind the wicker
chairs and pulled me after her.

The C.C.C. boys who were assembled on the dance floor, meanwhile, stayed glacially frozen. Smiles floated muzzily around their
faces. A droning rose from the room, a sound like dragonflies in
summer, and I realized that we were hearing the men's groaning
effort to stay in focus: to flood their faces with ersatz blood, to hold
still, hold still, and smile.

Then the chair tipped; one of our pursuers had lifted Clara up,
kicking and screaming, and began to carry her back to the dance
floor, where men were shifting to make a place for her.

"Front and center, ladies," the company captain called urgently.
"Fix your dress, dear. The straps have gotten all twisted."

I had a terrible vision of Clara caught inside the shot with them,
her eyes turning from brown to umber to the deathlessly sparkling
gold.

"Stop!" I yelled. "Let her go! She—"

She's alive, I did not risk telling them.

"She does not photograph well!"

With aqueous indifference, the camera lifted its eye.

"Listen, forgive us, but we cannot be in your photograph!"

"Let *go!*" Clara said, cinched inside an octopus of restraining
arms, every one of them pretending that this was still a game.

We used to pledge, with great passion, always to defend each
other. We meant it too. These were easy promises to make, when
we were safely at the boarding house; but on this mountain even
breathing felt dangerous.

But Clara pushed back. Clara saved us.

She directed her voice at every object in the lodge, screaming
at the very rafters. Gloriously, her speech gurgling with saliva and
blood and everything wet, everything living, she began to howl at
them, the dead ones. She foamed red, my best friend, forming the
words we had been stifling all night, the spell-bursting ones:

"It's done, gentlemen. It's over. Your song ended. You are news
font; you are characters. I could read you each your own obituary.
None of this—"

"Shut her up," a man growled.

"Shut up, shut up!" several others screamed.

She was chanting, one hand at her throbbing temple: "None of
this, none of this, none of this *is!*"

Some men were thumbing their ears shut. Some had braced themselves in the doorframes, as they teach the children of the West to do during earthquakes. I resisted the urge to cover my own ears as she bansheed back at the shocked ghosts:

"Two years ago, there was an avalanche at your construction site. It was terrible, a tragedy. We were all so sorry . . ."

She took a breath.

"You are dead."

Her voice grew gentle, almost maternal—it was like watching the wind drop out of the world, flattening a full sail. Her shoulders fell, her palms turned out.

"You were all buried with this lodge."

Their eyes turned to us, incredulous. Hard and yellow, dozens of spiny armadillos. After a second, the C.C.C. company burst out laughing. Some men cried tears, they were howling so hard at Clara. Lee was among them, and he looked much changed, his face as smooth and flexibly white as an eel's belly.

These men—they didn't believe her!

And why should we ever have expected them to believe us, two female nobodies, two intruders? For these were the master carpenters, the master stonemasons and weavers, the master self-deceivers, the ghosts.

"Dead," one sad man said, as if testing the word out.

"Dead. Dead. Dead," his friends repeated, quizzically.

But the sound was a shallow production, as if each man were scratching at topsoil with the point of a shovel. Aware, perhaps, that if he dug with a little more dedication he would find his body lying breathless under this world's surface.

"Dead." "Dead."

"Dead."

"Dead."

"Dead."

"Dead."

They croaked like pond frogs, all across the ballroom. "Dead" was a foreign word that the boys could pronounce perfectly, soberly, and matter-of-factly, without comprehending its meaning.

One or two of them, however, exchanged a glance; I saw a burly blacksmith cut eyes at the ruby-cheeked trumpet player. It was a guileful look, a what-can-be-done look.

So they knew; or they almost knew; or they'd buried the knowledge of their deaths, and we had exhumed it. Who can say what the dead do or do not know? Perhaps the knowledge of one's death, ceaselessly swallowed, is the very food you need to become a ghost. They burned that knowledge up like whale fat and continued to shine on.

But then a quaking began to ripple across the ballroom floor. A chandelier, in its handsome zigzag frame, burst into a spray of glass above us. One of the pillars, three feet wide, cracked in two. Outside, from all corners, we heard a rumbling, as if the world were gathering its breath.

"Oh, God," I heard one of them groan. "It's happening again."

My eyes met Clara's, as they always do at parties. She did not have to tell me: *Run.*

On our race through the lodge, in all that chaos and din, Clara somehow heard another sound. A bright chirping. A sound like gold coins being tossed up, caught, and fisted. It stopped her cold. The entire building was shaking on its foundations, but through the tremors she spotted a domed cage, hanging in the foyer. On a tiny stirrup, a yellow bird was swinging. The cage was a wrought-iron skeleton, the handiwork of phantoms, but the bird, we both knew instantly, was real. It was agitating its wings in the polar air, as alive as we were. Its shadow was denser than anything in that ice palace. Its song split our eardrums. Its feathers burned into our retinas, rich with solar color, and its small body was stuffed with life.

At the Evergreen Lodge, on the opposite side of the mountain, two twelve-foot doors, designed and built by the C.C.C., stand sentry against the outside air—seven hundred pounds of hand-cut ponderosa pine, from Oregon's primeval woods. Inside the Emerald Lodge, we found their phantom twins, the dream originals. Those doors still worked, thank God. We pushed them open. Bright light, real daylight, shot onto our faces.

The sun was rising. The chairlift, visible across a pillowcase of fresh snow, was running.

We sprinted for it. Golden sunlight painted the steel cables. We raced across the platform, jumping for the chairs, and I will never know how fast or how far we flew to get back to earth. In all our years of prospecting in the West, this was our greatest heist. Clara opened her satchel and lifted the yellow bird onto her lap, and I heard it shrieking the whole way down the mountain.

YUKO SAKATA

On This Side

FROM *Iowa Review*

TORU FOUND A GIRL sitting on the stairs in the midsummer heat when he came home from an early shift. Even from half a block away, she stood out against his decrepit apartment building. She sat, hugging her bare knees, in white cotton shorts, her long dark hair draped forward over both shoulders. The sleeves of her unseasonable denim jacket were rolled up to just below her elbows. There was a large canvas bag next to her, blocking the staircase. Through the afternoon heat everything shimmered uncertainly, and for a second Toru wondered if she wasn't an apparition. The insistent buzz of the cicadas created a kind of thick silence, numbing his senses.

Upon noticing him, the girl looked up with a hopefulness that made Toru feel apologetic. Suddenly he could smell his own body. He had come from making the rounds restocking vending machines and hadn't bothered to shower at the office when he'd changed out of the uniform. With his eyes to the ground, he tried to squeeze past her.

"Toru-kun." The girl stood up. Her voice sounded oddly thick.

For a moment they stood awkwardly together on the stairs. A mixture of soap and sweat wafted from her. Up close, Toru saw that her face was meticulously made up, her skin carefully primed, and her expectant eyes accentuated with clean black lines. He was slow to recognize what was underneath. But then he felt his heart skip a beat.

"Masato?" he said.

"Hello." As though in relief, she held out her hand, and Toru shook it automatically. Her fingers were bony but solid in his palm. "I go by Saki now."

"Saki?"

More than ten years ago, in junior high school, she had been a boy.

Toru tentatively invited her, or him, or whatever Saki was now, into his one-room apartment on the second floor. He didn't want to be seen with her on the stairs. His neighbors were mostly single men of meager means like himself, and with only thin walls between them, everyone did his best to keep to himself.

Saki took off her sandals and walked in, not minding the dusty tatami floor bleached from years of sunlight. Her toenails were painted the color of pomegranate. Next to the entrance were a metal sink, a two-burner stove, and an antiquated fridge that constituted Toru's kitchen. The opposite wall had a closet with sliding paper doors where he kept his clothes and bedding. There was a toilet in each apartment, but the bath was shared. A small, tilting bookshelf and a folding coffee table were the only pieces of furniture, and the white canvas bag Saki flopped down in the corner became the third-largest item in the room.

Saki opened and closed the bathroom door and walked around the room once, as though giving it a quick inspection. She then went to the sink and tried the faucet. The air in the small room felt even more stagnant than usual. Toru considered offering her something cold to drink, but he didn't want this unexpected visit to draw out.

"Sorry I don't even have AC," he said.

"Oh, this is just fine," Saki said, and bent down to turn on the fan next to the coffee table. "I don't like AC anyway."

Toru glanced at the back of her shapely calves and noted a long-healed scar forming a startling trench on the side of her right knee. The first thing he had felt on the staircase was a knot forming in his stomach, a forgotten seed of guilt he didn't care to inspect, and now it was threatening to grow. He hadn't thought of his classmate in years. But the longer he looked at her, this Saki, the more he realized that he wasn't as baffled as he might have been by the transformation. He remembered the slight neck that seemed to reach perpetually forward and the dense, long eyelashes that used to cast melancholy shadows over the eyes. She was, and had been, pretty.

"So." Toru cleared his throat. He had been staring. "How did you find me?"

"Oh, I just looked you up," Saki said. "There are ways. It's not that hard. Can I stay with you for a while?"

"Excuse me?"

"I need a place to stay. Just for a while."

Toru looked at her blankly. He was still in his shoes, standing just inside the door. "You mean here?" he said. "Why? What do you mean?"

"I'm in this predicament. A relationship problem, so to speak."

Toru felt the knot in his stomach become denser as he watched Saki drift to the open window. The only view he had was a narrow slice of southern sky between the walls of the adjacent buildings and the corrugated rooftop of a warehouse, but Saki gazed out as though at a refreshing country vista. Above her head hung boxers and socks and a thin, worn towel that Toru had hand-washed that morning.

"Well," Toru said. "I'm very sorry to hear that. I do feel sorry. But I wasn't expecting—I'm sure this isn't your best option. I mean, look at this place. There's barely room for myself."

"Oh, this is totally fine. I'm not particular."

Toru sighed. "Look, you don't understand. I'm afraid it's not fine," he said. "I have my own problems. For one thing, I have a girlfriend."

"That's a problem?" Saki tilted her head. "She's a jealous type?"

"No, no." Toru flinched. "That's not how I meant it. See, you don't even know me at this point. I'm barely managing day to day here. I'm surely not the best person to turn to in your situation."

"You don't know my situation yet. You haven't asked."

Although Saki's tone was matter-of-fact, simply pointing out his mistake, Toru was taken back by the truth of this.

"I don't want to pry," he said.

"It's really just for a while," Saki said, as though patiently reassuring a child. "I'll of course cook and clean."

"Don't you have other friends?" Toru said. "Does your family know you are here?"

Saki frowned at him. "If I had a family who cared where I was, don't you think I would go stay with them?"

When Toru failed to respond, Saki let out a small sigh and dropped her gaze to the floor.

"Here's the thing," she said. "I just got out of the hospital and I'm broke. I need a little time to sort things out."

"What, are you sick?" Toru said. "What happened?"

Saki bounced on her heels for a moment, fiddling with the hem of her shorts. "I was injured. Stabbed, actually, by my boyfriend." She paused, searching for something on his face. "He didn't know. That I was, you know. So."

Toru blinked. Then he blinked again.

"If you want, I can show you the wound." Saki grabbed the bottom of her shirt.

"Wait." Before he could think, Toru found himself across the room, still in his shoes, and seizing her wrists. Whatever was behind the fabric, he wasn't ready to see.

Saki was a horrible cook. When Toru came home the next day, she had prepared some curry, but it was straight out of a package. The vegetables were undercooked, the onion still tangy. She had added too little water, and the paste was not evenly dissolved. The rice was dry, even though she had used the same rice cooker Toru used every day. He was baffled that anyone could mess up the simplest of dishes.

"You shouldn't worry about cooking," Toru said, eating out of politeness and dripping with sweat. "You're—a guest, I suppose."

"Oh, it's no trouble." Saki had eaten less than a third of her bowl and was poking the vegetables around while Toru tediously worked on his. "It's the least I can do."

"No, really," Toru said. "Look, I'll prepare something simple after I come home. Okay?"

"Okay," Saki said. "If you insist."

Saki hadn't left the apartment all day. When Toru asked, she said she had mostly slept, read some, and listened to the radio. She then added, brightly, "You can't imagine how much I appreciate this. This is exactly what I needed."

The night before, he had conceded his thin futon to Saki and slept on top of his old sleeping bag. He couldn't bring himself to kick her out. Whatever sort of life Saki had lived since Toru had last known her he didn't feel inclined to imagine, but he couldn't help suspecting he'd had a hand in it. That life now all seemed to fit into her plain canvas bag. Everything that came out of it went back into it. If he were to pick up the bag and take it out like the trash, there would be no trace of her left behind.

For a few months at the beginning of eighth grade, Toru's life had revolved around Masato. Before his childhood friend Kyoko had singled out Masato as her crush a few weeks into school, Toru hadn't even taken note of him. Masato had been a quiet, fragile-looking boy who seemed to prefer solitude. Toru could only now surmise that he might have tickled maternal instinct in some girls. ("Don't you think he's adorable?" Kyoko had said. Toru had to search his mind to vaguely picture Masato's face.)

Earlier that spring, Toru had watched with bewilderment as Kyoko blossomed into something mysterious and fragrant next to him. He was desperately hoping that she would see a similar transformation in him and realize that he was no longer the silly neighborhood kid she could boss around. But Toru was her best friend. It had been to him that she confided her feelings for Masato. It had been he who had to help her get close to this taciturn classmate. He was enlisted to create many awkward coincidences for her to bump into Masato. He had to ask him to lunch, where Kyoko would casually join; find out his birthday and shoe size; and walk home with him so Kyoko would know which route he took.

For those few months, Toru hated Masato.

"What is your girlfriend like?" Saki said now, as they sat drinking beer after dinner. "Is she a good cook?"

Once in a while, Toru got to take home canned drinks that had passed the sell-by dates. If the timing was right, he got to pick a box of beer. It was one of the very few perks of his job.

"I actually don't know," Toru said. "She's never cooked for me. We never meet at either of our places."

"Why not?"

Toru didn't own a TV and was playing a movie on his old laptop, to have something when the conversation lulled. It was a black-and-white Kurosawa, something his girlfriend had lent him.

"Well, obviously this is not a place to bring a woman for a date," he said. He turned the beer can in his hands several times. "And she has a family."

There was a pause. "She's married?"

"Yes."

"Children?"

"Two. Boys, I think." Toru sneaked a look at Saki's face to gauge her reaction. She had her eyes on the computer screen, though he couldn't tell if she was watching. "So we meet at a hotel. Just a couple of times a month," he said.

"And eat at restaurants," she said.

He nodded. And he willed the conversation to cease there. His older girlfriend paid for meals and rooms most of the time, with her husband's money. He was not proud of it.

The evening air outside the open window smelled vibrant, as though the intensity of the heat had been skimmed off its surface and all the living things underneath were finally allowed to breathe. Occasionally trains went by just a few blocks away, but they sounded strangely muted and distant.

"Speaking of restaurants," Saki said, three beers later, "I have this recurring dream."

"About a restaurant?" Toru glanced at her. Having given up on the movie, she was leaning on the low windowsill, her elbow sticking outside and her cheek resting on the back of her hand. "A nightmare, no doubt."

"I don't know if it's a nightmare, quite. But I've had it for years. I'm in this crowded restaurant, with or without other people, the details always change. I place an order, but after waiting for a long time, I realize I'm not getting the food. So I go look for my server and find the kitchen closed in the back. I return to a different, dark room, and my food is on the table with plastic wrap over it, and there's a note stuck on it. Like a Post-it note. This makes me very sad, and the next moment I find myself in an empty house."

Toru waited. "And then? What happens in the empty house?"

"That's it," she said. "That's the end."

"Saki." Toru tapped her shoulder, but she didn't budge. While he finished the movie, she had fallen asleep on the floor. Her long hair hid most of her face, but he could see that her cheek was flushed and her mouth was open.

Toru moved the coffee table to make room for the futon next to her and rolled her over onto the sheet. She was alarmingly light. He observed her shoulder move up and down almost imperceptibly with her breathing, and noticed the imprint left on her temple from the floor.

The bottom of her shirt had ridden up a little. Toru was tempted for a moment to peek, to confirm the stab wound and, more importantly, to see how the subtle but unmistakable roundness of her breasts worked. Whether they were real.

Once, after walking home together, Toru had asked to use the bathroom at Masato's house. No one was home, and Masato invited him to stay for a snack. While Masato went to get things from the kitchen, Toru used the bathroom and poked around, just so he could report back to Kyoko. Masato's room, which he found down the hallway, was dim, with the curtains mostly drawn, and surprisingly messy. Strewn clothes covered most of the available surfaces, with textbooks and magazines and candy wrappers entangled in them, while the cream-colored walls remained strangely unadorned. There was something odd about the room, though Toru couldn't immediately put a finger on it. And then he saw what it was. Among the formless piles of clothes were several pairs of girls' underwear.

Saki twitched her fingers in her sleep. Toru stood up, picked up the empty cans, and turned the lights off.

"Don't you want to get out a bit?" Toru said to Saki a few days later. They had finished breakfast, and he was rinsing the plates. "Walk around or something? I guess you're still recovering, but I'm sure it'd feel better than sitting in this dingy room all day."

Saki looked up from the fashion magazine she was leafing through. In the evenings she would go to the convenience store near the station while Toru cooked dinner—the only time she would go out—and always come home with a new magazine. A small stack was starting to form on the floor beside the coffee table.

"I don't have a key," she said.

She was sitting on the floor in a pair of jean shorts, leaning against the table with one leg folded at her side and the other one, the one with the old scar, stretched out. Though they had just eaten, she was snacking on some potato chips. The fan next to her face mussed her hair every time it swung past, revealing her forehead.

"No one would break into a dump like this," Toru said. "There's nothing to take."

"But I have all my stuff here."

Toru put away the coffeepot and stood wiping his hands on the towel. "Trust me, nothing will happen while you take a little walk."

"The thing is," Saki said, "my apartment got broken into while I was in the hospital. The same boyfriend."

Toru sighed. He bunched the towel and tossed it on the dish rack.

"He systematically destroyed everything I owned," Saki said.

"Fine," said Toru, "I'll copy the key for you."

"Thank you," she said, and her smile made Toru wonder if he had been tricked. He still hadn't asked her when she intended to leave.

"Look, I won't even pretend to know what it's like." He sat down across the table from her. "But your situation sounds serious. Shouldn't you seek out some professional help?"

Saki went back to flipping through the magazine. From the open window the mechanical sound of cicadas seeped into the room and filled the little silence between them.

"Did you talk to the police?" he said. "I mean, this guy sounds like a psychopath. What did they do with him?"

"Nothing," Saki said. "I told them I was mugged. Didn't see any face."

"What?"

"The police won't do me any good. Trust me." Without taking her eyes off the pages, Saki reached for more potato chips and nibbled on them.

"Are you trying to protect this guy?" Toru said. "Is that it? After what he's done to you?"

Saki abruptly closed the magazine and tossed it onto the pile. "How about we go for a walk together?" she said.

Toru blinked. "Now? I have to go to work."

"Can I come along, then?" she said. "I'd like to see what you do with the vending machines."

She picked up a glass with some melting ice cubes at the bottom and tilted it back to get a trickle of water. The clinking of the ice cooled the stale air in the room by a fraction of a degree.

"I don't think that's a good idea," Toru said.

"But you're making the rounds all by yourself, right?" she said. "No one's going to know."

"I'm going to a different job today," he said.

Saki raised her eyebrows. "Oh?"

"I have this part-time job," he said. "A seasonal one."

"Well, what is it?"

Toru hesitated for a second. "I work at a cemetery."

"A cemetery?"

"You know it's Bon this month, but a lot of people can't make the trip these days. So they hire someone else to do it for them. Some people more than once a year, but mostly just for Bon. It's the peak season."

"So you go visit and clean the graves of people you don't know."

"Right."

"That sounds great," Saki said.

One step out of the air-conditioned train, the chorus of cicadas once again vibrated the heavy air. Toru's ears had grown numb to the incessant ringing, but he felt it loudly on his skin. There was not a hint of breeze and walking was an effort, as though wading through thick liquid.

In public with Saki for the first time, Toru felt self-conscious, his movements somehow encumbered by her bare-legged presence. The whole walk to the cemetery, Saki followed a few paces behind him at a leisurely pace, dangling a shopping bag of cleaning supplies. Toru thought she was favoring her scarred leg, but the unevenness in her gait was subtle enough that he could have been wrong.

Sometime in late fall, back in eighth grade, Masato had jumped from the third-story balcony at school. A group of male students who had been with him at the time said it had been a dare, just a joke, that no one had expected him to actually jump. Others who had seen it happen confirmed that he had voluntarily climbed over the railing. When the assistant principal spoke about the incident to the student body, he referred to it as "an accident resulting from reckless behavior." They were not to confuse selfish acts that inconvenienced many people with courage.

Masato broke a number of bones and didn't come back to school after he was released from the hospital months later. His family had supposedly moved to another town. But by then it was past winter break, and his empty desk had long since been taken. The rumors and hushed excitement had grown stale.

Toru and Saki stopped to buy flowers near the station and picked up boxes of sweets and fruits along the way for offerings.

"Wow," Saki said. "Fancy. All that for dead strangers?"

"I'll get reimbursed, of course." Toru neatly folded the receipts into his wallet. "And we get to keep the food. We have to take it home because we can't leave it out at the grave. It's just a gesture."

"I suppose that's what counts," she said. "A gesture."

The cemetery had sprawling paved grounds and no temple. Toru stopped at the management office to check in and pick up the assignment for the day, then went to fill a bucket with water.

"Whenever I think of a cemetery, I picture it in the summer," Saki said, watching Toru clean. "Quietly grilling under the sun, just like this."

Toru was on his fifth grave. Saki had closely observed the process the first time, and then had wandered off for a while to walk around the grounds before finding him again. This grave had a fairly new, elaborate headstone, its corners still sharp and its surface polished.

"I guess I do too." Toru had removed the wilted flowers and incense ashes from their receptacles and was sweeping the tiny plot of land. "Because we used to play in the cemetery near our grandparents' during the summer. But an old man chased us with a broom this one time, saying we'd be cursed for disturbing the peace of the dead." He halted the sweeping and looked around. "I just remembered that. One of my cousins yelled back, 'Soon, when *you* are stuck under one of these stones, I bet you'll wish you had some company!'"

Saki contemplated this for a second. "Do you think it's really peaceful there?" she said. "On the other side?"

Toru glanced at her. She was tracing the clean edges of the gravestone with her long finger. The sun was already high, and everything in sight had a bright shallowness to it. A tiny thunderhead poised over the distant treetops, but no shade was in sight. Just then, there was something so delicate about Saki that for a second Toru had an urge to shield her from the harsh light. He shook the thought away.

"I personally don't believe in the other side," he said.

"Then you don't think there'll be suffering, either?" she said. "Like punishment?"

The sweeping done, Toru poured some water on the gravestone and started wiping it down with a cloth. "You mean like Hell?"

"I don't know," she said. "Just some sort of consequence. Of your life."

"I've always imagined it'll just be complete nothingness. Back to zero," he said. "Would you get me the toothbrush?"

Saki bent down to search in the shopping bag. "Complete nothingness. That doesn't sound too bad." She handed him the toothbrush and rested her butt on the marble ledge marking the next plot, stretching out her scarred leg. "But what if you've done something horribly wrong in your life?"

"Like what?" Toru went on scrubbing the letters engraved on the stone. This one said TAJIMA FAMILY on the front, with individual names and years on the back. Some of the stones were so worn he could hardly make out the letters, while some of the new ones had a name or two in red letters, indicating people who were still alive. He never understood the rush, the urge to have somewhere to go after this life.

"Like if you've seriously harmed someone. Or killed someone."

"I don't know," Toru said. "You'd *live* with the consequences then, right?"

Saki remained silent for a second. Toru could feel her eyes on his back.

"What if that wasn't enough?" Her tone sounded provocative, but Toru couldn't be sure. "What then?"

Toru ladled more water onto the gravestone and placed fresh bundles of flowers in the vases. The sky was overbearingly wide open above them. His shirt clung to his back. The blinding sun was all around them, reflecting off the cement and white pebbles.

Kyoko and Toru never talked about Masato after the incident. Toru sensed Kyoko's intense shame and fear, and knew better than to bring up her crush on the bullying target. They acted as though nothing, not even a quiet ripple, had disturbed the smooth, continuous surface of their daily lives at school. But that meant they had to pretend that the months leading up to the fall had never happened, that this thing that had structured their days had never existed. The two of them hung out less and less, in a way that felt inevitable. It didn't occur to Toru until much later that Kyoko must have seen him as a threat, a ticking bomb that could be her undoing at any moment. That she might have desperately wanted to get rid of him. By the time they started the new school year in April, the two of them were going around in different circles.

"Of course," Toru said carefully, "it would be comforting to think there's something just about the whole thing in the end.

That those who've done wrong wouldn't ultimately get away with it. But I have a feeling it doesn't work that way. We probably have to work things out on this side."

Saki picked up one of the rough-edged stones at her feet and toyed with it, as if to read something in the texture of its surface. She then straightened up, pocketed the stone, and walked around the grave.

"God, it's hot," she said. "I should have brought my hat."

"You shouldn't just be standing around." Toru felt relieved. "You'll have a heat stroke. Maybe you should go home."

"I'm fine," Saki said. "I kind of like it here."

"Why don't you go inside for a bit, at least?" he said. "And you could get two more bundles of incense for me on the way back."

While she was gone, Toru finished laying out the offerings and putting the cleaning supplies away. Although it was close to Bon, there weren't many other people visiting the graves on a weekday. He heard some kids shrieking in the distance and their mother calling after them. There was an old woman several rows away, pulling weeds under a broad-rimmed straw hat. When Toru stood up to stretch his back, the woman looked up and nodded approvingly. Toru nodded in return. He then realized he had thrown away the fresh flowers that he had just placed in the vases. He searched for them in the garbage bag, cursing himself, and put them back. They looked slightly disheveled now, but then again, he and Saki would be the only ones to see them anyway. He couldn't think straight. It was the heat.

For a while after the incident, Toru occasionally found himself picturing the scene on the balcony. In his mind, there was a haunting fierceness to Masato's action. Toru hadn't been there, not exactly; he had been copying Kyoko's homework in the classroom, and when he'd looked up, sensing the commotion on the balcony, Masato was already on the ground eight meters below. But Toru sometimes imagined that Masato's eyes had actually sought him through the window, that it had been Masato's gaze that had made him look up. That their eyes had met. This couldn't have really happened, because all Toru could see from where he sat at the far end of the classroom were the backs of his classmates, indistinguishable in their gray uniform sweaters. And yet the more he thought about that day, the more vividly he could picture the look on Masato's face.

Did his classmates also see it—anger, hatred, defiance, or was it mere desperation?—flicker in those large but normally downcast eyes? Toru tried to imagine the discomfort spreading among the group of boys as Masato climbed over the railing, even as they sneered at his bluff. And the shock that must have rippled through them when he jumped. The brutal instantaneity of the fall, how there was no moment of suspense in which he seemed to become airborne, as in a movie, but how instead the body just hit the ground with a dull thump before they could grasp what was happening. Had there been time for Masato to feel the triumph, the satisfaction, before the pain came? Had he been able to see the astonishment and perhaps awe on his classmates' faces high above? Toru didn't even know whether Masato had fallen facedown or -up.

When Saki came back, she stood next to Toru and prayed with him. The clean grave smelled fresh from the evaporating water and the incense. Toru never knew what to say to the dead strangers, but he always put his palms together, closed his eyes, and thought something general and polite. This time, though, with his eyes shut, he could think only about Saki. He really needed to ask her to leave the apartment before he got entangled in some mess. Before it was too late.

But instead he said, "Shall we get something for lunch?" He felt lightheaded. "Something cold?"

Saki kept her eyes closed and finished her prayer before turning to him. "That sounds good," she said.

For the next few weeks, Toru went to clean the graves in the morning, and then worked the late shift refilling the vending machines. Now that she had the key, Saki seemed to go out regularly. Most days he would find her back in the apartment when he came home, reading her magazines and nibbling at sweets from the cemetery. Sometimes she would come back while he prepared dinner. They would always eat together, and afterward they would have some beer and watch a movie on his computer. Somewhere along the way, their days started to acquire a new, plain rhythm, hypnotic in its simplicity and almost indistinguishable from the routine he had established alone.

He spent one evening with his girlfriend, but he was distracted. The thought of Saki sitting around his apartment while he ate at a restaurant and had sex in an air-conditioned hotel room kept him restless. It was easy to picture her at the coffee table munching on potato chips for dinner, and he wondered if he should have prepared and left something for her. In bed, he found himself going rough on his girlfriend, as though trying to dig through his thoughts to the body beneath him. His girlfriend noticed.

"What's on your mind?" She was fixing her hair in the mirror, combing it back into her usual simple low ponytail. The room was by the hour, so they never lingered.

"There's a bit of a situation." Toru sighed, already dressed and sitting on the edge of the bed. "I should probably explain. It's just that I don't know—"

"If there's someone else, don't tell me," she said into the mirror, in a reassuring voice that he imagined would comfort her children. "I don't want to know. Just don't let me ever feel her presence. That's all I ask." Toru watched her scrape mascara from under her eyes with her neatly trimmed nails. Her hands were unadorned, for practical use. He imagined her at home, in her kitchen, cooking meals that he would never taste.

"Where do you go every day?" Toru said.

It had been a little over a month since Saki had arrived, and he had another early shift. He found Saki hunched over the coffee table, repainting her nails. They were the same pomegranate color as her toes. She pretended not to hear.

"You've been going out, right?" Toru said, pulling a T-shirt over his head. "Are you looking for a job?"

She finished painting the last nail and held her left hand to the light to inspect the glossy surfaces before turning her attention to him. "Why so curious suddenly? You sound like a jealous boyfriend."

It was his turn to remain silent.

"You want to know what I'm doing while you aren't looking?"

"I thought you were trying to get back on your feet."

"It's okay." She sounded playful. "You want to know?"

"You said just for a while. It's only fair."

"I'll tell you, but you have to keep it a secret." There was a glow in her eyes. "I'm on a mission."

"A mission?"

"I've been tracking down all the bullies from my past."

Toru could feel the weight of the familiar knot taking shape in his stomach.

"So I can go around getting back at them, one by one."

"Get back how?" Toru said.

"I'd show up with these giant scissors, you see," she said. "Of course I'd first seduce them, drug them, and tie them up naked. In whatever order works. Then I'd wait until they were fully awake. And while they were saying, 'I'm sorry, I was a jerk, I repent! Please, forgive me!' I'd chop their thing off. Like this, with both hands. Snip."

Despite himself, Toru felt a small chill at the base of his spine. They held each other's gaze, the last word hovering in the humid air between them. Toru thought he recognized those eyes, the ones that had sought him from the balcony through the window, with a flicker of something that was lost before he could grasp it. Then he remembered that this had happened only in his mind. He was unable to distinguish real memories from those he'd imagined. For instance, he was no longer certain that he had never intended for things to turn out the way they had. It wasn't that he had meant, really, to compel his classmates to go after Masato when he told them about his curious collection of girls' underwear. But couldn't he have predicted that there would be bathroom ambushes, jeering, and peeking?

"Look at you." Saki laughed out loud. "I'm joking. Of course I'm looking for a job."

Toru, feeling weary, picked up his sweaty undershirt from the floor and brought it to the sink. He ran it under the water, squeezing the stench out of the thinning fabric. "Well? Any prospects?"

Saki didn't respond, and Toru kept squeezing and rubbing, as though if he kept up with it long enough, he would be able to wash away his thoughts as well. When he finally wrung out the shirt, much more thoroughly than necessary, and turned around, he was met with Saki's patient eyes.

"Did you know you can see the sunset from your window?" she said.

"What?"

She said she could see the western sky change colors in his neighbor's window. Toru was rarely home before sunset, and when he was, he never thought to look out. That evening, as the sky turned from pale blue to light green to amber to pink to

crimson, they sat on the floor watching it, cut out in rectangular in the neighbor's windowpane. There was no way of knowing
if all that transformation was actually happening in the real sky
out of their sight, but there it was in the reflection, vivid and real
enough.

"Hey, I just thought of something," Saki said, once it was all
gone. "Do you know how to do the farewell fire?"

"No," Toru said. "My family never did the rituals. Why?"

"Wouldn't it be nice to do one of our own? I was listening to the
radio and they were talking about it. The different ways they do it
around the country."

"But Saki, the premise is that we've welcomed the spirits into
the house beforehand. Who are we going to send off?"

"You've been taking care of a whole bunch of graves. That
should be enough."

"I really have no idea how it's done."

"Let's just make it up, then," Saki said. "We don't have to be
proper. You said you don't believe in these things anyway. I want to
do the one where you let the lanterns float away in the river."

Saki rummaged through Toru's kitchen drawers and found
some plastic take-out containers and emergency candles. There
was no river in the area, so they decided an old irrigation ditch
on the outskirts of town would do. It was a meandering, twenty-
minute stroll through streets lined with small houses and two-story
apartments before the residential area gave way to an overgrown
rice field.

"I'm pretty sure none of this is legal," Toru said as they climbed
down the short slope to the ditch in the dark. "This is a fire hazard,
and it's littering. Do you know plastics never biodegrade? Ever?"

"Will you be quiet for a second?" Saki was leading the way, sure-
footed and in control. She was giddy. "Just let me have a little fun."

The night air near the water was ripe with a grassy smell and
crickets' chirping. In the moonless sky above, Toru thought he
could make out some stars if he squinted hard. Once they found a
little spot that was level enough, Saki lit the candles and prepared
her makeshift lanterns, five in all.

"Here, you have to do one too," she said.

They carefully lowered the plastic containers into the water, trying not to let them topple. They had to hold on to some roots
with one hand because the embankment's final drop was steep.

When they let go, the lanterns precariously bobbed up and down a couple of times and then, finding their balance, started to float.

"It's working," Saki said. "They're leaving us."

In the dark, the disembodied voice belonged to Masato. Only it had never sounded so cheerful back then, so certain. This—that despite the recent turn of events, perhaps Saki was at least more secure now in her body—comforted Toru.

They lowered the remaining three lanterns so that they could follow the others' paths. As the flickering flames drifted away, they reflected off the water and multiplied. They grew smaller and seemed to wander uncertainly, like spirits searching their way back. But Toru imagined that both he and Saki were letting go of some parts of themselves, shedding their pasts maybe, seeing them off to a better place.

"Bye-bye," Saki said. "I hope it's peaceful there."

Back in the apartment, with the neighbor's dark window no longer reflecting anything, Saki continued to look out with her elbow on the windowsill. As he prepared their dinner, Toru glanced over his shoulder every once in a while to find her in the same position. The sight was strangely reassuring. He thought perhaps this, the two of them on the fringe together, could work. Perhaps this was something he needed.

Toru was heading out to the station one morning when one of his neighbors caught up with him.

"Hey, 203," said the middle-aged day laborer whom Toru had seen several times in passing. "You're in 203, right? Wait up."

Toru nodded in acknowledgment but kept walking, and the man, who was shorter than he was, half-trotted beside him.

"So," the man said, "about that girl you got up in your room."

Toru glanced sideways at the man's deeply tanned, stubbly face. He thought he could smell alcohol on his breath, but he didn't seem confrontational. "Excuse me?"

"Come on now, there's no use playing dumb. You know the rules."

"What do you want?"

"Hey, didn't your mother teach you manners?" The man looked genuinely taken aback. "Slow down. I'm not trying to blackmail you or anything here. I could've complained to the landlord if I wanted to."

"Okay." Toru loosened his stride a little. "Then what is it?"

"That girl you've got. She's this, isn't she?" The man touched the back of his hand to his opposite cheek, in a gross approximation of femininity. "She a professional?"

"What? Of course not."

"Well, I don't know what the story is. I don't even want to know. But I wouldn't let her squat for too long if I were you."

Nearing the station, they were about to join a steady stream of commuters.

"I know that type," the man said. "The minute you let them into your life, they trample all over it. With their muddy shoes."

"What are you talking about?" Toru turned to face the man.

"I saw her bring a guy up to your room." The man evaluated Toru's expression. "Bet it wasn't something you'd arranged."

Toru stood there, his feet suddenly rooted to the hot asphalt.

"So here's some friendly advice," the man said. "Get her out of there."

A female voice announced the train Toru was supposed to catch. "I have to go," he said.

"Look, I know your lady issue's none of my business." The man was almost sympathetic. "I don't care what you do or with whom. But I don't want any fishy stuff where I live. I can't have police sniffing around, you know what I mean?"

"Sure," Toru said.

"I mean it. I'll tell the landlord if you—"

"I said okay," Toru said. "I understand."

"I've been wondering, Saki," Toru said, in that pocket of time just after dinner but before they were ready for the dishes, "if I could have more of a part in this, your situation, in some way. Longer term."

Two days before, after he had spoken with his neighbor, Toru had come home mid-shift to an empty apartment. He didn't know what he had expected to find, but he checked the futon sheet and tatami mat, perhaps for suspicious stains, and went through the trash. For a while he contemplated searching Saki's canvas bag, but then he suddenly became aware of what he was doing, a part of him coolly observing his discomposure from the outside, and felt disgusted. What exactly did he want to know, anyway? What was he going to do with the knowledge? He went back to work, sneaking out of his own apartment like a thief.

Saki looked up from where she sat across the table, leaning against the wall. They had the radio on and were listening to the weatherman predict the course of the first typhoon of the season. "What did you say?" she said.

"If I can help you find a job, a proper job," he said, testing the water, "maybe we can find another place. Together."

Saki picked up a chopstick and lightly tapped on an empty bowl. "I don't know," she said, "if that's going to work out."

On the radio, a young female announcer laughed at the weatherman's joke, and some cheerful music came on.

"Yeah?" Toru said. "Why not?"

Toru had remembered it was Saki's birthday. Masato's birthday. The date had been stored somewhere in his mind all these years, like a lock's combination that stuck with you long after the lock itself had been lost. He had bought two slices of prettily decorated cake on his way home, and the box was sitting in the fridge.

"It's been so good being here," Saki said, not looking at Toru but gazing at the dirty dishes on the table. "You have no idea. I think I almost got too comfortable."

Toru got up and turned off the radio on top of the fridge. "Well then, what's going to work out? What is your plan?"

"I don't know," Saki said. "But you can't help me more than you already have."

"What's this all about, then, Saki?" Toru felt a flash of anger somewhere deep behind his eyes. He sensed his plan to gently work out the tangle slipping away. "Tell me why you are here if I can't help you. Why you came to me."

Saki sat quietly for some time, as though contemplating the tip of the chopstick in her hand. "What would you like to hear?" she said almost kindly, now looking straight at Toru.

"Well, one thing for sure—that you don't bring your customers here again."

"What?"

"I know what you're doing." Toru couldn't stop. "A neighbor saw you. I don't know what you think I owe you; maybe you think I deserve this, and maybe I do. But how can you do such a thing? Have you thought of the consequences?"

Saki held his gaze, but Toru could see something retreat in her eyes, closing off. The fan slowly swung its head, back and forth, back and forth, just slightly stirring the air between them.

"That was my boyfriend's brother," Saki said, words exhaled like a resignation.

Toru stood still.

"I meant to tell you," she said, "but I hadn't figured out how to."

"He found you?" Toru said. "Is the brother also a psychopath? Did he do anything to you?"

"No, no." Saki halfheartedly waved her arms in the air, as though physically scattering the idea. "I've been going to see him. My boyfriend. His brother came to ask me to stop."

Toru felt weariness settling on him like fine dust, weighing him down. He thought maybe he should sit down, but that seemed to require too much effort. "Is that what you want?" he said. "To get back with this guy?"

"I don't know." Saki ran her hands through her hair and then grasped it in her fists, as though holding on to her head. "I really don't know."

Long after they had turned the lights off, Toru lay awake on his sleeping bag. He could hear Saki's regular breathing, but he knew she wasn't asleep either.

"Toru-kun," Saki said, eventually. "Do you remember what I used to look like?"

"I do," he said. "I do remember."

"Did you know you were my only friend at school?"

Toru stared out the window at the small patch of sky that contained nothing. "No," he said. Then, "Maybe."

"Well, now you do. You were. That's why I came to you."

Toru got up and dragged his sleeping bag over to where Saki lay on her side, her back toward him. He placed his hand on her waist. It was warm. When she turned over onto her back, he gently lifted the bottom of her shirt. In the dim light from the street lamp, Toru could see her torso littered with old scars and healed incisions. He reached his hand and felt them with his fingertips, as though reading Braille. Just below her left ribcage, he found one that had healed into a forceful indentation, like a diagram of a black hole bending space-time.

"That's the new one," Saki said. "All the others are from the

fall, back in school. Did you know I almost died then? Most of my
injuries were internal, from the impact. They had to cut me open
many times."

"I'm sorry," Toru said.

"He didn't mean it, you know. He didn't even know what he was
doing. It was one of those moments."

"It's okay," Toru said. "You don't have to defend him to me."

"He was so gentle and proper. You'd never imagine him hurting
anyone."

"Saki. If you think things will work out with this guy, you're totally deranged. You know that."

Saki made a sound that was halfway between a chuckle and a
sigh. "Yeah," she said. "I know."

Toru continued to trace the scars, trying to decipher something
from each of the textured edges, as though straining to hear someone whispering in a room next door. He kept his hand on Saki's
torso and lay down next to her.

"Did you think I came to you for a romantic reason?" Saki said.

Toru didn't say anything. He didn't know the right answer.

"Who knows," she said. "Maybe I did."

Like that, with his hand rising and falling with Saki's breathing,
he closed his eyes.

When Toru came home the next day, Saki wasn't there. Her white
canvas bag, which normally sat on the folded futon in the corner
of the room, was also gone. But she didn't leave her key, so Toru
cooked dinner and waited, just in case. On the windowsill where
she always rested her elbow, he found a stone he recognized from
the cemetery. When the food grew cold, he packed a lunchbox
and put it away in the fridge. The cake box still sat on one of the
shelves, unopened.

That night, the typhoon hit. It was already September. The rain
smashed onto the pavement with enough force to knock a child
down. It was as though someone had decided to waste the entire
world's supply of water on this town. The roaring replaced the
sound of cicadas, which had by then become such a constant that
Toru noticed it only in its absence. The new, powerful roar took
up every inch of the available space, filling the world with another
level of deafening silence.

Toru stood at his window, letting the stray splashes into the room. He picked up the stone and turned it in his hand, feeling its warm surface the way Saki had done, before putting it into his pocket. The neighbor's windowpane was pitch black now. A streetlamp stood illuminating a sheet of rain, waiting for someone to step into its cone-shaped spotlight. Toru took out his cell phone and held it in his hand for a long time before finally flipping it open. He counted seven rings before she answered.

"Hello?" It was the familiar voice, half-worried, half-pleased. "Why are you calling now? Do you need to reschedule?"

"Hi," he said, and cleared his throat. "No, I just wanted to make sure you weren't stranded somewhere."

He heard a chuckle. "What, like in a flood?"

"You know, with all this crazy . . ." He trailed off, the words suddenly escaping his throat without first collecting sound.

"Yeah?" she said. "Well, I'm fine. Don't worry. Listen, the kids are here, so I should go. Next Wednesday, right?"

He thought about the empty house in Saki's dream. In his mind, he was walking from one dark room to another, looking for something. The Post-it note. Wasn't there a Post-it note? He needed to find out what was written on it. But none of the rooms in the empty house had a table on which the plastic-wrapped plate of food could be placed, on which the note could be stuck.

"Toru?" the voice was saying. It was right in his ear, yet so far away. "Are you there?"

SHARON SOLWITZ

Gifted

FROM *New England Review*

THEY LIVED ACROSS from a rundown park on a street they jokingly called Park Place. They drove older cars, drove as little as possible for the sake of the environment. They had a cleaning service, so they wouldn't fight over who had left what where. But they rarely fought, in part because Allan was easygoing, in part because Thea was happy. Her job required travel (what fun!) but not enough to upset the applecart of the family. She made it to basketball games (Nate), violin recitals (Nate), and soccer matches (Dylan). When she was gone, Allan, who taught two courses a semester at a Research I university, took care of the boys. Amiably. Lovingly.

Was she lucky? She felt it, though less keenly than if she were less used to being lucky. The older of two girls, she had been deemed (so it seemed) the prettier and smarter early on, so it stuck. Which floated her through high school, sent her to the University of Chicago, and made her want to test herself—not just her luck but her limitations. Nixon was routed, the war over. Money and work were easy to come by and would be forever and ever, amen, world without end.

Her sophomore year she quit school without asking for a leave and moved in with a gifted, troubled boyfriend. She worked as a waitress, took classes in painting, then singing and acting; she auditioned for plays. She had other boyfriends amid the mysterious AIDS epidemic, went to bed with men whose names she didn't know, and once had asked for and received money. And she remained healthy; what luck! She could stay up far into the night at a bar where a boyfriend's band was playing, her pleasure in the music intensified by MDA, then get a couple of hours of sleep and still make it to work the next day. She could have an abortion in the morning, deliver correctly designated plates of food in the afternoon, and remember her lines (there weren't many lines) in the play she was in that night, with an occasional break to change her pad. To friends in law or medical school she would declare wryly: I'm downwardly mobile.

By her midtwenties her élan was flagging. Gaby, her sister, had married right out of college, taught fifth grade, and had two girls one after the other while her solid-citizen husband climbed his corporate ladder. They moved to Highland Park, threw dinner parties, gave to the Symphony and the United Jewish Appeal. Gaby started working out, cut her hair short, looked no-nonsense glamorous. At a downtown lunch, Gaby picked up the tab. And Thea could see sister lunches down the years, Gaby generously paying, and she grateful and ashamed. And now the balance had shifted, or else it was always like this but till now she hadn't understood: Gaby knew what she wanted and what she didn't want, while Thea wanted just about everything. If not everything, she would have nothing. She'd impress the theater world with her Portia and Gypsy Rose Lee, she'd reign over a salon where she and other brilliant people amused one another, or she'd shuffle through alleys with all her possessions in a shopping cart. One or the other.

The thought of pity (and in some cases, perhaps pleasure) from her family and friends induced the hot spurt of terror that returned her to action. She applied and was admitted to art school and earned not only her degree in design but the love of her department head, twelve years older than she was, but trim and sweet-natured with a warm, wry delivery. *Thea always pulls it off.* That was said of her. Which she publicly disputed but in her heart believed. She had slacked off a bit but the stars or Whoever was running the show was on her side. Then, wanting children, with a man who wanted them too, she managed that as well. Two boys, after age thirty. After two abortions weighing on her with their nasty irony.

Money had been a problem. And the swamp of early motherhood—pee and baby powder. But when Nate was twelve, old enough to watch Dylan after school the two or three days Dad taught (God bless academia), she was hired by a firm that built hotels all over Europe. It was better than fine. There was getting away and there was returning, pleasure and love, novelty and security. Her luck continued, no longer luck, even, but a blessing from on high. A superstitious person might have worried.

The night everything changed was her second in London. It was early September but chilly with rain. They'd viewed a site near Hampstead where a new Wyndham might go up. The English countryside looked stowed away and orderly, even when wet. In her poly-lined raincoat she was warm and dry. Later that day came the fun of drinks with Edward, their UK project manager, a man slightly younger than she was. He liked her mind, he said, and the shape of her nose, which some had deemed too prominent. At forty-three, it was pleasant to be desired. He had a nifty accent, a disconcertingly direct gaze, a ponderous but dry sense of humor. His ex-wife, Martha, had abandoned him for an MP. Not that he'd have preferred, he said, to have been replaced by an unemployed chimney sweep.

Thea liked Edward. If they slept together, Allan would never have to know. But in the fullness of her contentment she decided against. Before Allan, she'd had sex in what felt like a lifetime of variations. She loved Allan in bed, warm and generous as elsewhere. After the shared bill was paid, Edward invited her to his room. "In our next life," she said, and kissed his cheek, feeling not only attractive but a good person to boot. There was a line in the Old Testament: A woman's virtue is beyond rubies.

Alone in her queen-size hotel bed, she was reading *Anna Karenina,* a book she'd always wanted to read but till now hadn't had time for, when Allan called. They'd talked last night, emailed this afternoon. She didn't expect to hear from him till tomorrow. She felt a pulse of love for her husband, unlike Anna for poor Karenin. "Dahling," she said with the local articulation, "I'm *fright*fully glad to hear your voice." She felt giddy and free, while across the pond it was work time. Allan would be sitting out the end of his office hour (Tues., Thurs.: 4–5 p.m.). "I like your voice," she said. It was low and reverberant, surprising in a man of only average size, sexy coming out of the dark during a slide lecture. "Guess what I'm thinking?" She smiled into the phone. "When I get back I'm going to jump your bones." It was an idiom from her pre-Allan days, one he disliked. She cackled. "So, what's new on Park Place? Did Dylan finish his science project? Is Nate practicing his Torah portion?" Nate's bar mitzvah was scheduled for December. They'd just sent out the invitations. Nate had seemed pretty blasé. "Are you there, Allan?"

He coughed. In the long-distance silence her heart sped up. "Allan? What?"

He spoke shakily at first but soon gathered control. Nate was in the hospital. There was something in his abdomen, a mass of some sort. He went on but she absorbed no more. Dylan at the Rosenthals, Allan with Nate at Children's Memorial. What was a mass, exactly? She pictured peas; grapes. You have a walnut-sized mass in your left breast. Were they always compared to foods?

"It's the size of a football," he said.

He was angry with her for being gone, she thought. He was angry with her for not noticing that something was wrong with their son. She was angry with herself. What had she missed?

Later they would learn what they had overlooked: the swell of belly under Nate's loose shirts, his occasional shortness of breath, that he sometimes walked on his toes instead of his whole foot. None of the Five Warning Signs. There was some possibly hopeful news. Gail Elkin, the attending, thought the tumor was a Burkitt's, fast growing and thus sensitive to treatment. Rapidly dividing cells invited zapping. There were more tests but they would probably start chemo in the morning. A Burkitt's was a tumor of choice, so to speak, 90 percent survival at five years.

Allan sounded calm now and incredibly knowledgeable. She was shaking at the thought of Nate in the mortal 10 percent. She was used to being in the 10 percent group, along with other gifted children receiving extra work in math or art. She looked around the room though she didn't know what she was looking for. She had to go home. She had to call American Airlines. Or was it Continental? Shit, Wyndham had arranged it. She breathed in quick pants. Where was the printout? "Hold on," he told her. "I'm walking the phone back to Nate's room. He wants to talk to you."

She swallowed ferociously in order to speak to Nate without tears in her voice. But he was cheerful. The hospital was an interesting novelty. A nurse's aide, Kwan Lin, had played chess with him, and she wasn't that bad. He'd told Kwan Lin about the force of gravity, which was a property of every object that had any mass and created attraction between them. Everything has mass, he said, even a tiny hair! There's a pull between us and between everything.

Mass? She laughed so as not to cry at the pushy little word, suddenly ubiquitous, remembering how Nate had looked when she kissed him goodbye on Sunday morning, so tall she didn't have to bend. His round cheeks, sturdy legs, dark hair curling over his ears. He needed a haircut. "You sound like yourself," she whispered. "I love yourself."

Hanging up, she thought of Edward with self-loathing and terror. As if a mere idea, the glimmer of an adulterous thought, could become a cancerous mass inside her firstborn. She ransacked her purse and found her boarding-pass stub (British Airways) and, pleading her case, secured a flight back the next morning. And how to live through the night?

Both of her parents were dead, of different (she thought with a shudder) forms of cancer. She had friends she could have called. But Laura Beth was visiting her in-laws and Melissa, dear, smart, and scrupulous, had no children of her own and might feel awkward. There were Allan's parents, still mentally intact in Boca Raton.

She called her sister, who now worked in human resources at her husband's company. It turned out to be a mistake. Gaby started crying. Thea was furious at her sister's tears. That the mother had to comfort the aunt. He wasn't dead. "I'm hanging up, Gaby."

Lying alone in the unfamiliar bed, she wrapped her arms and legs around the rock-hard hotel pillow and tried to extract affection. She tried to teleport wellness to her son, not that she believed in such things. She pondered the mystery of Gaby's healthy children, and of Gaby herself who in high school had had thin orange hair and nervous boyfriends. In Highland Park her life was routinized; at any moment of the day Thea could pretty much guess where she'd be and even the attitude she'd be presenting (helpful, interested). Sister-in-a-bag? But it was suddenly clear to Thea that not just now but always Gaby had been the happier person. As kids in the hot backseat of a car on the way to visit ancient relatives, Gaby would fall contentedly asleep while Thea stared out the window, rethinking what had happened yesterday and what might happen later that day, and what to do to make things turn out as she wished.

*

The next day, Tuesday, was September 11, 2001, but the calamity of what would be called for years afterward 9/11, of the collapsed towers and three thousand dead, was lost on Thea, wandering through Heathrow like a sleepwalker. Her flight was canceled, there were no plans to reschedule. Hours later back at the hotel she called Allan, teeth chattering with frustration and bewildered fright.

His news didn't help. Nathan's tumor wasn't a Burkitt's, but that was all they knew. Until they knew what it was they couldn't treat it. In the meantime, seven a.m. Chicago time, Nate was about to have a needle inserted in his back to drain one of his effused lungs. He would get local anesthesia but it would hurt, and he wanted to talk to her on the phone during the procedure. Allan's voice tried to be soothing. Could she handle it?

"What's with his lung?" she said. "I thought it was his abdomen—"

"Try to be calm, honey. For his sake."

"Oh, please!"

She could feign calm. She had been calm telling her supervisor this morning why she was leaving—the Queen of Calm, *he'll be in the hospital till they find out what's wrong, we're being hopeful.* She thought of Allan walking the phone back to Nate's room and reminded herself how sturdy Nate was, he and Dylan both. They'd scrape their knees on cement, get knocked around on some ball field, and then screech and return to the fray. At the sound of Nate's voice, tears sprang to her eyes but she quickly gathered herself. "Hey, kiddo."

"Just talk, that's all," Nate said. "Keep talking."

Of course she could do that. "I'm coming home as soon as I can, at least by Friday, boy-o, and here's something to think about. What do you want me to bring you from England? How about a soccer jersey? Manchester Monkeys or something? Mollusks? Mall rats?!" She giggled frantically, it was hard to get the tone appropriately light, but she knew not to stop. "I'll tell you about the meeting yesterday. There was this zoning, historic-London person, garden party, old family, blue-blood type, she kept nixing anything that made our project a tiny bit distinctive. Regulation height, roof slope, that's it. Windows have to look just so. Choice of three products for facing, I know these details don't mean much but you get the general picture?" She mimicked the woman's BBC accent: "*In our small arena we try to maintain continuity. Respect for the past.* Like we Americans were yokels. Hicks!" Nate uttered what sounded like a whimper. "What, honey?"

"It was just cold on my back, the cotton or whatever—keep talking, Mom!"

She swallowed fast. "I talked to Aunt Gaby last night, she's going to come down to see you, with Cousin Emma? Maybe Ava too. I'll be home Friday, did I just say that?"

"I don't know, Mom. But here's what I want from England, a Red Hot Chili Peppers CD. With their autograph. Do you think you can get it, dude?"

Then in a patch of silence, in which she was thinking how to get hold of this group, the Chili Peppers—she had to write the name down so she wouldn't forget—and wondering if other twelve-year-olds called their moms *dude*—she heard a scream. She dropped the phone, dropped to her knees, clambered for it. "Honey? I'm here, Nate, love—"

Half a minute later he was marveling, "That was the worst pain I ever felt." She was weeping; she couldn't hide it. "Mom, what's the matter?"

"You're so brave," she whispered. Then, before another sob blossomed, "Let me talk to Dad, okay?"

That night the group from the Chicago office went out to a pub. They didn't know about Nate, she didn't want to tell them, nor did she want to be with them without their knowing. So she arranged another solo dinner with Edward. He no longer attracted her, on the short side, round face, thinning hair; Allan's was graying but full. But he listened while she told him the facts of Nate's illness and tried to describe her state of mind, and he seemed to feel for her. His sister's boy had had leukemia at two, and at six now he was doing fine. *Thank you, Edward.* He loved cricket and fifties-era Hollywood movies, and his ordinariness was bubble wrap for her sore mind, separating her in London from the terrors of Chicago. He didn't have children and didn't think he wanted them. He wasn't sure he'd ever get married again. Once was enough (after Martha). By the time their plates were removed Thea was certain that even if she were single, he was no one to spend her life with. Despite his crisp consonants and former marriage he seemed not quite formed, a lad.

He had the tact or decency not to re-instigate their flirtation, but that night, unable to sleep, she put on her robe, padded down the softly lit hall to his room, and knocked on his door. It was two a.m. Sex was rushed, awkward, but her own room yawned with confusion and terror. She put her arms around Edward, breathed his unfamiliar set of odors, slept and woke and slept. The next day she avoided him, and that night instead of staying at the hotel he went home to Brighton where he had a house. On Friday she flew home.

Naturally in Chicago she rarely thought about Edward. The night with him was a mere episode, a piece of craziness or weakness that arose from her fear — utterly wrong and shameful, but negligible in light of what was going on at Children's Memorial. Nate underwent test after test, until — it took a full week — the doctors determined that the tumor was a PNET, a primitive neuroectodermal tumor, an atypical form of Ewing's sarcoma that afflicted fewer than four hundred children every year in the United States. Good: they knew what it was. Bad: it was aggressive. Unlike Burkitt's, it responded sluggishly to chemotherapy. Survival at two years, 30 percent.

Thea and Allan sat on a hard couch in a small private room while Gail Elkin relayed the numbers. Another doctor was there as well, a lanky, youngish Fellow in pediatric oncology; he provided a positive spin. Each case was different, each child different; in cancers this rare, obviously stats were unreliable. Good cop, bad cop. That the numbers were much worse than those for Burkitt's Thea understood, but her mind resisted further conjecture. She held Allan's hand. She was glad Nate wasn't there.

Nate received only the name for his tumor and the illusion of choice as to protocol, both of which had been first described to his parents. It came down, essentially, to two grades of chemo, regular or heavy-duty. Elkin, a small, clear-eyed woman of about forty with, no doubt, many other patients to see, was terse and unambiguous. The more aggressive regimen offered a better chance for a cure but the side effects were worse. His hair would fall out. He might suffer, among other things, nausea, diarrhea, mouth sores, anemia, and damage to kidneys, bladder, and heart. In the end it could kill him. The Fellow tried to change the emphasis. There were ways to protect a patient from each of these problems. They would take good care of Nate.

Nate had set down the joke book he was reading. He lay back

against his pillow, pleasurably awed with the power he had to de-
termine the course of his life. To Thea, the choice seemed a crapshoot. Like choosing the door behind which you'd find either a
princess to marry or a tiger to tear you to pieces—or worse, since
in Nate's case, there could be tigers behind both doors. But Nate
kept his eyes on Dr. Elkin, gravely and without fear, liking the idea
of a challenge or maybe just the word "aggressive." Go for the gold!
Allan made a fist, Nate did too, and they knocked them together,
males signaling solidarity. Thea asked question after question,
forgetting the answers, delaying the onset of whatever would happen. Her heart pounded as if she were working incredibly hard,
although it was clear to her that there was nothing she could do.

Gaby drove down to the hospital that evening with a Dave Barry
book for Nate, his preferred bedtime reading since his hospitaliza-
tion. Thea felt the pull of their sisterhood, a blood camaraderie in
the face of external threat. Perhaps—though it took positive thinking much too far—the ultimate effect of Nate's illness would be to
warm and deepen their kinship. Their father, who had mistrusted
any bond not based on blood, would press them to call each other.
There were no other siblings.

Waiting for the elevator at the end of visiting hours, Thea was
sufficiently warmed by her sister's kindness to Nate to ask about her
children. Her daughter Emma would be going into high school.
Emma was smart and ambitious, recommended for AP math and
biology, Gaby said. "Following in her aunt's footsteps."

"I hope not," said Thea with mock horror that had an under-
lay of real horror. Still, she genuinely liked the idea of her niece
excelling in high school as she had. She liked the absence of her
familiar surge of envy. She put her arms around her sister. They
held each other murmuring encouragements.

"You're postponing the bar mitzvah, right?" said Gaby. "I'll help
you make the phone calls. In fact I'll do it all for you, just give me
the list."

"Thank you," said Thea.

Gaby took a deep breath. "I'm so afraid," she said, "we're going
to lose him."

It took a moment for Thea to take in her sister's words. Her
brain shrank in the cave of her skull. "Where does this *insight*
come from?"

Gaby looked confused.

Then the elevator door opened. Inside, a girl was strapped into an elaborate wheelchair, her mother beside her. The little girl's head kept jerking, and the mother put tender hands on her daughter's cheeks and held her head, looking straight into her eyes. "It's okay, Lizzie. We'll get you your Baclofen." The sisters rode down without speaking while the woman murmured to her daughter, a hum in which Thea labored to separate her rage from her fear and to isolate both emotions from her response to the woman with the damaged child. Lizzie. Elizabeth. She hadn't brought her coat and the spring night was cool but she walked Gaby to her car. She had to swallow many times in order to speak, and her voice was wire-thin. "How could you say that to me?"

"Say what?" Gaby shook her head. "I'm sorry. I didn't mean—"

"Where did you get it, all your medical expertise?"

"Please, I don't want you to be—" Gaby looked at her. "You're freezing, let's go inside at least."

"You don't know anything about it," Thea cried. "Are you God?"

"You're right, I don't know, I only heard—" Gaby clapped a hand to her mouth. "Shut me up. I won't say anything else, I promise."

She couldn't let up. "It's like you *want* him to die or something."

Gaby moaned. "You don't really believe that?"

Thea was crying. "I can bear this as long as I think he'll be okay in the end." Sobs heaved up her throat, one at a time, like large abrading stones.

"Please. Of course he'll be okay!"

Gaby apologized over and over again. She took back everything, called herself a stupid moron, refused to leave the parking lot till Thea forgot the blather she'd spoken. Which came from her being ignorant and neurotic, talking to fill nervous space, that's all. "I swear to God!" she cried. They hugged goodbye. Thea rode the elevator back to Nate's floor, counting breaths to subvert all thought-horrors. And managed to do so in a faint, partial way by construing Gaby as unconsciously jealous of her. Thea had boys, Gaby girls. *I'm afraid we're going to lose him.* The words seethed with clairvoyance, or worse, like the report to the family after emergency surgery. Did Gaby feel the same blood rivalry that she had felt toward Gaby all her life? She fervently hoped so.

*

For a month Nate remained in the hospital while they tried to re-solve his pleural effusion. Thea was given leave from work, and she and Allan took turns, one of them sleeping in a pull-out chair in Nate's room while the other was home with Dylan. Nate would be discharged only to return to the hospital the following day. He was nauseated, weak, sometimes feverish. "The Side-Effect King!" said the Fellow, whom they had come to term the Good Doctor (Elkin, brusque and pessimistic, was the Bad Doctor). Gradually, though, Nate's lungs cleared, and the tumor, as aggressive as it was, began to shrink. In December it was decided that for the duration of his protocol, unless he spiked a fever, he would spend only five days a month in the hospital, for his nastiest rounds of infusions. Thea returned to London.

In Chicago when she'd thought about Edward, it was mainly to figure out how to disengage without hurting his feelings, not that she knew whether he was attached to her in such a way as to be wounded. A single night together, a few hours two long months ago: it would be arrogant—no?—for her to worry un-duly about him. Either way, she would be cordial and faintly re-gretful. They would have lunch, during which she would touch briefly on her family troubles. She would be sad and brave, he, respectful.

Over their actual lunch, though, her legs trembled and she couldn't stop talking. Gaby was no doctor but Thea feared her as prophetess. *I'm afraid we're going to lose him.* She gave him Gaby's words in Gaby's tone, as close as she could come to it, along with the tale of their ancient rivalry. He described problems with his hyper-assured, wealthy brother, then pointed out an ambiguity in Gaby's "I'm afraid." In the mouth of an authority figure the words might preface a decree, a declaration of something slated to hap-pen (*I'm afraid we're going to have to let you go*), but colloquially all they expressed was personal feeling. Unless Gaby was a witch or a doctor, she was simply, genuinely, *afraid!* Thea closed her eyes, waiting for something to wash over her—irritation with Edward's attempt at solace, or relief. She felt relief.

After that, as long as she was in England, Thea didn't want to let Edward out of her sight and he seemed to need her too. In private they started holding hands.

*

One of the problems with cancer treatment—not the big thing, the fear of pain and death, but the immediate, tangible thing— was the itinerary, the journey, its relentless sameness. There was no peak, no rise and fall. No fever that broke or didn't, no surgery that stemmed or failed to stem the bleeding. In moments of relative lightheartedness Thea would describe it architecturally. If cancer treatment were a house, it was ranch style, if a guesthouse, a motel; graphed, it was a sine curve. There was no focal point, no place for eye or mind to rest. No goal, only bouts of infusions, after which Nate would get sick and then recover enough for the next one.

Of all Nate's therapeutic poisons the worst was the one he received in the hospital. Adriamycin sounded like an antibiotic, familiar and benign, but it was blood-red in the bag over the bed, and draped with a pillowcase so that Nate wouldn't see it and gag. It was evil in other ways too, gave him sores in the back of his throat, a track of shingles across his chest, a constant fever of 101, and lowered his red count to where he sometimes needed a transfusion. "Mom," he said once, holding a paper cup of orange juice that he couldn't swallow, "I don't think I'm getting better."

Allan was in the room too and he cried, "You *are!*" as if insistence would change things. As if simple utterance had power. Thea's mouth was trembling. She couldn't walk out and leave her son with the message her departure would give, but she couldn't let him see her face. Face averted, she kept her voice steady. "Remember what the doctors said, honey? Ups and downs? Tomorrow will be an up."

But even when Nate seemed, or perhaps actually was, better, she was walking around on the constant verge of tears that she couldn't emit, even when she was alone, for fear of losing control of herself. Sometimes, she thought, it was better for Nate when she wasn't there. The parents' job was to amuse the sick one without showing how worried they were. On Adriamycin nights when she and Allan alternated sleeping at the hospital, she took on her tours of duty like a soldier, bearing the pain of Nate's pain, but Allan seemed almost to enjoy his. Drowsing in the hospital's all-night fluorescent twilight to the tune of beeping, humming, or a roommate's television, Allan said he felt at peace. Nate would be feverish or nauseated or hurting, but when it let up, for Nate it was gone, and for him too. They would play chess or gin rummy.

He would read to Nate and help with the schoolwork he was trying to keep up with. Nothing mattered, said Allan, beyond the blue-and-yellow curtains (a sailboat pattern) of the hospital room. He and Nate were two shipwrecked sailors on an island. They lived moment to moment. There was a sweetness.

Thea thought but didn't say that the island was gradually sinking. And if Allan didn't say it, he seemed to know it. Her worst moments weren't at the hospital but at home with Allan. It was hard to make love with him, though they still accomplished it from time to time. Harder was the moment they pulled away from each other, when she caught his eye and saw his fear, which mirrored and multiplied hers.

Her refuge was London, where she spent—was required to spend—five days each month. There was her work and there were her nights with Edward, who declared he was falling in love with her. She wasn't in love with him and she didn't believe he loved her (he possibly romanticized her, an older woman, woman of tragedy), but she could get lost in the sound of his unfamiliar voice, the touch of his unauthorized hands, the eternal novelty of the foreign city, the way as a child she had lost herself in books of fantasy.

All winter and spring Nate did well, even according to Elkin. His bar mitzvah was rescheduled for July. The cantor came to the house or the hospital, wherever Nate was ready for practice, and Nate practiced seriously. He sometimes spiked a fever but he was less fatigued than most kids in his situation, hospitalized only for the Adriamycin. To keep his white count high enough to ward off infection, Thea and Allan had learned to infuse him at home with immature white cells called G-CSF. They would set up the apparatus in the living room while he read a book or watched TV, and they admitted to enjoying it, injecting new cells into Nate's bloodstream that would grow into the adult cells that the chemo had zapped. Having overcome her fear of hurting her son, Thea could push the needle straight down through his skin into the port with the steady hand of a good nurse. Most of the time he went to school, and when school let out, if he was well enough he'd spend two weeks at a sleep-away camp for kids with cancer. Then the bar mitzvah. In the meantime, an altruistic Jewish organization had assigned him Avi, an eighteen-year-old Chabad-Lubavitcher.

He didn't preach, just visited him in the hospital and took him and Dylan out to play laser tag and video games when Nate was home. At home, friends came over like friends of anybody. When his count was low the friends had to wear surgical masks, and they did so with gravitas. No one cheated.

Once when Nate was unusually lively, a problem arose, albeit a small one. Nate and Assad had started roughhousing, which looked like so much fun that Thea didn't stop it. The port dislodged and required a trip to the ER, but the next day his temperature was normal. Thea described the event to Gaby, who visited frequently and kept all dire predictions to herself. "It was nice going to Children's for something they could fix," Thea said. "I felt like an ordinary mother."

"I know exactly what you mean."

It was Saturday morning. Allan was playing racquetball. The sisters sat together at the kitchen table, Thea pretending, as usual, to be more upbeat than she really was. Assad was over again, and Nate and Assad were such good friends, and Nate and Dylan were getting along too, the younger boy welcome in his brother's group. From time to time three-way laughter came in from the TV room. Then Gaby said, so casually it seemed rehearsed, that she was thinking of going back to school. Nursing school.

"Nursing?"

The question was automatic, a placeholder. Gaby's face was pink. She had been feeling lately that she was wasting her life. Since she had her BA, she could be an RN in two years. She took Thea's hand in her surprisingly moist one. "I don't know why I feel so guilty. Or nervous about this. I already applied, Thea, and I was accepted."

Thea congratulated her but had to amplify her enthusiasm. It seemed, oddly, that their shaky balance was tilting again. As if she couldn't thrive or even live without Gaby fixed in place like the North Star. Sister-in-a-bag, sister lesser; less interesting. What was wrong with her?

Until now, Thea hadn't told anyone about her affair, not even her closest friends. She didn't want to participate in hushed talk or field private looks of concern or complicity, which would make Allan nervous or suspicious. He was not insensitive. If she needed a confidante, she would not have chosen Gaby, whom she was habituated to outmaneuver. Still, perhaps to best her sister in the arena of surprise revelations, or simply in the throes of her age-old jealousy, Thea told her about Edward. How it began. What it was like. What *he* was like. To her relief, Gaby made no suggestions. There was no inkling of disapproval. *Your English lover!* she said, fascinated, and Thea went deeper and deeper into the experience, the disgust and thrill of touching another man's skin, the exhilaration of law-breaking, the color of the sky at dusk through her hotel window, Edward's smooth, youngish face. As she spoke, like fish rising to the surface of murky water, the image reassembled before her. As if a membrane between the two worlds were breaking down. She felt a ghostly frisson.

"You could really screw me," she said to Gaby.

"I would never," cried Gaby. "Do you really think I'd tell anyone?"

No, that wasn't it. She knew her sister would keep her secret. And there was more to say, what Thea was at this point only beginning to understand. Edward wasn't glamorous; he wasn't even that interesting. He was a comfort, a distraction. In some ways she felt as guilty about Edward as she did about Allan.

But before she could follow the train of thought to where it might enlighten her, Nate ran into the room, not on his toes as he had walked with the tumor growing in his belly, but on his whole foot, heel-toe, heel-toe. He opened the freezer, took out a quart of chocolate ice cream, carried it back to the den. "Yo, hombres!" he called out. "I bring sustenance."

Gaby was looking at Nate with what seemed pure pleasure, and Thea regarded her sister, whom she used to envy and still did, though Thea was taller by an inch and thinner, even now, by three to ten pounds. Today Gaby looked neither pretty nor ugly. One day Gaby would be a nurse. Thea felt Nate's presence in that realignment. Another link between the families. Thicker webbing.

She closed her eyes, conscious of Gaby, the boys in the den, the May sun warming them through the window. Of her own face she could summon no mental image. She wasn't fortune's favorite. No special treatment would be given her. This ripple of peace with its curl of joy could come to an ordinary person just the same. But it would be stupid not to embrace it.

Secret Stream

FROM *ZYZZYVA*

NATHAN WAS PEDALING along on Third Street at a robust twenty-five miles per hour when he spotted her, a feminine mirage in black that forced him to stop. Even before his brakes had finished squealing he began to laugh and shout. "Hey, what are you doing up there?" The woman was stuck to the top of a chainlink fence, trying to reach the sidewalk on a stretch of Third Street where Nathan never saw anyone on foot. It's a cliché about Los Angeles that no one walks, but on that shortcut to the Westside it's actually true. There are no pedestrians on Third Street and thus no crosswalks. The resulting fast and free flow of traffic feels like a memory of the city's unencumbered past, and Nathan biked that stretch like a guy driving a Porsche: he was in a hurry, he cut people off, and he didn't stop to take in the sights, except in this special case when a lithe woman in need appeared before him, attached to the top of a fence.

The barrier in question sealed off the street and the public from the undulating, artificial pastures of a private golf course. A broken strand of the fence had hooked into the woman's jeans: like a steel finger, it seemed to be pulling her down as she tried to free herself.

"You're fleeing the golf course," Nathan said.

She was about thirty years old, with lips glossed burnt umber, and the flat soles of her ankle-high black boots were caked in mud. On the other side of the fence two men in shorts were standing on the seventh green with clubs in hand, studying the geometry of their putts and squinting up at the noon sky. A thin layer of high clouds had drifted over the city, weakening the sun into a yellow stain, and all the shadows had been erased from the world below, confusing the golfers as they tried to read the dips in the grass beneath their shoes. They were therefore oblivious to the fence climber nearby.

"It's actually a country club," she said.

"And you're not a member."

"I'm trapped."

In the moment it took Nathan to get off his bike so that he could help her, she freed herself and leaped off. Her hair rose in a cloud of raven strands and fell with a splash as she bounded onto the sidewalk. With a few quick swipes of her hands, she brushed some blades of grass and dried mud splashes from her jeans.

"Well, that was embarrassing," she said.

She took a small nylon bag from her back and removed a notebook and pencil from it, and Nathan suddenly ceased to exist for her as she sat on the sidewalk, her back against the fence. Nathan watched her begin to draw and wondered which of the city's arty tribes she belonged to.

"Hi," Nathan said, insisting, because she was dark-skinned and pretty and he felt the need to know why she was trespassing on a golf course. "Excuse me, but . . . what are you doing?"

"I'm following the water."

As soon as she said "water" Nathan heard it and felt it: the sound of liquid flowing, dripping, moving through the air, causing oxygen molecules to shift and cool. Looking behind her, on the other side of the fence, he saw a stream. About three feet wide and four inches deep, it curved around some bunkers near the seventh green, and then fell sharply, broadcasting a steady, metallic sound as it disappeared into a concrete orifice beneath Nathan's feet.

"Fucking country club," Nathan said. "They shouldn't be wasting water like that." It was the middle of August, after all. In the middle of drought-parched LA.

"No," the woman said. She stopped drawing and looked at the water again. "It's not theirs. So they can't be wasting it."

"Well, who does it belong to, then?"

The woman paused for a second and answered with an amused smile. "The underworld, I guess."

*

Sofia was her name and she described herself as a "river geek." She said she was mapping the creek that ran through the golf course. And also its "tributaries." It was an ancient stream, she told him, born from a spring at the base of the Hollywood Hills, "bubbling up from the underworld." She showed Nathan her map, a series of blue pencil lines over a street grid she had pasted into her notebook. "It's groundwater," she said. Before reaching the golf course, the stream flowed into downtrodden Hollywood proper, around assorted industrial buildings and parking lots, and also through a junior-high campus and the television studios of KTLA. Sofia described all these things with a reverence that Nathan found disturbing: he sensed that she'd been doing this mapping expedition of hers alone, for weeks, and had never talked to anyone else about it until this moment.

Nathan returned the map to Sofia. He saw that the water in the culvert moved quickly, and was crystalline, as if it were some sylvan stream. This can't be, Nathan wanted to say. This supposedly natural body of water was trickling under his feet on Third Street, in a wealthy neighborhood called Hancock Park that was surrounded by low-slung, less-wealthy Korean, Filipino, and Salvadoran neighborhoods that were themselves near the geographic center of approximately five hundred square miles of asphalt and concrete.

"The flow never stops. Not even in the summer," Sofia said. "This creek was here before the country club. Before everything around you."

Sofia spoke these words and turned quiet, as if to allow the sound of the stream to make the truth of its presence clear to him. She was shy and a loner, like him, he thought. Nathan considered himself a loner, though none of his friends did, especially his women friends, all of whom were fervent cyclists: they thought he was charismatic and often very funny (when he was riding a bike), though clueless when it came to women. Clueless Nathan now concluded that Sofia's lonesomeness was deeper and more interesting than his own, more attuned to the mysterious and the sublime. She wore a silver scarab clip in her hair, a jeweled stud in her nose, and looking at her made Nathan feel unkempt and underdressed, which is a ridiculous thing for a man on a bicycle to feel.

Nathan told her he was mapping something too. He was scouting routes for a club of his that met at night and cycled to the most obscure LA landmarks they could think of. If she was a river geek, he was a bicycle geek, a map geek, a history geek.

"Our last one was the Tour de Smells. We went to a meat-packing plant in Vernon, a garbage dump in the Valley. Our group is called The Passage of a Few People Through a Rather Brief Moment in Time. We meet every two weeks." Sofia wrinkled her brow in confusion as he explained this, as if he was describing some exotic cult. He removed a piece of paper from the bag on his back and gave it to her: it was a hand-drawn map of the route he was currently working on, marked with labels such as *Abandoned Synagogue* and *SDS Hangout.*

"You have beautiful penmanship," she said.

"Maybe I can help you," Nathan said. He was a teacher, and classes were out for summer. His days were free and he could follow the stream with her and take notes, he said. Awkwardly, he asked for her number.

"I don't have a phone," she said, and Nathan knew instantly that this was true, because she paused and her dark eyes shifted nervously when she was forced to reveal this private thing about herself.

"Let's meet again at this same place tomorrow," he said. "At this same time."

"Okay, but without your bike," she said. "Because we need to go places a bike can't reach."

When they met at the culvert the next day, Sofia was dressed in black again. Her fingernails were also painted black. She led him south, down a gently curving street of assertive mansions, her black boots gliding over the sidewalk with steps that felt like flowing water to Nathan. Sofia was carrying a new map covered with topographical lines, and she studied it as they turned west and passed a buffet of overdone tributes to assorted architectural styles: a mini Monticello here, a bloated Tudor cottage there. "This street follows the old streambed," Sofia said. "The city buried it, like, a hundred years ago. But the water's still flowing down there. In a big drainpipe."

A block later they reached another fence, and stood above another culvert from which the stream emerged, moving slower, wider and shallower, flowing into a tangle of branches and bushes.

Without a word Sofia climbed the fence and landed with a

splash in about an inch of water. "Technically, I'm pretty sure this is trespassing," Nathan said as he followed her. Sofia marched along the water, pulling back branches for him. Where is this woman taking me? he wondered, and after a few paces he got his answer, as they entered an open space where the suddenly dry air seemed to vibrate under a liberated, ferocious sun. The space was a kind of meadow, framed by two mansions, each so abundant with backyard paraphernalia, Nathan felt as if he'd entered the prop closet of a studio dedicated to making movies about suburban American excess. He saw competing steel barbecue machines with gauges and propane-tank attachments; one stood before a tiled-roofed Spanish-style mansion, the other at the base of a turret-topped Moorish castle, as if ready to prepare steaks and burgers for a medieval army. Next to the Spanish mansion a pathway of flat stones led to a child's climbing structure made of fiery redwood. The Moorish castle's domain included a marble dining table and a tennis court of emerald cement.

Sofia's stream snaked through this gaudy landscape, making two gentle turns inside a channel sunken in crabgrass. "I just want to look at it for a while, if you don't mind," Sofia said, and she sat down on the grass with her sleeved arms wrapped around her knees. The water flowed in a smooth, flat current, like a bonsai-shrunken version of the Mississippi.

Nathan looked up at the windows of the multistoried mansions around them and wondered if the people inside would call the cops.

"Really, you just want to sit here?" Nathan said.

Sofia nodded with a gentle, wordless insistence. He joined her for a second, sitting on the grass. The water was silent here, and the houses were silent too, though the birds in the trees around them were engaged in a jazz improv of tweets and hoots and cackles.

After five minutes Nathan mumbled, "I'm going to keep on exploring. I'll meet you, uh, downstream, I guess."

Sofia didn't look up to acknowledge Nathan as he walked away. He was disturbed by the aching weirdness of what he was doing, trespassing amid fake backyard ecologies, the creek leading him on a midday sleepwalk past olive trees, a rosebush, assorted cacti, grapevines, and four cypress trees that loomed over him like monstrous green sentinels. He stepped over a low wooden fence and heard high-pitched yelling. Peering through a patch of ferns, he saw a swimming pool and two boys in bathing suits. One of the boys stopped at the edge of a diving board and stared at Nathan when he stepped out into the full sunlight. Nathan waved. The boy waved back and jumped into the pool with a percussive splash.

Nathan followed the stream into more backyards until he reached another culvert and climbed over it to the safety of a public street. As he waited for Sofia to appear, he looked back at the stream, admiring the way it trickled and whistled in the wind. The city tried to tame the water, but it still followed some prehistoric course through the subdivided and built-up land. The stream had a lifespan measured in geological time, and looking at it, Nathan felt at one with the centuries, the millennia, and the epochs. Maybe that was why Sofia followed it, why she was back there in someone's yard staring at it. When she looked into the stream, she was looking at timelessness.

Nathan waited forty minutes before Sofia finally appeared, her feet splashing in the water. She caught his eye and raised the corners of her lips in what might have been a smirk. Or maybe just a smile. He reached out to help her climb up to the street, and she allowed him to keep his hand clasped to hers a moment longer than necessary.

"Thank you for waiting for me," she said.

On the bus ride back home that afternoon Nathan thought about how smart and beautiful Sofia was, and how their private obsessions with public spaces matched, and he wondered if he'd finally found the ideal loner with whom to share his solitude. He wondered what he might say or do the next time they met, now that he'd clasped her hand.

When they met the following day, Sofia led him toward the southwest. "I'm glad you came back," she said. "I thought I'd scared you off yesterday." She gave him a playful look that caused a warm electricity to pass through his spine.

"Yeah, trespassing isn't usually my thing," he said. "But following a secret stream is pretty wild, pretty audacious, I must say."

Sofia led him away from Hancock Park and the houses began to shrink, and the streets widened and filled with more cars, which were driving faster, and the people inside these vehicles had darker skin tones that more closely matched hers.

"I think I know where this stream hits daylight again," she said.

"Where?"

"You'll see."

As they walked past a sixth, seventh, and eighth block, Sofia told him about the river and its history. She'd spent many hours in the Central Library, she said, immersed in the accounts of California amateur geologists and naturalists of the nineteenth and twentieth centuries, looking for references to streams and groundwater. In Sofia's universe, natural history was never erased, and water could still flow underneath the six lanes of Olympic Boulevard, and listening to her Nathan felt ashamed of the modern-day thoroughfare and the way he'd enjoyed its straightness, speeding toward the glass ghosts of downtown towers on the smoggy horizon. All these years in LA, he'd been unaware that he was riding over a stream whose old Spanish name Sofia had just revealed to him.

"El Arroyo del Jardín de las Flores," Nathan repeated.

"Correct."

He wanted to walk alongside Sofia, but she kept drifting one or two paces ahead. "What is it you do?" he asked finally, and the question caused her to slow down. "For a living?"

"Nothing, right now. I used to work in a museum no one ever visited," she said. "A state park that got closed down. It was an old rancho with lots of beautiful and rusty old things inside."

They reached a park surrounded by tall modernist office buildings whose painted cement skins were flaking in the sun. "I know this park," Nathan said. "I always thought it felt like Manhattan in the desert." A glass tower stood nearby, about eight stories tall, smothered in dust and slowly dying, its several hundred windows long unwashed. They climbed down a gentle, lawn-covered slope, to the spot where a large corrugated tube emerged from the grass. El Arroyo del Jardín de las Flores now resembled the flow from an oversized kitchen spigot, seeping into a crevice between the park's lawns, trickling through foot-tall reeds.

"The stream used to flood every winter," Sofia said. "That's why there's a park here. No one could build on this land."

Sofia found a spot overlooking the creek and sat down. Nearby a child of about seven was building a bridge over the creek with his father. They had fashioned a little roadway from pieces of eucalyptus bark, tree branches, and dried reeds. Nathan watched the boy and his father work with steady, playful purpose, bringing palmfuls of mud from the streambed and tufts of grass and more twigs, and using them to cover the surface of their roadway, until the bridge itself started to look like a specimen of jungle flora. The boy took three miniature cars from his pocket and put them on the road-way, and then he stepped back and watched the stream flow un-derneath.

The boy and his father and their bridge made Nathan feel con-tent, nostalgic for his own boyhood, but they had no effect on Sofia. Sitting there, staring at the stream, she looked like a woman trying to imagine a world without civilization. Or like a woman straining to understand some ferocious and overwhelming idea contained in the water's flow.

"You don't have to stay here with me," she said, suddenly. "I'm fine alone."

"No, I don't mind. It's peaceful here," Nathan said, though he was lying, because he knew he would never get used to the idea of sitting in one place, in the middle of summer, just to look at flow-ing water. "My ex-wife got laid off too," he said, to make conversa-tion. "She worked for the county. In social services."

"How long were you married?"

"Sixteen months."

"I was engaged," Sofia said, keeping her eyes on the stream. Three sparrows fluttered over the water and landed nearby, and they began playing a game of hopscotch on the grass, bounc-ing into the stream and bouncing out. "He was a drummer," she said. "He died four years ago this month. Of pneumonia, which is crazy." For some reason the silence that followed was not filled with an overwhelming sense of tragedy. The sparrows disappeared and the water flowed. Sofia had been a loner before, Nathan con-cluded, and she would still have been following this stream, alone, even if her drummer had lived to marry her. A very faint breeze drifted over the grass and Nathan felt the glass skins of the mod-ernist office buildings dissolving into sand in the sun.

"I just like to spend time with the water," Sofia said. "You under-stand. Right?"

"What do you see?" he asked. "When you look at the stream?"

"It's not what I see. It's what I feel."

"What do you feel?"

"That it's been waiting here for me to find it."

Nathan did not know what to say to this. He didn't believe in fate. When he discovered cool things on his cycling explorations, he didn't think it was his destiny to find them. But he couldn't say any of that, and instead he felt defeated at his inability to take their conversation to a place that didn't feel so anchorless. Her communion with the stream was making him feel anxious. He needed to keep moving, and he looked at her pleadingly, as if to say, Can't we just keep on exploring? But she didn't notice or care about his discomfort. Instead, she took out a book to read.

"If you want, I could read this to you," she said. "It's poetry. This one is called 'The Idea of Order at Key West.'"

The poem described a woman standing on the edge of the ocean, singing. Nathan listened for the argument of the poem, or the story it told, but there didn't seem to be one. Eventually he began to focus on the sound of Sofia's voice instead, the precise and slow whisper with which she read each line. The poem filled up her solitude with awe and wonder, especially when she read the line "The sky acutest at its vanishing." But the poem itself made less sense to Nathan the longer it went on. When she finished he couldn't think of anything to say other than the exceedingly lame comment, "It's beautiful."

"If you don't mind, I'd like to wait here until the sun goes down," she said finally. "I want to see the stream fade in the light."

The summer sunset was at least five hours away. Nathan decided he couldn't sit that long. He'd wished he'd brought his bicycle, instead of having to take the bus back home again.

"So," he said. "At this same place, at the same time, tomorrow?"

"Sure."

Before Nathan left for the bus stop, he walked over to examine the bridge the boy and his father had built an hour earlier. A line of ants was crawling over it. In their shuffle march, the ants were crossing the stream from north to south, as if they'd undertaken a mission of exploration to new, undiscovered lands.

On the bus ride back home, Nathan remembered the first line of the poem: *She sang beyond the genius of the sea.* He imagined a conversation in which Sofia talked about the poem and explained it to him. Nathan would then share his own introspective musings and talk about how he channeled his curiosity about the city into his riding, exploring on his bicycles (he owned three). He imagined sharing his passion for the city's geography with Sofia, telling her about routes that led to destinations that the city's haters called "nowhere," though in Nathan's mind each of those places was definitely somewhere. And finally, he imagined that Sofia would actually find all of this interesting and agree to go riding with him.

But when Nathan saw Sofia again at the park, he instantly understood the absurdity of his fantasy. Their eyes met and she said with a smile, "We're almost done."

Nathan followed her silently. They left the park and walked along Pico Boulevard for a mile until they reached a brick cube labeled LIQUOR. She led him around to the back, to a small parking lot of eroded asphalt, and a fence topped with barbed wire.

"Here it is," she said. They walked up to the fence and looked ten feet down into a muddy slough littered with bottles, white plastic bags, and the desiccated corpse of a cat. At the bottom, a strip of tar-black water not more than four inches wide moved slowly westward.

"Bummer," Nathan said.

"Yeah, it's pretty ugly. Let's keep going."

The water advanced between rows of cinderblock buildings, and then it slipped under Venice Boulevard, a street so wide, flat, and long, it swallowed up all the city around it, as if it were a corridor cut through space-time that would suck them up and spit them out in some other dimension. Venice Boulevard finally guided them to a concrete basin with vertical walls, the kind of domesticated "river" for which LA was infamous. El Arroyo del Jardín de las Flores fed into this channel from a rectangular hole in one of the sidewalls: like a slaughtered animal, it bled a black stain onto the concrete.

"That's it?"

"Yes."

Nathan looked at his watch: it was late, and he thought they should continue their trek tomorrow. "So," he said. "At this same place, at the same time?"

"No," Sofia said abruptly. "This is where our stream ends. Our stream is a tributary of this thing you see here, which used to be a real river."

"Ballona Creek," he said.

"It flows into the ocean, over by the Marina," she said. "I've been there a dozen times."

"Me too."

"So you know: Ballona Creek is a straight, manmade ditch going into the ocean," she said. "It just makes me feel empty, going there. I don't know why."

"Maybe if I go there with you, you'll feel different."

Sofia shot him a skeptical look, and then studied him, as if she were measuring him somehow, or assessing the value of their incipient friendship.

"Okay, then," she said.

As he rode the bus home Nathan thought a lot about Sofia's tepid "Okay, then." He quickly came to the conclusion that she wouldn't be there to meet him the next day.

When he woke up the next morning, he was certain Sofia wouldn't be there. If he wanted to see Sofia again, Nathan thought, the best strategy would be to seek out more streams and hope that his path crossed with hers again. For a moment Nathan imagined a life in which he pursued a river obsession as madly as Sofia did, following streams under skyscrapers, past football stadiums, factories, and tenements, selling off his bicycles as he surrendered himself completely to this new quest. He'd buy all sorts of river-hunting paraphernalia: divining rods, maybe, or waterproof shoes, and one day he'd run into Sofia at some hidden urban wetland and they'd resume their riparian wandering together.

The hour of their meeting came and went and Nathan didn't leave home. It was the way he'd handled relationships with women since his wife left him: he preempted disappointment.

Instead, that afternoon, in the hours before sunset, he rode his mountain bike up the dirt paths that led to the top of Mount Hollywood. From that perch he took in the sprawl of the city and imagined the aquifers percolating inside the mountain below his feet, and the water that escaped to follow secret channels through the city. Nathan thought about Sofia's thin fingers drawing a map of the stream with colored pencils, and he thought about the sound of her voice reading the poem. He'd found a copy online and now he read it on his smartphone. *The sea was not a mask / No more was she.* The poem continued to perplex him, as if it were written in a code understood only by women who stared at streams.

A few days later Nathan returned to Ballona Creek on a road bike. He did not expect to find Sofia, and he glided quickly past the point where they had last spoken. He was going to follow Ballona Creek to the ocean. There was a bike path the last few miles.

Fed by several more tributaries, Ballona became a creek worthy of the name in its final stretch. He reached the beach, and then pedaled past it, because the path continued on a breakwater that jutted into the sea. When the path ended, Nathan stopped and took out his phone. He read more lines from the poem — *The heaving speech of air, a summer sound / Repeated in a summer without end . . . The meaningless plungings of water and the wind.* The words unsettled him and he decided not to read them again.

Nathan preferred the certainty of maps, and he imagined the place where he was standing as represented on a map: the fixed black line of the bike path, and a dot for the path's terminus. Below his feet the cold Pacific swallowed up the freshwater from Ballona Creek. He thought of the thin flow of El Arroyo del Jardín de las Flores swirling and dissolving in the estuary, transformed into foam and green droplets laden with algae. When he looked up at the horizon, the sea was as big and blue and welcoming as he remembered it. The ocean swayed, it rose and fell, and it played with the light and the moving air. Nathan realized, suddenly, that he was seeing Sofia's poem and its "plunging waves" and "gasping wind" come to life, and this thought caused him to laugh out loud. He felt surrounded by a presence that was feminine and circular, as if he were standing inside the warm and soothing whirlpool of a woman's thoughts. Nathan stared at the water and allowed his mind to drift. When he looked down at his watch again, he realized he had been standing there, looking at the ocean, for an hour.

JOHN EDGAR WIDEMAN

Williamsburg Bridge

FROM *Harper's Magazine*

To be absolutely certain I rode the F train from my relatively quiet Lower East Side neighborhood to 34th Street and set myself adrift in the crowds around Penn Station and Herald Square. Short subway ride uptown in dark tunnels beneath New York's sidewalks, twenty-five, thirty minutes of daylight above ground, among countless bodies hurtling ahead like trains underground, each one on its single-blind track.

Quick trip yesterday, so today I'm certain and determined, though not in any hurry. Why should I be? All the time in the world at my disposal. All mine the moment I let go. How much time do you believe you possess? Enough perhaps to spare a stranger a moment or two while he sits on the Williamsburg Bridge, beyond fences that patrol the pedestrian walkway, on an extreme edge where a long steel rail runs parallel to walkways, bikeways, highways, and train tracks supported by this enormous towering steel structure, sky above, East River below, this edge where the bridge starts and terminates in empty air.

I heard Sonny Rollins play his sax on the Williamsburg Bridge once and only once live one afternoon so many years ago I can't recall the walkway's color back then. Definitely not the pale red of my tongue when I wag it at myself each morning in the mirror, the walkway's color today at the intersection of Delancey and Clinton Streets where I enter it by passing through monumental stone portals, then under a framework of steel girders that span the 118-foot width of the bridge and display steel letters announcing its name. Iron fences painted cotton-candy pink guard the walkway's

flanks, and just beyond their shoulder-high rails much taller barriers of heavy-gauge steel chicken wire bolted to sturdy steel posts
guard the fences. Steel crossbeams, spaced four yards or so apart,
form a kind of serial roof over the walkway, too high by about a
foot for me to jump up and touch, even on my best days playing
hoop. Faded cross-ties overhead could be rungs of a giant ladder
once upon a time that slanted red up into the sky, but now the
ladder lies flat, rungs separated by gaps of sky that seem to open
wider as I walk beneath them, though if I lower my eyes and gaze
ahead into the distance where the bridge's far end should be, the
walkway's a tunnel, solid walls and ceiling converge, no gaps, no
exit, a cul-de-sac.

Tenor-sax wail the color I remember from the afternoon, decades ago, I heard Sonny Rollins the first and only time live. Color
deeper than midnight blue. Dark, scathing, grudging color of a
colored soldier's wound coloring dirty white bandages wrapped
around his dark chest. It was a clear afternoon a sax turned darker
than the night. Color of all time. Vanished time. No time. Color of
deep-purple swirls I mixed from ovals of pure, perfect color in the
paint box I found under the Christmas tree one morning when I
was a kid. An unexpected color with a will of its own brewed by a
horn's laments, amens, witness. That's what I remember, anyway.
Color of disappointment, of ancient injuries and bruises and staying alive and dying and being born again all at once after I had
completed about half the first lap of a back-and-forth hump over
the Williamsburg Bridge.

Walking the bridge an old habit now. One I share with numerous other walkers whose eyes avoid mine as I avoid theirs, our
minds perhaps on the people down below, people alive and dead
on tennis courts, ball fields, running tracks, swings, slides, jungle
gyms, benches, chairs, blankets, grass plots, gray paths alongside
the East River. Not exactly breaking news, is it, that from up here
human beings seem as tiny as ants. Too early this morning for
most people or ants, but from this height, this perch beyond the
walkway's fences, this railing along the edge of the Williamsburg
Bridge, I see a few large ants or little people sprinkled here and
there. Me way up here, ants and people way down there all the
same size. Same weight. Same fate.

So here I am, determined to jump, telling myself, telling you,
that I'm certain. Then what's the fool waiting for? it's fair for you

to ask. In my defense I'll say I'm aware that my desire to be certain is an old-fashioned desire, "certain" an obsolete word in a world where I'm able only to approximate, at best, the color of a bridge I've crossed thousands of times, walked yesterday, today, a world where the smartest people acknowledge an uncertainty principle and run things accordingly and own just about everything and make fools of the vast majority of the rest of us not as smart, not willing to endure lives without certain certainties. I don't wish to be a victim, a complete dupe, and must hedge my bets, understand that certainty is always relative, and not a very kind, generous, loving relative I can trust. Which is to say, or rather to admit, that although I'm sure I'm up here and sure this edge is where I wish to be and sure of what I intend to do next, to be really certain, or as close to certain as you or I will ever get, certainty won't come till after the instant I let go.

Many years passed before I figured out it had to be Sonny Rollins I heard one afternoon. Do you know who I mean? Theodore Walter Rollins, born September 7, 1930, New York City, emerges early fifties "most brash and creative young tenor player." Flees to Chicago to escape perils of NYC jazz scene, reemerges 1955 in NYC with Clifford Brown, Max Roach group—"caustic, often humorous style of melodic invention . . . command of everything from arcane ballads to calypso." Nicknamed "Newk" for resemblance to Don Newcombe, star Brooklyn Dodgers pitcher. Produces string of great albums (1956–58). Withdraws again, no public performances (1959–61), practices on the Williamsburg Bridge "to get myself together" after "too much, too soon." Brushes up on craft and returns with album, *The Bridge.* Another sabbatical, Japan, India (1969)—more time "to get myself together . . . I think it's a good thing for anybody to do." Returns (1971) to perform publicly, etc., etc. All this information I quote available at Sonny Rollins website; cocaine addiction, ten months he did at Rikers for armed robbery not in website bio.

Once I decided it had to have been Sonny Rollins playing, my passion for his music escalated, as did my intimacy with the Williamsburg Bridge. Recently, trying to discover where it ranks among New York bridges in terms of its attractiveness to jumpers, I came across alexreisner.com and a story about a suicide in progress on the Williamsburg Bridge that Mr. Reisner claimed to have witnessed. Numerous black-and-white photos illustrate his piece. In some pictures a young colored man wears neatly cropped dreads, pale skin, pale undershorts, a bemused expression, light mustache, shadow of beard, his hands curled around a rail running along the outermost edge of the bridge where he sits. Water ripples behind, below, to frame him. His gaze downcast, engaged elsewhere, a place no one else on the planet can see. No people there, no time there where his eyes have drifted, settled. His features regular, handsome in a stiff, plain, old-fashioned way. Some mother's mixed son, mixed-up son.

If I could twist around, shift my weight without losing balance, rotate my head, and glance over my left shoulder, I'd see superimposed silhouettes of the Manhattan and Brooklyn Bridges downriver, grand cascades of steel cables draped from their towers, and over there, if I stay steady and focused, I could pick out the tip of the Statue of Liberty jutting just above the Brooklyn Bridge, Lady Liberty posed like sprinters Tommie Smith and John Carlos on the winners' stand at the 1968 Mexico City Olympics, her torch a black-gloved fist rammed into the sky: We're number one. Up yours.

Dawns on me that I'll miss the next Olympics, next March Madness, next Super Bowl. Dawns on me that I won't regret missing them. A blessing. Free at last. Not up here because I didn't win a gold medal. Not up here to sell shoes or politics. Nor because my mom's French. Not here because of my color or lack of color. My coloring pale like the young colored man in website photos who sat, I believe, precisely on the spot where I'm sitting. Color not the reason I'm here or the reason you are where you are, wherever you happen to be, whatever your color. Ain't about color. Speed what it's about. Color just a gleam in the beholder's eye. Now you see it, now you don't.

On the other hand, no doubt color does matter. My brownish skin, gift of the colored man my mother married, confers added protection against sunburn in tropical climates and a higher degree of social acceptance generally in some nations or regions or communities within nations or regions where people more or less my color are the dominant majority. My color also produces in many people of other colors an adverse reaction hardwired. Thus color keeps me on my toes. Danger and treachery never far removed from any person's life regardless of color, but in my case danger and treachery are palpable, everyday presences. Unpleas-

ant surprises life inflicts. No surprise at all. Color says, smiling,
Told you so.

Gender not the reason I'm here either. A crying shame in this
advanced day and age that plenty of people would tag my posture
as effeminate. Truth is, with my upper body tilted slightly backward, weight poised on my rear end, arms thrust out to either side
for balance, I must press my thighs together to maintain stability,
keep my feet spread apart so they serve as bobbing anchors.

Try it sometime. Someplace high and dangerous, ideally. You'll
get the point. Point being of course any position you assume up
here unsafe. Like choice of a language, gender, color, etc. A person's forced to choose, forced to suffer the consequences. Like
choosing which clothes to wear on the Williamsburg Bridge or
not wear. I've chosen to keep my undershorts on. I want to be remembered as a swimmer, not some naked nut. Swimmer who has
decided to swim away with dignity intact in homely but perfectly
respectable boxers.

Just about naked also because I don't wish to be mistaken for
a terrorist. No intent to harm a living soul. No traffic accidents,
boat accidents caused by my falling body, heavier and heavier, they
say, as it descends. No concealed weapons, no dynamite strapped
around my bare belly. I've taken pains to situate myself on the
bridge's outermost edge to maximize the chance I hit nothing but
water.

And contrary to what you might be thinking, loneliness has not
driven me to the edge. I'm far from lonely. In addition to my undershorts I have pain, grief, plenty of regrets, and prospects of
a dismal future to keep me company, and when not entertained
sufficiently by those companions I look down below. Whole shitty
world's at my feet. My chilly toes wiggle like antennae, chilly thighs
squeeze together not because of fear or loneliness but like my
mother's hands when they form a steeple, and you might think
she's about to pray, but then she chants: This is the church / Here's
the steeple, a game Mom taught me in ancient days. I can't stop a
grin spreading across my face even now, today, when she starts the
rhyme, steeples her pale long elegant fingers. I'm a sucker every
time.

Yes, Mom, one could say I drink a lot, Mom, and drink perhaps
part of the problem, but not why I'm up here. Drink a bad habit, I
admit. Like hiring a blind person to point out what my eyes miss.

But drink simpatico, an old old cut buddy—I gape at his antics, the damage he causes, stunned by the ordinary when it shows itself through his eyes. Only that, Mom. Nothing evil, nothing extreme, nothing more or less than the ordinary showing itself as a gift. The ordinary revealed when I'm drinking. You must know what I mean. I'm the hunter who wants to shoot it, wants to be eaten.

French my dead mother's mother tongue and occasionally I think in French. If another person appeared next to me sitting on the steel rail where I sit and the sudden person asked, What do you mean mother's tongue? What do you mean thinking in French? I would have to answer: To tell the truth, I don't know. Carefully speak the words aloud in English, those exact words repeated twice to keep track of language, of where I am, to keep track of myself. Desperate to explain before we tumble off the edge. Desperate to translate a language one and only one person in the universe speaks, has ever spoken.

What words will I be saying to myself the instant I slip or pitch backward into the abyss? Will French words or Chinese or Yoruba make a difference? Will I return from the East River with a new language in my head, start up the universe again with new words, or do I leave it all behind, everything behind forever, the way thoughts leave me behind? East River behind me, below me. River showing off today. Chilly ripples scintillate under cold, intermittent sunshine. Water colors differently depending on point of view, light, wind, cosmic dissonance. Water shows all colors, no color, any color from impenetrable oily sludge to purest glimmer. Water a medium like white space yet white-space empty—thin ice, a blank page words sprint across until they vanish. White space disguises itself as spray, as froth, as bubbles, as a big white splash when I fall backward and land in the East River, my ass-backward swan dive, swan song greeted by white applause, a bouquet of white flames while deep down below, white space swallows, burps, closes blacker than night.

With my fancy new phone I googled the number of suicides each day in America. By speaking a few words into my phone I learned 475 suicides per year, 1.3 daily in New York City. With a few more words or clicks one could learn yearly rate of suicide in most countries of the civilized world. Data more difficult obviously to access from prehistory, the bad old days before a reliable someone started counting everything, keeping score of everything, but even ancient numbers available I discover if you ask a phone the correct questions in the proper order, answers supplied by sophisticated algorithms that estimate within a hairsbreadth, no doubt, unknown numbers from the past. Lots of statistics re suicide, but I could not locate the date of the very first suicide or find a chat room or blog offering lively debate on the who, when, why, where of the original suicide. You'd think someone would care about such a transformative achievement, or at least an expert would claim credit for unearthing the first suicide's name and address, posting it for posterity.

Suicide of course a morbid subject. Who would want to know too much about it? I'm much more curious about immortality and rapture. If a person intent on suicide is also seeking rapture, why not choose the Williamsburg Bridge. Like the young man in the website photos who probably believed his fall, his rapture, would commence immersed within the colors of Sonny Rollins's tenor sax, Sonny's music first and last thing heard as water splashes open and seals itself. Rapture rising, a pinpoint spark of dazzle ascending the heavens, wake spreading behind it, an invisible band of light that expands slowly, surely as milky-white wakes of water taxis that pass beneath the bridge, expand and shiver to the ends of the universe.

Sometimes it feels like I've been sitting up here forever. An old, weary ear worn out by nagging voices nattering inside and outside it. Other times I feel brand-new, as if I've just arrived or not quite here yet, never will be. Lots to read here, plenty of threats, promises, advice, prophecies in various colors, multiple scripts scrawled, scrolled, stenciled, sprayed on the walkway's blackboard of pavement. I've read that boys in Central Asia duel with kites of iridescent rainbow colors, a razor fixed to each kite's string to decide who's king. Clearly my kite's been noticed. Don't you see them? Bridge crawling with creepy cops in jumpsuits, a few orange, most the color of roaches. Swarms of them, sneaky fast and brutal as always. They clamber over barriers, scuttle across girders, shimmy up cables, skulk behind buttresses, swing on ropes like Spider-Man. A chopper circles. One cop hoots through a bullhorn. Will they shoot me off the bridge like they blasted poor, lovesick King Kong off the Empire State Building? Cop vehicles, barricades, flashing lights clog arteries that serve the bridge and its network of expressways, thruways, overpasses, and underpasses that should be pumping traffic noise and carbon monoxide to keep me company up here.

With a cell phone, if I could manage to dial it without dumping my ass in the frigid East River, I could call 9-1-1, leave a number for SWAT teams in the field to reach me up here, an opportunity for opposing parties to conduct a civilized conversation this morning instead of screaming back and forth like fishwives. My throat hoarse already, eyes tearing in the wicked wind. I threaten to let go and plunge into the water if they encroach one inch further into my territory, my show this morning.

Small clusters of people-ants peer up at me now. What do they think they see tottering on the edge of the Williamsburg Bridge? They appear to stare intently, concerned, curious, amused, though I've read numerous species of ant and certain specialists within numerous ant species are nearly blind. Nature not wasting eyes on lives spent entirely in the dark, but nature generous too, provides ants with antennae as proxies for vision and we get cell phones to cope with the blues.

Shared cell-phone blues once with a girlfriend I had high hopes for once who told me about a lover once, her Michelangelo, gorgeous, she said, a rod on him hard as God's wrath, is how she put it, a pimp who couldn't understand why she got so upset when he conducted business by cell phone while lying naked next to naked her, a goddamn parade of women coming and going in my bedroom and Michelangelo chattering away as if I don't exist, him without a clue he was driving me crazy jealous, she said, her with no clue how crazy jealous it was driving me—the lethal combination of my unhealthy curiosity and her innocent willingness to regale me with details of her former intimacies, her chattering away on her end and me listening on mine connected and unconnected.

Not expecting a call up here. If I could explain white space, perhaps I could convince everyone down there to take a turn up here. Not that it's comfortable here, no reasonable person would wish to be in my shoes, I'm not even wearing shoes, tossed overboard with socks, sweatshirt, jeans, jacket, beret, stripped down to skivvies, and intermittent sunshine the forecast promised not doing the trick. Each time a cloud slides between me and the sun, wind chills my bare skin, my bones shiver. On the other hand, the very last thing any human being should desire is comfort. World's too dangerous. Comfort never signifies less peril, less deceit, it only means your guard's down, your vigilance faltering.

On the bridge one day dark, thick clouds rolling in fast, sky almost black at two in the afternoon, I caught a glimpse of a man reflected in a silvery band of light that popped up solid as a mirror for an instant parallel to the walkway's fence, a momentary but crystal-clear image of a beat-up, hunched-over colored guy in a beret, baggy gray sweats, big ugly sneakers scurrying across the Williamsburg Bridge, an old gray person beside me nobody loves and he loves nobody, might as well be dead, who would know or care if he was dead or wasn't, and this man scurrying stupid as an ant in a box, back and forth, back and forth between walls it can't scale is me, a lonely, aging person trapped in a gray city, a vicious country, scurrying back and forth as if scurrying might change his fate, and I think, What a pitiful creature, what a miserable existence, it doesn't get any worse than this shit, and then it does get worse, icy pellets of rain start pelting me, but between stinging drops a bright idea—universe bigger than NYC, bigger than America, get out of here, get away, take a trip, visit Paris again, and even before the part about where the fuck's the money coming from, I'm remembering I detest tourism, tourists worse than thieves in my opinion, evil and dangerous because tourists steal entire lands and cultures, strip them little by little, stick in their pockets everything they can cart back home and exchange for other commodities until other lands and cultures emptied and vanished, tourists like false-hearted lovers worse than thieves in the old song, you know how it goes, a thief will just rob you and take what you have, but a false-hearted lover will lead you to the grave.

Once upon a long time ago I had hopes love might help. Shared rapture once with a false-hearted lover. I'll start with your toes, she whispered, start with your cute crooked toes, she says, your funny crooked toes with undersides same color as mine, skin on top a darker color than mine, and when I'm finished with your toes, she promises, my false-hearted lover promises, I'll do the rest. Hours and hours later she's still doing toes, she's in no hurry and neither am I. Enraptured. Toes tingle, aglow. How many toes do I own? However many, I wished for more and one toe also more than enough, toe she's working on makes me forget its ancestors, siblings, posterity, forget everything. Bliss will never end. I read *War and Peace, Dhalgren, Don Quixote,* and think I'll start Proust next after I finish *Cane* or has it been Sonny Rollins's mellow sax, not written words, accompanying work she's busy doing down there. Whole body into it, every tentacle, orifice, treacly inner wetness, hers, mine. Time seemed to stop, as during a yawn, blink, death, rapture, as in those apparently permanent silences between two consecutive musical notes Sonny Rollins or Thelonious Monk blew, or between heartbeats, hers, mine, ours. A hiccuping pause, hitch, an extenuating circumstance.

It's afterward and also seamlessly before she starts on my toes and she's still in no hurry. No hurry in her voice the day that very same false-hearted lover tells me she's falling . . . slipped out of love.

Shame on me but I couldn't help myself, shouted her words back in her face. Who wouldn't need to scream, to grab her, shake her, search for a reflection in the abyss of her eyes, in the dark mirror of white space. I plunged, kicked, flailed, swallowed water, wind, freezing rain.

Sad but true, some people born unlucky in love, and if you're jinxed that way it seems never to get any better. No greeting this morning from my neighbor ghost, not even a goodbye wave. Can't say what difference it might have made if she had appeared, I simply register my regret and state the fact she was a no-show again this morning in the naked space above her window's bottom ledge.

We speak politely in the elevator, nod or smile or wave on streets surrounding the vast apartment complex or when we cross paths in the drab lobby of section C of the building we share. Not very long after I moved into my fifteenth-floor one-bedroom, kitchenette and bath, the twin towers still lurked at the island's tip, biggest bullies on the block after blocks of skyscrapers, high-rises, the spectacle still novel to my eyes, so much city out the window, its size and sprawl and chaos would snag my gaze, stop me in my tracks, especially the endless sea of glittering lights at night, and for the millisecond or so it took to disentangle a stare, my body would expand, fly apart, each particle seeking out its twin among infinite particles of city, and during one such pause, from the corner of one eye as I returned to the building, the room, I glimpsed what might have been the blur of a white nightgown or blur of a pale, naked torso fill the entire bright window just beyond my kitchenette window, a woman's shape I was sure, so large, vital, near, my neighbor must have been pressing her skin against the cool glass, a phantom disappearing faster than I could focus, then gone when a venetian blind's abrupt descent cut off my view, all but a thirty-inch-wide band of emptiness in my neighbor's window, increasingly familiar and intimate as the years passed.

What if she had known that today her last chance. A showing as in Pentecost. No different this morning, though it's my last. Her final chance too. Sad she didn't know. Too bad I won't be around tomorrow to tell her so we can be unhappy about it together, laugh about it together. Her name, if I knew it, on the note I won't write and leave behind for posterity.

Posterity. Pentecost. With a phone I could review both etymologies. Considered bringing a phone. Not really. Phone would tempt me to linger, call someone. One last call. To whom? No phone. Nowhere to put it if I had one. Maybe tucked in the waistband of my shorts. Little tuck of belly already stretching the elastic. Vanity versus necessity. So what if I bulge. But how to manage a call if I had a phone and someone to call. Freeing my hands would mean letting go of the thick railing, an unadvisable maneuver. Accidental fall funny. Not my intent. Would spoil my show. A flawless Pentecost this morning, please.

"Posterity," "Pentecost": old-fashioned words hoisting themselves up on crutches, rattling, sighing their way through alleys and corridors of steel girders' struts, trusses, concrete piers. Noisy chaos of words graffitied on the pedestrian walkway: DHEADT REFUSE, EAT ME, JEW YORK, POOP DICK DAT BITCH, HONDURAS. Ominous silence of highway free of traffic as it never is except rarely after hours, and even during the deepest predawn quiet a lone car will blast across or weave drunkenly from lane to lane as if wincing from blows of wind howling, sweeping over the Williamsburg Bridge.

"Why" the most outmoded, most vexing word. Staggering across the Williamsburg Bridge one morning, buffeted by winds from every direction, headwind stiff enough to support my weight, leaning into it at a forty-five-degree angle, blinded by the tempest, flailing, fearing the undertow, the comic-strip head-over-heels liftoff, and I asked myself, Why the fuck are you up here, jackass, walking the bridge in this god-forsaken weather, and that question—why—drumming in my eardrums, the only evidence of my sanity I was able to produce.

Why not let go. Fly away from this place where I teeter and

totter, shiver, hold on to a cold iron rail, thighs pressed together, fingers numb from gripping, toes frozen stiff, no air in my lungs.

Always someone's turn at the edge. Are you grateful it's me not you today? Perhaps I'm your proxy. During the Civil War a man drafted into the Union Army could pay another man to enlist in his place. This quite legal practice of hiring a proxy to avoid a dangerous obligation of citizenship enraged those who could not afford the luxury, and to protest draft laws that in effect exempted the rich while the poor were compelled to serve as cannon fodder in Mr. Lincoln's bloody unpopular war, mobs rioted in several northern cities, most famously here in New York, where murderous violence lasted several days, ending only after federal troops were dispatched to halt the killing, beating, looting, burning.

Poor people of color by far the majority of the so-called draft riot's victims. A not unnatural consequence given the fact mobs could not get their hands on wealthy men who had hired proxies and stayed behind the locked doors of their substantial estates in substantial neighborhoods protected by armed guards during the civil unrest. Colored people on the other hand easy targets. Most resided in hovels alongside hovels of poor whites, thus readily accessible, more or less simple to identify, and none of them possessed rights a white man was required by law or custom to respect. Toll of colored lives heavy. I googled it.

So much killing, dying, and after all, a proxy's death can't save a person's life. Wall Street brokers who purchased exemption from death in the killing fields of Virginia didn't buy immortality. Whether Christ died for our sins or not, each of us obligated to die. On the other hand, the moment you learn your proxy killed in action at Gettysburg, wouldn't it feel a little like stealing a taste of immortality? Illicit rapture. If suicide a crime, shouldn't martyrdom be illegal too? Felony or misdemeanor? How many years for attempted martyrdom?

When you reach the edge you must decide to go further or not, to be free or not. If you hesitate you get stuck like the unnamed fair-skinned young colored man in Reisner's photos. Better to let go quickly and maybe you will rise higher and higher because that's what happens sometimes when you let go—rapture. Why do fathers build wings if they don't want sons to fly; why do mothers bear sons if they don't want sons to die.

When I let go and topple backward, will I cause a splash, leave a mark? After the hole closes, how will the cops locate me? I regret not having answers. The plunge backward off my perch perhaps the last indispensable piece of research. As Zora Neale Hurston said, You got to go there to know there.

But no. Not yet. I'm in no hurry this morning. Not afraid either. I may be clutching white-knuckled onto the very edge of a very high bridge, but I don't fear death, don't feel close to death. I felt more fear of death, much closer to death, on numerous occasions. Closest one summer evening under streetlights in the park in the ghetto where I used to hoop. Raggedy outdoor court, a run available every evening except on summer weekends when the high-fliers owned it. A daily pickup game for older gypsies like me wandering in from various sections of the city, for youngblood wannabes from the neighborhood, local has-beens and never-wases, a run perfect for my mediocre, diminishing skills, high-octane fantasies, and aging body that enjoyed pretending to be in superb condition, at least for the first five or six humps up and down the cyclone-fenced court, getting off with the other players as if it's the NBA Finals. Ferocious play war, harmless fun unless you get too enthusiastic, one too many flashbacks to glory days that never existed, and put a move on somebody that puts you out of action a couple weeks, couple months, for good if you aren't careful. Anyway, one evening a hopped-up gangster and his crew cruise up to the court in a black, glistening Lincoln SUV. Bogart winners and our five well on the way to delivering the righteous ass-kicking the chumps deserved for stealing a game from decent folks waiting in line for a turn. Mr. Bigtime, big mouth, big butt, dribbles the ball off his foot, out of bounds, and calls a foul. Boots the pill to the fence. Waddling after it, he catches up and plants a foot atop it. Tired of this punk-ass, jive-ass run, he announces. Motherfucker over, motherfuckers. Then he unzips the kangaroo pouch of his blimpy sweat top he probably never sheds no matter how hot on the court because it hides a tub of jelly-belly beneath it, and from the satiny pullover extracts a very large pistol, steps back, nudges the ball forward with his toe, and—*Pow*—kills the poor thing as it tries to roll away. *Pow—Pow—Pow*—starts to shooting up the court. Everybody running, ducking to get out of the way. G'wan home, niggers. Ain't no more gotdamn game today. *Pow*. King of the court, ruler of the hood. Busy as he is during his rampage, brother finds time to wave his rod in my direction. What you looking at, you yellow-ass albino motherfucker. Gun steady an instant, pointed directly between my eyes long enough I'm certain he's going to blow me away and I just about wet myself. Truth be told, with that cannon in my mug maybe I did leak a little. In the poor light of the playground who could tell. Who cares, is what I was thinking if I was thinking anything at that moment besides dead. Who knows. Who cares. Certainly not me, not posterity, not the worker ants wearing rubber aprons and rubber gloves who'll dump my body on a slab at the morgue, drag off my sneakers, snip off my hoop shorts and undershorts with huge shears before they hose me down. Sweat or piss or shit or blood in my drawers. Who knows. Who cares.

A near-death experience I survived to write a story about, a story my mother reads and writes a note about on one of the pamphlets she saved in neat stacks on top of and under the night table beside her bed, each one containing Bible verses and commentary to put her to sleep.

I saw the note only after Mom died. A message evidently intended for my benefit, but she never got around to showing it to me. She had underlined words from Habakkuk, the pamphlet deemed appropriate for the first Sunday after Pentecost—"Destruction and violence are before me; strife and contention arise —law becomes slack and justice never prevails . . . their own might is their God"—and in the pamphlet's margin she had printed a response to my story never shared with me.

Of course I had proudly presented a copy of the anthology containing my story to my mother, one of two complimentary copies, by the way all I ever received from the publisher as payment. Mom thanked me profusely, close to tears, I believe I recall, the day I placed the book in her hands, but afterward she never once mentioned my story. I found her note by chance years later when I was sorting through boxes full of her stuff, most of it long overdue to be tossed. Pamphlet in my hand and suddenly Mom appears. Immediately after reading her note, I rushed off to read all of Habakkuk in the beat-up, rubber band–bound Bible she had passed on to me, the Bible once belonging to my father's family, only thing of his she kept when he walked out of our lives, she said, and said he probably forgot it, left it behind in his rush to leave. I searched old journals of mine for entries recorded around the date of the pamphlet, date of my story's publication. After this flurry of activity, I just about wept. My mother a busy scribbler herself, I had discovered, but a no-show as far as ever talking about her writing or mine. Then a message after she's gone, ghost-message Mom doesn't show me till she's a ghost too: This reminds me of your story about playing ball.

Why hadn't she spoken to me? Did she understand, after all, my great fear and loneliness? How close I've always felt to death? Death up in my face on the playground in the park. Probably as near to death that moment as any living person gets. Closest I've ever felt to dying, that's for damn sure. So absolutely close and not even close at all, it turns out, 'cause here I sit.

Yo. You all down below. Don't waste your breath feeling sorry for me. Your behinds may hit the water before mine.

At the last minute, for comfort's sake, for the poetry of departing this world as naked as I arrived, maybe I will remove these boxers. Why worry about other people's reactions. Trying to please other people a waste of time at my age. I understand good and well my only captive audience is me. Any person paying too much attention to an incidental detail like shorts is dealing with her or his own problems, aren't they, and their problems by definition not mine. I have no words to soothe their pain.

Can't seem to get underwear off my brain this morning. Not mine, we're finished with mine, I hope, though a woman's underwear that day in Paris, my undershorts today on the Williamsburg Bridge surprisingly similar, made of the same no-frills white cotton as little girls' drawers used to be. I'm seeing a lady's underwear and recalling another unlucky-in-love story. Last one I'll tell, I promise. A civil war precipitated by underwear. Not a murderous war like ours between the states. A small, bittersweet conflict. Tug-of-war when I pull down a lady's underwear and she resists.

I was young, testing unclear rules. I wished/wish to think of myself as a decent person, an equal partner, not a tyrant or exploiter in my exchanges with others, especially women. Which means that whatever transpired in Paris between a lady and me should have been her show, governed by her rules, but I was renting her time, thus proxy owner of her saffron skin, slim hips, breasts deep for a young woman. Why not play. Wrap a long, black, lustrous braid around my fist, pull her head gently back on her shoulders until her neck arches gracefully and she moans or whimpers deep in her throat.

I asked her name and when she didn't respond immediately, I repeated my French phrase— *Comment t'appelles-tu*—more attention to pronunciation since she was obviously of Asian descent, a recent immigrant or illegal, maybe, and perhaps French not her native language. Ana, I thought she replied, after I asked a second, slower time. Then I shared my name, and said I'm American, a black American— *noir,* I said, in case my pale color confused her. I asked her country of origin— *De quel pays?* Another slight hesitation on her side before she said *Chine*—or she could have said Ana again or the first Ana could have been China, I realized later. Her name a country. Country's name spoken in English, then French, an answer to both my inquiries.

Her eagerness to please teased me with the prospect that perhaps no rules need inhibit my pleasure. I assumed all doors open if a generous enough tip was added to the fee already collected by a fortyish woman on a sofa at the massage parlor's entrance on rue Duranton. In my mind, only unresolved issue the exact amount of *pourboire.* I didn't wish to spoil our encounter with market-stall haggling, so like any good translator I settled for approximate equivalences, and we performed a short, silent charade of nods, looks, winks, hands, blinks, fingers to express sums and simulate acts, both of us smiling as we worked.

I trusted our bargain had reduced her rules to only one rule I needed to respect: pay and you can play. Her bright, black eyes seemed to agree. Resistance, they said, just part of the game, Monsieur. Just be patient, *s'il vous plaît.* Play along. I may pretend to plead—no no no no—when your fingers touch my underwear, but please persist, test me.

Easy as pie for a while. Underwear slid down her hips to reveal an edge of dark pubic crest. Then not so easy after she flops down on the floor next to the mat, curls up knees to chest, and emits a small, stifled cry. Then it's inch by inch until underwear finally dangled from one bobbing ankle, snapped off finally and tossed aside. A minute more and not a bit of shyness.

Wish I could say I knew better. Knew when to stop, whether I paid or not for the privilege of going further. Wish I believed now that we were on the same page then. But no. Like most of us, I behaved inexcusably. Believed what I wanted to believe. Copped what I could because I could. No thought of limits, boundaries. Hers or mine. No fear of AIDS back then. Undeterred by the threat of hordes of Chinese soldiers blowing bugles, firing burp guns as they descend across the Yalu River to attack stunned U.S. troops, allies of the South in a civil war, Americans who had advanced a bridge too far north and found themselves stranded, trapped, mauled, shivering, bleeding, dying in snowdrifts beside the frozen Chosin Reservoir.

No regrets, no remorse until years later, back home again, and one afternoon Sonny Rollins practicing changes on the Williamsburg Bridge halts me dead in my tracks. Big colors, radiant bucketfuls splash my face. I spin, swim in colors. Enraptured. Abducted by angels who lift me by my droopy wings up, up, and away. Then they let go and I fall, plunge deeper and deeper into swirling darkness.

Am I remembering it right, getting the story, the timing right, the times, the fifties, sixties, everything runs together, happens at once, explodes, scatters. I will have to check my journals. Google. Too young for Korea, too old for Iraq, student deferments during Vietnam. Emmett Till's exact age in 1955, not old enough to enlist or be on my own in New York City, slogging daily like it's a job back and forth across the Williamsburg Bridge those years of Sonny's first sabbatical. When I hurried back to rue Duranton next morning to apologize or leave a larger tip, it was raining. No Ana works here, I believe the half-asleep women on the sofa said.

I wish these dumb undershorts had pockets. Many deep, oversize pockets like camouflage pants young people wear. I could have loaded them with stones.

Before I go, let me confide my final regret: I'm sorry I'll miss my agent's birthday party. To be more exact, it's my agent's house in Montauk I regret missing. Love my agent's house. Hundreds of rooms, marvelous ocean views, miles and miles of wooded grounds. One edge of the property borders a freshwater pond where wild animals come to drink, including timid, quivering deer. Stayed once for a week alone, way back when before my agent had kids. Quick love affair with Montauk, a couple of whose inhabitants had sighted the *Amistad* with its cargo of starving, thirsty slaves in transit between two of Spain's New World colonies, slaves who had revolted and killed most of the ship's crew, the *Amistad* stranded off Montauk Point with a few surviving sailors at the helm, alive only because they promised to steer the ship to Africa, though the terrified Spaniards doing their best to keep the *Amistad* as far away from the dark continent as Christopher Columbus had strayed from the East Indies when he landed by mistake on a Caribbean island.

I know more than enough, more than I want to know, about the *Amistad* revolt. Admire Melville's remake of the incident in *Benito Cereno* but not tempted to write about it myself. One major disincentive the irony of African captives who after years of tribulations and trials in New England courts were granted freedom, repatriated to Africa, and became slave merchants. Princely, eloquent Cinqué, mastermind of the shipboard rebellion, one of the bad guys. Cinque, nom de guerre of Patty Hearst's kidnapper. Not a pretty ending to the *Amistad* story. Is that why I avoided writing it? Is the Williamsburg Bridge a pretty ending? Yes or no, it's another story I won't write.

Under other circumstances, revisiting my agent's fabulous house, the ocean, memories of an idyll in Montauk might be worth renting a car, inching along in bumper-to-bumper weekend traffic through the gilded Hamptons. My agent's birthday after all. More friend than agent for years now. We came up in the publishing industry together. Rich white kid, poor black kid, a contrasting pair of foundlings, misfits, mavericks, babies together at the beginning of careers. *Muy simpático*. Nearly the same age, fans of Joyce, Beckett, Dostoevsky, Hart Crane. (If this was a time and place for footnotes, I'd quote Crane's most celebrated poem, "The Bridge"—"A bedlamite speeds to thy parapets / Tilting there momentarily"—and add the fact that Crane disappeared after he said, "Goodbye—goodbye—goodbye, everybody," and jumped off a boat into the Gulf of Mexico.) We also shared a fondness for Stoli martinis in which three olives replaced dry vermouth, and both of us loved silly binges of over-the-top self-importance, daydreaming, pretending to be high rollers, blowing money neither had earned on meals in fancy restaurants, until I began to suspect the agency's charge card either bottomless or fictitious, maybe both. *Muy simpático* even after his star had steadily risen, highest roller among his peers, while my star dimmed precipitously, surviving on welfare, barely aglow. How long since my agent has sold a major piece of my writing, how long since I've submitted a major new piece to sell? In spite of all of the above, still buddies. Regret missing his party, Montauk, the house. House partly mine, after all. My labor responsible for earning a minuscule percentage of the down payment, *n'est-ce pas?* For nine months of the year no one inhabits the Montauk mansion. In France vacant dwellings are white space poor people occupy and claim, my mother had once informed me. Won't my agent's family be surprised next June to find my ghost curled up in his portion of the castle.

Last time in Montauk was when? Harder and harder to match memories with dates. One event or incident seems to follow another, but often I misremember, dates out of sync. Sonny Rollins's sax squats on the Williamsburg Bridge, changes the sky's color, claims ownership of a bright day. Was I in fact walking the bridge those years Sonny Rollins woodshedding up there? I'll have to check my journals. But the oldest journals temporarily unavailable, part of the sample loaned to my agent to shop around.

I'm sure I can find a university happy to pay to archive your papers, he said.

Being archived a kind of morbid thought, but go right ahead, my friend. Fuckers don't want to pay for my writing while I'm alive, maybe if I'm dead they'll pay.

Stoppit. Nobody's asking you to jump off a bridge. Nothing morbid about selling your papers. Same principle involved as selling backlist.

So do it, okay. Still sounds like desperation to me, like a last resort.

Just the opposite. I tempt publishers with posterity, remind them the best writing, best music, never ages. Don't think in terms of buying, I lecture the pricks. Think investment. Your great-great-grandkids will dine sumptuously off the profits.

Truth is, I've got nothing to sell except white space. You know what I mean: white space. Where print lives. What eats print. White space. That Pakistani guy who wrote the bestseller about black holes. Prize client of yours, isn't he? Don't try and tell me you or all the people buying the book understand black holes. Black holes. White space. White holes. Black space. What's the difference?

White space could be a bigger blockbuster than black holes. No words . . . just white space. Keep my identity a secret. No photos, no interviews, no distracting particulars of color, gender, age, class, national origin. Anonymity will create mystery, complicity—white space everybody's space, everybody welcome, everybody will want a copy.

The *Amistad* packed with corpses and ghosts drifts offshore behind me. Ahoy, I holler and wave at two figures way up the beach. No clue where we've landed. I'm thinking water, food, rescue, maybe we won't starve or die of thirst after all. The thought dizzying like too much drink too fast after debilitating days of drought. Water, death roil around in the same empty pit inside me. The two faraway figures scarecrows silhouetted against a gray horizon. They must be on the crest of a rise and I'm in a black hole staring up. Like me they've halted. I'm not breathing, no water sloshing inside me, no waves slap my bare ankles, roar of ocean subsided to a dull flat silence, my companions not fussing, not clambering out of the flimsy rowboat behind me. Everybody, everything in the universe frozen. Some fragile yet deep abiding protocol, ironclad rules obscure and compelling, oblige me to wait, not to speak or breathe until those alien others whose land this must be wave or run away or beckon, draw swords, fire muskets.

The pair of men steps in our direction, then more steps across the whitish gray. They are in booths making calls, counting, calculating with each approaching step, each wobble, what it might be worth, how much bounty in shiny pieces of silver and gold they could collect in exchange for bodies, a rowboat, a sailing ship that spilled us hostage on this shore.

My friends, calls out the taller one in a frock coat, gold watch on a chain, his first words same words Horatio Seymour, governor of New York, addressed in 1863 to a mob of hungover, mostly Irish immigrants, their hands still red from three or four days of wasting colored children, women, and men in draft riots.

I'm going to go now. What took you so long? I bet you're thinking, or maybe you wonder why, why this moment—and since you've stuck with me this long, I owe you more—so I'll end with what I said to my false-hearted lover in one of our last civil conversations when she asked, What's your worst nightmare? Never seeing you again. Come on. Seriously. Seeing you again. Stop playing and be serious. Okay. Serious. Very super-serious. My worst nightmare is being cured. Cured of what? What I am. Of myself. Cured of yourself? Right. Cured of who I am. Cured of what doesn't fit, of what's inappropriate and maybe dangerous inside me. You know. Cured like people they put away—far away behind bars, stone walls, people they put in chains, beat, shock with electric prods, drugs, exile to desert-island camps in Madagascar or camps in snowiest Siberia or shoot, starve, hang, gas, burn, or stuff with everything everybody believes desirable and then display them in store windows, billboard ads, on TV, in movies, like perfectly stuffed lifelike animated cartoon animals.

Lying naked in bed next to naked her I said my worst nightmare not the terrible cures or fear I fit in society's category of people needing cures. Worst nightmare not damage I might perpetrate on others or myself. Worst nightmare, my love, the thought I might live a moment too long. Wake up one morning cured and not know I'm cured.

P.S. The other day, believe it or not, I saw a woman scaling the bridge's outermost restraining screen. Good taste or not I ran toward her shouting my intention to write a story about a person jumping off the Williamsburg Bridge, imploring her as I got closer for a quote. "Fuck off, buddy," she said over her naked shoulder. Then she said: "Splash."

Contributors' Notes

Other Distinguished Stories of 2015

*American and Canadian Magazines
Publishing Short Stories*

Contributors' Notes

CHIMAMANDA NGOZI ADICHIE is the author of a story collection and the novels *Purple Hibiscus, Half of a Yellow Sun,* and *Americanah.* She divides her time between Nigeria and the United States.

• This story was inspired by a friend who once told me that he had lied about a househelp when he was a child, the househelp was fired, and he —my friend—has carried the regret with him for years.

I am drawn as a reader to stories of childhood told in an adult voice, stories full of the melancholy beauty of retrospect. I am interested in the regrets we carry from our childhoods, in the idea of "what if" and "if only."

I think of Okenwa's attraction to Raphael as a certain kind of first love, a childhood first love, that early confusing emotional pull, that thing filled with an exquisite uncertainty because it does not know itself and cannot even name itself.

MOHAMMED NASEEHU ALI is from Ghana. He is the author of *The Prophet of Zongo Street,* a collection of stories. Ali's fiction and essays have appeared in the *New York Times, The New Yorker, Mississippi Review, Bomb, Gathering of the Tribes, Essence, Open City,* and other publications. He is the recipient of fellowships from Yaddo and the Dorothy and Lewis B. Cullman Center for Scholars and Writers. Ali lives in Brooklyn, New York, and teaches undergraduate fiction at NYU's creative writing program.

• In 1993, the West African nation of Ghana witnessed a dramatic change. After ruling the country with an iron fist for twelve years, the socialist-leaning, anti-West friend of Muammar Gaddafi and Fidel Castro —the military dictator Flight Lieutenant Jerry John Rawlings—discarded his signature military garb, donned civilian clothing, and was sworn in as the democratically elected president of Ghana's Fourth Republic. Today, twenty-three years later, Ghana is heralded as the most stable and strongest democracy in sub-Saharan Africa. But before this glorious story, and even before the coup d'état that brought J. J. Rawlings to power in 1981, there was the coup of June 4, 1979, the putsch that introduced the then twenty-nine-year-old airman to the Ghanaian political scene. Though the regime —called the Armed Forces Revolutionary Council—lasted only three months, the violence it unleashed on Ghanaians was unprecedented, and the carnage would forever scar the hearts and minds of the citizens who lived at the time. During those three oppressive months Ghanaians witnessed the rounding up and killing (by firing squad) of every single living former head of state and their top commanders. The regime's War on Corruption, which turned out to be a war against anyone who was rich, directed its guns and venom at business people and traders. The atrocities visited upon the Ghanaian public were horrendous and too numerous to mention here, but they included the public humiliation of wealthy business people "suspected" of hoarding, smuggling, or profiteering; the public stripping and flogging of market women who had sold provisions above the "controlled price"; the bombing of houses in which "contraband" goods were found, even if the goods didn't belong to the homeowner; the assault, jailing, and even killing of any individual who dared voice dissent, no matter how slight. Businessmen and businesswomen were beaten to a pulp and paraded through city streets; many died while in custody, and those who managed to escape lost all their property to the state.

I was a young boy when this carnage took place, and even though I didn't suffer any direct physical harm or any palpable emotional or psychological distress, the events of the summer of 1979 remain the most impactful of my life. The fear and the confusion of the adults in my life, and their helplessness in the face of such brutality, are what I try to capture in "Ravalushan."

TAHMIMA ANAM is a writer and anthropologist. In 2013, she was named one of Granta's Best of Young British Novelists. She is a contributing opinion writer for the international *New York Times* and a judge for the 2016 Man Booker International Prize. Born in Dhaka, Bangladesh, she was educated at Mount Holyoke College and Harvard University and now lives in Hackney, East London, and Tamworth, New Hampshire.

• On April 24, 2013, an eight-story commercial building called Rana Plaza collapsed in a northern suburb of Dhaka, Bangladesh. When the rescue operations were called off, the death toll was confirmed at 1,130, making it the deadliest accidental structural failure in modern history. The garment-factory workers who died in Rana Plaza had been evacuated from the building the day before, but were ordered back on-site on the morning of the collapse. "Garments" was born out of that terrible tragedy, but when I went to write the story, it became centered on female friendship among three factory workers and their attempt to find security, love, and humor amid the brutal realities of their lives.

ANDREA BARRETT is the author of six novels and three collections of stories: *Ship Fever,* which received the National Book Award; *Servants of the Map,* a finalist for the Pulitzer Prize; and *Archangel,* a finalist for the Story Prize. She lives in western Massachusetts and teaches at Williams College.

• When I was in college, I spent a few weeks at the marine biological laboratory at the Isles of Shoals. The island and its creatures enchanted me, although I knew nothing, then, about the history of the area. Twenty years later, still largely ignorant, I set a story called "The Littoral Zone" there.

Many more years passed before I became aware of Celia Thaxter, her gardening books, and her family's connection to the islands. Writing a story called "The Island," in which I invented the character of Henrietta Atkins, a young student at the 1873 session of a summer school for the study of natural history, I began to think more about the late-nineteenth-century passion for marine biology. Its more demure fringes—collecting and preserving seaweeds, studying tidal pools, drawing and examining invertebrates—were, like certain kinds of botany, relatively welcoming to women then, and I began to wonder if Henrietta and her friend Daphne might explore those fringes later in their lives.

The story grew as I began to study the history of the Isles of Shoals and to read not only about Celia Thaxter but also some of the guides to the seashore written and illustrated by women naturalists in the late nineteenth and early twentieth centuries. The headnotes beginning each section of the story are freely adapted from one of them.

SARAH SHUN-LIEN BYNUM is the author of two novels, *Ms. Hempel Chronicles* and *Madeleine Is Sleeping.* Her stories have appeared in many magazines and anthologies, including *Glimmer Train, The New Yorker, Ploughshares, Tin House, Georgia Review,* and *The Best American Short Stories* 2004 and 2009. She lives in Los Angeles with her family.

• I wrote the first two thousand words of this story over a decade ago. I wrote them while at a beautiful writers' residency in the Hudson Valley, and just before I arrived, I'd learned that I was pregnant. It was too early in the pregnancy to announce it, and I spent most of my two-week stay feeling as if I was hiding something, and also experiencing fairly mild yet constant morning sickness. I remember lying on the floor of my room and reading *The Man Who Loved Children* and a biography of Montgomery Clift. Through the farmhouse walls I could hear the sound of the other writers tapping on their keyboards. I escaped by taking long walks along the highway, and since I found myself with nothing else to write about, I would return each day and write down a few sentences about what I'd seen on my walk. That was all I managed to produce during the residency, and I didn't have high hopes that it would turn into anything.

Many years later, I thought I should try taking the advice that I often give my students who have difficulty with plot, which is to borrow one from somewhere else. The pages I had written and abandoned long before seemed like good material to experiment on. I turned to fairy tales for guidance, as I often do, and for a while I imagined that the marvelous house that so enchants the narrator might turn out to be a sort of Blue-beard's castle, with a cache of dead wives waiting inside. But somehow this didn't feel correct: too redolent of Angela Carter. I also thought about the story of Hansel and Gretel, the ways in which the house and all its trap-pings stir the narrator's hunger—and then I pushed away this possibility because I couldn't imagine introducing a Hansel. I wanted the narrator to act alone. And maybe it was the idea of a woman wandering, curious and alone, that led me to remember Goldilocks, and the more I considered it, the more inevitable it felt. Inevitable because William James had appeared in the draft ten years earlier, a detail that had surfaced mysteriously and served, as far as I could tell, no real purpose. Once I knew what story I was writing, however, James then brought his bear into the tale; his presence no longer seemed accidental, but in fact quite right. I am grateful to Linda Swanson-Davies and Susan Burmeister-Brown for giving the story a won-derful home.

TED CHIANG is a graduate of the Clarion Science Fiction and Fantasy Writers' Workshop. His fiction has won four Hugo, four Nebula, and four Locus awards. His collection *Stories of Your Life and Others* has appeared in ten languages and was recently reissued. He lives near Seattle, Washington.

• There are actually two pieces titled "The Great Silence," only one of which can fit in this anthology. This requires a little explanation.

Back in 2011 I was a participant in a conference called Bridge the Gap, whose purpose was to promote dialogue between the arts and the sciences. One of the other participants was Jennifer Allora, half of the artist duo Allora & Calzadilla. I was completely unfamiliar with the kind of art they created—hybrids of performance art, sculpture, and sound—but I was fascinated by Jennifer's explanation of the ideas they were engaged with.

In 2014 Jennifer got in touch with me about the possibility of collabo-rating with her and her partner, Guillermo. They wanted to create a multi-screen video installation about anthropomorphism, technology, and the connections between the human and nonhuman worlds. Their plan was to juxtapose footage of the radio telescope in Arecibo with footage of the endangered Puerto Rican Parrots that live in a nearby forest, and they asked if I would write subtitle text that would appear on a third screen, a fable told from the point of view of one of the parrots, "a form of interspecies translation." I was hesitant, not only because I had no experience with video art, but also because fables aren't what I usually write. But after they showed me a little preliminary footage I decided to give it a try, and in the following weeks we exchanged thoughts on topics like glossolalia and the extinction of languages.

The resulting video installation, titled "The Great Silence," was shown at Philadelphia's Fabric Workshop and Museum as part of an exhibition of Allora & Calzadilla's work. I have to admit that when I saw the finished work, I regretted a decision I made earlier. Jennifer and Guillermo had previously invited me to visit the Arecibo Observatory myself, but I had declined because I didn't think it was necessary for me in writing the text. Seeing footage of Arecibo on a wall-sized screen, I wished I had said yes.

In 2015, Jennifer and Guillermo were asked to contribute to a special issue of the art journal *e-flux* as part of the 56th Venice Biennale, and they suggested publishing the text from our collaboration. I hadn't written the text to stand alone, but it turned out to work pretty well even when removed from its intended context. That was how "The Great Silence," the short story, came to be.

LOUISE ERDRICH is a member of the Turtle Mountain Band of Chippewa and lives in Minnesota. She has written poetry, memoirs, and novels, including *The Plague of Doves* and *The Round House,* her most recent, which won the National Book Award. She and her daughters own Birchbark Books, a small independent bookstore in Minneapolis.

· This story has its roots in journals kept by fur traders, traditional Ojibwe and Cree stories, and descriptions of early missions on Madeline Island. I worked on it very slowly, over years, accumulating it as background for a character in a novel. It became a story, then dispersed into the novel *LaRose,* then collected into a story again. I have four daughters, and the competence and decisiveness of young girls, like The Flower, has always astounded me.

YALITZA FERRERAS was recently a Steinbeck Fellow in Creative Writing at San Jose State University. Her writing appears in *Colorado Review* and the anthologies *Wise Latinas: Writers on Higher Education* and *Daring to Write: Contemporary Narratives by Dominican Women.* She received an MFA in creative writing from the University of Michigan, where she won the Delbanco Thesis Prize, and is the recipient of fellowships from Djerassi Resident Artists, the San Francisco Writers' Grotto, and Voices of Our Nation. She was raised in New York and the Dominican Republic and currently lives in San Francisco, where she is working on a novel and a collection of short stories.

· When I was five years old I became obsessed with the power of volcanoes after watching a documentary about Pompeii. The reenactments of people's last moments, as fire and ash rained from the sky, were horrifying and beautiful—all the things you don't want a five-year-old to see. I then embarked on a lifelong investigation into what made the earth kill all those people in such a dramatic fashion.

My obsession came at a time when I was being shuffled back and forth between family in the Dominican Republic and New York out of necessity, as my parents worked double shifts in Brooklyn factories. At the time, I didn't fully understand why I couldn't be with them and all the reasons why people leave their homes for faraway lands. I missed my parents so much, and I didn't know if I was supposed to be Dominican or American, but I did know that I wanted to be a part of something solid and immovable. I wanted to stay put, and I also wanted to be a force even though I felt small and voiceless.

Years later, my geological explorations led me to a terrifying incident at a Hawaiian lava field, which I wrote about in "An Alphabetical List of Famous Geologists and the Failed Geologist Who Loved Them," an essay for Yiyun Li's undergraduate creative nonfiction class at Mills College. I felt infinitely inspired to take creative chances and used an alphabetized list of geologists and their discoveries as the narrative drive. When I fictionalized the essay to expand its scope, I realized the list was made up mostly of men and was devoid of people of color. This exposed the real engine of the story: the quest for power by someone who feels powerless. The story became about how Leticia embodies this desire.

LAUREN GROFF is the author of a story collection, *Delicate Edible Birds,* and the novels *The Monsters of Templeton* and *Arcadia.* Her latest novel, *Fates and Furies,* was a finalist for the National Book Award, the National Book Critics Circle Award, and the Kirkus Prize. Her short fiction has been published in journals including *The New Yorker, The Atlantic,* and *Ploughshares,* and in the PEN/O. Henry and Pushcart Prize anthologies. Groff's work has also appeared in three previous editions of *The Best American Short Stories* and in *100 Years of the Best American Short Stories.* She lives in Gainesville, Florida.

• Years ago, when I had almost no money, I took a friend up on an offer she'd made, out of spontaneous generosity, to spend a month with her family in the house they were renting for the summer in Champagne, France. They are gracious. They hid their surprise when I showed up. My friends are nothing like the characters in the story, but they do have wealth greater than mine by orders of magnitude, and not only could I not treat them to the dinners they had in Michelin-starred restaurants nearly every night, I couldn't pay for my own seat at the table. The only way I could thank them was to do some of the more menial tasks around the house: cleaning the kitchen after our late nights drinking old champagnes, running to the village to buy *viennoiserie* at dawn, trying to get stains out of the rugs, picking the cherries from the tree next to the house. By the end of the visit, we were all brimming with emotion, and though I was grateful, a mean little part of me was resentful at having to put myself in the position of toady. My friends, on the other hand, acted beautifully, but since then they've vacationed only with friends of equal means.

Also, I love the song "Au Clair de la Lune"; it was the lullaby I sang to my boys every night for the first few years of their lives, and they can sing it too, without knowing the French words—which is useful, because, like all great children's entertainment, the song contains a double-entendre for the parents who have to sing it over and over, a story of lusty Harlequin trying to get into his friend Pierrot's pants, failing, and then having a wild night with the neighbor lady.

MERON HADERO was born in Ethiopia and immigrated to the United States with her family as a child after living briefly in Germany. She graduated from Princeton and Yale Law School before receiving an MFA from the Helen Zell Writers' Program at the University of Michigan. Her other stories have appeared in *Boulevard, The Offing, The Normal School* (online), and the anthology *Addis Ababa Noir* (forthcoming). She's a member of the San Francisco Writers' Grotto and is currently working on a novel and a short story collection.

• I got the idea for this story when a relative was traveling to Addis Ababa, and I was going store to store with family, rushing to find a special type of cereal with raisins and a very specific style of stretch pants for someone in Ethiopia. I thought this was a pretty funny, almost surreal mission, but these two countries can feel so removed from each other that this experience felt heightened and urgent.

When I thought about this suitcase, I imagined a little portal between two worlds opening up for just a moment, then closing, and then another little portal would open up again somewhere new when someone else was making the trip, then it too would slam shut, and so on. I imagined all of these tiny channels between hard-to-bridge worlds opening and closing, which felt very personal, whimsical, and also tense. Because of the inherent scarcity of physical exchange between such communities, every opportunity for connection, even a seemingly mundane one, has weight. This scarcity, I thought, might also call into question, shift, or emphasize interpersonal dynamics and relationships in complicated ways. I came to recognize this as a complex, ripe moment to explore through fiction.

SMITH HENDERSON is the author of *Fourth of July Creek,* a 2014 New York Times Notable Book. This novel won the 2015 John Creasy (New Blood) Dagger Award and the 2014 Montana Book Award and was a finalist for the 2015 PEN Center USA Award for Fiction, the James Tait Black Prize, the Center for Fiction's Flaherty-Dunnan First Novel Prize, the Ken Kesey Award for the Novel, and the Texas Institute of Letters Jesse H. Jones Award for Best Work of Fiction. The book was also long-listed for the 2016 Dublin Literary Award, the Folio Prize, and the VCU Cabel First Novelist Award. Henderson's short fiction has appeared in anthologies and in journals such as *Tin House, American Short Fiction, One Story, New Orleans Review, Witness,* and *Makeout Creek.*

Born and raised in Montana, Henderson now lives in Los Angeles, California.

• For some reason, "Treasure State" didn't require much to get into shape. I'd read an article about some clever rural burglars, and the whole story just fell out of my head—*thunk!*—like an ingot onto the desk. I knew why the brothers were doing what they were doing. I knew they would be traveling in a long circle—on the run, but not quite, not really—and I knew where the story would end. Above all, I knew the characters and the deep impoverishment that spooked them into their desperation.

Sometimes you get lucky and the gods just give you a whole story instead of a sentence or an evocative moment or whatever scant thing it is that sets you off searching. It might happen again, but I'm not counting on it.

Lisa Ko is the author of *The Leavers,* the novel that won the 2016 PEN/Bellwether Prize for Socially Engaged Fiction; it will be published in 2017. Her short fiction has appeared in *Apogee Journal, Narrative, One Teen Story, Brooklyn Review,* and elsewhere. A fiction editor at *Drunken Boat,* she has been awarded fellowships from the New York Foundation for the Arts, the Lower Manhattan Cultural Council, and the MacDowell Colony. She was born and lives in New York City.

• I've been working, sporadically, on a linked collection about the Kwan family for years, and "Pat + Sam" is the family's origin story. I wrote the first draft in a fever dream at an artists' residency in 2010, after three weeks of binge-editing my novel. It took me two days to get that first draft out of my head and five years of revisions and submissions to get it out into the world.

I'd previously written stories with the two characters in the present day, as retirees, and others from the points of view of their daughters, but always wondered what got them together in the first place. I started the story knowing how I wanted it to end, with a particular image that had been chasing me, a man and woman in bed, physically close but emotionally distant, weighing the compromises they're about to make. I often write to find out why my characters make the choices they do, the deals they make with themselves, the decisions that reverberate—in this case, as a very long marriage. I built the scenes leading up to that ending on what I already knew about Pat's daughters and her first husband's recent death, Sam's immigration, what it was like to be Chinese American in Jersey and NYC in the early 1970s. The story came together when I stopped resisting the alternate points of view. Although Pat and Sam don't know what the other is thinking, the reader does.

I listened to two songs on repeat while writing, both of which worked their way into the narrative: James Brown's "Lost Someone" (live at the Apollo Theater in 1962) and "I'll Be Waiting" by The Lotus, a sixties Hong Kong band. Both songs are about yearning, but they share a sweetness as well, a ramp-up to a screaming chorus, a sense of youthful anticipation and a wistfulness for something that might not have even happened yet. That crackly vintage sound doesn't hurt, either. I gave these songs to Sam for his personal soundtrack, which then gave the story the texture it craved.

BEN MARCUS is the author of several books, including *The Flame Alphabet* (2012) and *The Age of Wire and String* (1995). His most recent book is *Leaving the Sea* (2014). His stories have appeared in *Conjunctions, Harper's, The New Yorker, Paris Review, Granta, Tablet,* and other publications. He has also edited two story anthologies: *New American Stories* (2014) and *The Anchor Book of New American Short Stories* (2004). He lives in New York with his family.

• This story began for me with a kid pulling away from his parents, declaring he no longer loves them. Not in a rebellious or antic way, but coldly, rationally. The parents have to figure out how to respond. Do they make room for this development or wagon-circle their child with even more love? And then they have to navigate each other as well. Coparenting, such a mysterious and fraught collaboration. From these opening conditions in the story it seemed important to keep things plausible and see how the drama played out.

CAILLE MILLNER is the author of *The Golden Road: Notes on My Gentrification*. Her essays and fiction have appeared in *Michigan Quarterly Review, Paris Review Daily, Joyland,* and other publications.

• "The Politics of the Quotidian" is my first published short story. It took me a year to write it—eighteen drafts. I made most of the big choices at the beginning. The heroine is facing a common contemporary problem. She's talented, she's a striver, and she's a person of color who's failing to make her way in a historically homogeneous institution. I knew that I wanted to start the story not with anger but with her feelings of exhaustion, shame, and sadness. I knew that there should be a few laughs, because the setting is academia and academia's a bit ridiculous. One of my favorite books is Vladimir Nabokov's wonderful academic comedy, *Pnin*.

Finally, I knew that I would take one big risk—identifying only those characters who had been accepted by the institution. It fit with the themes of the story and with the heroine's discipline, philosophy. But many drafts later, it still wasn't right. The missing piece, I realized on draft seventeen, was why she became interested in philosophy in the first place.

What's your character's motivation? The question is such a cliché. It's probably the first chapter of *Screenwriting for Dummies.* But once I answered it, every other element took on a new resonance. That's when I knew the story was finished.

DANIEL J. O'MALLEY'S stories have appeared in *Alaska Quarterly Review, Gulf Coast, Ninth Letter, Meridian,* and *Third Coast,* among other publications. He was born and raised in Missouri and currently lives in West Virginia, where he teaches at Marshall University.

• A few summers ago, my friends were out of town, so I was picking up their mail and turning on lights in the evening to make their apartment appear inhabited. Then some days I just more or less inhabited it. I'd go over with a book and a drink and sit for a while. Their apartment was on the second floor, with a screened porch that overlooked my own downstairs apartment across the street. One afternoon I was sitting up there, and I started imagining this boy. He was looking out of a window and he could see an elderly couple on a bridge. The first draft happened quickly. I wrote it there on the porch, on a small pad of paper. For a few weeks I played around with the sentences. About a year later, I did some more tinkering, and the story went on a bit longer so the boy could try to make sense of some things.

KAREN RUSSELL is the author of the story collections *St. Lucy's Home for Girls Raised by Wolves* and *Vampires in the Lemon Grove,* the novella *Sleep Donation,* and the novel *Swamplandia!* She is a graduate of the Columbia MFA program, a 2011 Guggenheim Fellow, and a 2013 MacArthur Fellow.

• Recently, I moved to Oregon, a happily haunted state where the past cohabits with the present—you see this everywhere, in the architecture, in the cemeteries, in the web of trails and campsites. I live in Portland, where Mount Hood is like a senile triangle on our horizon, flickering in and out of view. Last summer, I took my family on a trip to see the stunning Timberline Lodge, a ski resort in the Mount Hood National Forest built by the W.P.A. and the C.C.C. in the 1930s. An army of young men, fighting the nationwide depression by raising a winter wonderland, a fantasy lodge. Black-and-white photographs of these workers' faces I found poignant and haunting. There is a trapped-in-amber quality to their hope and hunger still sparkling in the past.

What stopped me in my tracks was the ski lift—all of the frozen chairs, hanging in space, mobbed by dragonflies. A chairlift in July is somehow a terrifying sight—another uncanny gift from Oregon. Like those photographs, stare at it long enough, and you are possessed by the lurching illusion that it's about to start moving . . .

For me, "The Prospectors" is a story about two young women whose hopes are not unlike those of the C.C.C. boys. Our history reveals cycles of boomtowns and ghost towns, greed, optimism, frenzied speculation, collapse, and the resuscitation of hope. I wanted the story to explore what it might feel like for two friends to mature in the middle of such a boom-to-bust cycle. I thought of Clara and Aubby as being inspired by the speculators and adventurers and prospectors of the nineteenth century: the question that Clara asks, "Who would we be, if we lived somewhere else?," launches them into a sort of co-authored speculative fiction. They are striking out on their own, and the *real* gold they're panning for is horizon light.

The word "prospecting" wound up feeling very resonant to me. The idea of staking not just a literal but an existential claim, trying to moor yourself in space. Clara and Aubby do this for each other—their friendship is an anchor. They go to a party where their hosts demand that the young women mint them into reality; what could be more dangerous than refusing to do this for a person? I loved the idea of a story about two friends who survive the painful collapse of a fantasy, of a phantom structure of reality, and live to tell the tale.

YUKO SAKATA's stories have appeared in *Missouri Review, Zoetrope: All-Story, Iowa Review,* and *Vice.com.* Born in New York, she grew up in Hong Kong and Tokyo and has an MFA in creative writing from the University of Wisconsin–Madison. She currently lives in Queens with her husband and young daughter.

• The story began with the setting: Japan, summer, the sound of cicadas thick in the air. I keep returning to Japan as the setting for my stories because I am intrigued by the place and its culture as something simultaneously my own and foreign, and this gives me an awkward yet curious distance from which to explore it as a fictional environment. In it I found Toru, the character similar to myself in temperament and nothing much else, and followed him to the end (albeit many times over).

SHARON SOLWITZ's collection of stories, *Blood and Milk,* won the Carl Sandburg Prize from Friends of the Chicago Public Library and the prize for adult fiction from the Society of Midland Authors; it was a finalist for the National Jewish Book Award. Awards for her individual stories, published in magazines such as *TriQuarterly, Mademoiselle,* and *Ploughshares,* include the Pushcart Prize, the Katherine Anne Porter Prize, the Nelson Algren Literary Award, and grants and fellowships from the Illinois Arts

Council. A story appeared in *Best American Short Stories 2012*. Currently her essay on Alice Munro can be found in *Writer's Chronicle*, and a story online on the *American Literary Fiction* website. Her most recent novel, *Once, in Lourdes,* is under contract. She teaches fiction at Purdue University and lives in Chicago with her husband, the poet Barry Silesky.

• In my grad school days, in a daylong workshop run by Gordon Lish —former editor from *Esquire,* then at the "red hot center" of the literary universe—participants read the first line of whatever they were working on and Lish allowed them to continue if the line passed muster. My first line, "My sister is not as pretty as I am," failed on account of *adorability* (his term). My self-promoting, self-aggrandizing narrator would put a reader off. The story should be told, said Lish, by the less pretty sister. But that pretty woman has always interested me, someone who started life with all the fairy's gifts.

Fast-forward twenty years, and our son Jesse dying of cancer. After the blank, and the grief, and the intermittent depression, came a time when I wanted to write about Jesse, not by plumbing my memory for details and nuances, but by writing the story of his illness as if it were happening to someone else. I don't know why; it was all I wanted to write. Now I'm in the midst of a collection of interrelated stories, or maybe it's a novel in stories, about a fictional family with a boy with cancer. The mother in my book, Theadora, had been, in high school, prettier and smarter than her younger sister.

HÉCTOR TOBAR is the author of four books, including the novels *The Tattooed Soldier* and *The Barbarian Nurseries.* His nonfiction work *Deep Down Dark: The Untold Stories of Thirty-three Men Buried in a Chilean Mine and the Miracle That Set Them Free* was a finalist for the National Book Critics Circle Award and the Los Angeles Times Book Prize and a New York Times bestseller; it was adapted into the film *The 33. The Barbarian Nurseries* was a New York Times Notable Book and won the California Book Award Gold Medal for fiction. Tobar earned his MFA in creative writing from the University of California–Irvine and has taught writing and journalism at Pomona College and the University of Oregon. He is the son of Guatemalan immigrants.

• "Secret Stream" grew out of my long love affair with the city of Los Angeles. Like the story's protagonists, Sofia and Nathan, I too am a loner who has found respite in solitude by wandering through LA's peculiar natural and manmade landscapes. The subcultures of stream mappers and bicycling historians actually exist in Southern California: I wrote about them back in my days as a columnist with the *Los Angeles Times.* The stream itself is real too, but remains unknown to most Angelenos. I've always been awed by the implausibility of finding natural springs and flowing groundwater in a place that's so dry and asphalt-covered. The boy that Sofia and Nathan see building the little bridge over the stream with his father—that's me, more than forty years ago. I grew up in Hollywood, and playing in a creek in nearby Griffith Park is one of my earliest childhood memories.

JOHN EDGAR WIDEMAN is an "old head, retired from university teaching." Recently elected to the American Academy of Arts and Letters, he is the author of more than twenty works of fiction and nonfiction, including *Brothers and Keepers, Philadelphia Fire,* and the story collection *God's Gym.* He is the recipient of two PEN/Faulkner Awards, the Rea Award for the Short Story, a MacArthur "genius" grant, and many other awards.

• It doesn't ever get any easier to write—why should it—the urge/impulse/need/stamina are the gifts as a writer I value most—even readers less important than the good luck to want to write most mornings when I wake up.

I walk the Williamsburg Bridge lots and lots because it is close to my apartment on the Lower East Side. I walk everywhere around the city but most often the bridge—long—sometimes like pacing in a cell, sometimes like riding a big sky-blue Pegasus. Sport, pastime, destination unknown, nowhere else to escape to, dark tunnel, the light I'm pretty sure won't be there when tunnel ends. Simple really—very much like the impulse to write a story. I've often got no idea where the thought to cross the bridge comes from or where it will land me, but my feet and body parts get a chance to speak along with whatever else happens to be along for the ride that day—Olé—off we go, humping away. Who knows what evil lurks in the minds/hearts of us all. A story desires and sets out to see what is there —and sometimes finds a bridge—with a history, names, walkers, jumpers, memories, etc.—so starts across.

Other Distinguished Stories of 2015

American and Canadian Magazines Publishing Short Stories

Able Muse Review
African American Review
AGNI
Alaska Quarterly Review
Alimentum
Alligator Juniper
American Athenaeum
American Short Fiction
Antioch Review
Apalachee Review
Appalachian Heritage
Apple Valley Review
Arcadia
Arkansas Review
Armchair/Shotgun
Arts and Letters
Ascent
The Atlantic
Baltimore Review
Barrelhouse
Bayou
The Believer
Bellevue Literary Review
Bellingham Review
Bellowing Ark
Blackbird
Black Clock
Black Denim Lit
Black Warrior Review
Blue Lyra Review

Blue Mesa Review
Bluestem
Bomb
Booth
Bosque
Boston Review
Boulevard
Brain, Child: The Magazine for Thinking Mothers
Briar Cliff Review
Bridge Eight
Callaloo
Calyx
Camera Obscura
Carolina Quarterly
Carve Magazine
Catamaran Literary Reader
Chariton Review
Chautauqua
Cherry Tree
Chicago Quarterly Review
Chicago Review
Cimarron Review
Cincinnati Review
Cleaver Magazine
Coe Review
Colorado Review
Columbia
Commentary
The Common

Confrontation

Conjunctions

Consequence

Copper Nickel

Crab Orchard Review

Crazyhorse

Cream City Review

Crucible

CutBank

Daedalus

DailyLit

December

Denver Quarterly

Descant

Dogwood

Ecotone

Electric Literature

Eleven Eleven

Epiphany

Epoch

Esquire

Event

Fairy Tale Review

Fantasy and Science Fiction

Farallon Review

Faultline

Fiction

Fiction Fix

Fiction International

The Fiddlehead

Fifth Wednesday

Five Chapters

Five Points

Fjords Review

Florida Review

Flyway

Fourteen Hills

Free State Review

Freeman's

Fugue

Gargoyle

Gemini

Georgetown Review

Georgia Review

Gettysburg Review

Ghost Town/Pacific Review

Glimmer Train

Gold Man Review

Good Housekeeping

Grain

Granta

Green Mountains Review

Greensboro Review

Grey Sparrow

Grist

Guernica

Gulf Coast

Hanging Loose

Harper's Magazine

Harpur Palate

Harvard Review

Hawaii Review

Hayden's Ferry Review

High Desert Journal

Hotel Amerika

Hudson Review

Hunger Mountain

Idaho Review

Image

Indiana Review

Inkwell

Iowa Review

Iron Horse Literary Review

Isthmus

Italian Americana

Jabberwock Review

Jelly Bucket

Jewish Currents

The Journal

Joyland

Juked

Kenyon Review

The Lableter

Lady Churchill's Rosebud Wristlet

Lake Effect

Lalitamba

The Literarian

Literary Review

Little Patuxent Review

Little Star

Los Angeles Review

Louisiana Literature

Louisville Review

Lumina

Madcap Review
Madison Review
Make
Manoa
Massachusetts Review
Masters Review
McSweeney's Quarterly
Memorious
Meridian
Michigan Quarterly Review
Mid-American Review
Midwestern Gothic
Minnesota Review
Mississippi Review
Missouri Review
Montana Quarterly
Mount Hope
n + 1
Narrative Magazine
Nashville Review
Natural Bridge
New England Review
New Genre
New Guard
New Letters
New Madrid
New Millennium Writings
New Ohio Review
New Orphic Review
New Quarterly
New South
The New Yorker
Nimrod International Journal
Ninth Letter
Noon
The Normal School
North American Review
North Dakota Quarterly
Notre Dame Review
One Story
One Throne Magazine
Orion
Oxford American
Oyster Boy Review
Pak N' Treger
Pangyrus
Parcel

Paris Review
Pembroke Magazine
The Pinch
Pleaides
Ploughshares
PoemMemoirStory
Post Road
Prairie Fire
Prairie Schooner
Prism International
Profane
Provo Canyon Review
A Public Space
Puerto del Sol
Pulp Literature
Raritan
Redivider
River Styx
Room Magazine
Ruminate
Saint Ann's Review
Salamander
Salmagundi
Santa Monica Review
Seattle Review
Sewanee Review
Shenandoah
Sierra Nevada Review
Slice
Sonora Review
So to Speak
South Carolina Review
South Dakota Review
Southeast Review
Southampton Review
Southern Humanities Review
Southern Indiana Review
Southern Review
Southwest Review
Sou'wester
StoryQuarterly
Subtropics
The Sun
Sycamore Review
Tahoma Literary Review
Tampa Review
Third Coast

This Land
Threepenny Review
Timber Creek Review
Tin House
Transition
TriQuarterly
upstreet
Virginia Quarterly Review
War, Literature, and the Arts
Water-Stone Review
Waxwing Magazine

Weber Studies
West Branch
Western Humanities Review
Willow Springs
Witness
Yale Review
Yellow Medicine Review
Your Impossible Voice
Zoetrope: All-Story
Zone 3
ZYZZYVA

THE BEST AMERICAN SERIES®

FIRST, BEST, AND BEST-SELLING

The Best American Comics

The Best American Essays

The Best American Infographics

The Best American Mystery Stories

The Best American Nonrequired Reading

The Best American Science and Nature Writing

The Best American Science Fiction and Fantasy

The Best American Short Stories

The Best American Sports Writing

The Best American Travel Writing

Available in print and e-book wherever books are sold.

Visit our website: *www.hmhco.com/bestamerican*